Songs of Naamah

A Novel of King David's Harem

Gayle A. Walhof

Inscript

Inscript Books
A Division of Kingdom Christian Enterprises
PO Box 611
Bladensburg, MD 20710-0611

Paperback ISBN 978-1-957497-50-1

I dedicate this book to . . .

My husband, Duane - without him this book would not exist. Who knew, high school sweetheart of mine, that we would go down this road?

To our two children, Jesse and Jamie, who never gave up their confidence in me as an author.

To my two friends who kept believing in me and both told me, "You did not hear God wrong!" – Elaine and Debbie. And to my friend, Mary Jo, who stood quietly by my side with gentle empathy whenever I needed it.

To our darling young grandson, Theodore, who filled me with joy when I felt none granting me perseverance when I felt like giving up. I pray, my little Theo, that you will always have God in your life - both in good times and bad times - and like Naamah and myself, your walk with Him will forever grow.

To Yahweh who, in one way or another, kept pushing me and prodding me to keep going until this book was completed and published. Without Him this book would have been only a dream.

Acknowledgements

Thank you does not cover what I owe my editor, Jeanette Windle. She pushed, challenged, redirected, fine-tuned, and encouraged me at every step of this project. It was sometimes a tough road, but she kept me on track. She is a very gifted editor, and this book would never have come to fruition without the guidance she provided.

A special thanks to my team at Dove Christian Publishers/Inscript Books for believing Songs of Naamah was worthy of publication and for their expertise and help on this journey.

Thank you to my husband, Duane, and children, Jesse and Jamie, whose prayers and support kept me writing.

Thank you to my prayer warriors and support crew – my high school girlfriends, Deb, Karen, Gwen, and Faith; my friend and coworker, Amy; my friend, Jonneke; and my women's Bible study gals, Laura, Elaine, Eileen, Kaitlyn, Sharon, Tess, and those who have since left our group. Your prayers and reassurance were God's tools to push me forward when I thought I had nothing left to give to this project.

To my Beta readers – Jeanne and Debbie – thank you for your positive feedback and technical advice. Your scrutiny was essential to the completion of this work and your uplifting reviews gave me fortitude.

Thank you to family, friends, and coworkers – you know

who you are. You are the people who thought to ask about my journey in writing and offered encouragement whenever I was discouraged. Even if it was just a simple question, your interest in the book kept me moving forward. I owe a debt of gratitude to each and every one of you.

Above all, I thank my Father in heaven. He was in every aspect of writing this book. I truly was Yahweh's vessel in telling Naamah's story. To God be the glory!

Endorsements

What a beautiful and captivating story from start to finish. Gayle took the Biblical story of David and added a fictional twist with his concubine, Naamah. Gayle's meticulous research is evident in the vivid descriptions of the era and the characters. Naamah is a beacon of hope for anyone who has had a trauma in their life. With the love of God, family, and friends we all will find our voice and "sing" again.

Debbie

I found Songs of Naamah hard to put down once I started. I thoroughly enjoyed it and was duly impressed with Gayle's writing skills. Wow!

Jeanne

Chapter 1

Thrashing about on her mat, Naamah felt the thorns slicing into her back. The lips of the man who had thrown her behind the thornbush sought her own, the stench of his hot breath strong in her nostrils.

"No! Stop!" Naamah continued her battle with this evil phantom who had turned the peace of night into the nightmare she'd already survived. He was not daunted at her resistance but simply moved his foul-smelling mouth to her neck. Somehow, he managed to pull Naamah's dress from her body.

"No! No! No!" A hand covered Naamah's mouth, muffling her cries. She no longer felt the pain of thorns stabbing into her back, just the heavy body of the man who had pinned her down. Her arms and thighs throbbed where he had bruised her. Any will to fight left her, and she begged Yahweh that it might soon be over.

"Naamah! Please wake up! You must wake up!" As Naamah calmed, abandoning her fight with the shadow of the man who haunted her, the hand covering her mouth slowly lifted. Naamah's eyes fluttered open to see only darkness. But she sensed the presence of her beloved sister Zahara hovering over her.

"Were you dreaming again of that terrible night?" Zahara asked.

"Yes." Naamah sat up from her mat. As her eyes adjusted to dim moonlight shining through a distant window, she looked around to check whether she'd awakened her parents whose room was next to the one she shared with Zahara.

As though reading her thoughts, Zahara whispered, "No, you didn't wake them up. Though I'm thankful you came out of your dream or Mother would have woken up for sure. You were calling out quite loudly."

"I'm sorry." Naamah's body shook with her soft weeping. "The nightmare of that night is as real as if it were happening again right now."

"Oh, Naamah." Leaning forward above the sleeping mat, Zahara wrapped her arms tightly around her younger sibling. She waited until Naamah's tears subsided before suggesting, "Come, let's sit against the wall until all thoughts of this nightmare have passed."

The two quietly pulled their mats closer to the outer wall and joined hands as they sat together. Naamah rested her head against Zahara's shoulder. "I don't know if I would have survived this, Zahara, if I didn't have you to talk to."

"You are stronger than you think," Zahara murmured in reply. "That you managed to hide this from our family is amazing to me. I would have been useless for weeks! Perhaps months!"

Zahara's statement was true. Eighteen months older than Naamah at almost sixteen, Zahara was a beautiful young woman who already carried her slim figure with elegance. But she was far more extraverted and carefree. If she'd survived the physical trauma, the emotional scars would have permanently damaged her joyous spirit. Nor would she have managed to suffer in silence even to protect the family's reputation or her own. In truth, Naamah wondered how she herself had managed to hide her trauma this long. The only things that had kept her going were her cries to Yahweh in the night and the unstinting sympathy of her beloved sister.

"Zahara," Naamah asked softly, "can I tell you something?"

"Of course, my dear sister. Surely you know that you can tell me anything."

"I'm terrified someone will find out about the horror done to me," Naamah admitted.

"I can understand that." Zahara placed her other hand over the one she was holding and stroked it gently. "But there is no reason for anyone to find out. Surely you know I would never tell another soul."

"Of course I know that, Zahara. But since I am not yet betrothed, the law says the man who raped me could come to Father and demand I be given to him in marriage. He could insist I gave myself to him willingly. All he must do is pay Father fifty shekels of silver. Then he could never divorce me for as long as he lives." Naamah's voice rose in panic. "Zahara, I do not want to marry a man capable of such violence."

"Hush, or we will awaken our parents!" Zahara moved over to rest her own head against Naamah's. "Please believe me that if Father knew what this beast had done, he would never betroth you to him no matter what the law permits. And he would believe your account that you were forced against your will over any man speaking against you. But it does not matter because this man will not speak to Father."

Naamah sighed. "You are fortunate you already know who

you will marry."

"Yes. And that Amos is a very good man," added Zahara.

The sisters sat silently together, listening to the night sounds of sheep and cattle, a breeze stirring the olive grove, and Father mumbling in his sleep. After a few minutes, Naamah spoke again anxiously. "But what if Father betroths me to another man who discovers my secret on our wedding night? He would have every right to send me away as an outcast if he finds out. He could even have me stoned to death."

At her sister's quick indrawing of breath, Naamah regretted sharing such dark thoughts. "Never mind. I didn't mean to worry you. Let's not dawdle over such a dreary subject or we will never get back to sleep."

Adjusting her mat, Naamah lay down in a pretense of sleep. Beside her, Zahara took two deep breaths before relaxing into soft snores. Still wide awake, Naamah tried not to think of the assault. But her mind could not banish the memories. Why had that beast of a man chosen her to brutalize? Naamah had been told more than once that she was beautiful, the dark hair and eyes of her people contrasting with skin somewhat fairer than most while even at fourteen her bust and hips were more curvaceous than her older sister. Yet the village had many women more alluring. So why her?

She deliberately turned her thoughts from such evil. Naamah chose to focus instead on the people who loved her and the familiar surroundings that provided a feeling of comfort and safety. As the oldest of four living brothers, Naamah's father Abdiel was the patriarch of their clan. As such, his house was the largest in their small village. Abdiel's own father had built his home on a hillside so that all available land could be planted in olive orchards, vineyards, and grain fields.

His father had died suddenly when Abdiel was still under thirty. As the oldest, he and his wife Alzbetah had left the two-room home his father had built for each of his four sons and moved in with his mother. That small home had now passed on to Naamah's older brother Gavriil and his bride Rivka.

These were all built around a sizeable courtyard connected by a tall mudbrick wall that provided protection if needed against marauding Philistines or bandits. A corral just outside with a thatched shelter against the elements held goats, sheep, and oxen at night. Should the village come under attack, the animals would be herded for safety into the courtyard.

Other clan members had similar multi-family compounds, all close enough to make up a sizeable village. It would have been easier to build homes on each nuclear family's farmland instead of having to hike out from the village each day. But Israel had been founded as a nation at war, and it was far safer to cluster together than to allow clan members to be picked off individually.

Along with the tiny room where Naamah and Zahara slept on mats, a larger one with an actual bedframe where their parents slept, and a couple storerooms that could be used as bedrooms if needed, the home had a sizeable central living space with a stone fireplace for cooking, eating, working, or just resting. Mats and cushions made it easy to transform a room in moments from dining or entertaining guests to a work space for weaving or leather work.

Naamah's favorite part of their home was the courtyard because there she could fellowship with aunts, uncles, and cousins who lived in the interconnected homes opening onto the courtyard. This was where they all gathered to worship Yahweh on the Sabbath. Where the women congregated to work when weather cooperated. Where Naamah herself led singing with her Aunt Antje to alleviate the boredom of mundane tasks.

No, she wouldn't think about that. She hadn't been able to sing since the night of her rape. Maybe she never would again.

As she often did when struggling to get back to sleep, Naamah prayed for each family in their compound. The homes that belonged to Abdiel, his three brothers, their children, and grandchildren now numbered thirty-seven total inhabitants. One by one, Naamah lifted each family before Yahweh. Uncle Malkiel and Aunt Abela with their three married sons and six grandchildren. Uncle Eelis and Aunt Antje with their two married sons, a daughter who lived with her husband's family, and five grandchildren. Uncle Janek and Aunt Ahava with their married son and two unmarried daughters who still lived at home. Her own family, including her older brother and his wife.

As Naamah finally drifted off to sleep, her last thought was to wish she could once again sing and play music.

Chapter 2

Naamah awoke to her mother shaking her shoulder. "Naamah, you need to get up! Today we journey to Jerusalem for the Sukkot festival."

Zahara was sitting up on her mat but looked as though in a fog. Alzbetah clicked her tongue in disapproval. "I can't remember the last time I had to actually shake you two to get you to wake up. And today of all days!"

She yanked away the woven blankets covering each daughter, leaving them shivering in the morning chill. "That will wake you up! Come, there is much to do today. Or should I call your father to get you out of bed?"

Naamah smiled at Zahara, who winked back at her. Both knew their kind, long-suffering mother too well to take her severe words seriously. Folding their blankets and rolling up their mats, they placed the bedding on a shelf and began dressing for the busy day ahead.

Both girls wore wool tunics dyed yellow using pomegranates. The robe Naamah wore over her tunic and the sash about her waist were dyed blue using wood chips. Zahara's robe and sash were more of a lilac color, which came from myrtle. Alzbetah's robe and tunic were shades of bronze.

"Your father will want you girls to help pick choice figs and olives for the trip," Alzbetah continued. "Also palm fronds and branches to make our Succoth shelter. The countryside will be stripped bare by the time we get there."

The Sukkot festival was one of Naamah's favorite times of year when Yahweh's people celebrated the ingathering of the harvest and Yahweh's miraculous protection for Israel during forty years of wandering in the wilderness. Once in Jerusalem, they would build a shelter with the gathered palm fronds and branches. For the seven days of the feast, they would live in the shelter as their ancestors had done in the wilderness.

Contentment banished the memory of last night's nightmare as Naamah worked alongside her mother and sister. They took joy in even simple daily tasks such as preparing food and keeping their home neat. Naamah knew her mother's inner peace and positive attitude came from her trust in Yahweh. Alzbetah's life hadn't been easy. She had given birth to six children, but only three had survived childhood.

Nine at the time, Naamah remembered vividly the death of her little brother Ilya, who was only three when he ran into the path of a heavy-laden ox cart and was killed by one of the wheels. All women knew it was a grim task to raise a child to adulthood with the difficulties of childbirth, disease, and accidents. Certainly, Naamah had seen many women in her family mourning the loss of children.

But Naamah had also witnessed first-hand a resilient faith in her mother above others who had gone through loss. Her steadfast faith, joy, and kindness made Alzbetah beautiful even if she had grown plump over the years, a few strands of silver streaking her dark hair, lines of both laughter and grief etched around her mouth and eyes.

Naamah was pouring olive oil from a waist-tall jar into a smaller one for the trip when her father entered their home. Since he spent much of his day in the sun and wind, Abdiel's bronzed skin was as weathered and wrinkled as boot leather. Alzbetah looked up from the dried figs, olives, goat cheese, and warm loaves of bread she was setting aside for a meal along the way. "Good morning, Abdiel."

"Good morning, Father," Naamah and Zahara chimed together.

"So you girls are finally out of bed! I had thoughts we might have to leave you behind." While his tone was gruff, Naamah knew her father was as kindly and forbearing as her mother.

"It's my fault, Father," she spoke up quickly. "I had a bad dream in the night and kept Zahara up so late it is no wonder she overslept."

"We aren't so far behind," Alzbetah broke in reassuringly. "We have almost everything ready as far as the food and blankets."

"Good. Then why don't Naamah and Zahara come with me, and we will pick the best olives and figs we can find from this year's harvest for our offering to Yahweh," Abdiel suggested. "I already have the first wheat set aside. Only the finest for our God."

Following their father to the orchard, Naamah and Zahara helped Abdiel fill two baskets of the most perfect figs and olives, then wandered down a slope to a shallow stream, searching for bamboo and palms that could still spare a few fronds. By the time they returned home, Abdiel had the ox yoked to the family cart. Alzbetah was loading bedrolls, baskets, jars, and a bulging wine skin into the cart bed.

"Here is the last." Emerging with a bundle of fresh-baked loaves wrapped in palm fronds, Alzbetah closed the door of the house behind her. She set the bundle in the cart, then checked her daughters to ensure their headscarves were modestly pulled down on their forehead so no hair showed. She adjusted her own scarf so the end covered her mouth and nose, a precaution against the wind and dirt of the road.

Doing the same, Naamah smiled to see the same joyous anticipation in her own heart radiating from her mother's and sister's eyes above the soft material of their scarves. Shaking his head, Abdiel announced mournfully, "We're going to be the last arrivals in Jerusalem!"

But the twinkle in his eyes belied his tone, and by the time the family exited the compound, the ox plodding patiently toward the dusty road leading out of town, the rest of the villagers were just starting to form a caravan. Naamah looked about to see where her aunts, uncles, and cousins were in this procession. Uncle Malkiel, Uncle Eelis, and their families were still emerging from the compound. Uncle Janek, the youngest of Abdiel's brothers, and his family along with Naamah's brother and sister-in-law, Gavriil and Rivka, were a few families ahead of them in the procession.

Seeing his parents, Gavriil steered his wife toward the ox cart. Uncle Malkiel and Uncle Eelis fell in with their carts and family behind Abdiel's party. Abdiel led the way as they exited a gate between two walled compounds that led from the village onto the main highway leading to Jerusalem. Their small group soon turned loud and large as they joined an unending line of people, carts, beasts of burden, and animals meant for sacrifice that had come from more distant towns and villages. Naamah was grateful to be traveling in such a large group. Even though it was only six miles, or a short half-day journey, to Jerusalem, it was safer to make this trip together rather than being alone on the road.

Most of the crowd was walking except for those who preferred to drive their carts and children too small to keep up, who perched on top of their family's provisions. Mothers with small babies carried them in a sling fashioned from a shawl. As they continued toward Jerusalem, Naamah saw farmers working hard to finish their olive harvest by beating the limbs of the olive trees, causing the fruit to fall.

Along the way, new groups of pilgrims emerged from sideroads to join the procession. There were now as many people stretched behind Abdiel's party as up ahead. Glancing back, Zahara exclaimed, "I'm sure glad we don't have to travel as far as some of these people. Though it would be fun to see some of the towns they come from. Like Bethlehem."

"That wouldn't be so hard," replied Naamah. "It's less than an hour from our village. I know Father has been there to sell our harvest in the market. What made you think of Bethlehem in particular?"

Zahara shrugged. "I guess because we're going to the city where King David resides and Bethlehem was where he was born. In any case, I will probably never see it. Women never get to travel. Look at Mother. She hasn't been anywhere but Jerusalem for the festivals since she married Father. It doesn't seem fair that Father and Gavriil and the other men can travel to sell and buy but women can't leave home except to marry or attend the festivals."

Her vehemence surprised Naamah. If she never left the safety of her family again, she would be happy. Even being on this hard, dusty road with so many other people was making her heart pound. Zahara reminded Naamah of their assignment to look for additional palm fronds for their shelter. But this meant scrambling up the hillside and down into ravines in competition with many others also seeking the perfect fronds.

Tagging at Zahara's nimble heels, Naamah tried to push her anxiety down. Zahara spotted her trembling hands. "You are perfectly safe, Naamah. I won't leave your side."

"Yes, I know." Naamah forced a smile. "I keep bracing for that man to jump out from behind a rock or bush. It is just something I have to get over. Like the nightmares."

Zahara put her arm around Naamah's shoulders. "And like not being able to sing anymore since you encountered that man?"

Chapter 3

Naamah's face flushed deep-red as she realized her sister had noticed what no one else in the family had commented on. Naamah had indeed not made a note of music since the man's violent attack.

"I didn't mean to upset you," Zahara said gently. "I just miss your sweet voice, and I am so angry that man stole your gift of music with all the other evil he has done. But I know you will find it again soon. I can feel it in my spirit!"

"I pray you are right, my sister," Naamah responded.

Zahara stopped suddenly in her tracks. "Listen! We must be getting close to Jerusalem."

Naamah stopped as well. Sure enough, singing and music could be heard in the distance. Already in response, people in the procession were pulling out instruments. Naamah's sharp ear identified cymbals, bells, lyres, and a shofar. Voices rose in praise to Yahweh. Women and girls began dancing up the road.

Naamah's own favorite instrument was the lyre, which her Aunt Antje had taught her to play before she was even five years old. Naamah spotted Aunt Antje not far ahead playing her lyre as she walked alongside their family cart. Zahara joined in, singing and dancing with abandon. Part of Naamah longed to offer her gift of music to the Lord as she'd done on such pilgrimages for years. But she simply couldn't find it in herself to sing or dance.

Moving away from her sister, Naamah found a spot to walk alongside her father's ox, essentially hiding herself from celebrating family members. She caught her mother's eye on her from the other side of the cart. Forcing a smile, she waved at Alzbetah, hoping to cut off any queries as to why the family songbird wasn't singing. Thankfully, her mother's gaze didn't linger.

The city of Jerusalem was built on a number of hills, so the final segment of road leading to the entry gate wound steeply upward. Abdiel and the rest of the crowd didn't turn in at the gate but followed the base of the massive stone wall encircling the city until they arrived at a steep uphill trail leading to a bluff overlooking the city. They were all winded by the time they reached the spot Abdiel had chosen for their sukkot.

As she helped her parents unload the cart, Naamah looked across a narrow valley dividing the bluff from an even higher hill, the Mount of Olives, where she could make out the white linen panels that marked the outer courtyard of the tabernacle. This had been moved from its permanent location inside Jerusalem's fortifications to a wide, flat threshing ground near the top of this mountain in order to accommodate the multitudes of worshippers arriving for the Sukkot festival.

Directly across from the Mount of Olives on the highest hill was the original fortress of Jerusalem, which King David had conquered from the Jebusites and made his capital. Rising above the fortifications was King David's palace. Its polished stones gleamed in the bright sunlight, and terraces dropped down to the perimeter wall.

The homes of the wealthy spilled down the hillside, those of King David's top advisors closest to the palace. These mansions were two-story buildings with verandahs around an inner courtyard. With minimal land area available inside the city, the flat roofs were used for additional living space, high parapets surrounding them and thatched shelters or small guest quarters constructed on top. Poorer homes clustered in the dark ravines between hilltops where the sun reached only a few hours a day. Around each city gate was a marketplace where merchants and farmers sold their goods.

Already, there were multitudes everywhere Naamah looked, pitching shelters on hillsides, squeezing through the streets, and crowding the markets around the gates. From past experience, Naamah knew the crowds would only become larger as the Sukkot festival progressed. The thought of so many people brought her both comfort and fear. Comfort in the protection of so many family members, including her stalwart father, brother, and uncles. Fear that she might run into the man who raped her.

No, she wouldn't go there again. She deliberately chose another focus for her thoughts. "I wonder what it would be like to live in such a beautiful palace."

Zahara dumped an armload of fronds next to the lengths of bamboo her father had tied off to form uprights. "I certainly wouldn't mind trying it for myself."

Alzbetah shook her head in disapproval. "The life of luxury always looks nice from the outside, but I can assure you the wealthy have problems of their own. For one, it is common knowledge our king and many of the wealthy have multiple wives and concubines. I, for one, would not like to share my husband with other women. I think that leads only to jealousy and difficulties."

"And I think less talk and more work would keep us from difficulties right now!" Abdiel interjected, looking around.

With that, the three women buckled down to putting up the sukkot. Bamboo poles formed the corners with a lashing of smaller bamboo and sticks as rafters and palm fronds as thatch. The remaining fronds were enough to weave rough walls on two sides. Alzbetah hung a blanket across the third, leaving open the side facing the tabernacle. It was tall enough for all but their father to stand up comfortably. A few feet away, Gavriil and Rivka had erected a much smaller shelter barely large enough to creep inside for sleeping. They would be joining the rest of the family for everything else.

Zahara and Naamah helped their mother bring in items they would need immediately, including sleeping mats, blankets, and a pottery water jar. The rest were left stored in the cart. Alzbetah assembled a simple evening meal of bread, olive oil, olives, and a few figs while the two girls spread a tanned goat hide in front of the shelter as a makeshift table. Once the food was set out, Father led the family in prayer. "Blessed are you, O God, our Lord, King of the World."

"Who brings forth bread from the ground," the family responded in unison.

By the time they'd eaten and the meal was cleared away, night had fallen, and they all retired to sleeping mats crowded close together inside the shelter. Another spare blanket was hung over the entrance to provide some privacy.

Sleep eluded Naamah as she listened to the sounds of thousands of people confined together. Snores, murmurs, and occasional shouts mingled with the lowing of cattle and baaing of goats and sheep. She could hear from the soft snores that the rest of her family had found the comfort of rest. That her body was so tired yet she could not sleep increased her irritation.

Naamah finally pushed back her blanket and rose silently to her feet. If she could just step out into the open air and stretch a moment, maybe she'd be able to relax. She tiptoed barefoot toward the glimmer of light that was campfires and moonlight shining around the edges of the blanket blocking the entrance. Lifting the blanket aside, she stepped through.

Once outside, Naamah felt as though she were standing in the midst of an enormous city with sukkots as far as she could see. The moon was high and bright. The tiny cookfires dying down all across the hilltop looked like stars fallen to earth. Naamah turned to look across the valley where King David's palace stood. Moonlight glistening on polished stone painted it with a serene beauty. What would it be like to live in such a place?

Even from this distance, the moonlight was bright enough that Naamah could make out a male figure pacing back and forth along a palace terrace. She couldn't distinguish facial features, but he walked impatiently as though suffering from her own insomnia. Several other men stood stiffly along the parapet bordering the terrace. Moonlight glinted on metal breastplates, spears, swords. Palace guards, undoubtedly. So who was the man they guarded?

Naamah's curiosity was piqued when the man strode over to the parapet to stare downward at the wealthy neighborhood below the palace walls. Following his gaze, Naamah spotted another moving figure on a rooftop not twenty feet below the palace terrace. A cloak or robe billowed in the night wind. Naamah had no idea if the figure was male or female until the man on the terrace strode a few feet to snatch up a torch, then hurried back to the parapet.

As he leaned over, the torch flame cast light on the figure below, now motionless, head tilted to look upward. Naamah drew in her breath at the sight of unveiled hair and delicate female features. The man and woman stood there unmoving, simply staring at each other, for a long moment. Then one of the guards stepped forward. Whether he spoke, Naamah couldn't tell at that distance, but the man abruptly stepped back and handed the torch to the guard. Restored to shadows, the woman slipped away. A moment later the rooftop was empty.

Who were they? Had Naamah imagined the almost palpable emotional connection between those two engrossed gazes?

Chapter 4

The man had now left the terrace as well, a reminder Naamah needed to get back to her own sleeping mat. At least her excursion had achieved its purpose as by the time she'd pulled the covers over her shoulders, fatigue overtook curiosity, and she finally fell asleep.

The family ate their morning meal the following day to the bawling of sheep, goats, and cattle being prepared for the morning sacrifice. As they finished, Abdiel announced, "I have made a decision. I know we want to worship Yahweh at the tabernacle. But now that all our children are old enough to appreciate the experience and we have a new daughter in the family …"

Abdiel gave Rivka a fatherly smile.

"… I feel it's important this year that we witness every part of this festival. Beginning with the high priest filling his water pitcher from the pool of Siloam inside the city walls. We can then travel with him to the tabernacle and see him pour out the water on the altar. By then the crowds will be great, so we may not be able to offer our own sacrifice today. But before the end of the festival, we will ensure we have sacrificed our best to Yahweh."

The remnants of the meal were quickly stowed away, the ox fed and watered. The family then headed down the steep trail toward the city gate where they had first arrived in Jerusalem. The path was crowded with pilgrims heading up to the tabernacle and others like their own family heading into the city. Naamah and Zahara linked arms to keep from being pushed off the trail.

Once down in the valley and through the gate, the narrow cobblestoned streets and buildings prevented sight of the palace or hilltop where the tabernacle was pitched. The family followed excited crowds until they emerged at a series of spring-fed pools on the lower southern slope of Jerusalem, a vital part of the city's water system when it was a Jebusite fortress. Naamah's excitement rose as she spotted the high priest in his distinctive dress walking toward the Pool of Siloam with a gleaming pitcher of pure gold. Musicians began playing instruments as the priest dipped the pitcher into the crystal-clear spring water.

Naamah and her family fell in step as the crowd turned to follow the high priest and musicians across the valley and up the slope of the Mount of Olives toward the tabernacle pitched at the top. As on their journey to Jerusalem, many in the crowd began dancing and singing to the joyful instrumentals of the musicians as they climbed.

As expected, by the time they reached the threshing grounds where the tabernacle had been pitched, the crowds were so large it was impossible to get close to the white linen walls of the tabernacle. They stood for a while listening to the mass choirs of Levites singing psalms of ascent on opposite sides of the tabernacle and priests in the crowd reading the Law of Moses to those within earshot. But as the sun rose hot and bright overhead, Abdiel led the way back to the shade of their sukkot shelter.

"We have plenty more days to worship Yahweh at the tabernacle," he consoled. "For now, Father God knows our hearts and that we are worshipping Him even from a distance, and He is pleased."

They spent the afternoon building a small fire, cooking a hot meal, then resting while they listened to the music of choirs and instruments, all but Naamah breaking into song when the lyrics were a familiar psalm. The following morning, they were up before sunrise. After a hasty meal, they started down the hillside to the valley floor, then across and up the slope of the Mount of Olives. As others with the same idea began pouring from sukkots pitched on every slope and hilltop in sight, Abdiel urged his family to quicken their pace.

Even with their early start, the tabernacle courtyard was crowded by the time they passed through the beautifully woven tabernacle entrance embroidered in blue, purple, and scarlet. Abdiel managed to find room for his small family near the altar where the priest would offer burnt offerings to Yahweh. Standing on tiptoes, Naamah watched the high priest pour water from the golden pitcher onto the altar.

"Please, Lord, save us," he cried above the murmur of the crowd. "Hear our prayers."

The priest then related how Yahweh had led the people of Israel through the wilderness, appearing by day as a pillar of smoke and by night a pillar of fire. It was a familiar story, and Naamah's attention wandered to the musicians standing on ridges further up the mountainside toward the summit, awaiting the signal to play and sing. Every time the family came to Jerusalem for a festival, Naamah was astounded at the number of musicians, many times more than lived in their village. Along with entire choirs were musicians playing various sizes of lyres, cymbals, bells, shofars, trumpets, timbrels, drums, and flutes.

As the high priest fell silent, the entire body of musicians burst into a psalm of praise. For the first time since the assault had stolen her voice, Naamah found herself leaning forward in wonder and joy. All around her, voices joined in. "Happy is every man on whom guilt rests, and he who having sinned is now with pardon blessed."

As the melodious song swelled louder and louder, many in the multitude broke into joyous dance. Naamah could feel her fingers strumming invisible lyre strings, and one foot tapped in time to the instruments. Music was indeed returning to her soul. Now if she could just find her voice!

Then a Levite stepped forward from among the musicians. As the high priest motioned the crowd to silence, the Levite began leading the musicians in a song of response.

"Give thanks to the Lord, for He is good," sang the leader.

"His love endures forever," the musicians chanted.

"Let Israel say," the speaker continued.

The musicians responded, "His love endures forever."

Back and forth, the leader and musicians sang out in praise to Yahweh.

"Let the house of Aaron say."

"His love endures forever."

"Let those who fear the Lord say."

"His love endures forever."

At this point, the Levite turned to invite the congregation to join in on the refrain. It was a familiar ritual, and all the crowd roared out, "His love endures forever."

The Levite called out the final paean of thanksgiving. "Give thanks to the Lord, for He is good."

Naamah could no longer hold back. Her pure, sweet tone rang out over all the voices around her. "His love endures forever!"

She was so caught up in the music she didn't notice Alzbetah and Zahara were no longer singing until Zahara elbowed her. Mother and sister were staring at Naamah with expressions of pure joy.

"You did it!" Zahara whispered. "You found your voice!"

By the final evening of the Sukkot festival, Naamah was joining the worship of Yahweh in song with full joy and abandon. She only wished the lyre she and Aunt Antje shared back at home was in her grasp now, allowing her to try out some of the new music the Levites had presented during the festival. The family had presented all their firstfruits and other offerings to the Lord.

That final evening, they found a spot close enough to the front of the crowd to witness four priests pouring oil into four golden candelabras, each with golden bowls. When the lamps were lit, the evening sky was set aglow, and the sweet fragrance of incense drifted across the crowd.

"Isn't it beautiful?" whispered Zahara.

"I'm so glad I came," Naamah whispered back. "All the music, the worship of Yahweh, I think it has made me whole again."

Early the next morning, the family tore down the sukkot, then began the return trip to their village. While not the same excitement as traveling toward Jerusalem, they were all looking forward to getting home. Alzbetah and Zahara were chatting about exotic fabrics they'd seen in the marketplace and how they might possibly replicate them on their own loom. Uninterested in new clothing, Naamah tuned them out. A psalm of ascent she'd heard the Levite choirs singing several times over the past week bubbled to the top of her mind. She broke into song.

"I rejoiced with those who said to me, 'Let us go to the house of the Lord.' Our feet are standing in your gates, O Jerusalem. May there be peace within your walls and security within your citadels. For the sake of my brothers and friends, I will say, 'Peace be within you.'"

Her mother and sister broke off their discussion to stare at Naamah. Zahara exclaimed, "That is beautiful! I have never heard it before."

"Of course, you have, sister," replied Naamah. "The Levite choirs sang it last only yesterday."

"It's new to me as well, Naamah," Alzbetah added. "Not that I was paying as much attention to the music as you were."

"It is a new song," Naamah conceded. "The priest who announced it said it was composed by King David."

"Leave it to you to learn a song when you've only heard it once," Zahara chuckled.

"Well, I'm just thankful to hear you singing again," Alzbetah interjected. "I was beginning to worry we were working you too hard or something was weighing on your heart."

She directed a tender smile at Naamah. "Or someone. You do know, daughter, that if there is an appropriate young man on whom you have set your heart, you can speak to me, and I will speak to your father. How do you think your brother and sister found such perfect matches?"

Leaning in, Zahara whispered to Naamah, "I think you no

longer need to worry about your secret."

"Sing it again for us, Naamah," Alzbetah encouraged.

Her face flushed with joy, Naamah let her pure, sweet soprano ring out so that all around fell silent to listen. "I rejoiced with those who said to me, 'Let us go to the house of the Lord.' Our feet are standing in your gates, O Jerusalem. May there be peace within your walls and security within your citadels. For the sake of my brothers and friends, I will say, 'Peace be within you.'"

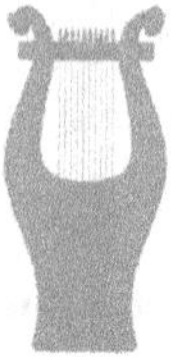

Chapter 5

Striding down the cobblestone street from the palace grounds, Hushai was too caught up in frustration with his close friend King David to enjoy the murmur of voices, aromas of cooking, laughter, and occasional music of a busy city settling in for the night.

"The constant pacing is not at all like my friend and king," Hushai muttered to himself. "Nor indeed his lack of focus."

Watching King David pacing everywhere in the palace had left Hushai exhausted. The only conclusion he'd come up with was that the king was seeking to fill some void in his life. Though he couldn't think why David should feel a void with all the advantages he enjoyed. Not to mention the women pursuing him in and out of his harem.

Hushai had seen it over and over. A glimpse of the well-built, handsome king in his fine robes with thick, black hair flowing from beneath his gold crown was enough to melt most women's hearts, even married ones. Hushai had never been able to compete with his illustrious friend, but nor did he wish to. He was only too happy to enjoy one wife who had aged graciously with him and maintained his modest household in a comfortable tranquility King David could envy.

"Why do I worry so?" Hushai demanded of himself. "David's other advisors simply listen, give their recommendations, and go home."

Hushai's long friendship had begun with a Jebusite lord named Araunah. The Jebusites were hostile toward the Israelites and had turned Jerusalem into a formidable fortress from which they could dominate surrounding Israelite towns and farming communities. Despite this, Hushai had formed an amicable relationship with Araunah, renting out the Jebusite's threshing floor atop the Mount of Olives to process his clan's wheat harvest. Araunah was at least respectful of Hushai and other Israelites. When Araunah learned that Hushai had trained as an architect under King Hiram of Tyre, he'd convinced the Jebusite chieftain that Hushai could be an asset in improving the defenses of their fortress.

Helping the Jebusites increase their dominion over the local Israelite population was the last thing Hushai desired. But he wasn't given a choice. Assessing the citadels and fortifications of Jerusalem, Hushai discovered that the system of water tunnels that made Jerusalem so impregnable connected to a shaft that led beyond the city foundations.

About the same time, Hushai learned that Israel's young new king, who had been crowned in Hebron some twenty miles south of Jerusalem, had pledged to end Jebusite domination once and for all. Slipping out of the city, Hushai had obtained a private audience with King David, where he'd revealed that the only way into the impregnable fortress was up the water shaft he'd uncovered. Using his knowledge of the fortress, he'd led David and his men into the city unspotted by the Jebusite garrison. It was an unqualified victory for the young king, who in turn began fortifying Jerusalem as his own capital.

Hushai still remembered vividly when King David had sent a messenger summoning him to appear before the king. He'd assumed David might have further questions as to the citadel's layout and defensive secrets. Instead, David had praised Hushai for his architectural expertise, then informed him that Hiram, the powerful king of Tyre, was so impressed with David's meteoric rise as a leader he'd offered an alliance and now wanted to build him a palace.

David had placed Hushai in charge of working with King Hiram's architects, craftsmen, and stone masons. Hushai also advised David on how to use the tunnels, water cisterns, fortifications, and hilly geography to make Jerusalem increasingly secure against the most powerful army. By the time the palace was complete, Hushai had risen from palace architect to David's most trusted advisor and close friend.

From the palace, it was only a short walk for Hushai past several large compounds belonging to David's commander-in-chief Joab and surviving Mighty Men. Entering his own spacious compound, he allowed his majordomo to remove his colorful outer robe. His wife Nasya came forward to greet Hushai with a kiss on his cheek. "You look tired, my husband."

"Tired, frustrated, and maybe a little worried," responded Hushai. "Israel's armies have marched as they always do at this time of year. But for the first time, King David has remained behind. I don't know what he's thinking!"

He broke off, realizing this was more than he should have voiced aloud. Nasya led the way towards a low table already covered with food. "We can talk more over our meal."

Hushai and Nasya settled themselves on cushions, and Hushai offered a quick prayer of blessing. Knowing how hungry he always was when he returned home from the palace, Nasya served her husband a hefty helping of goat stew with lentils, then set dishes of olives, cheese, honey, and fresh bread close enough to serve himself.

"I'm sorry to hear your day has been frustrating," Nasya commented as she filled her own dish. "I was hoping you might have had some time to visit Reuel while you were at the palace. You have a better chance of catching him there than at home! It seems he's gone before I awake and comes home only to sleep when he doesn't remain overnight at the palace. Who knew a scribe's trade involved so much work?"

Hushai stifled a sigh. This was a conversation they'd had more than once. "Reuel is not just a scribe. He is training to be able to gather and correlate information from all over the kingdom and beyond that is of value to the king. You know Yahweh gave our son great gifts that benefit the building of our nation. To be able to remember anything he hears and reads in many languages and repeat it however much time has passed. To be able to draw anything he has seen. Above all, to be so upright and trustworthy the king need fear no treason. These are treasures few kings possess. Which is why Reuel reports directly to me as I report to King David alone. As to his absence—"

Hushai paused. "—let us just say there is no need for concern, but he will not be home for a few days."

Nasya sniffed. "So what you are saying is that he is no scribe but a spy! Like Salmon who spied out Jericho for Joshua and ended up marrying the Moabite courtesan Rahab!"

"Salmon happens to be an ancestor of King David by Rahab the Moabite," Hushai reminded. "And it was Rahab's faith in Yahweh that led to her being spared with her family when the walls of Jericho were levelled by Yahweh. In any case, a spy infiltrates enemy territory. Your son is serving the king of Israel to provide the very best information so our king can make wise decisions. And he spends most of his time in the palace inscribing or translating what has been gathered and in no danger at all. If anything, he finds himself bored and frustrated that he can't march to war with so many young men of his acquaintance."

"Well, for that at least I can be thankful," Nasya conceded. "Which brings up a more important matter. You seem to forget that it is high time a marriage is arranged for Reuel. If I am to see so little of my son, at least provide me a daughter-in-law and grandchildren."

"You are right, Nasya. It isn't that I have forgotten. I've simply been so caught up in my concerns for King David that I've repeatedly pushed the matter aside." Hushai reached out and took his wife's hand tenderly in his own. "Now if I promise I will make finding a wife for Reuel my top priority, can we speak of other things?"

Nasya's frown immediately melted into an affectionate smile. "Yes, my dear husband. And I do not mean to make your position as advisor to King David seem unimportant. No one knows more than I how valuable your guidance and friendship are to our king."

"I'm glad you feel that way." Hushai reached for an olive stuffed with marinated garlic cloves. "And I've just had a thought that might resolve my other concern. Do you remember when King David appointed our dear friend Asaph over the Levite singers and musicians to minister before Yahweh in the tabernacle?"

Nasya nodded. "I certainly do. Our king was a great

musician raising his voice to Yahweh long before he was king. I remember when I was still a child how he played for King Saul when the king's spirit was troubled. Who could have guessed then he would one day be our king? We are so blessed to have a king who understands the power of music to impart Yahweh's message to the human soul. I am especially blessed when Asaph and his musicians sing the songs King David himself has written to proclaim God's goodness and love."

"Yes, music has always meant much to King David," Hushai agreed. "King Saul saw this gift from Yahweh in David. It is why he summoned David to his court so that David's playing could sooth his anxious soul. If I could just find such a musician as David was, I wonder if perhaps music could sooth King David's own melancholy."

Always practical, Nasya countered, "It isn't enough to find a skilled musician. Asaph has many such among the ranks of the Levites. Like David, such a musician would need a special anointing from the Lord. Do you know anyone you believe has such an anointing?"

"No, I don't," Hushai responded with renewed frustration. The couple finished their meal in silence. As they arose, a pair of servants entered to clear the table. Nasya began giving her usual litany of instructions for morning chores. Exhausted, Hushai headed for their bed chamber, then paused to turn back. He waited until the servants left the room to speak.

"Lest I forget, I too will be out of town for a while. Perhaps as long as two weeks. We have received reports of some formidable new fortifications built by the king of Syria to protect his capital of Damascus. King David would like me to check out the reports and see if there are any innovations we could employ here. We are on good terms now with

Syria, and I have arranged a visit, ostensibly to discuss trade agreements. Their textiles and sword-work are far superior to anything we have here. But my priority will be a close look at the new fortifications and if possible a talk with their architects and look at the blueprints. I have no doubt they will want a corresponding visit to see what we've done here."

Nasya sighed. "I will miss you. But I shouldn't complain over both husband and son being out of town when so many women have sent their husbands and sons off to war."

She grinned impishly. "Maybe I will invite Uriah's wife Bathsheba and some of the other wives whose husbands are accompanying Joab and the army, and we will have our own women's celebration while you are gone."

"That is a good idea. Why should you sit home worrying over your husband and son, as I know you will, when there is nothing you can do? You work too hard as it is, so it will warm my heart to know you are enjoying my absence."

Nasya stepped close to hug her husband. Their marriage had been an arranged one all those years ago when they were both much younger and slimmer without streaks of gray in their dark hair. But she'd never ask for those days back as when they looked at each other now, it was through eyes of love.

"There is one thing I will do," she said softly. "I will pray night and day to Yahweh for your protection."

Chapter 6

"Peace be with you" had been echoing in Naamah's mind ever since the family arrived home from the Sukkot festival. Tomorrow was the Sabbath, Israel's God-appointed day of rest and worship. Like the rest of the family, Naamah would bathe this evening to come before Father God clean and wholesome.

For her bath, Naamah used the family's bathing basket. Woven beautifully by Zahara, this contained jars of ashes and oils from various plants, animal fat, rosemary, marjoram, a pumice stone, and a few sponges. Naamah mixed ash with fat to sponge down her body. After scraping off the grime, she applied oil to protect her skin, then rosemary and marjoram for their lovely scent. She didn't need the pumice stone, which Abdiel used to scrub the embedded dirt of farming from his hands and feet.

Bath complete, Naamah crawled into bed, savoring the fresh, tingly feeling of cleanliness. The next morning, she and Zahara helped Alzbetah with a light morning meal before gathering in the courtyard with the rest of the clan. Since no work was done on the Sabbath, they'd already prepared the Sabbath feast the previous day to be served after the worship service as had the other clan women.

As the oldest male in their clan, Abdiel took very seriously that he was the leader. Parents were to teach their children to love and serve Father God, and Abdiel believed children should understand that Yahweh was there in every aspect of their lives. For this reason, he took the opportunity on the Sabbath when the entire clan was gathered to teach the young children the great ancient stories of the Israelite people.

The clan gathered in the courtyard, seated cross-legged on spread-out blankets. Awnings and a few potted citrus trees provided shade from the merciless sun. Abdiel recounted the story of Moses leading the Israelites out of Egypt.

"Moses told Pharaoh, 'The Lord God of Israel says to let my people go.' But Pharaoh responded arrogantly, 'Who is the Lord, that I should obey Him?' It was then that Yahweh-Yireh—the Lord who will provide—sent the ten plagues, beginning with water turning into blood."

The children hung on every word as Abdiel detailed all ten plagues. "Then the Lord God swept Pharoah's entire army into the sea. Not one of them survived."

His audience joined Abdiel in singing the song of Miriam, Moses's sister, that immortalized that day. "I will sing to the Lord for He is highly exalted. The horse and its rider, He has hurled into the sea."

The zeal for Yahweh evident in Abdiel's voice as he shared the ancient accounts made Naamah proud. She thought of the small cylinder Abdiel had fastened to the doorpost at the entrance to their home. Inside was a tiny parchment scroll declaring that their family loved Yahweh with all that was within them and pledged to follow Yahweh and His laws.

Naamah desired to have the depth of faith her father displayed.

Once the worship service was over, the clan women retrieved the woven cloths used for dining and spread them out in the courtyard, then set out all kinds of appetizing fare—rewarmed lentil and bean stews, bread with oil for dipping, goat's cheese, figs, grapes, dates, pomegranates, and honey. After all had eaten their fill, Abdiel ended the meal with a blessing.

The women cleaned up while the children ran and laughed and played. The men hunkered down in a corner of the courtyard to talk of livestock and crops. As the sun dropped behind the mountains, Naaman felt a deep contentment. Mothers put small children to bed. Men tired from a week of hard work sought their mats, knowing they'd have to be up before dawn. Others still gathered in the courtyard and on the rooftops, enjoying the glories of the heavens Yahweh had spread out overhead.

Naamah's family had retired to their mats when she caught the sweet sounds of Aunt Antje singing with her lyre across the courtyard. "O God, You are my God. Earnestly I seek You. My soul thirsts for you, my body longs for You, in a dry and weary land where there is no water. On my bed I will remember You. I think of You through the watches of the night. Because You are my help, I will sing in the shadow of Your wings."

As her aunt's voice faded away, another song rose to Naamah's mind. It was a long time since Naamah had sung the words, but tonight she sang them in a barely audible soprano. "May God be gracious to us and bless us and make His face shine upon us. May all the peoples praise You, O God. May all the peoples praise You. Then the land will yield its harvest, and God, our God, will bless us. God will bless us, and all the ends of the earth will fear Him."

As Naamah ended her song of praise to Yahweh, it was replaced by the quiet breathing of Zahara and continued snores of Abdiel and Alzbetah. Maybe her older sister was right that Naamah was finally putting her secret behind her. She soon followed her family into blissful slumber.

The following morning, Naamah, Zahara, and Alzbetah joined the other clan women in the courtyard where they talked and sang as they worked together. Naamah and Zahara focused on grinding grain into flour, a tedious task that could occupy several hours a day. Aunt Antje and Alzbetah sat nearby experimenting with a new pattern for storage baskets they were braiding.

Naamah had always shared a special bond with Aunt Antje, who understood and fostered Naamah's passion for music. She found great pleasure in her niece's talent on the lyre, and by the time Naamah was six years old had admitted with joy rather than envy that Naamah had surpassed her own expertise. She heard her aunt comment to her mother, "I certainly enjoyed the Sukkot festival. Especially hearing the Levite choirs singing our king's beautiful praises to Yahweh."

Aunt Antje raised her voice in one of King David's psalms. Naamah was thankful she'd found her voice and could join the other women as they sang, "Lift up your heads, O you gates, lift them up, you ancient doors, that the King of glory may come in. Who is He, this King of glory? The Lord Almighty—He is the King of glory."

The impromptu chorus had just fallen silent when Aunt Antje suddenly looked up, "I think I just felt a raindrop!"

Standing up, Alzbetah eyed the sky. "It looks like we're in for a rainy afternoon. Daughters, bring that flour in before it gets wet."

Naamah, Zahara, and Alzbetah spent the afternoon weaving baskets to the soft, relaxing drumming of rain on the roof. Alzbetah had entered the store room to select food items for supper when Naamah heard a loud thud followed by her mother's annoyed exclamation. "Ach, I tipped over the water jar!"

The two girls rushed in to help Alzbetah pick up the vessel and deal with the mess. The jar in question was a large one, almost waist-high, into which smaller carrying jars were poured, necessitating several trips to the well. Only a couple inches of water still remained at the bottom once they'd settled the jar back upright. Grabbing a twig broom, Zahara swept the excess water out the door into the courtyard.

Alzbetah turned to Naamah. "Daughter, I will need you to go to the well. We have saved some of the water but not enough to last until morning."

"But it is raining," Zahara interjected.

Alzbetah waved a hand toward the courtyard, where water dripped from eaves and tree branches but no longer drummed against cobblestone. "It is barely drizzling, unfortunately, or I would just refill our jar from the rain. And Naamah won't melt if she gets a little wet."

"I could go for her!" Zahara continued. "Or we could go together and bring more water. That way we won't need to go tomorrow."

Naamah knew full-well Zahara was trying to protect her from going to the well by herself, aware how much Naamah feared being out alone since her rape. But their mother was looking increasingly puzzled and perturbed.

"Well, yes, you could." Alzbetah looked sharply from one daughter to the other as though suspicious of something not being said. "But I need one of you here to help prepare supper, and I've already told Naamah to do it. Is there some reason why she should not?"

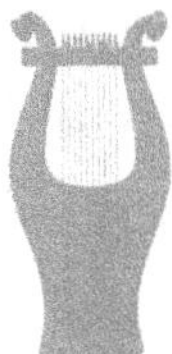

Chapter 7

There was no easy answer to that. Shrugging defeat behind her mother's back, Zahara silently mouthed the words, "You can do it!"

Nodding ascent, Naamah donned her cloak and picked up the carrying jar. Exiting the compound, she trekked along the muddy path toward the well. This was on the far side of the village just inside the gate opening onto the narrow track that in turn led to the main road between Bethlehem and Jerusalem. In times of conflict, the gate would be closed and barred, protecting the town's water source and residents. But in recent years since King David had brought peace to the region, the gate stood open, allowing villagers free passage to fields and orchards and the occasional caravan access to the open green where the well was located so they could water their animals and fill their water bags.

The rain had driven residents indoors, and this wasn't an hour when women flocked to fill their water jars, so Naamah found herself alone on the path. At first, she felt nervous, walking as quickly as she could and eyeing every shadow lest someone jump out at her. When she safely reached the final corner where a street of connected houses gave way onto the village green, she broke into a song of thankfulness.

"It is good to praise the Lord and make music to Your name, O Most High. To proclaim Your love in the morning and Your faithfulness at night to the music of the ten-stringed lyre and the melody of the harp. For You make me glad by Your deeds, O Lord. I sing for joy at the works of Your hands. How great are Your works, O Lord."

Still singing, Naamah rounded the corner to approach the well, now just a dozen paces ahead. Her voice trailed off in sudden shock. Ahead of her milling around the well was an entire entourage of men and livestock. Several men wearing the plain cloaks, leather breastplates, and swords of soldiers had created a bucket brigade to ferry water from the well into nearby troughs where horses and camels drank thirstily.

Standing a short distance away and several paces closer to Naamah was a man in much finer clothing, including a striking blue robe of the finest fabric. A silver flagon was raised partway to his lips as though he'd been interrupted mid-sip. The man's steely-dark gaze was focused on Naamah herself.

Naamah's immediate reaction was such panic she almost dropped the jar. Stumbling, she steadied the jar with one hand while reaching with the other to pull her scarf across her lower face. She took a stealthy step back toward the corner around which she'd just emerged. But before she could escape, the man took a step in her direction and called out, "Daughter of Israel, don't be afraid! Step forward!"

His voice was commanding but also kindly, and Naamah abruptly made up her mind that he had no intention of harming her. In any case, the other men with him had all swung around at his upraised voice and were staring at her. There was no way she could escape them all. She'd just have to trust that the ancient laws of hospitality, which would never deny water to a thirsty stranger, went both ways and this clearly wealthy traveling party would not abuse the hospitality of their village.

Timidly, Naamah sidled several steps closer and held out her pottery jar, half in offering and half as a shield. "Shalom, s …sir! W…would you like some fresh water from our well? I would be happy to fetch some for you."

The man smiled, and this time his kindliness was unmistakable as he lifted his silver flagon and answered gently, "That won't be necessary. As you can see, my servants have brought me refreshment. But there is something you perhaps may have to offer. Am I correct that it was you we heard singing just a few moments back?"

Naamah could feel her cheeks flushing under her scarf, "Yes, sir. I …I found myself overcome with praise to Yahweh for His protection and blessings to me and my family."

"Then indeed you have a voice that is a wondrous instrument to our Lord God!" the man exclaimed. "Would it be an imposition to ask you to sing again the melody we heard?"

Naamah felt uncomfortable under the intensity of his eyes. But she could see no reason to deny his request, and she was so thankful this was all he'd asked that she poured her relief and thanksgiving into her voice as she sang, "It is good to praise the Lord and make music to Your name, O Most High … I sing for joy at the works of Your hands."

By the time she finished, the entire traveling party was listening in mute respect. Their leader blinked rapidly several times as though fighting back emotion before speaking. "That was truly beautiful. Where did you learn that song?"

"Thank you!" Naamah responded. "That song is one of those

I composed several years ago."

"Several years ago?" The man sounded astonished as he looked Naamah over from head to foot. "But you are only a child now! Are you sure someone didn't teach you the song?"

"Yes, sir. I remember well the day I composed it to express my gratitude for Yahweh's blessings," Naamah informed him. "And I was not so young. Perhaps seven or eight years old."

"Then Yahweh has indeed provided you with a gift!" affirmed the man. "Do you play instruments as well?"

"Just the lyre." Naamah couldn't contain her enthusiasm. "I have been playing since I was a small child."

"And do you play as well as you sing?"

"My Aunt Antje, who taught me to play, tells me that I do," Naamah answered honestly.

"What is your name?" the man continued his inquiry. "And who is your father? Where do you live? I may want to speak to him."

"My name is Naamah. My father is Abdiel." Naamah pointed back through the village streets to the family compound up on a hill. "We live up there."

"It has been my pleasure to meet you, Naamah." The man took the reins of a tall mahogany stallion from one of his men. He vaulted into a finely-worked leather saddle. "I pray we may meet again sometime soon."

He gestured to the soldier who had brought him the horse. "Draw our songster some water in return for her kindness."

As he spurred his horse toward the town gate, he called over his shoulder, motioning towards the sky, "And you may want to hurry."

His subordinate reached with a smile for Naamah's jar. Bemused, Naamah stood there as he quickly filled the jar and handed it back to her. She'd never had a man wait upon her before rather than the other way around. It warmed her heart that the richly-dressed stranger and his men somehow recognized in her what her own family never had, a Yahweh-gifted musician, not just a lowly female.

Hefting the jar to her shoulder, Naamah watched the party gallop out the gate before beginning the trek home, deep in thought. Why had the man said he'd like to speak to her father? She'd be worried she'd done something to offend if his praise hadn't been so sincere. Was he serious about praying they'd meet again soon? What did this all mean?

"Well, he's right about one thing," Naamah declared aloud as thunder rumbled and fresh rain began to fall. She hurried as fast as she could on the muddy path, slipping and sliding now that she was going up-hill. Despite the difficulty balancing her jar, she didn't mind getting wet. Rain was always scarce in this region, therefore always a welcome reminder of Yahweh's promise to the Israelites, "I will send you rain in its season."

The words combined with the beat of raindrops against the clay jar to become a new song forming in her mind. As lyrics and music wove together, Naamah pushed the strange conversation with the man at the well from her mind. It most likely meant nothing, and she would undoubtedly never see him again.

Chapter 8

Hushai arrived home just in time for the evening meal with a quickness to his step and a lightness in his mood. He waited to share his good news with Nasya until they'd finished their meal and were enjoying a glass of wine together. "I believe I may have found a solution for King David's melancholy."

"Wonderful!" Moving closer to Hushai, Nasya looked directly into his face. "Out with it, my husband."

Hushai relaxed back into his floor cushion with a grin on his face. It was such a joy to have good news to share rather than the stresses of the palace as of late. "Just today returning from Syria, I came across a young girl with the voice of an angel. Now before you get too excited, I must still involve Asaph. After all, he knows more about music than I do. But I can say this. From what I heard, I believe she could do for King David what our king did for King Saul."

"You mean, soothe his spirit?" questioned Nasya.

Hushai nodded.

"Well, tell me how this came about," Nasya pushed. "Tell me about her!"

"We'd stopped at a well just a few leagues from Jerusalem

to water the animals when a girl walked up to fetch her own water. She was singing as she walked, and her voice was more beautiful than a nightingale. I think I frightened her with my stares, but her voice was so lovely I couldn't help myself. I felt immediately she was an answer to my many prayers."

"Go on," Nasya coaxed. "Was she lovely to look at?"

"I paid no attention to such things!" Hushai said severely, though his eyes twinkled. "In any case, it had been raining, and little was to be seen under her muddy cloak and scarf. I needed to know more about her, so I asked her several questions. She told me she has played the lyre since a very little girl and that she began composing music when she was seven or eight years old."

"So she has a gift," interjected Nasya. "Much like our son."

"Yes," agreed Hushai. "Naamah—that is her name—has the gift of music and poetry. Her words are as lovely as her melody. Our son Reuel has the gift of an artist's eye and a scholar's ear to be able to draw any image exactly as he saw it or remember and write any word he has heard or read."

"An artist and a scholar," responded Nasya thoughtfully. "I supposed that describes our son's gift, but I still do not understand it." She paused, then added pensively, "It might be nice if this young woman could meet our son. Even if their gifts are in different areas, at least they would understand the passion behind each other's gifts."

Hushai's twinkle deepened as he smiled at his wife. "I know what you are thinking. And perhaps you are right that this girl may be right for our son as well as our king. I did get her father's name, so I can speak with him once I have spoken with Asaph. I hope to approach Asaph tomorrow."

The following morning, Hushai walked past the palace to the

tabernacle, which had been pitched within the fortress grounds once the Sukkot festival had ended. Entering the gate of finely twisted linen, he requested one of the Levites on duty to call for Asaph. As he waited, he looked around the courtyard with its bronze lavar and altar, the white linen panels and gold pillars of the courtyard wall, and the tabernacle tent itself under its covering of animal hides.

Impressive as a place of worship for wandering tribes in the wilderness. But after so many centuries, the weavings and hides were getting worn, the brass tarnished. Now that Israel was a great nation no longer moving from place to place, Hushai wished that King David would consider building a temple to Yahweh, one far more splendid than this folding tent, to give glory to their great God. Perhaps Hushai should bring it up at their next advisory meeting.

The Levite soon returned, followed by Asaph. As always, the chief musician wore a simple linen tunic and robe, both white, with a colorful sash, today's a deep blue. Asaph led Hushai to his own administrative quarters as chief musician within the palace near the administrative quarters of the king's chief scribe.

Hushai had a profound esteem for Asaph, whom King David had elevated to oversee hundreds of singers and musicians in leading daily worship before Yahweh. A Levite and skilled songwriter who wrote distinctive, forceful, and spiritual music, Asaph excelled in passing on the purposeful practice and understanding of music in worship to others. But what Hushai admired most about Asaph was that he remained a humble man despite all his talents and high position.

After a few moments of casual conversation, Hushai began. "Master Asaph, I am going to need your expertise. I had a chance meeting with a young girl who has the voice of an angel. She also plays a lyre. I was surprised to discover that she has already been writing music. If she is as good as I think she is, perhaps she could play or sing for our king when times are stressful for him. The idea came to me when I considered how King David played for Saul and soothed his spirit. But I am no expert when it comes to music, which is why I am coming to you."

Asaph seemed very interested, almost leaning on Hushai's every word. "She is not only gifted both vocally and with the lyre but writes her own music? That is less common."

"That is what she told me. The song she sang was an exquisite psalm of praise to Yahweh but not one I've ever heard before. Still, I don't have your wide knowledge of music. Perhaps if you heard her, you would know if she is telling the truth."

"Then indeed, we should go meet this girl," Asaph responded. "It may be that you have found a new musician for the king's court. But we had better find out more about her first."

"It is but a two-hour ride to Naamah's home. That is her name. If we leave at first light tomorrow morning, we will have ample time not only to examine her gifts but find out more information about her family."

"I will plan on that. Let's meet outside the entrance to the palace."

Hushai bid farewell to Asaph. Somehow, he felt he was beginning a journey ordained by Yahweh.

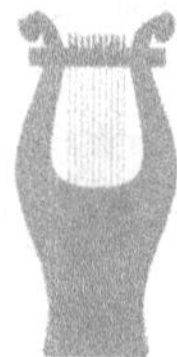

Chapter 9

A sound of hoof trots drew Naamah's glance to the tall, wood double doors of the compound gate, which stood open during the day for easy access. She gasped audibly and dropped the stone with which she'd been grinding flour.

"Naamah, what is it?" Zahara looked up with a frown from her own grinding. "What is the matter?"

"It's the man from the well. He's here!"

"The man from the well? What do you mean?"

Naamah was at a loss for words. A party of half a dozen horsemen had dismounted on the packed-earth track outside their home. Two were dressed in fine robes, including the man who'd admired her singing the previous day. The remainder were in the same soldier's garb she'd seen at the well. She saw among them the soldier who had filled her water jar.

"Do you know these men? Do you know what this is about?" Zahara grilled Naamah.

"No, I don't know any of them," Naamah whispered back. "But the one in the blue robe liked my music."

"He liked your music?" Zahara spoke with too much fervor, drawing the attention of Alzbetah, who was seated under an awning putting the final touches on her new basket pattern.

"What are you two talking about?" Setting down her basket, Alzbetah rose to her feet and walked over to the gate. "What in the world!"

Approaching the gate, the man in blue said courteously, "I am looking for Abdiel and his daughter Naamah. Is this his home?"

"It is." Alzbetah gave Naamah a sharp look. "But my husband is in the orchards. Shall I send someone to request his presence?"

"Please. It is important I speak with him. I have come from Jerusalem."

"Zahara, go find your father!" Alzbetah ordered brusquely.

Naamah knew her mother well enough to be aware she was dying of curiosity as to how these strangers knew her daughter by name. But she wouldn't ask in public. As Zahara jumped to her feet and scurried out the gate, Alzbetah turned to the visitor with a courteous smile. "You must be tired from the trip. May I offer you and your men water? Or perhaps a cup of wine?"

"Thank you, but it was not our intention to disturb your work," the man responded. "We will wait for your husband outside."

As soon as the man had returned to his party, Alzbetah swung around to Naamah. "What is going on? How do these men know you? What have you done?"

"Nothing!" Naamah responded weakly. "As I told Zahara, I met the man in the blue robe yesterday at the well. It was for just a few moments. He said he liked my singing. He asked my name and who my father was. Then he rode away."

"Hmmph!" Alzbetah snorted. It was a sound that in her mother's repertoire had a thousand meanings, but her expression softened, and Naamah knew she was no longer in trouble. "We will see what he wants of your father."

It was no more than ten minutes before Zahara and Abdiel showed up outside the gate. Their hard breathing made clear Abdiel had felt such an unusual visit merited coming at a full run. Entering, Zahara returned to her flour grinding. The rest of the women and children scattered around the courtyard returned to their own tasks, though furtive glances out the gate made clear everyone was as curious as Naamah as to the horse party's reasons for visiting their hilltop home. It was a full half-hour before Abdiel entered the courtyard.

"What is it, Abdiel?" cried Alzbetah. "Why are you staring at Naamah? Has she done something wrong?"

Abdiel shook his head, apparently to clear his mind. "On the contrary. Naamah's singing seems to have caught the attention of one of King David's advisors named Hushai. He shared this information with Asaph, King David's chief musician. They came here today to hear her sing and play the lyre."

Abdiel rubbed the back of his neck as an astonished murmur swept the courtyard. "They had many questions. What tribe we are from. If we are faithful worshippers of Yahweh. If we attend the festivals. What we do for a living. How Naamah's gift came to be known. And on and on."

Alzbetah and Zahara both looked at Naamah with questions written all over their faces. Naamah's jaw dropped as her face flushed, and she looked at her father in unbelief. Abdiel went on, "They want to speak to Antje as well since she taught Naamah how to play the lyre."

Under the awning where Aunt Antje had been working on baskets with Alzbetah, Naamah's aunt got to her feet. "I will bring out the lyre."

While Aunt Antje scurried into her own quarters, Abdiel hurried inside to bring out carpets and cushions that were used for Sabbath services. He clapped his hands. "Let us clear this area!"

Within moments, the household women had cleared away their various tasks while Abdiel spread out carpets and cushions under the awning to form a comfortable resting spot. He urged his two guests to make themselves comfortable. "Please rest! And let me bring water for your feet and wine for your refreshment."

Hushai and Asaph entered the compound. Already, Zahara was rushing forward with water and a towel. As they settled themselves under the awning, she slipped off their sandals and washed the dust from their feet. By the time she had finished, Abdiel had poured wine into two cups of finely worked silver only used for weddings and other special occasions.

Carrying the lyre, Aunt Antje exited her residence and handed it to Naamah. Naamah sank down onto one of the carpets a few feet from the awning and settled the lyre in her lap. Only then did she glance timidly toward the visitors.

Catching her eye, Hushai smiled warmly. "Good day, Naamah. Did I not promise I would return? And do you know who this is?"

He gestured toward his companion. Naamah nodded mutely. She swallowed before she could get any words out. "Yes, Asaph, King David's chief musician. I have seen him many times at the festivals. His music is like listening to angels. It is my dream to make such beautiful music to our Father God. Though perhaps that is a conceit for a village girl like me."

She broke off, flushing with embarrassment. What would these important men think of her presumption in putting herself in the category of Asaph's elite musicians? But Asaph's expression was kindly as he responded, "It is never a conceit to wish to praise our God in music. And Hushai tells me you have a gift of song that equals the best of the temple musicians. Shall we find out if he is right?"

Chapter 10

Naamah swallowed again. She had never been so nervous, and she wasn't sure she could get a note out of her throat right now. Asaph leaned forward. "Don't be afraid, child. And do not even think of us. Just pick up your instrument and raise your voice in praise to Yahweh. But first, I have a few questions for your teacher."

At Hushai's request, Aunt Antje joined them, and Asaph began to question her. Naamah was in such a state of shock she only heard bits and pieces but recognized that Asaph was asking about Naamah's musical ability, the age at which Aunt Antje had begun working with her, the songs she'd composed, and more. The older woman showed none of Naamah's bashfulness and answered each question forthrightly.

Finally, she turned to Naamah, "They would like to hear you play now, dear."

Naamah was so nervous she was afraid her fingers were too stiff to play. Her fingers strummed a jangling chord. Seeing her distress, Hushai said gently, "Turn away from us, think of your gratitude to Yahweh, and sing the song I heard at the well."

His kindness gave Naamah strength and she began to pluck

the strings. Very soon, she lost herself in the music that took her to a place of peace. "It is good to praise the Lord and make music to Your name, O Most High. I sing for joy at the works of Your hands."

"Beautiful!" cried Asaph as the last note floated across the courtyard and Naamah stilled the strings with both palms.

Naamah's eyes flew open at the sound of his voice, and her heart skipped a beat. It began to calm as she saw her father and Aunt Antje smiling at her. Naamah recognized a look of pride on both of their faces.

Asaph looked over at his companion. "Hushai, you were right. I have rarely heard a voice so beautiful nor someone who can play the lyre in such a way that it draws you into a place of blissful peace."

Asaph turned to Naamah. "How many songs have you composed on your own?"

Naamah pondered a few moments. "I don't know. At least several dozen. I could count them if you wish it."

Asaph waved a hand. "Never mind that. Can you remember all of them?"

"Yes," Naamah answered honestly. "You see, they just come to me, often brought on by circumstances. Once I have the entire song in my mind, I can recall it as often as I like."

"That is good for now," Hushai interjected, looking at Asaph. "But I think she should have them written down so they can be used for other purposes. And there may come a time when they are more difficult for her to recall."

"Yes," Asaph agreed. Under his breath, Naamah heard him say, "Such a gift!"

Hushai turned to Abdiel. "The two of us would like to speak with you privately."

"Well, I never …" Alzbetah's voice trailed off at a stern glance from her husband. Abdiel exited the courtyard with the two visitors. It was just a few minutes before Naamah heard the swift clop of hooves as the horse party rode away.

Abdiel reentered the courtyard. "They are going to speak with King David."

"Speak with King David?" Alzbetah repeated, looking stupefied. "Whatever for? What would the king want with our daughter?"

Abdiel smiled at Naamah. "The king's advisor and chief musician have been seeking a court musician to play for King David when he is tired and in need of solace as our king played for King Saul when he was young. After witnessing your gift, Naamah, they believe you may be that person. They want you to go to the palace to play and sing for the king."

Naamah stood in shocked silence, but her mother was quick to speak. "How can she sing for the king? She is but a girl! Court musicians are men!"

"Miriam, the sister of Moses, was not a man but led the women in singing to Yahweh after Pharaoh's army was defeated," Abdiel pointed out peaceably. "In any case, they have given us until tomorrow to prepare Naamah to travel. Then they will send someone to fetch her."

& & &

"Reuel, we are only sparring for practice and to get some exercise." His friend parried Reuel's powerful sword stroke with difficulty. "You're not supposed to actually kill me!"

Seraiah, who oversaw the palace scribes such as Reuel, had instructed that all scribes should be proficient in hand-to-hand combat. This was to ensure they could hold their own if called to the battlefield on courier duty. Seventeen-year-old Reuel, who had his father's jet-black hair and steely, inquisitive gaze, took this directive seriously.

Reuel lowered his sword. "Fine. I must get back to the palace anyway. Tomorrow we will run the streets of Jerusalem and lift rocks to build our muscle strength."

"You certainly enjoy this more than I do," his friend interjected.

"Not really." Reuel walked off.

Reuel enjoyed the feeling of being strong, but this didn't take away from his passion for his job—that of a scribe. He'd found a certain joy and intrigue in the written word since he was a young child and had discovered he could read a passage just once and remember it verbatim.

Reuel quickly changed from the kilt he'd worn for combat practice into the tunic and robe of a scribe and hurried to exit the training grounds. Realizing he was late, he hastened through the palace corridors, passing storerooms, guards quarters, libraries piled high with scrolls and stone tablets, and finally ended where he felt most at home, the scriptorium where the scribes spent their days. Reuel walked to the table where he worked. Seraiah, who did not let anything pass by his eagle eyes, took notice and immediately strode over to give Reuel an assignment.

"A descendant of Korah came to me with a song he composed. However, he is not able to write it down. So I am giving you that task. He should be here shortly to speak the words to you."

"Very well." Reuel began to lay out his tools, which included animal skins he'd turned into fine parchment, ink made from gallnuts, and his pen, a quill with the top cut at a precise angle and length.

Just then, Asaph entered and walked directly to Reuel. "Reuel, would you fetch one of the ancient scrolls for me? I need it for that song we spoke of yesterday. I thought I could complete the song without the scroll, but now I realize I will need it as a reference."

With his ability to recall anything he'd read, Reuel knew exactly where the scroll Asaph needed was stored. He was thrilled to handle one of the ancient accounts of their ancestors such as Abraham, Isaac, Moses, Joshua, and all the judges. Reuel cherished the feel and smell of the scrolls as well as the words written on them. He cheerfully did as Asaph requested and headed to the specific library room where the scroll was housed.

Chapter 11

Just as Hushai had said, two men appeared early the following morning to take Naamah to the palace. Naamah was the first to notice as in her anxiety she'd been up early and had climbed to their rooftop to keep an eye out. The two men rode in a cart with fine carvings on it pulled by two oxen. Abdiel hurried out to meet them.

When he came back inside, the entire extended family had gathered in the courtyard to say goodbye. Naamah wore her best robe she normally kept for Sabbath and festivals, though the handspun fabric seemed inadequate for a king's palace. Her mother was bustling around to cover up her wet eyes, filling a cloth with bread, cheese, and a small waterskin.

Sensing his wife's angst, Abdiel took her hand. "This is a great opportunity for our daughter, Alzbetah. She may be able to fully use her gift."

"But what if King David likes her?" Alzbetah pleaded. "Where will she stay? At the palace? Will she travel back and forth from home to Jerusalem? I just do not understand."

"You are right, Alzbetah. Some of this is very uncertain right now. But Hushai has assured me he will look after Naamah.

If need be, he said Naamah could stay with him and his wife. I am sure she will be able to come home for visits, and we can visit her when we travel to Jerusalem for the festivals."

Alzbetah looked very unsure about this plan. Abdiel continued, "I trust him, Alzbetah. In any case, I also inquired of my cousin, who has worked as a stone mason under Hushai. He is not just the king's advisor but the architect who oversaw the building of King David's palace. My cousin assured me Hushai is not only kind and wise but a sincere follower of Yahweh."

Alzbetah wiped away an escaping tear as she left her husband's embrace to hug Naamah instead. "Oh, my daughter, what an honor has come to you! Just to be asked to play before the king is a great credit to you. This gift was given to you by Yahweh, and you must go and do your best. We will deal with the outcome whatever that may be."

As Alzbetah released Naamah, Aunt Antje took her place. She was holding her lyre. Setting it down, she hugged her niece. "I am so proud of you, child! And I'm sure King David will be astonished when he hears you. One thing I know is that you are a far more gifted musician already than I could ever aspire."

Naamah returned the hug fervently. The deep bond between Naamah and her aunt was different than the love she felt for the rest of her family because it was born out of sharing a mutual gift, that of music. As she released her aunt, she was stunned when Aunt Antje picked up her lyre and placed it in Naamah's hands. "Take this with you. Having your own lyre will give you calm, and I will be blessed and honored to have you play my instrument before our king."

"It will remind me of you!" Taking the precious gift, Naamah followed her father outside to the cart. The whole family went with her. Abdiel pulled his daughter into his arms for a farewell embrace. "We will pray for you, Naamah. We will trust that Yahweh has a grand plan for your life."

Zahara seemed at a loss for words, but Naamah noted that her sister's eyes were dark with fear of the unknown. As the two embraced, Zahara whispered into Naamah's ear, "I want you to do well, but I want you to remain home with us more."

Abdiel broke the moment. "You must go now, Naamah."

Everything was a blur to Naamah as she mounted the cart with the help of her father. She was afraid to look back at her family. If she did, she felt she might jump off the cart and rush back into her mother's arms, never having found the strength to grasp this opportunity that Yahweh had provided for her. She found comfort in gripping the lyre to her chest.

Naamah settled into the back of the cart while the two men sat on the driver's seat in front of her. One was tall and muscled in the same dress as the soldiers who had accompanied Hushai. The other was small and plump with long black curls and far too dark of skin to be an Israelite. He wore a colorful robe of fine fabric. He had no beard growth, and his skin looked soft for an adult male. He was clearly someone who had never had to spend time toiling in the fields under a hot sun.

The oxen leaned into their harness, and the cart began to move. Other villagers poured outside as they drove through the center of the village. Naamah's exciting news had clearly traveled ahead of them.

They had barely cleared the village gate when the smaller man began complaining bitterly about the bumpy ride in the wagon. Naamah was fascinated to notice his voice was high-pitched like a woman. His hand movements, the multiple jangling silver bracelets on each arm, and the toss of his head also seemed feminine. Or perhaps such mannerisms were a norm for men in whatever nation from which he'd come.

As the road wound past familiar terraced olive groves and vineyards on rocky slopes, Naamah gradually settled into calm. Occasionally, she fingered her lyre, though she didn't break into song. When the walls of Jerusalem rose up ahead, Naamah could feel panic rising within her. As they entered the city gate, the cart wheels clattered on stone-paved streets.

Spread out on both sides of the gate was the market, which Naamah never got to explore thoroughly during the Sukkot festival due to the crowds. The scents of horses, camels, sheep, and goats fought the aromas of exotic spices and honeyed sweetmeats. Her eyes were tantalized by bright-colored tapestries, ivory, copper, shawls, and scarves. She wished she could enjoy the sounds of shoppers haggling, but fear was taking a hold of her heart.

The oxen continued through the city and up a hill. At the top was King David's palace, which Naamah had only seen from a distance across the valley. Up close, the site was intimidating with its high stone fortifications. Once guards waved the cart through an entrance, Naamah saw an immense building of carved stone, marble columns, and cedar surrounded by multiple stepped terraces and beautiful gardens. It was said that the cedars had come all the way from the mountains of Lebanon when King Hiram built the palace for King David.

Her family's farming background allowed Naamah to identify many varieties of trees. Palm. Pomegranate. Mulberry. Fig. Pine. Olive. Evergreen. Added to the perfume of flower beds and sage, the entire palace grounds gave off such a wonderful fragrance that Naamah again felt calm return to her heart and mind.

The oxen plodded around to a far side of the palace and

stopped outside of a narrow door. A guard stepped forward to help Naamah out of the cart. She hugged the lyre close to her chest. The small, plump man hopped down with an agility surprising to his appearance. As the cart moved off, he waved Naamah forward impatiently. "Come with me. Hushai has asked that I provide you with a new tunic and robe before you see the king. Oh, and my name is Chinua."

Chapter 12

Chinua headed down a long corridor, Naamah staying close behind for fear of getting lost. There were corridors branching off in all directions and countless people walking swiftly. This was a maze she'd never be able to retrace should she lose her guide. She was thankful for the lyre that shielded her body from the curious stares of so many pushing past her.

At last, they entered a room filled with chests and shelves and hooks from which hung items of clothing. On the shelves were folded robes, veils, sandals, perfume flasks, and other items Naamah didn't recognize. Grabbing a tunic from one of the hooks, Chinua held it up to Naamah, only to replace it with a tunic from another peg. Once he found a tunic that met his approval, he handed the daffodil-yellow garment to Naamah. "Put this on while I find a robe for you."

Naamah stood with the lyre in one arm and yellow tunic in the other. "Here?"

Chinua continued sorting through the robes, clearly oblivious to anything else around him. Unsure what she should do, Naamah just stood holding the tunic and her lyre. Holding out a linen robe in the same soft yellow as the tunic, Chinua stated the obvious. "You have not changed!"

Naamah blushed as bright as crimson.

"I understand," Chinua sighed. "I will exit the room. You will put on this yellow robe and the tunic you are now holding."

Once Chinua left, Naamah placed her lyre on the floor and hustled to change. She was just finishing when Chinua returned. He frowned. "Let me see your hair. We do not have very much time. They are expecting us soon."

He fussed with Naamah's hair, combing it with his fingers before adding a cloudlike length of material a darker bronze than the tunic to replace her dusty headscarf. Again, Naamah could feel her face flushing. She was thankful when Chinua decided he had done what he could. "Come, it is time for us to go to the throne room. Bring your lyre."

Naamah scurried to follow Chinua through more corridors. She wished she could find this grand spectacle of the palace exciting, but her heart was beginning to beat very fast in her chest. Too soon, she followed Chinua into an antechamber with a floor of polished white stone and walls painted in bright colors with black symbols and pictures. Massive stone pillars were spaced along this hallway. Between them hung gold lamps waiting to be lit when darkness fell.

The antechamber held several couches made of cedar carved in a decorative fashion and covered in a fine purple fabric embellished with red embroidery. Naamah sighed with relief when she spotted Hushai and Asaph smiling at her from one of the couches.

As she approached, they stood.

"Are you ready, Naamah?" asked Hushai.

"I believe I am."

"I think it would be best if you begin by singing and playing your own composition you sang for us," Asaph instructed.

"Yes, I will do that."

Hushai turned to Chinua. "Will you wait here? I will give instructions once we know the king's wishes."

Hushai and Asaph led the way toward huge cedar double doors. A guard swung the doors open while another announced their arrival to King David. Naamah caught her breath as she followed Hushai and Asaph into the enormous throne room. Like the corridor, the floor was of polished white stone that swept up to a throne of ornately carved cedar.

On the throne sat a handsome man dressed in fine purple robes, thick black hair lightly flecked with grey flowing from beneath a gold crown. He looked bored, mechanically tapping a gold scepter topped by a large red jewel against his other hand. Naamah had no doubt she was gazing on King David.

On the far wall opposite the throne was a floor-to-ceiling mural divided into three sections. Naamah immediately grasped that each mural depicted a scene from King David's life. The left panel showed a young David killing the giant Goliath with a sling and a stone. The panel on the right was a scene showing David the warrior and his mighty men defeating the Philistine armies. The middle panel was a depiction of King David being crowned king. To Naamah's surprise, the huge room was otherwise empty of people.

"This is the young woman of whom I told you, my king. Her name is Naamah." Hushai's voice drew Naamah back to the present.

King David focused his attention on Naamah. "She is fair enough of face."

Naamah blushed, clutching her lyre close, as the king's eyes roved over her body. Hushai spoke with a sharp familiarity that surprised her. "It is not for her face that we have brought her here, my king, but for her gift of song. Truly one that could only come from Yahweh Himself."

Hushai turned to Naamah. "My child, why don't you play for your king?"

Asaph motioned for Naamah to take a seat on a cushioned couch against a wall to the left of the throne. She felt as though she was going to faint. Raising her lyre, she breathed a quick, desperate prayer. "Help me, Yahweh! Help me!"

As she'd done the previous day, Naamah closed her eyes and tried to shut out all around her but the music. "It is good to praise the Lord and make music to Your name, O Most High."

When the song finished, she shifted into another of her own compositions. "May God be gracious to us and bless us and make His face shine upon us. May all the peoples praise You, O God. May all the peoples praise You. Then the land will yield its harvest, and God, our God, will bless us. God will bless us, and all the ends of the earth will fear Him."

This time, she let her voice and the lyre die away into silence. She opened her eyes. King David was leaning forward on his throne. She jumped at the sound of his voice, "Where did you learn that song?"

Naamah glanced at Hushai. When he gave her a reassuring nod, she said diffidently. "I composed it myself."

King David looked over at Hushai. "Just as you said, my friend. Indeed, this young woman does have a very special anointing of Yahweh's spirit. And she is very beautiful."

Sitting back in his throne, King David rolled his scepter back and forth in his hands, seemingly pondering something. Then he spoke decisively. "I believe this young woman's music may comfort me when my soul is in turmoil. I will take her as a concubine and personal musician. She will be placed in my harem."

Naamah's heart plunged down to her sandals. A concubine would be required to have intimate relations with King David. What if he uncovered her secret? He could easily order her stoned to death with such a discovery!

"Hushai, take Naamah immediately to the harem and have her prepared to be part of my court," King David went on. "Then send word to her father and pay him a substantial mohar."

Naamah glanced at Hushai, whose face looked like he'd been struck by lightning. King David continued, "And Asaph, you must make sure her musical abilities are used to their full potential. I am thinking her compositions should be written down so that they may be used in worship to Yahweh."

King David's face was suddenly alight, his boredom gone. "I am riding out with Joab to inspect the new chariots arriving from Damascus. But perhaps tonight I will call for—." He gave Naamah a closer look. "—Naamah, right? I will call for Naamah, and she can teach me more of these compositions. Perhaps we can sing together."

The king smiled at Naamah. But instead of feeling comforted, she felt terrified. She to sing along with the sweet psalmist of Israel, as the king had been characterized? How had she ended up in such a place? She suddenly wished she'd never raised her voice in song at the well.

Chapter 13

King David was now on his feet and heading out of the throne room in restless, powerful strides. Naamah suddenly recognized that walk. King David must have been the man she'd seen pacing the terrace during the Sukkot festival. But who had been the woman down below the parapet? Perhaps she could find out whose rooftop that had been.

Asaph was already on his way out of the throne room. Hushai beckoned Naamah to follow him. As though sensing her turmoil, he slowed his steps and glanced back to smile at her compassionately. This small kindness gave her strength to clasp the lyre to her chest and continue her journey out of the throne room one step at a time.

Chinua was waiting in the antechamber. As Asaph walked off, Hushai addressed Chinua. "Naamah is to become part of the harem. I will leave it to you to make sure she is comfortable and cared for. Make sure Semere understands she is not only to be a concubine but the king's personal musician. He may call often for her to play and sing for him. Beginning with this evening."

Naamah's heart sank even further as Hushai walked

slowly away. Even though she'd only met the king's advisor three times, he'd been at least a semblance of familiarity and connection to her family in this strange place. She followed Chinua out of the antechamber and down a hallway. They were about to turn the corner down another corridor when Naamah suddenly realized she wouldn't be returning home that night as she'd believed.

In fact, what would happen once she entered the king's harem? Would she ever see her family again? She was fearful of a life without her family. But she was even more terrified of King David finding out about her secret.

Stopping dead in her tracks, Naamah lost her grip on her lyre, which almost fell to the ground before she somehow caught it. Seeing that Naamah was no longer following him, Chinua hurried back to her. "What has happened? Are you ill?"

Tearing up, Naamah replied, "I want to go home! I do not want to be a concubine! I came to sing for the king, not to enter a harem! Now I will not see my family again!"

"That is not true," Chinua assured. "Your mother, sisters, and other female family members are permitted to visit you in the harem. And I am sure there will be times you can visit your home if it is not too far."

"Truly?"

"Truly. Now would you like me to carry your lyre for you? You must be very tired."

Looking at Chinua, Naamah realized that however odd he might seem, he was being kind. "No, thank you. I appreciate the offer, but I prefer to keep it with me. It reminds me of my family."

Naamah also realized that whether or not she was afraid, she must go forward into this new life Yahweh had placed before her.

"Help me, Yahweh! Help me!" she whispered with each step as she followed Chinua through the palace.

Exiting the maze of hallways, Chinua led Naamah into a room crowded with shelves and tables where a tall, bronze-skinned man in yellow-orange robes was overseeing what looked like a physician's store of bottles, jars, ointments, pastes, and powders of all colors in glass and pottery containers.

"Semere, this is Naamah. King David has chosen her as his newest concubine. I was instructed to tell you that King David has also appointed her his personal musician and may call upon her at any time. She needs the proper attire and beauty treatments."

Semere immediately approached Naamah, taking in every piece of her body with his penetrating gaze. Naamah could feel the heat rise in her face, and she clutched the lyre even closer. Silently taking the lyre from her grasp, Semere continued his evaluation. To himself, he mumbled, "Skin fairer than most and smooth for a villager. She has done one thing right remaining out of too much sun. A delectable body. She is already a vision. With proper beauty treatments, we will refine her into a delicacy worthy of our king. Take her on into the harem and begin your work."

Naamah was thankful when Semere handed her back her lyre. Chinua led Naamah through another short corridor into a part of the palace that seemed to be its own entity. Numerous rooms opening onto verandahs surrounded a courtyard open to the sky. Like her own home, any number of women of various ages with their children were sitting, working, playing. But here were several times the women and children living in her father's compound.

Chinua led the way into a room that had one large bed plus a small one. Both beds were low to the floor. Two walls had seats built against them where one could sit and talk or embroider or do other things. On another wall was a large storage chest. The cold mosaic floor was covered with a rug of many colors. Shuttered windows, now swung open, looked out onto the courtyard.

Before Naamah or Chinua could say a word, a woman silently entered the room. Naamah had never seen someone so tall, especially for a woman. She immediately noted the penetrating blue eyes, nose shaped liked the beak of an eagle, skin much fairer than Naamah's, and the palest hair Naamah had ever seen, a yellow almost the same hue as Naamah's tunic. The woman looked at Naamah with the same assessing stare as Semere.

"Akilah, this is Naamah, King David's latest concubine," said Chinua, "Semere has assigned her to me for beauty treatments. I knew Shiphrah had a room to herself, so I thought she could share with Naamah. You will be responsible for her as well as Shiphrah."

Without even taking a breath, he continued, "You would not believe what a trial it has been today obtaining her. Sitting on a hard seat for hours. A ridiculously bumpy road. Then the stench of the oxen!"

Chinua waved his hand in front of his nose as if reliving the torture of the smell. Dryly, Akilah retorted, "I am sure it was awful for you."

Chinua didn't seem to notice the mocking tone in Akilah's voice. "I believe the best place to start is with the bath. Akilah, I will have you take care of that."

Naamah had so many questions piercing her mind. What

was this bath they spoke of? Who was Shiphrah? Where had this woman Akilah come from that her coloring was so odd? And her size! Should Naamah be afraid of this tall female?

"Would you like me to store this for you?" Chinua reached for the lyre Naamah still carried.

Naamah shrunk away, feeling she might break into tears, "No, I have already said it is all I have of my family. I want to keep it with me!"

Chinua stopped his motion, and once again Naamah saw kindness in his face. "Of course. Then we will find something to keep it in here in your room. Meantime, you can set it here while we take you to the bath."

He gestured to the large bed. Reluctantly and carefully, Naamah laid the lyre down. Chinua returned to his practical manner. "Akilah, find her a new tunic on your way. Something with a little more color. I was way too rushed when I chose this one."

"I agree. Yellow makes pale skin look sallow, a reason I never wear it." Akilah started for the door. "Come, Naamah, follow me."

Chinua walked with them only a short distance before disappearing down a hallway. Naamah's heart felt heavy as she followed Akilah back into the maze that was the palace. She felt as though she was walking into an unknown world and future. Coping with this female giant who might or might not be someone to fear was one more new challenge when she was already exhausted.

As it was, Akilah glared at every person they encountered. Naamah noticed they all gave the tall woman a wide berth as they passed. Akilah stepped briefly into a storeroom to grab a tunic in soft blue and a brightly woven basket filled with finely engraved alabaster jars. Several corridors later, they descended a stairway into a large, exquisitely decorated room. There was a row of decorative columns, and the walls were painted with pastoral murals. Benches of polished white stone lined three of the walls.

In the middle of the room was a large sunken pool several times the length of a tall man. Naamah was horrified to see a dozen other undressed women already in the pool. All of them were staring directly at her.

"There are other women here!" Naamah exclaimed under her breath.

"Why, of course," Akilah responded. "This is the royal bath."

Seeing the alarm and doubt in Naamah's face, Akilah was gentle. "I will be right here with your towel and clean tunic when you have completed your bath. Here is the soap you will use."

"But … my clothes will be off! These women will see my body!" Naamah could feel her face turning a bright shade of crimson.

Akilah chuckled quietly. "Who bathes with their clothing on? If your town is too small for proper baths, have you never been swimming in a river with your sisters and female family members?"

"Not unclothed!" Naamah could see she had no choice but to disrobe. As she began to do so, Akilah whispered, "Do not attempt to cover yourself as you enter the pool. Walk in as though you have done this many times or the other women will have reason to talk about you."

With a gulp, Naamah entered the pool where steps had been created for this purpose. She held her head high even though she knew there was a red hue to her entire body in her embarrassment. Akilah handed Naamah the soap and a sea sponge. The fragrance was similar to the mixture Naamah used at home, though she thought she detected olive oil rather than the animal fat her mother used to make soap for the family.

Akilah then removed from the basket what looked like some type of blade made of a shiny black stone and held to a white stone handle by strips of leather. Stropping the blade back and forth on a piece of leather, Akilah held it out to Naamah handle-first. Puzzled, Naamah took it, her discomfort rising as she felt the eyes of the other women following her.

Akilah whispered, "The razor is for your lower private area. All wives and concubines use this tool to shave that smooth."

The scarlet returned to Naamah's face as she fumbled with this unexpected task. She was grateful Akilah stayed near to whisper instructions on how to use the scary device. Once she had completed her bath, Naamah stepped out of the pool and into the towel Akilah held out for her. Akilah used her tall body to shield Naamah from the stares of the other women.

"You will get used to it," Akilah encouraged, sorting through the remaining jars in her woven basket. "And they will get used to you."

At a loss for words, Naamah simply wanted to get clothing back on. Before she could do so, Akilah pulled out a jar. "This is frankincense. Do not be alarmed. I am simply going to massage it into your hair and body with this oil."

Naamah found the smell of musty pine, citrus, and spice vaguely familiar. Akilah pulled out another jar. "And this is myrrh, which I will use to perfume your body."

When Akilah had finished rubbing both substances all over Naamah's body from hair to the soles of Naamah's feet, Naamah asked timidly, "May I get dressed now?"

A smile lightened Akilah's formidable features. "Yes, of course. Here is your new tunic."

Naamah was thankful to cover her body. She was also grateful for the compassion that Akilah had shown to her. Perhaps she'd found a friend in this towering woman rather than someone to fear.

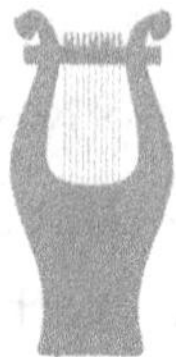

Chapter 14

Which was more than Naamah could say for the other women. Not one of them had spoken to her before Naamah and Akilah left the pool room. On the journey back to her quarters, Naamah felt comfortable enough with her towering companion to bring up a topic she'd been mulling over all day. "Akilah, I do not understand Chinua."

"No one understands Chinua," Akilah retorted.

"I mean, the way he looks and speaks. It is—" Naamah lowered her voice so no one walking past could hear. "He seems at times as though his body and voice do not know whether he is a man or a woman."

"Oh, I understand what you are asking," Akilah replied. "You see, Chinua is not really a man any longer. Eunuchs such as Semere and Chinua are placed in charge of the harem since men such as these no longer desire the bodies of women."

Naamah could feel her face burning flame-red even though she was uncertain what Akilah meant. Rather than continue such a discussion, Naamah remained quiet until they reached her room. She was thankful Akilah didn't pursue the topic either.

Chinua was in the room when they returned. Naamah immediately noticed another bed and chest had been brought in. The chest had been propped open, and Naamah could see her lyre nestled inside on a pile of robes. Just then, a woman entered the room holding a little girl by the hand. Taller than Naamah though nowhere near as tall as Akilah, she had fine features and a fair complexion. Where sunshine from the window touched her dark hair, it had a reddish tint. Though slender, she looked as if she might be pregnant.

The little girl, who was a miniature of her mother, stopped dead in her tracks at the sight of Naamah. "Mommy, who is that lady? And why was my bed moved over there?"

Chinua directed his answer to the woman. "Shiphrah, this is Naamah. She will be your roommate, so we had to make some changes to your room. Semere and I have decided that Akilah will act as maidservant to both of you."

Shiphrah smiled at Naamah. "Welcome to the harem. This is my daughter, Amaris."

"I am three," announced Amaris.

Naamah leaned down to the level of the little girl. "Hi, Amaris! I am glad to meet you. My name is Naamah. I hope we will be friends."

Shiphrah looked at Naamah with a smile of gratitude as Amaris nodded shyly at Naamah's suggestion.

"We still have much to do before the evening meal," announced Chinua.

"Yes," agreed Akilah. "We have not chosen any cosmetics yet for Naamah's face."

Shiphrah touched Naamah's arm gently. "Listen to them. You do not want to give the other women fodder by appearing without make-up and so drawing attention to yourself."

"There you see," Chinua interjected. "Shiphrah understands. As I said, we have much to do."

"Come, Amaris. Let's go play with the other children in the courtyard and leave these three to work together." Taking her daughter's hand, Shiphrah smiled at Naamah. "I will be back to accompany you to the evening meal. It is nice to have a friend with you when you enter that world."

At least her new roommate seemed friendly. Yahweh must be watching out for Naamah by placing her with Shiphrah. Chinua was already digging through the basket that Akilah had taken to the bath. "Have you ever created eyebrows? Or used eyeliner?"

Naamah shook her head no.

"Then I will show you how it is done. The paint is in these glass containers. And these reeds are to apply the paint."

Chinua took his time creating eyebrows that pleased him, then used eyeliner to accent Naamah's eyes. He also applied rouge to her cheeks. When he handed Naamah a bronze mirror, the face looking back at her looked much older, a full-grown and quite alluring woman.

"Now, let me see your teeth." Chinua grabbed Naamah by the jaw.

Naamah was becoming accustomed to Chinua's demands and obediently opened her mouth.

"They do not seem to be in bad shape yet. We must begin the care of her teeth so she can keep them for many years." Chinua took another juglet from the basket. "Open up again."

With his fingers, Chinua rubbed a dry powder mixture all over Naamah's teeth. She opened her eyes wide in disgust, choking out her words around the foul substance. "What is that?"

Akilah laughed. "It is bad, is it not? He will not get near me with that concoction of his. It is powdered ash from ox hooves, myrrh, powdered burned eggshells, and pumice. He also claims it works as a breath freshener. Yuck!"

Once Chinua had his fingers out of Naamah's mouth, she tried to talk without drooling. "How do I get rid of it? Am I supposed to swallow this rubbish?"

Chinua snatched up the towel. "Akilah, bring her water to rinse her mouth."

Akilah poured water from a flagon sitting on one of the wall benches into a tin cup. After rinsing it around, Naamah was handed a bowl in which to spit the dirty water. She repeated with clean water.

When she was done, Chinua opened the new chest and pulled out a bundle deposited beside the lyre. "I visited the royal seamstress and hand-picked items for Naamah."

The apparel Chinua unfolded were all of fine fabric and brightly colored. Akilah helped Naamah into the new clothing one by one. First was a tight sheath dress of fine linen the color of golden walnut. This had a front panel intricately embroidered with red and green with an accent of yellow.

Akilah then wrapped a soft yellow belt around Naamah's waist followed by a cloak of fine wool woven in stripes of cream, red and green. There were leather sandals with tiny tinkling bells on them.

"And the headband." Chinua handed Akilah a band of leather embroidered in yellow and adorned with gold droplets that would dangle across Naamah's forehead. As Akilah placed the headband on Naamah, Chinua was obviously delighted. "Ah, she is a beauty!"

"Yes, you are beautiful, my lady," added Akilah .

"You most certainly are, Naamah." Shiphrah and Amaris reentered the room. "Are you ready for supper?"

Naamah nodded wordlessly, overcome at her new finery.

"Amaris, you go with Akilah to eat with the other children," said Shiphrah. "I will take Naamah to eat with the women."

Amaris happily hopped across the room and took Akilah's hand, clearly in no way intimidated by Akilah's fierce demeanor.

Shiphrah guided Naamah down a hallway she hadn't yet traversed. Naamah could soon hear women's voices. Together, Shiphrah and Naamah entered a hall where two long, low tables of cedar wood were laid out, a much longer one perpendicular to the other. Dozens of women were crowded around both. Shiphrah nodded at the shorter table on the far end of the hall as she led Naamah to an open spot halfway down the longer table. "That is for the king's wives. We concubines sit here."

Naamah sank cross-legged onto a soft rug between Shiphrah and a woman somewhere in her late twenties or thirties. In her seated position, the table was just high enough for Naamah to reach for bowls and platters of lentil stew, parched grain, cheese, and a stewed mutton dish set along the center of the table. But she was too nervous to eat or even fill the silver cup placed in front of her from the flagons of wine that were interspersed with the food. Never had she dined in finer accommodations than a woven cloth spread out on the ground.

Accepting a piece of flatbread from Shiphrah, she kept her head down, nibbling halfheartedly. All around, she heard the shrill voices and laughter of other women. Were they speaking to her?

Naamah felt Shiphrah nudging her and realized a question had been addressed to her. Raising her eyes, she saw an encouraging smile on the face of a pretty young woman across the table. "So where are you from, Naamah?"

Naamah managed to get out an answer. Then the woman beside her said, "Shiphrah tells us you have your own lyre and that you played for the king this afternoon. You must be very talented."

"Perhaps you will play for us," the woman across the table added. "We all love to sing, but no one here is expert on an instrument."

Naamah relaxed. These women weren't so different from her own sister and mother and aunts and girl cousins and other village women to whom visitors with new stories and skills to alleviate the sameness of each day were always welcome. "Of course, I would be happy to. Perhaps even this evening if I am not called by the king."

By the end of the meal, Naamah was conversing freely. She told of her own village and family. The other concubines told of how they'd been chosen for the harem, some during the king's wandering years before he'd captured Jerusalem, others as gifts from other kingdoms. A tall black-skinned young woman with a short cap of tight curls almost like a lamb's mane was Nubian. Another with copper skin, a high-bridged nose, and waist-long extremely curly hair was a gift to David from the king of Syria in Damascus.

They chattered about their children, their latest attire and jewelry, beauty treatments, even disagreements with other harem women, but not about the king. It was as though King David was a taboo topic. Which made sense if all these women were vying for the king's favor. Unlike Naamah, who would be happy if the king never called for her again.

But one thing was evident. Despite the luxurious accommodations, food, and drink, these women lived a very prescribed and even boring life cooped up in a cage that might be golden but was a cage nonetheless. At least Naamah had her music.

"You did well," Shiphrah reassured Naamah as they headed back to their room. Amaris had stayed behind to play with the other children. "I am so glad you have joined us. You will fit in nicely with the rest of us. It is not a bad life. And soon perhaps you will have children of your own like Amaris and this coming little one."

Shiphrah patted the slight bulge of her belly. But her kind words didn't have the effect she'd intended. Naamah stopped dead in her tracks, her eyes suddenly welling with tears at the reminder that she wasn't here for a pleasurable visit but the rest of her life.

"I don't want to fit in here," she whispered. "I want to go home. I only came to play for the king. No one asked me if I wanted to stay!"

"No one ever asks us women what we want. Do you think any of us were given a choice to come here?" Shiphrah took Naamah's hand and squeezed it. "But it will get better. And believe me, Naamah, it could be a lot worse. I'd rather be the king's concubine than married to the old goatherder with three dead wives who tried to purchase me for his fourth before I caught the king's eye on his last campaign against the Moabites."

As the tears fell, Shiphrah said nothing more but just continued to hold her new friend's hand. Naamah's mind was empty from anxiety and fatigue. She couldn't think of words or songs. The only thing that ran continuously through Naamah's spirit was a simple prayer. "Help me, Yahweh. Help me!"

Chapter 15

Hushai's morning meal and rest revitalized him. Above all, the opportunity to speak with Nasya, whose practical nature routinely eased his worries. When he'd shared why Naamah wouldn't be staying with their family after all, she'd assured him that she'd still keep Hushai's promise to her parents to watch out for the girl, whether visiting her in the palace or inviting her to their home. Hushai was grateful that Nasya understood the concern he felt for Naamah, having been responsible for bringing her to King David's attention.

What Hushai hadn't shared was his great disappointment that Naamah was no longer a potential wife for Reuel. With both of them such unusually gifted individuals, they would have common ground on which to build a good marriage. Now none of that would come to fruition thanks to the king's impulsive decision to seize Naamah for himself alone. Did he not have enough women in his harem?

Upon entering the palace, Hushai hurried to the throne room. A full report on what he'd learned of the new Damascus fortifications had been waylaid by the flurry of finding Naamah and bringing her to the palace. The king had instructed Hushai to deliver a private report this morning. But he found only a few guards on duty in the antechamber and throne room.

"Where is King David?" Hushai asked the closest guard. "I was instructed to meet with him here."

"Yes, he is expecting you. King David said he was going to take a walk on the terrace until you arrived."

An even larger set of doors than those leading to the antechamber opened from the throne room directly onto the terrace. It was through here that visiting dignitaries and their entourages approached the throne. Stepping outside, Hushai saw the king a good fifty paces to the right standing at a parapet that overlooked the neighborhood in which Hushai and many others of the king's top administrators had their residences.

Hushai strode over to join his friend. Looking down, he recognized the rooftop almost directly below. It was that of Uriah, one of King David's top thirty Mighty Men who had fought at his side even while King Saul was still trying to kill David. Of Hittite descent, Uriah's family were long-time converts to the worship of Yahweh, as evidenced by Uriah's name, which meant "Yahweh is my Light."

Hushai knew Uriah was with Joab and the armies of Israel besieging the Ammonite city of Rabbah. So what was the king finding of such interest in Uriah's home? Hushai was appalled when he looked down to see a woman with tumbled dark hair and beautiful features stepping out of a large portable copper bath with nothing but a thin strip of toweling wrapped tight around her body.

Hushai immediately recognized Uriah's wife Bathsheba. Young enough to be Uriah's daughter, the woman had been barely nubile when Uriah first brought her to the encampment in Hebron in the earliest days of David's reign over just his own tribe of Judah before the death of Saul's son Ish-Bosheth led to all of Israel pledging their support to David. Uriah had moved his household to Jerusalem along with the rest of David's closest companions when the fortress became David's capital. Hushai had glimpsed Uriah's wife only occasionally and at a distance when the woman had joined his own wife and other women of David's court at temple festivals and other celebrations.

With her face and hair uncovered and her thin covering revealing every curve of her body, she was certainly an alluring sight. And she had to know her rooftop bath was fully visible from the parapet above. As immediately confirmed by the king's longing whisper. "Bathsheba! What a beautiful woman! So fair of face and tongue and thought. Uriah does not deserve her!"

"My king!" Hushai interjected urgently.

King David shook himself from the spell which seemed to hold him. "Hushai, what are you doing here?" After a moment, he continued, "Oh, yes, your report on the Damascus fortifications."

Hushai bowed, "Yes, my king."

King David patted Hushai on the back. "Come then, my friend. Let us get some work done."

Hushai headed back across the terrace. King David did the same, but suddenly turned back to one of the guards. Hushai heard his low order distinctly. "Send messengers to the wife of Uriah and have her come to me."

Hushai was stunned, his mind racing. Had his dear friend and king, anointed to the throne by Yahweh's own prophet, the sweet psalmist of Israel who had restored the worship of Yahweh from one end of the land to the other, truly instructed that the wife of one of his most loyal warriors be brought to him? What could this mean? Surely not what it sounded! Was this more of the dark melancholy that seemed to shroud King David lately?

"Naamah!" Hushai whispered to himself. Maybe her beauty and God-anointed gift of music was the antidote for King David's black moods and obsession with another man's wife. Much though he'd been disappointed to forfeit the young woman as a wife for Reuel, perhaps it was to prevent the king from a terrible misstep that Yahweh had placed Naamah in Hushai's path. After all, Yahweh had removed Saul from the kingship over disobedience to His command. What dreadful consequence might result from Saul's replacement deliberately breaking the sixth commandment by taking his loyal servant's wife?

& & &

"Naamah, Naamah, wake up!"

Reluctantly opening her eyes, Naamah found Shiphrah leaning over her and shaking her by the shoulder. It had been a restless night of sleep. Her cries to Yahweh throughout the night had been interspersed with brief periods of sleep brought on by exhaustion and high emotions. She could tell by the sunlight slanting in the open window that it was now late in the morning.

"You are being called for, Naamah," Shiphrah added.

Sitting up, Naamah recognized the tall, dark-skinned eunuch—whatever that meant as she'd still been given no clear explanation—she'd met in the room she had thought was a physicians' storeroom. What had his name been? Oh, yes, Semere. And by his demeanor, he held authority over Chinua and Akilah. He was carrying the most exquisite lyre Naamah had ever seen. Made of cypress wood, it was highly polished with a gold inset forming a star and lion for the house of King David at the very top. Naamah could see her own reflection dancing in the sheen.

Semere held out the lyre. "Chief Musician Asaph has chosen this lyre specifically for you. The king wishes for you to have the finest instrument in both beauty and sound to play in his court."

Naamah gasped with pleasure as she took the shining lyre into her hands. "For me?"

She gently plucked a chord. The pure harmony made Aunt Antje's lyre, fine though that was, sound like a jangling noise. A reminder that her aunt was without an instrument while she now had two. She looked up at Semere.

"This is beautiful. And I thank the king and Chief Musician Asaph for such a treasure. It is the most beautiful gift I've ever owned. But I do not need two instruments. Would it be possible to send my own lyre back to my family?"

The tall eunuch nodded regally. "Of course. I have been asked to arrange for a message from Hushai and a mohar for your father to be sent to your family. I can send the lyre as well."

Setting down her new treasure, Naamah hurried over to her chest and pulled out Aunt Antje's lyre. As she passed it to Semere, he asked, "Is there a message you would like to send to your family with this?"

Naamah hesitated. What she really wanted to say, she didn't

dare. Which was that she didn't want to be here and wanted her father to come immediately and retrieve her. Though looking at the new lyre, she felt a stirring of excitement at the thought of playing something so beautiful for her king and his court. As Shiphrah had said, maybe being here wasn't so bad. "Just tell them, please, that I am well and that the king has expressed approval of my music."

"Very well." Semere again dipped his head. "One other thing. After the evening meal, tonight, you are to go to King David. So you may want to take the remainder of the day to acquaint yourself with your new instrument. I will return when the time comes to escort you."

Naamah's heart froze with fear. Was the king summoning her to play again — or for more? Suddenly all the beauty treatments and fine new clothing took on a terrifying perspective. Was tonight when her secret would finally be discovered? And by the king, no less?

Chapter 16

Naamah's entire body went rigid, and she couldn't move. Chinua was still prattling on. "Is she going to play for the king or give him pleasure in bed? Which it is makes a great difference in how I am to dress and prepare her. Even the oils and perfumes will be different for a bed experience than if she is to entertain. Or is it to be both? That complicates the decision."

Seeing the color totally drained from Naamah's face, Shiphrah intervened. "Chinua, calm down or you will only add to her anxiety. Why, you are making *me* nervous! Naamah, why don't you play us a melody with your beautiful new lyre. We have plenty of time before you need to prepare for the king. And do not fear. We have all been to the king many times. He is a kind man as well as a passionate one. He will be gentle with you."

Shiphrah's words were not the reassuring ones her roommate believed. But Naamah picked up the lyre. The sounds were so beautiful she soon lost herself in the music. She was astonished to raise her head sometime later and discover that the room, doorway, and even hall beyond were crowded with harem women listening in rapt silence. The light had faded.

Akilah stepped forward and lifted the lyre from Naamah's hands. "It is time to begin preparations, my lady."

A murmur of disappointment rose from Naamah's audience. Shiphrah stepped forward, making a shooing motion with her hands. "And the rest of you. It is time for the evening meal. You, Ziphorrah." She beckoned to one of the younger concubines. "Bring Naamah some food on a tray. It is too late for her to dine properly. And not too much. She does not want to go to the king on a full stomach."

The next hour was a blur for Naamah. She attempted to eat something from the tray brought her while Akilah and Chinua laid out still another outfit and the ubiquitous basket of ointments and makeup.

"I have heard of a new way to perfume the whole body," commented Chinua, shaking out a robe.

"What is that?" asked Akilah.

"You start a small fire in a clay bowl, then add perfumed oil much like burning incense. The woman crouches over the bowl with her tunic and robe draped over her head to form a tent. As she perspires, her skin and clothing absorb the fragrance of the oil, leaving her thoroughly perfumed by the time the fire burns out."

"Well, we do not have time for that!" Akilah exclaimed.

"Not tonight but perhaps next time," Chinua replied. "You know the women of this harem will do anything to get an advantage."

"Our Naamah doesn't need such an advantage," Akilah retorted. "But I agree the women will do anything. I saw the king's first wife Michal the other day with a nasty substance all over her face. It smelled terrible."

"Oh, that is a new treatment for age spots," explained Chinua. "Quite popular for older women."

"But what is it?" Shiphrah asked. "And does it work?"

"It's the excrement of lizards," Chinua revealed gleefully. "As to whether it works, do you see any fewer wrinkles on that old crone's face?"

"What?" Akilah and Shiphrah chimed together.

"You're just making that up!" said Shiphrah. "That's awful!"

"Not at all," Chinua responded. "It is very popular in Egypt, where all the best beauty treatments are born. So is crocodile dung, though that is harder to obtain here in Israel."

Naamah realized she was thankful for the banter between her three companions. It took her mind off her fear and gave her something to think about other than her secret. She whispered a thank you to Yahweh for these new friends.

Once Naamah had finished eating, Chinua hurried from the room while Akilah helped Naamah into her new outfit. By the time Naamah was dressed, Chinua entered with new sandals in one hand and oil perfumed with balsam in the other. He sprinkled the balsam on the sandals. "When Naamah walks or clicks her heels, the fragrance will be released. Brilliant, is it not?"

"You are a wonder," Akilah said dryly, brushing out Naamah's hair. "It must be hard to contain such brilliance!"

Chinua scowled up at the tall woman. Naamah intervened hastily. "Akilah, I have been meaning to ask, are all your people so tall and fair?"

"Indeed, yes, my lady," Akilah responded. "The Amorite people are known for being among the tallest on the earth. Except for the giants, of course. The Nubians may be as tall, though of course they are black of skin and look very different."

"Amorites!" Naamah exclaimed. "But I thought the Amorites were enemies of Israel."

Naamah flushed as she realized her statement could be construed as rude. But Akilah just shrugged. "Men fight wars. Women pay the price. Much of my nation was destroyed by the Israelites under Joshua when they first came into Canaan. But the Jebusites who built the fortress of Jerusalem were among the remnants of our race."

Akilah paused briefly to sprinkle gold dust across Naamah's curls. "When King David captured Jerusalem, I alone survived of my family. I was but a small girl and spared from annihilation like the males and women who had reached puberty. Most of the other children were sent into slavery in Damascus. But Abigail, one of King David's wives, took me as her maidservant. It was she who taught me to worship Yahweh."

"I am sorry," Naamah whispered. And here she had been whining about her own lot! "You have such a story to tell."

Akilah shrugged again. "Yahweh has been good to me. And I use my height to my advantage. I put on my fierce demeanor, and those who like to make trouble stay away from me."

Retrieving the mirror from the basket, Akilah handed it to Naamah. "Enough of stories. Take a look at yourself. Naamah, you are beautiful! No king could desire more."

Gazing into the mirror, Naamah was amazed. Not even her earlier transformation could have prepared her for what she saw. Gold dust sparkled in her long ebony curls like stars in the night sky. She still wore the gold headband with droplets dangling onto her forehead. But her dress was now the creamy-white of fresh milk with gold threads elegantly embroidered into the fine linen. Tiny shards of gold set into the bodice glimmered as Naamah moved. Around her waist was a wide belt of vibrant teal also embroidered with gold threads.

"I truly look beautiful!" Naamah lowered the mirror. "Thank you, Chinua. Thank you, Akilah!"

There was no more time to admire herself as just then Semere showed up in the doorway. All her pleasure at her new appearance abruptly drained away. The danger she feared was now upon her. As she picked up her new lyre and followed Semere from the harem, she prayed in silent fervor. *God of Israel, I am so afraid King David will find out I am not a virgin. Protect me, Father God, protect me. You can keep my secret hidden forever. I am not sure what to pray for, Yahweh. I just know I need you. Go with me, Father God. Just be with me.*"

Semere was silent as they navigated the labyrinth that was the palace. It was now fully dark outside, and the shadows dancing in the glow of the gold lamps seemed to take on the form of the man who had sprung out to rape her. Naamah could barely force her feet to move. Semere became so impatient at waiting for her to catch up that he finally grabbed the lyre from her hands, tucked it under his massive arm, and grabbed her wrist with his free hand to tug her after him.

Suddenly, Naamah was reminded of a psalm King David had written when he was on the run and taken captive by the Philistines. It had been a favorite story her father told from Israel's most recent history. "When I am afraid, I will trust in you. In God, whose word I praise, in God I trust. I will not be afraid. What can mortal man do to me?"

The beat of her heart calmed to the familiar words, pushing out the fear. As Naamah quickened her pace, Semere released her to walk on her own. Over and over, she repeated silently the king's inspiring words. It was a reminder that even the great king was still a mortal man and Yahweh was in control.

Naamah almost bumped into Semere when he abruptly stopped. It was then that she looked up and shook herself from her thoughts. They were in a corridor that reminded Naamah of the antechamber with its polished white floor and colorful walls that led into the throne room. But this was on a much smaller proportion. In the light of a pair of gold lamps, Naamah recognized Hushai standing outside a single panel door of cedar covered with carvings.

Semere looked surprised to see the king's advisor. "My lord, I wasn't expecting to see you here at this hour. Did you have further instructions for me?"

"Not at all," Hushai said calmly. "But since it was I who recommended Naamah's presence and gift of music to the king, I want to make sure personally that all goes well tonight. You may leave, and I will escort Naamah from here."

Bowing slightly, Semere handed Naamah's lyre back to her and turned to leave. Hushai looked down at Naamah with a smile that was kindly but also seemed to hold worry. Was Hushai as apprehensive about the king's reaction as Naamah? Or perhaps he simply felt responsible for having taken her away from her family.

"I pray you are adjusting to the palace," Hushai commented. "I see you have received the lyre."

"Yes, thank you. It is a truly wondrous gift."

"Yes, well, music has always spoken to the king's soul. It is to be hoped that with such a beautiful instrument, your exquisite voice, and your playing will elevate the king's spirits. I will now take you to his bedchamber so you can play for him."

The word "bedchamber" once again awoke Naamah's terror. She clung to the lyre as though it could protect her as Hushai signaled a guard standing at attention outside the carved door to open it. As he did, Hushai looked down at Naamah and said with quiet gentleness, "I hope you will believe me, child, that none of this was my intention when I brought you here. Asaph and I believed you would be a blessing to our king with your music. That the king would choose to make you his own was unexpected to us both."

Naamah could hear the implied apology in the advisor's careful words. Just knowing he cared was a comfort. She smiled at Hushai bravely. "It is Yahweh who brought me here, and I am happy to serve our king."

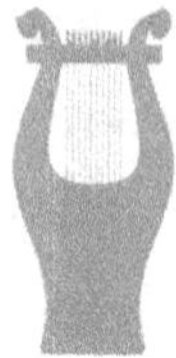

Chapter 17

Hushai rested his hand on Naamah's shoulder in a brief affectionate squeeze, then motioned her to enter the door in front of him. The room into which they stepped was like no bedchamber Naamah had ever seen, being almost in size to her parents' entire home. The first section was designed for sitting with a long, wide couch of carved cedar wood piled high with brightly colored cushions along one wall. In front of the couch was a low table of the same cedar. The walls were painted in red, yellow, and cream with a top border filled with symbols and pictures. A lion skin covered the white stone floor.

On another wall was a fireplace. A wide arch beside the fireplace led into another section where Naamah glimpsed a huge bed waist-high off the floor with a mattress as big as her bedroom at home. A doorway stood open onto a garden. Windows on either side showed a panoramic view of Jerusalem and the Mount of Olives across the valley. Standing at one window was King David.

"My king," began Hushai. "As we discussed, here is Naamah, your new concubine, who will play her lyre for you."

King David turned from the window, but he seemed distracted, and Naamah wasn't sure he'd even heard Hushai.

"You said you wished her to play for you again tonight," Hushai continued. "If you will allow it, I know her music may bless you."

The king's brooding glance moved to Naamah, then back to his advisor. "Very well, she may play for me." He smiled slightly. "And you may leave, dear friend. I know well your wife is wondering why you are not yet home. You do not need to hover as though your pretty songster needs protecting."

Hushai's rueful smile emphasized the close friendship between the two men. He turned to Naamah. "May Yahweh be with you, child."

Then he was gone. King David sprawled out on the couch. Naamah stood where she'd been left, unsure of where she was to perform.

"I find that it is the most comfortable to play while sitting," King David commented. "Come, sit with me here on the couch."

Jolting herself out of her stupor, Naamah moved to the far end of the couch from the king and settled the lyre on her lap. What did you play for a king? Then the words rose again to her mind as they had during her long walk. Softly, she played and sang, "When I am afraid, I will trust in you. In God, whose word I praise, in God I trust. I will not be afraid. What can mortal man do to me?"

As the last notes died away, King David spoke musingly, "So it isn't just your own compositions you sing. I was not so much older than you when I wrote those words after the Philistines seized me in Gath. Now play me one of your own songs. Perhaps the one you sang in my throne room."

Naamah's fingers began moving again across the lyre, this time more confidently. "May God be gracious to us and bless us and make His face shine upon us. May all the peoples praise You, O God. May all the peoples praise You. Then the land will yield its harvest, and God, our God, will bless us. God will bless us, and all the ends of the earth will fear Him."

When she finished, King David gazed at her for what seemed a long time. Then he said sincerely, "That is every bit as beautiful a praise to our God as any psalm I have written. We must ask Asaph to teach it to the choirs for worship at the tabernacle."

Naamah caught her breath. "A song of mine at the tabernacle?"

"Why not?" The king's smile held humor. "We sing songs composed by Miriam, the sister of Moses, and the prophetess Deborah. Why not one by Naamah, the concubine of David?"

King David ended any further discussion. "Now, sing me another. The first you sang in my throne room."

Naamah began obediently, "It is good to praise the Lord and make music to Your name, O Most High. To proclaim Your love in the morning and Your faithfulness at night to the music of the ten-stringed lyre and the melody of the harp."

She broke off as a guard opened the door and stepped inside. "My king, the woman you summoned has arrived."

Without further instruction, a woman entered the antechamber. She was tall and beautiful, her dark hair and eyes contrasting vividly against pale-gold skin and wine-red lips. She carried herself with the almost arrogant assurance that men found her desirable. A sky-blue tunic draped her body gracefully, her small waist accentuated by a darker blue sash that was the same shade as her cloak.

King David rose to his feet. "Bathsheba, my dear, you have come!"

Bathsheba fell to her knees before the king in a posture of adulation. But her dark eyes held smoldering passion while the half-smile on her red mouth was both bold and intimate. Naamah sucked in her breath in sudden realization. Just as she'd recognized the king's restless stride, so now she recognized the exquisite features she'd last seen half-cloaked in torch light. This was the woman King David had been watching from the palace parapet that first night of the Sukkot festival with such intent focus that Naamah had sensed the emotional bond between them from a mountain ridge away!

King David's gaze, as heavy with passion as Bathsheba's own, did not move from the newcomer's face as he waved a hand toward Naamah. "Leave us!"

Naamah almost dropped her lyre as she scrambled to her feet. She hastened to the door just as King David reached down and lifted Bathsheba to her feet. They were already moving toward the arch that led to the bed by the time Naamah was outside. The guard closed the door behind her. They both stood looking at one another, unsure what to do.

"I believe I should go back to the harem," Naamah finally stated. "But I am not sure I can find the way."

"I will find someone to guide you," the guard replied. "Just wait here a moment."

He walked a few paces down the corridor and around a corner. A moment later, he returned with another guard.

"Follow me." The new guard led Naamah down corridor after corridor until at last he knocked on a door that looked familiar. Semere opened the door. Behind him was the workshop where Naamah had first been introduced to him.

He gave Naamah a dark look. "What happened? Why have you left the king?"

"He … he had someone else with him," Naamah explained. "He told me to go."

Thankfully, Semere asked no questions, just guided Naamah back to the harem. As they walked, Naamah's heart returned to a normal rhythm. While she remained confused at the passionate exchange between King David and Bathsheba, her main emotion was profound relief. Yahweh had answered her prayer, and once again she'd been spared the terror of her secret being found out.

Stepping into her room, Naamah spotted Shiphrah and Akilah fussing around Naamah's bed. They jumped back startled when they saw Naamah. "What are you doing back already?"

Moving further into the room, Naamah saw what they were doing. Her bed was now piled with several soft blankets and an embroidered pillow. Spread out on top was a tunic of thin material worn for sleeping. At the foot of the bed was a small cedar wood chest opened so Naamah could see the treasures within. Along with all the cosmetics and perfumes Chinua had used were an intricately carved ivory spoon, a bronze mirror, and several gold hairpins.

Naamah looked at the two women, confused. Shiphrah smiled gently. "All of these things are yours now that you are a woman of the king's household."

"And there is one more thing." From beside the bed, Akilah lifted out another exquisite box that had an unusual shape, "Chief Musician Asaph had this delivered for you. It is to hold your lyre when it is not in use."

With Akilah's help, Naamah placed the lyre in the box, then

set the box against the wall right next to her bed. She gave each of the two women who were already becoming her friends a quick hug. "How do I ever thank you?"

"Thank us by finding a good life here with us," Shiphrah responded. Akilah was silent, but there was a smile of pleasure on her face as she helped Naamah out of her finery. Snuggling into the soft blankets, Naamah was hopeful that by focusing on the acts of kindness shown to her throughout the day, she'd be able to sleep in this strange place.

But almost immediately, Naamah found herself in the bushes along the road fighting for her life. Vulgar hands touched her body, but this time she somehow knew they were the hands of King David. She cried out in panic, "Help me, Yahweh! Help me!"

Then in her dream, Naamah heard Aunt Antje playing her lyre and her mother's loving voice singing, "When I am afraid, I will trust in you. In God I trust. I will not be afraid. What can mortal man do to me?"

Naamah reached for her own lyre to join in but at that moment awakened to find she'd been wrestling her new blankets. She looked over to make sure she hadn't roused Shiphrah or Amaris. They were breathing the deep breaths of slumber. Lying back down, Naamah gave silent voice to the words going around and around in her tortured mind. *Help me, Yahweh! Help me!*

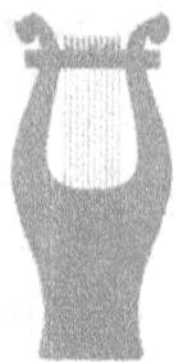

Chapter 18

The following morning, Shiphrah could see from Naamah's fatigued expression that she'd had a troubled night. After breakfast in the dining hall, she encouraged Naamah to join her and Amaris in the bright sunshine of the courtyard. This was quite different from the courtyard in Naamah's own home. For one, it was many times larger and included flowerbeds, shade trees such as palm, pomegranate, fig, and olive, and sweet-smelling bushes interspersed with walking paths. Stone benches were scattered under the trees and in the center of the courtyard so the women could visit together.

As Shiphrah led the way out into the sunshine, Naamah saw many women and girls she'd seen at meals scattered around working on embroidery, combing each other's hair, or simply relaxing in conversation. Children ran around the benches and along the paths while babies were rocked in their mothers' arms.

As Amaris ran off to join the other children, Naamah commented, "I have noticed most of the children here are girls. Do the boys not stay with their mothers?"

"Only until they are fully weaned," Shiphrah responded. A

sad expression flitted across her face. "Then it is not considered appropriate for them to remain in the women's harem. Above all, because they are the king's sons who must grow into great warriors. My son Jerimoth is now seven years old, and he has been in the quarters for the king's sons since he was four."

Pride replaced the sadness. "As a son of the king, he is being taught to read and write and the arts of war. He is already strong and agile for his age, so I have no doubt one day he will be a great warrior like his father the king. Perhaps even one of the king's Mighty Men, to which even the son of a concubine can aspire."

Shiphrah glanced over at Amaris, arguing vociferously with another little girl her age, and placed a hand on her belly. "But I cannot help hoping this new little one will be another daughter like Amaris so we need not be parted until her marriage. We are allowed to see our sons on Sabbath and sometimes festivals when they are not receiving instruction. But it is not the same, and we are not permitted to have them visit the women's quarters."

Shiphrah guided Naamah across the courtyard. "But let us not speak of sad things. There is someone I would like you to meet. Her name is Abigail."

"Abigail?" questioned Naamah. "Oh, yes, Akilah mentioned her. She is the king's wife who took Akilah as her handmaid, is she not?"

"Yes, Abigail is one of King David's earliest wives long before he was king," answered Shiphrah. "But she is not haughty with the concubines like some of the other wives. She is kind to all of us. Most importantly, her joy and calm come from her trust in Yahweh."

Shiphrah motioned to a tall, stately woman in a shimmery

blue robe who was seated on a bench fingering a small lap harp under the shade of a pomegranate tree. Though the age of Naamah's mother or a bit older, the woman showed no gray in the long, straight black hair held back by a golden band nor more than the tiniest of laughter wrinkles on her beautiful oval features.

"Abigail has often told us the story of how in Yahweh's favor she became the king's wife. Her first husband was a mean, churlish drunk who offended King David and his men unforgivably after they had protected him from harm. They were on the point of killing his entire household when Abigail stepped in to make peace. Yahweh struck her husband down for his evil behavior, and the king rewarded her godly wisdom by taking her as his wife. She tells us her story as a reminder that even if our situation is not what we would have chosen, Yahweh will work out our life path for good if we but place our faith in Him just as He did for Abigail despite the evil husband to whom her parents sold her.'"

"She is certainly very beautiful," Naamah murmured agreement. "And not just because of her outward beauty. I see wisdom and goodness in her face and eyes."

As they reached the bench where Abigail was now standing, Shiphrah introduced Naamah. A cordial conversation followed. Already, Naamah felt a friendship forming with this woman who had such a quiet joy about her. When several other women approached to chat with Abigail, Shiphrah led Naamah through the courtyard, identifying some of the other wives and concubines present—Michal, Ahinoam, Maacha, Haggith, Abital, Eglah, Jytte, Seraphina, Chaya, Bilhah, Zahra, Atefah, Brielle, Tahlia.

"And the girl over there is Tamar, the king's daughter by

Maacha, daughter of King Talmai of Geshur across the Jordan River. She is just ten years of age. But because of her status as daughter and granddaughter of kings, she already has a marriage arranged with a younger son of the king of Moab once she becomes nubile. That will be some years, of course. Her older brother Absalom is King David's third-born son, which gives her even higher status than many of the king's wives."

Shiphrah lowered her voice. "Abigail's son Daniel was the king's second son after his first-born Amnon. But sadly, Daniel was killed in battle some years ago with no children of his own, so poor Abigail sees the children and younger women of the harem as her daughters and grandchildren, having none of her own."

Shiphrah's words changed Naamah's thoughts of Abigail from awe to compassion. How sad to lose one's only child! The news strengthened Naamah's determination to be a friend to the older woman. If Abigail was partial to the harp she held, perhaps they could even make music together.

Shiphrah didn't even try to introduce Naamah to any of the other wives, not one of whom bothered to waste a glance on the new concubine strolling by. Tall for her age and already developing the beauty of a young woman, Tamar was as lavishly dressed for a stroll in the courtyard as Naamah had been for the king's presence the night before, the ten-year-old turned out to be affable and unpretentious when Shiphrah introduced them.

When Shiphrah boasted of Naamah's musical gifts, Tamar immediately beseeched Naamah to tutor her on the lyre. "I have always wanted to learn, but my mother tells me I am too clumsy. How talented you must be to be playing for my father when you are not so much older than me!"

"I am four years older, but I was playing long before I was your age," Naamah said with a smile. "I am sure with practice you will be capable of learning. When you are free, just come and find me."

"Tamar!" At her mother's raised voice and beckoning gesture, Tamar hurried over to join Maacha, but she threw a friendly grin at Naamah behind her mother's back. Naamah had no doubt she'd made another friend. If still a child, one much closer to her own age than the harem women she'd met to date.

Chapter 19

Shiphrah left Naamah's side to chase after Amaris, who had disappeared into the bushes. Just then, Akilah approached. "You have visitors, my lady."

"Visitors?" Naamah responded, stunned. "Are you sure you have the right person? Who would I know to visit me here in the palace?"

"Well, one is your mother. The other, I do not know."

"My mother!" Naamah gasped. Joy filled her heart. "Then take me to them immediately."

"They are waiting in the smaller courtyard where women of the harem receive guests."

Naamah followed Akilah back into the palace and down a corridor not yet familiar to her. They entered a small courtyard that had a gate leading through the outside wall of the palace grounds. Two women were seated on a bench under an olive tree. They jumped up as Naamah entered.

"Mother! Zahara!" Naamah rushed into the embrace of her mother and sister.

"Oh, my daughter, I have missed you!" exclaimed Alzbetah. "Even though it has only been a short time since you left."

"And I you! I am so happy you have come! Zahara, you haven't changed at all!"

"Well, it has been only a couple days!" Zahara teased, hugging Naamah tight. She lowered her voice. "Who is that giant woman who brought you here? I've never seen a woman that tall or with such pale hair and skin!"

"Oh, that is my maidservant Akilah," Naamah said nonchalantly.

Zahara gave her a sharp glance. "How swiftly you have changed, sister, to be speaking of having servants at your beck and call."

Naamah flushed. "I didn't mean it like that. It is solely because I am now in the king's harem. I share Akilah's services with my roommate and her daughter. Come, let me show you my quarters."

Akilah had been waiting a discreet distance away at the entrance into the palace. Naamah led her mother and sister at Akilah's heels through the corridors to her sleeping quarters. She discovered some pleasure in their astonished exclamations at the polished stone floors, colorful murals, and tall columns that had been new to Naamah just days earlier. Perhaps she was growing used to all this splendor.

Naamah lifted her new lyre from its storage case. "This was given to me as a gift by King David. Chief Musician Asaph chose it himself so that I may play my very best when the king summons me."

"Yahweh has truly favored you, daughter," Alzbetah said slowly. She looked from the beautiful instrument to the ornate beds with their soft blankets and pillow, the carved chests, and brightly painted walls. "I have always known your gift was meant for far greater things than our small village. But I never dreamed of anything so fine as this. I fear you have grown far beyond our family. With all this, you may not even want what we have brought you today."

"Never!" Naamah responded fiercely. "Yahweh has provided for me here, and I am even finding friends. But nothing will ever replace my family."

Choking back sudden tears, she forced a smile. "What is it you have brought me? I cannot wait to see!"

Reaching into her bag, Alzbetah handed Naamah a blanket woven in stripes of blue and yellow between the tan. Naamah immediately recognized it as the blanket her mother had been weaving for Naamah to take to her new home when she eventually married. Alzbetah had finished a similar one with blue and red stripes for Zahara just before her betrothal.

Naamah could no longer hold back her tears as she realized her mother and sister must have worked non-stop to complete it after Naamah had been taken away. "Oh, Mother! I will cherish this even more because I know how much you hate weaving."

The rest of the morning passed quickly as the three women curled up on Naamah's bed, exchanging news of the family for stories of Naamah's experiences to date in the harem. Naamah played the new lyre softly for her mother and sister so as not to attract attention. At noon, Shiphrah stopped by with Amaris on their way to the mid-day meal, and Naamah introduced them.

Not anxious to share her precious time with her mother and sister, Naamah asked Shiphrah to have Akilah bring a tray to their room. Once again, Alzbetah and Zahara showed astonishment at the ample choices of food as well as Naamah's easy summoning of a servant. To Naamah, it began to feel as though a wall was going up between her family and her new life.

Finally, Alzbetah stood up with a sigh. "We must leave, Naamah, if we are to reach home by dark."

Naamah now knew the way to walk her mother and sister back to the smaller courtyard and its gate leading beyond the palace walls. A guard stationed outside on the terrace opened it so Alzbetah and Zahara could slip outside. As they left, both promised to visit again, if not soon, then when the family came to Jerusalem next for a festival.

Once they were gone, Naamah rushed back to her room, where she hugged the blanket to her chest and wept into her pillow. Soon, she felt a warm hand stroking her hair.

"Don't cry, Naamah!" Shiphrah said sympathetically. "You will see them again soon. Until then, I hope you will consider us your family."

"Yes, don't cry, Naamah," Amaris's childish voice piped up. "You still have us to love you! Did you not say Yahweh brought you here? Then He wants you to be happy with us!"

Despite her youth, the little girl sounded so like her mother in her efforts to be comforting that Naamah's tears turned into a laugh. She sat up, wiping the tears from her eyes. "You are right, Amaris. I miss my family dearly. But I am happy to have met you and your mother. And I will stop crying."

"Good!" Amaris bounded joyously out the door and down the hallway. Naamah and Shiphrah smiled at each other, then Naamah spread her blanket across her bed and rose to her feet. "I think I could use a bath. Are you interested in coming with me?"

"Of course! And Amaris too if I can catch the little rascal!"

That night as Naamah crawled into bed and tucked her mother's blanket under her chin, she prayed silently with genuine gratitude, *Thank You, Yahweh, for this day and for the visit from my mother and Zahara. Thank You for the friends You had in place here before I even arrived. Thank You for Shiphrah and Amaris. And now I have this gift from my mother.*

She soon drifted off, joining her roommates in peaceful slumber.

Chapter 20

Naamah awoke the following morning with a smile on her lips and a song in her heart. *You make me glad by Your deeds, O Lord. I sing for joy at the works of Your hands.*

As she dressed, the words bubbled up joyously in her mind. Heading out of the room to breakfast with Shiphrah and Amaris, she allowed her voice to break free. "It is good to praise the Lord and make music to Your name, O Most High. To proclaim Your love in the morning and Your faithfulness at night to the music of the ten-stringed lyre and the melody of the harp."

The mention of harp and lyre reminded Naamah of her previous thought to find out if the king's wife Abigail might like to join her harp to Naamah's lyre. But this in turn brought to mind with a sudden jolt King David's command to get this composition and others Naamah had sang for him written down. The encounter with Bathsheba and her abrupt dismissal from the king's presence along with the emotions of her mother's and sister's visit had driven the king's order completely from her mind.

"If only I could do it myself," Naamah lamented quietly.

While she loved playing musical instruments and composing songs, she'd regretted since the first time she'd seen a village elder read from one of the Books of Moses that women weren't allowed to learn reading and writing as men were.

"What do you wish you could do yourself?" Shiphrah asked curiously. "And where did you learn such a beautiful song? I have been in the palace and listened to the temple choirs for more than ten years. Yet I have never heard that one."

"The song is of my own composition which I sang for King David," Naamah responded distractedly. "He instructed me to have the words written down, but I am unsure how I should proceed. The king mentioned something about going to see someone named Seraiah. But I have no idea who that is. I just wish I could write the words down myself."

"Very few people know how to write down words, especially women," Shiphrah replied. "But I know who you mean. Seraiah is King David's chief scribe. We can ask Akilah to take you to the scriptorium after breakfast."

"If you can just tell me the way, I am sure I can find it myself," Naamah said. "It is about time I learn the palace."

"My lady, that is not possible!" The shocked response was from Chinua, who was just hurrying towards them down the hall. "You must never leave the women's quarters alone. That is why I am here. Semere sent me to summon you. Chief Musician Asaph has sent word that you are to sing for the king this afternoon before his court, and Semere wishes to settle on your full wardrobe so it isn't necessary to find you new clothing each time the king summons you."

Shiphrah interjected, "There are women in the harem who will look for any opportunity to rid themselves of a rival for the king's attention. If you were seen outside the harem alone, rumors would immediately spread that you were sneaking around unattended to pursue an intimate relationship with someone other than King David. No king can allow his wives or concubines to be with any other man. Even if the rumors were not true, your fate would most likely be death in one way or another."

Chinua added, "Most of the harem women simply want to survive in peace. But there are those who will be happy to stab you or any other in the back if they believe you hold the king's favor. Especially the wives, who all want their sons to come before the king's attention."

Did that include outside women like Bathsheba? Why was it okay for a king to welcome to his bedchamber a woman clearly not a part of his household from what Naamah had glimpsed the night of the Sukkot festival, but a woman could be condemned to death for simply walking down a hall alone? As with her rapist, it seemed to Naamah there was one set of rules for women and another far more generous set of rules to permit men to act as they pleased. It wasn't fair!

"I can escort you after we see Semere," Chinua consoled her.

"But breakfast first," Shiphrah said firmly. "Naamah has enough filling her day without doing so on an empty stomach."

By the time Semere and Chinua picked out another dozen outfits for Naamah's permanent wardrobe, Naamah no longer felt in any way nervous of the tall, black-skinned harem overseer. As with Akilah, Semere's unusual size and appearance might give him the semblance of fierceness, but he showed himself gentle though firm with those under his care.

"Come back with your lyre someday," Semere invited, piling the new acquisitions into a chest. "My old ears would be blessed to hear this music that has caught the attention of the king and his chief musician."

"I will do that," Naamah promised with a smile. But her stomach tightened again with nerves as she followed Chinua back into the hall. She had at least met Asaph but knew nothing about Seraiah. Would he even believe that the king had sent Naamah to him?

Chinua escorted Naamah into a large room as long as the harem dining hall but wider with columns running down the middle. Numerous tables were covered by rolls of parchment and papyrus, bowls of ink, grinding pestles and mortars, and feathered quills with sharpened tips stained in various colors Naamah guessed must be instruments of writing. Most of the tables had one, two, or even three men on stools with quill in hand or standing bent over the various items. Against the inner walls opposite tall windows were shelves piled high with scrolls.

"You are fortunate. Seraiah is here." Chinua guided Naamah across the room to a large table with an ornate chair worthy of a prince—or the royal chief of scribes. But the man sitting there was small and thin, his thinning hair and beard streaked with white. He looked too ordinary and nondescript for such an important personage until he raised his eyes at Naamah's approach and their shrewd intelligence seemed to drill right into her soul.

Chapter 21

Chinua showed no nervousness at all in approaching the chief scribe. Naamah was beginning to think the plump eunuch was on friendly terms with everyone in the palace. "Master Seraiah, this is Naamah, the king's new court musician and concubine. She has been sent here about a song she has composed that the king would like recorded."

"Ah, yes." Seraiah studied Naamah thoughtfully. Like his sharp gaze, his voice belied his ordinary appearance. Deep and resonant, it could have been a musical instrument on its own. "I have been hearing of this young woman and her unusual gift. Asaph himself tells me that were she male she might be another young David when he sang for Saul. He did tell me that she has some songs of a quality to be used in the tabernacle worship he wished to see recorded among the other psalms."

Seraiah addressed Naamah directly. "Now, child, tell me of this song. No, perhaps it would be easier if you sing it for me."

Naamah's face flushed. "I do not have my lyre with me. But if you truly want me to sing, I will do so. Though I feel my compositions are receiving far more praise than they deserve. After all, there are so many gifted musicians in service to the king and tabernacle. I am only a woman who loves to sing and make music in gratitude to Yahweh. I could never compare my songs to the psalms of worship and praise I have heard sung by Chief Musician Asaph and the Levite choirs at the festival."

"If King David and Chief Musician Asaph see that Yahweh has given you a gift, then it is so!" Seraiah said firmly. "It is good to accept such gifts in a humble manner as coming from Yahweh and not by our own doing. But it is not humility to deny our gifts. On the contrary, you are demeaning the very blessing God has given you not to recognize it for what it is. Now, sing the song for me."

Seraiah's encouraging smile gave Naamah the courage to sing unaccompanied. She chose the second of the compositions she'd sung King David. "May God be gracious to us and bless us and make His face shine upon us. May all the peoples praise You, O God. May all the peoples praise You. Then the land will yield its harvest, and God, our God, will bless us. God will bless us, and all the ends of the earth will fear Him."

In the reverie of her song, Naamah had closed her eyes, raised her hands, and tilted her face upward in attitude of prayer. As her voice died, she opened her eyes to see Seraiah grinning before her. All across the room, she could see scribes all on their feet silently looking at her.

"Praise Yahweh!" Seraiah's voice echoed throughout the large hall. "Asaph is right. You have a remarkable gift. I cannot wait to hear you play your lyre."

"I only wish I could write the words down myself," Naamah murmured. "It has always been my desire that I might learn to read and write."

"All in good time. But for now, I believe I have the perfect scribe to work with you on transcribing your song. He too has been given a unique gift from Yahweh, but he is also one of the best copyists among the palace scribes. Reuel?"

A tall, broad-shouldered young man not many years older than Naamah and far more muscular than she would ever have expected of a scribe hurried over from a nearby table. Seraiah waved a hand toward Naamah. "Find a parchment scroll and take down the song this young woman has just sung. Choose a fresh one and mark the scroll 'Songs of Naamah' as I have no doubts this will be first of many of her compositions we will be recording."

Reuel led Chinua and Naamah to his work table. It was immediately obvious to Naamah that the young scribe was serious about his job. His desk was laid out in an organized fashion with all his tools ready to use. From a shelf, he chose an unused parchment scroll and carefully unwrapped it, then chose a quill and bowl of black ink. As he worked, Naamah studied his face. Something about his features, the shape of his mouth, the narrowed inquisitive gaze he directed at her, even his jet-black hair that tumbled to his shoulders, neither curly nor wavy but something in between, felt familiar. And yet she was sure she'd never seen him before.

Settling himself on his stool, Reuel picked up the pen and began writing. At first, Naamah assumed he was following Seraiah's instructions to mark the scroll. But as he kept writing without so much as looking up at her, Naamah grew increasingly annoyed. Finally, she spoke. "Do you want me to sing my composition or just recite the words."

"Neither," Reuel said without looking up. "I heard the words when you sang them. Now I am writing them down."

It was the first time Naamah had heard Reuel's voice. It too seemed vaguely familiar. With her musical ear, she knew it wasn't a voice she'd heard before, but it was close. Shrugging off the mystery, she demanded, "How can you write down my entire song from hearing it once?"

She broke off as he set down his quill and began reading what he'd transcribed. "May God be gracious to us and bless us and make His face shine upon us."

His melodious voice rolled on and on to the last words of Naamah's composition. "God will bless us, and all the ends of the earth will fear Him."

By the end, Naamah's annoyance had given way to amazement. Seraiah had mentioned this young man having a unique gift like her own. She now realized what at least part of that gift must be. Naamah remembered every song she'd composed and even those she'd heard just once from the Levite choirs to be able to sing them again and again. Reuel must be able to do something similar with writing down words he'd only heard once.

Pushing his stool back, Reuel asked impatiently, "Now do you have another song you would like transcribed? If so, simply sing the words or speak them, and I will write them down."

Naamah opened her mouth, closed it again, then opened it. "I have one other I sang for the king. It is easier for me to remember the words if I sing them."

She began the first song she'd sung for King David. "It is good to praise the Lord and make music to your name, O Most High."

This composition was much longer than the first. She sang the final line. "The Lord is upright. He is my Rock, and there is no wickedness in Him."

As before, every person in the room was silent, their rapt

eyes on Naamah, when she finished. Seraiah called out from his work station, "Well done, child. A true hymn of praise to our Father God."

Reuel continued writing without hesitation. Naamah waited until he was finished, still skeptic. But when Reuel read back his transcript, every word was precise to what she'd written. It seemed Seraiah was right in his choice of a scribe to work with her. If only he didn't seem so scornful and dismissive of her actual music, unlike the awed reaction of the other scribes.

Naamah was alone when she returned to her room. She was elated that a song of hers had been recorded in the archives of tabernacle music but dejected that she had to depend on a supercilious young man to both write down and read back her own words. If there was only some way she could bypass the need to depend on such a man.

Wistfully, she took her lyre out of its case and sat on the bed, her fingers gliding gently across the strings. As she softly played and sang the words Reuel had transcribed for her, the memory of his swift, expert movements stiffened her resolve. She didn't know how, but one way or another, mere woman or not, she wasn't going to rest until she'd found a way to learn how to both read and write for herself the words Yahweh gave her in praise to His name.

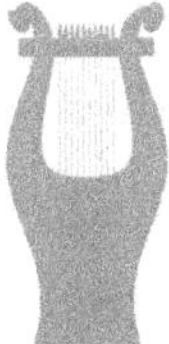

Chapter 22

Naamah carried her lyre as she trailed Semere to the throne room. She had finally learned through a discreet conversation with Shiphrah exactly what it meant to be a eunuch. She'd been horrified to learn of young boys and even pubescent youths being mutilated so they could be used to care for wealthy men's harems or dedicate their lives to specialized learning and crafts without the distraction of marriage and family.

But Semere and Chinua seemed content with their lot. So Naamah put this fresh information from her mind and resolved with renewed compassion to add both eunuchs to her growing circle of friendship as she never could with a full male. After all, was it so different from her own indeterminate situation neither embraced by a man like Shiphrah and the other women of the harem nor free to marry and have a family of her own?

It was now several weeks since Naamah had been called to the king's bedchamber. Almost every day, she'd been summoned to play and sing softly in the throne room or even at the king's meals or gatherings in the smaller council chamber where King David discussed affairs of the kingdom with his advisors and military commanders.

But the summons was always arranged by Chief Musician Asaph as he did all music for the palace or tabernacle. Not once had Naamah been called again alone to the king. Nor had King David again spoken to her. Occasionally, he'd glanced her way when she played one of his own compositions such as "The Lord is my Shepherd" or "When I am afraid, I will trust in You" as though acknowledging her familiarity with his music.

While thankful not to find herself in the king's embrace, Naamah wondered if it was Bathsheba occupying King David's thoughts and bed. If other wives and concubines had been summoned, they weren't close enough acquaintances for her to have noticed.

This time, Semere escorted Naamah into a corner of the council chamber. A long oval table piled high with scrolls, maps, even missives on clay tablets was crowded with the king's advisors and commanders, many of whom Naamah recognized by now. Among them was Hushai, whom she hadn't seen since her first day in the palace. She'd learned from the discussions that Hushai was on an expedition to the front lines where the king's commander Joab was besieging the Ammonite capital of Rabbah far across the Jordan River to the east.

Hushai smiled at Naamah as she took her place on the chair provided for her but continued addressing the group. "As you remember, this new war with the Ammonites rose because Hanun, king of the Ammonites, mistreated our ambassadors, shaving them and cutting off their robes at the buttocks before sending them back to King David in shame. In fear of retaliation, they hired an army of Aramean mercenaries. But our king defeated them so completely the Arameans are now afraid to help the Ammonites."

Naamah didn't sing while the men spoke but played softly in the background. In truth, she was always surprised she wasn't banished from the room when these learned men spoke of lofty kingdom affairs. Whether she was somehow trusted not to repeat what she heard or they simply believed her too ignorant as a young woman to understand their discussions she had no idea. But she found what she was learning fascinating.

Hushai went on, "With the Arameans defeated, Joab has advanced with our armies to the very walls of Rabbah, which he now has under tight siege. But there he is at a stalemate since the Ammonite defenses are strong, and our forces continue to lose many men every time we attack the walls. Joab requests more men, above all, archers, and more weapons, including all arrows available to launch against Hanun's men shooting at our men from the walls. He also asks for more supplies as the siege could take weeks."

Naamah lost interest in the following discussion, letting her fingers move from one psalm to another as the council weighed troop movements, available supplies, and other military details that were a foreign language to her. The group had broken up and all but Hushai and the king were filing from the council chamber when Naamah saw a man push through those exiting. She immediately recognized him as the guard who had ushered Bathsheba into the king's bedchamber the night she'd played for him.

Striding over to the king, the guard handed King David a small scroll, then spun on his heel and left. King David's expression brightened with expectation as he broke the wax seal. But the moment he read its contents, his face turned red with rage. Crumpling the scroll in his hand he shouted, "Leave me."

The room erupted into confusion as the advisors quickened their exit of the chamber. Only Hushai ignored the command, instead approaching King David. Still playing softly, Naamah was unsure if the order was for her as well. She softened the sound, hoping to go unnoticed.

"My king, what is it?" Hushai asked with deep concern. "Has bad news come? What can I do to assist you? Please, my king, whatever it is, I will do anything to alleviate your pain."

Naamah was astonished at the change Hushai's words brought to King David's demeanor. His rage softened to warm affection. "I know you would, my friend. But in this case, there is nothing you can do. Now, please leave me. I need to be alone to think."

King David glanced over at Naamah, "Completely alone."

Gathering up her lyre, Naamah followed Hushai from the chamber. The same guard who'd brought the message closed the door behind them, leaving King David in the solitude he'd ordered. Naamah was bursting with curiosity at what had just happened but knew better than to speak. In any case, it was clear Hushai knew no more than she did.

Hushai physically shook himself as if to clear his mind from the atmosphere that surrounded them. Then he smiled warmly down at Naamah. "It is good to see you again, Naamah. I apologize that I have not checked on you as I promised your father. I have been away from the city. But Asaph has kept me informed that you have settled in well and continue to please the king with your music. And now that I've returned, I have a message to pass on from my wife Nasya. She was disappointed when you were not able to stay with us as was the original arrangement with your father, and she would very much like to invite you to our home."

Naamah was surprised but delighted at the invitation. "I would like that very much, thank you, if I can get permission to leave the palace."

"I will make arrangements," Hushai said. "Including a proper escort. I will send news with Semere once I have spoken to my wife. It may take some days as Nasya leaves tomorrow for a visit to her own family."

Chapter 23

Several days later, Naamah was awakened to the sound of Akilah's voice. "Are the pains becoming closer, my lady?"

"Yes," groaned Shiphrah.

Naamah immediately threw off her covers. "Shiphrah is in labor?"

"She appears to be." Akilah began helping Amaris change into her daytime clothing. "I will take Amaris to one of the other mothers. She should not be here at such a time as this."

Naamah began dressing. "Give me a few moments, and I will be ready to help."

By now, Shiphrah's groans had drawn three other concubines, Jytte, Brielle, and Adah. Jytte was one of the oldest concubines, a petite, quiet woman. Akilah whispered, "Jytte is the midwife for the concubines. She was a midwife to Abigail and others of the wives before King David was king. She is so skilled she was taken into the harem to care for the king's sons and daughters."

Akilah smiled at Naamah. "As you were for your music."

The last to arrive was Abigail. She immediately walked over to Shiphrah's bed, took Shiphrah's hand in her own, and began praying. "Our Father God, Yahweh, be with this Your daughter as she brings another new life You have created into this world."

Shiphrah's groans quieted. Abigail looked over at Naamah. "Why don't you play for her to bring calmness in her time of pain."

Naamah pulled her lyre from its case and began playing softly. While Abigail went on praying, Jytte issued directions, giving each person a task. Adah massaged Shiphrah's shoulders and back while Brielle gently wiped her face and body with damp cloths. Jytte stripped away the bedcovers under Shiphrah and spread out an old cloth that bore stains of previous deliveries. As the morning continued, Naamah saw increased concern on Jytte's face.

"Naamah!" called Shiphrah through clenched teeth. "Sing for me, Naamah. Sing for me."

Fearful her friend might lose her baby or even her life, Naamah searched her mind for a song. None she knew seemed appropriate for this dire situation. Then she opened her heart and mind to Yahweh and allowed His presence to bring new words to her.

"Blessed are all who fear the Lord, who walk in His ways. You will eat the fruit of your labor. Blessings and prosperity will be yours. Your wife will be like a fruitful vine within your house. Your sons will be like olive shoots around your table. Thus is the man blessed who fears the Lord. May you live to see your children's children."

As the last word left Naamah's lips, Shiphrah cried out and gave birth to a healthy baby girl. Taking the baby, Jytte gently washed the little body with water that contained salt and a dash of wine. With fresh sea sponges, she went over the baby's body again, this time with olive oil, then wrapped the child in linen swaddling.

As she did so, the other two concubines sponged Shiphrah down, removed the soiled cloth under her, and spread fresh bedding. They then helped Shiphrah into clean clothing. When they were done, Jytte handed the little one to her mother. Throughout, Abigail audibly gave thanks to Yahweh for the newborn baby girl while Naamah returned to soft lyre music.

"Her name is Gia," whispered Shiphrah. "It means Yahweh is gracious."

To Naamah, Akilah murmured, "If it were a boy, Shiphrah would not have been able to name it. The king gives boys their name at the time of their circumcision on the eighth day after birth."

Almost immediately, Shiphrah and Gia both fell into a deep sleep. The other women slipped out quietly, all but Jytte, who as midwife would remain to keep vigil until she was certain there were no afterbirth complications. In the hall, Abigail turned to Naamah. "The song you sang was beautiful. I have never heard it before."

"I composed it just now for Shiphrah." Naamah smiled joyously. "It is the first new song that has come to me since I came to the palace. A reminder that I should go to the scribes to have it written down while it is still fresh as Chief Musician Asaph has asked me to do."

"Then I hope you will come back and teach it to me," Abigail said warmly. "You blessed us all greatly with your praise to Yahweh. I do not think Shiphrah would have given birth so easily and safely without your words and music to calm her. It is clear Yahweh's spirit rests upon you."

Naamah's heart swelled with pleasure that this wise, godly woman could possibly want to learn from her. "That would be my delight and privilege."

Finding Chinua to accompany her, Naamah headed through the corridors to the scriptorium. Seraiah spotted her the moment she arrived at the door. "Naamah! What brings you here so soon?"

"I have composed another song. I wanted to record it as soon as possible."

"Of course!" Seraiah looked delighted. "I would like to hear you sing, but I am just leaving now for the tabernacle. I will let Asaph know we have a new song for the choirs to learn. Perhaps you can sing it for both of us later. Meanwhile, have Reuel write it down."

Reuel was at his usual table, so focused on his work he didn't even look up as Naamah and Chinua walked over. Naamah watched over his shoulder as his pen made swift, concise marks on the parchment. If she couldn't read, Naamah by now recognized the shapes of words. This was very different, and she quickly realized that he was drawing male features. Not one that looked Hebrew but with a long curled beard cut squarely across the bottom, a haughty face with hooked nose, and a tall, ornate headdress.

"He looks almost alive!" Naamah commented. Her voice startled Reuel so that ink sprayed from his quill.

"I am so sorry!" she apologized abjectly. "I didn't mean to disturb you. I hope I have not ruined your drawing."

"It is okay," Reuel replied, dabbing at the ink drops with a scrap of leather. "See? I have made these drops part of his hair. It is my own fault for not seeing you approach. Sometimes I get so caught up in my work, I do not notice what is going on around me."

"I understand," Naamah smiled. "It is the same for me when

I am creating a new song."

Reuel looked thoughtfully at Naamah. "Is that why you are here? Because you have a new song?"

"Yes. I composed it just this morning. Seraiah told me to bring it to you to record."

"Then we will get to work immediately." Reuel carefully set aside the drawing he'd been making and walked over to a shelf, where he lifted down the scroll assigned to her compositions.

As he unrolled it, Naamah pointed to the inscription he'd placed at the top on her last visit. "These markings. Seraiah said to write 'Psalms of Naamah.' Does this mean one of these markings is my name?"

"That is correct." Reuel's expression was almost friendly as he pointed out a grouping of symbols. "This is your name."

"Could you teach me to write it?" Naamah asked eagerly. "I've been wanting to learn to read and write for a very long time."

Naamah broke off as the friendliness abruptly evaporated from Reuel's face.

Chapter 24

"**I**'m sorry!" Naamah said hastily. "I had no right to ask such a thing."

Reuel's expression thawed again. "It is never wrong to wish to learn. Even a woman. It is just—" He glanced from Naamah around the room, where every scribe had turned their eyes to the visitors. "I do not think it would be permitted or appropriate for me or any other scribe in the palace to teach you. Speak with Seraiah. If he agrees, perhaps there is someone among the eunuchs with the knowledge to teach you."

Naamah felt her face burn. She had come to feel so comfortable with Chinua and Semere and even Reuel in the limited role of scribe she'd forgotten how taboo and in fact dangerous it would be for the king's concubine to be spending time with a male. Even in her own home, her father would never have permitted his wife and daughters to learn from a male teacher.

"I understand."

Reuel kept his eyes on the scroll. Did he fear she might get him in trouble as Shiphrah had warned should anyone level accusations of illicit interaction? "Then why don't you begin, and I will write down your new song."

Turning away, Naamah sang the song she'd composed for Shiphrah to a nearby pillar while Reuel's quill clicked and scratched across the parchment. When she was done, Reuel added the final marks, then carefully laid the scroll onto another table to dry. They both stood looking at the words lying there.

"Thank you, Reuel," Naamah said quietly. "And please let Seraiah know that I am happy to come back and sing it for him if he wishes."

"You are welcome." Shifting so no one in the room could see, Reuel allowed a small smile to warm his lips. "I am sure you will soon be back with another song."

It was another week before Hushai sent word through Semere that his wife was expecting Naamah for the evening meal at their home. She was accompanied by Akilah, but Hushai also sent a palace guard as an escort. Cradling her newborn, Shiphrah encouraged Naamah to enjoy her time away from the harem.

Hushai's home was just a short walk from the palace in the wealthy neighborhood Naamah had seen just below the palace terraces. In fact, from the turning of the streets, the door on which the guard knocked couldn't be far from the house where Naamah had seen Bathsheba staring up at the king. Affixed to the doorpost was a mezuzah that held a small parchment with Yahweh's commands written on it. It brought a pang of homesickness, though this one of worked silver was far more ornate than the one her father Abdiel had on the doorpost of their own home.

Like most homes, the entrance opened into a courtyard surrounded on three sides by verandahs and a narrow stairway that led to the roof. But unlike her family compound, this house had two stories with ornate lattices on the upper-story windows. A manservant instructed Akilah and the palace guard to wait in a small antechamber to the left of the entrance, then led Naamah through a door off the verandah and up a wide polished-mosaic staircase to the second story.

The room into which Naamah was ushered looked to run one full side of the house, as large as her own father's entire living quarters in the family compound. There were woven rugs and piled cushions for lounging and chests against the walls. All the shutters overlooking the courtyard were open, allowing the cool evening breeze to blow through the latticework.

Naamah could smell pleasing aromas as she entered. A low table surrounded by large, flat cushions was already covered by bowls and platters filled with food. Nearby stood Hushai and a tall, plump woman about the same age. The woman rushed forward to envelope Naamah in a hug and kissed her solidly on both cheeks. "My child, I am so delighted to finally meet you! We had so hoped to have you as a daughter in our home while you served at the palace. But at least for this evening, I hope you will let me consider you a daughter of the house!"

"Naamah, this is my wife Nasya," Hushai said dryly when his wife released Naamah. "As you can see, she has been very eager to meet you."

"And why not? I have always longed for a daughter, have I not?" With a chuckle, Nasya took Naamah's hand and drew her forward toward the table. "Come, child, we are all family here so do not stand on formality. I am sure you must be hungry."

Nasya wrinkled her nose. "And the food in the palace! Say what you like, I never find what comes out of the palace kitchens to have the flavor of my own pots. David and his men spent too many years in a war camp. None of them really care what the food tastes like so long as there is plenty of it!"

Naamah was astonished at the casual familiarity with which Nasya referenced the king. A reminder that Hushai's family like many others of the king's administration had known David long before he was king when he and his men were just a war band of fugitives in the wilderness.

Before any more conversation could ensue, a new arrival entered. "Mother. Father. Forgive me for arriving tardy."

Naamah recognized the voice before she did the tall, muscled figure. Her astonishment burst out of her. "Reuel! What are you doing here?"

She broke off, blushing at her inadvertent rudeness.

Reuel looked just as astonished. "I live here. But what are *you* doing here?"

"Reuel is our son." Nasya looked from Naamah to Reuel. "But how can you possibly know each other? I was told you play and sing for the king, Naamah. But I was not aware Reuel would be present."

Naamah suddenly understood why Reuel had looked vaguely familiar when they met. Hushai must have looked very much like Reuel in his youth. She responded to Nasya's questioning look. "The king commanded that the songs I composed be written down. Seraiah assigned Reuel to transcribe them into a scroll. On two occasions, I sang my songs and your son wrote them down."

"Interesting," Hushai commented. "It had occurred to me when I first heard Naamah sing that her songs should be captured so others might be blessed by them as well. I suggested as much to Asaph, but since I have been traveling these past weeks, I had no idea my own son had been assigned to the task."

"It has been a pleasure." For the first time, Reuel smiled openly at Naamah. "The words and melodies both are beautiful, and I find them repeating over and over in my mind as prayers to Yahweh when I fall asleep at night."

This time Naamah's red cheeks were from happiness. The entire evening was one of wonderful food and conversation. The love she saw flowing between Hushai and Nasya reminded her of her own parents. Even Reuel, who didn't address her directly again but included her amiably in the general conversation, was an agreeable reminder of her own brother, Gavriil.

Chapter 25

Reuel found himself distracted the next morning as he finished the portrait of an Assyrian merchant and suspected spy he'd been detailed to document for identification. The latest of Naamah's compositions played over and over in his mind. *Your wife will be like a fruitful vine within your house. Your sons will be like olive shoots around your table. Thus is the man blessed who fears the Lord.*

What would it be like to come home each night to a wife and children? Reuel had rarely thought about it before, far more interested in his combat training and all the knowledge available in the palace library than thoughts of a future. But yesterday's simple fellowship around the family table, the loving affection between his parents, had stirred something in him.

Even Naamah's presence was a reminder of what their family might be had his mother been able to birth other children, a younger sister to tease and protect. When a wife was chosen for him, would she have the intelligence, talents, and beauty of Naamah? Reuel dismissed that thought quickly. Even thinking about one of the king's women was dangerous.

His musings were interrupted as Seraiah approached his table. "Reuel, King David is in need of your services immediately. You will be carrying a message to the battlefront for Commander Joab and possibly bringing back a response, so pack your travel case."

Reuel jumped to his feet. This was why he practiced so hard to be battle-ready like Joab's top warriors in hopes the time would come when he could distinguish himself on the field of battle and not just sitting at a scribe's table in the palace. "I will prepare immediately. Do I have time to deliver this to Ahithophel?"

He held up the finished drawing. Ahithophel was King David's other chief advisor along with Hushai. Unlike the fortifications and architecture that were Hushai's expertise, Ahithophel specialized in diplomacy and spy craft. He'd been suspicious that the wealthy Damascus merchant whose caravan was making its rounds from one to another of David's newly built cities and fortresses was actually an infamous Assyrian military commander spying out Israel's defenses. Reuel had been sent to observe the merchant for himself and create a likeness Ahithophel could send to Damascus to verify the man's true identity.

Seraiah lifted the drawing carefully so as not to smudge still wet ink. "Well done. Your eye for detail is remarkable. I will ensure this reaches Ahithophel. You go straight to the king."

Reuel wasted no time collecting his travel case of fortified leather that held various sizes of papyrus and parchment, a sealed vessel of black ink, quill and reed stylus made from reeds, wax, and a seal. As the son of King David's closest advisor and personal friend, he'd grown up as much a part of the king's household and family as King David's own sons.

With his unique gifts, he'd been undertaking assignments of increasing importance and trust. But Reuel had never served the king directly in his official capacity as a scribe, and he found himself more nervous than he would have expected.

In the antechamber to the throne room, Reuel saw his father exiting the throne room. Hushai's eyebrows rose at the sight of his son.

"I was sent to take down a message for the king," Reuel explained. "I will be taking it to Commander Joab."

What to Reuel was an exciting adventure was commonplace to the king's top advisor. Hushai simply commented, "It's about time they were giving you more responsibility. You'll find David in his council chamber. I will let your mother know you will be gone a day or two."

When Reuel entered the throne room, it was crowded with people awaiting an audience with the king, but the throne was empty. Stationed around the perimeter were uniformed guards with spears and swords. They all recognized Hushai's son. Reuel walked on past to the council chamber. As a guard ushered him in, Reuel saw that King David was the only one present in the room. Setting his travel case on the table, Reuel began taking out his materials.

King David gestured for him to stop. "I don't want a written message. I've chosen you because I know I can trust you implicitly as I trust your father. I am sending you with a message for Joab. Tell him this. Send me Uriah the Hittite."

"Send me Uriah the Hittite?" Reuel echoed. The message seemed far too simple and innocuous to be entrusted to Reuel rather than one of the usual messenger teams that took communications to the battle front and back. "Is that all?"

King David began pacing around the table, his restless

strides increasing Reuel's nervousness. "The message is not what matters. Surely you will not forget something so brief. What matters is that you give this message only to Joab and in his presence alone."

"And if he asks why the Hittite has been sent for? Why should he believe my word alone?"

"That is not your concern!" All knew the king was a man of fiery passions and could display as hot an anger as warm generosity. But in all the years that King David had been like an uncle to his friend's only son, Reuel had never witnessed that anger directed his way. He swallowed hard.

The king lowered his bellow to a normal speaking tone. "As to why he should believe, he will believe because you are Hushai's son, but also because of this."

King David held out his hand. Reuel was stunned to see in his palm the king's seal. "Prepare your scroll and your wax."

Hands trembling, Reuel took out a blank square of papyrus. Folding it, he used a nearby lamp to melt a tiny blob of wax onto the crease. King David smashed his seal into the wax. "There. You have the proof the message comes from me. But the words are for Joab's ears alone."

By afternoon, Reuel and a detail of six soldiers were galloping on horseback out of Jerusalem on the dusty road east skirting the Salt Sea and crossing the Plain of Moab. By evening, they caught up with a supply caravan and reinforcements, mostly new recruits, destined for the siege of Rabbah. The two-day trek was long and grueling for Reuel. Despite his routine of combat training, he could feel the long hours he spent daily on a stool by the time he rolled off his horse in the Israelite army encampment just before sunset the second day.

A distance of an easy arrow shot separated the encampment

from the walls of the Ammonite capital. A sensible precaution considering the rows of armored archers Reuel spotted along the wall. He easily located the Israelite commander's tent as this was taller than all surrounding tents and covered with rare black goat's skins to identify it from a distance.

Reuel presented his folded blank message stamped with the king's seals to the pair of guards standing on either side of the entrance flap. One guard ducked inside. A moment later, a powerful voice commanded, "Enter!"

Ducking into the tent, Reuel paused for his eyes to adjust to the dimness inside. Two oil lamps hanging from poles illuminated a table piled high with rolled parchments, remnants of food, and a tanned hide on which was marked out in black charcoal what looked like a simplified map of the Ammonite city and its environs. To one side were rolled up sleeping mats and a pair of chests that stood open, revealing clothing and parts of armor.

Several men stood around the table. One held a short length of burnt wood with which he'd clearly been making additions to the map. But Reuel immediately recognized the man to whom he'd been sent. Not just because he had the same build and facial structure of King David. Joab's mother Zeruiah was one of King David's older sisters, and Joab had been at his uncle's side since the two were both barely out of their teens and fleeing from a murderous King Saul. Like the king, Joab was powerfully built and muscled from decades of fighting Israel's enemies though he too must be into his fifth decade at least.

But Reuel didn't need that likeness. He'd been in the war leader's presence with his father often enough from early childhood since Joab and Hushai were King David's closest companions and counsellors. Still, Joab had little time or patience to waste on children, and by the time Reuel was old enough to join other Israelite young men flocking to fight under Joab's command, Hushai had grasped the value of his son's gifts for more subtle uses than a battlefield. Steered into his present profession of scribe, Reuel doubted if he'd exchanged so much as a greeting with the commander since he'd reached puberty. Would Joab even recognize him now that he was full grown?

That question was immediately put to rest. The commander immediately strode over and clapped Reuel on the shoulder. "Son of Hushai, I don't need to ask who you are. You look just as your father did when we first met. You have grown tall and strong since I saw you last. Why are you not here with me instead of ruining your eyes with the labors of a scholar? I will have to speak to your father about sending you to me to become a warrior."

Joab didn't wait for Reuel to respond. He held out his hand. "I am told you bring me a message from the king."

"Yes, sir." Reuel lowered his voice to reach only Joab's ears. "But it is for your ears alone by orders of King David."

"Then come with me." Joab glanced over his shoulder toward the table. "Uriah, continue your explanation of what the scouting party has brought back. I will read it myself."

Reuel started at Joab's words. The man holding the burnt wood lifted it in acknowledgement. He was short for an Israelite but massively powerful with tight black curls. His eyes were slightly slanted with virtually no brows or lashes compared to the large oval eyes with long lashes typical of the Israelites. The differences made sense now that Reuel knew this must be the Uriah of whom King David had spoken. He'd identified the man as a Hittite, one of the mountain peoples who had lived in Canaan before the Israelites arrived from Egypt.

Joab ducked out the entrance flap, and Reuel followed. Once they were a few feet away, Reuel handed Joab the parchment stamped with the king's seal. Breaking it open, Joab raised his eyebrows to see that it was blank.

"King David commanded me not to write the message down," Reuel explained. "He said to give it to you alone in private. It is just this. Send me Uriah the Hittite."

Reuel expected some kind of interrogation, at minimum a demand as to why the king would make such a mystery of such a simple request. But Joab didn't say another word to Reuel. Striding inside, he announced, "Uriah, you and your men will be riding back to Jerusalem in the morning with the king's messenger."

Chapter 26

After more than two months of peaceful sameness, Naamah was feeling increasingly at home in the palace. Especially after a second visit from her mother and Zahara helped erase lingering homesickness. Each time she'd been called to appear before King David, it was only to provide music. She began to feel increasingly confident her secret would never be discovered.

Still, tonight Naamah felt tranquility slipping away as she followed Semere through a doorway that was new to her. The room beyond was a large one with the biggest table she'd ever seen running down the center, even larger and broader than the concubine dining table in the harem quarters. She guessed this was the palace banqueting hall.

But this was no dignified banquet. Large quantities of food and wine were set out along the table. The room was filled with several dozen men milling about, cups of wine in one hand, food in another. Many wore battle armor, and the smell was to Naamah an unpleasant combination of barnyard, male body odors, perspiration, and wine dregs. She'd smelled something similar when her father, brother, and uncles came in from a long day of hard work under the hot sun, but nothing this strong.

Loud, slurred voices and raucous laughter made clear the group had been indulging in strong wine for quite some time. Among them was King David, sprawled loosely across an ornate chair that could almost be a throne on the far side of the room at the head of the table. To Naamah's surprise, Reuel was also present, looking uncomfortable but chatting with the other men as though he knew them. He shot Naamah a quick look, then turned away.

King David lifted a golden wine cup. "Uriah, good friend, you have been here long enough. And you have been fighting courageously for many months without a respite. Go on home, wash your feet, and enjoy your wife before you must return to the battle. The beautiful Bathsheba has surely been missing the embraces of her husband."

There was a rumble of lewd appreciation from the other men. Naamah held back as Semere steered her toward a small couch in a far corner behind the king but close enough for her music to reach him. "Why am I here? This does not seem a gathering appropriate for a woman to be present. Did the king truly request my presence?"

"Not precisely," Semere responded in a low voice. "It was Hushai who made the request. He is hoping your music will bring some calm before the situation gets out of hand."

Naamah saw Hushai walking toward them. His expression was passive, but Naamah had now spent enough time in his presence to recognize the worry in his eyes. He nodded to the couch and headed back toward King David.

As Naamah settled her lyre on her lap, she heard one voice raised loud in reply. "My king, my commander Joab with the ark of God and the armies of Israel and Judah are camped in the open country facing danger from the Ammonites. I came only to make the report you requested as to how your soldiers are and how the battle is going. So how could I alone go to my house to eat and drink and make love to my wife while my men who have accompanied me sleep in the open at the entrance to the palace? As surely as you live, I would not do such a thing!"

Enthusiastic applause from the other men greeted the statement. Though the short, stocky man in full battle gear who had spoken looked to Naamah more Canaanite than of Israel, his accent and words sounded like a true God-fearing Israelite. And unlike the others, he sounded completely sober.

But it was the name King David had mentioned that caught Naamah's attention. This Uriah was the husband of Bathsheba? Then the rooftop on which she'd once seen the beautiful woman locked in intense gaze with King David must be the home to which the king had referred. Why then had this Bathsheba been in the king's chambers? Why was King David now encouraging her husband to go home to her?

A knot of disappointment twisted in Naamah's chest. She might be just fourteen years of age and new to ways of the palace. But if a king might enjoy as many wives and concubines as Yahweh gave him, Naamah knew what the law said about adultery with another man's wife. How could a king known as a man after Yahweh's heart, a king who had written so many psalms of praise to Father God do what would be a capital sin for any other man? Or was there some piece of information Naamah lacked that would explain the discrepancy?

Naamah began playing softly, but she doubted the music was having any calming effect on these boisterous men. Watching attentively as she played, she saw the troubled expression in Hushai's eyes deepen. She saw quick rage cross King David's face before the king raised a wine cup toward Uriah and announced jovially, "The decision is yours, though for your own sake I should command you to go home. Stay here in Jerusalem one more day before you head back to Rabbah. You have earned the rest. And if you will not go to your wife, then I will send the gift I have prepared for your courage and valor in battle to your home to await your return."

King David gestured toward a small ornate golden chest sitting on the table in front of him. At his nod, Hushai opened it. Its contents, spilling over with gold coins and glittering red, amber, and green jewels, were enough to bring momentary silence even in that drunken revelry. "Bathsheba will appreciate the gift if you do not."

"My king, this is far too great a gift!" Uriah protested. "It is my pleasure to serve you and the God of Israel. I need no reward for doing that which is my duty!"

Whatever the response, Naamah didn't hear. But the party returned to its boisterous noise, drowning out Naamah's soft playing and song, and she noticed a short time later that the treasure chest was no longer on the table. She continued playing until Hushai approached and tapped her on the shoulder. "Child, you may as well leave. Your songs of praise have not reached the heart of the king as I hoped."

Naamah was thankful to leave, but as she settled into her own bed for sleep, her heart remained as troubled as the expression in Hushai's kindly dark eyes.

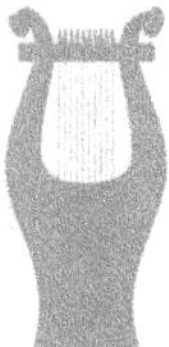

Chapter 27

In the three days since returning from his trip to Rabbah, Reuel settled back into his work as a scribe. He was relieved to hear from Seraiah that not only was Ahithophel satisfied with his drawing but that it had been recognized by an informant in Damascus as the suspected Assyrian spy.

Reuel wondered briefly if while he was gone Naamah had pursued his suggestion to inquire whether there was a eunuch who might have the education to teach her to read and write. Many highborn captives brought back from other nations were made eunuchs in order to make use of them as scholars and advisors for their new lord or tutors to the nobility. Perhaps even among those teaching the king's sons might be someone to satisfy Naamah's desire.

The thought was a reminder of Naamah's appearance at the festivities for Uriah and his men the night before. While Reuel had known the young woman was both a concubine and musician dedicated to the king, it had been a shock to see her in such circumstances. That said, he had been impressed at the skill of her playing, as gifted in touch on the lyre's strings as the voice he'd heard in the scriptorium.

A guard entered the room, walking right past Seraiah to approach Reuel. Reuel recognized him as the same who had been sent to summon him a week earlier. "King David requires your presence to carry a message to the battlefront."

At his table, Seraiah nodded assent. Gathering his tools, Reuel followed the guard. This time he was taken to the throne room. The entire party with whom Reuel had arrived back in Jerusalem three days earlier was gathered around King David, seated on his throne. They were bathed, hair and beards washed and braided, leather and linen tunics clean, and wearing full battle gear, including freshly polished breastplates, swords, and bronze belts, a far cry from the travel-worn, dirty party that had arrived three days earlier.

King David's hooded gaze took in Reuel's arrival as he addressed the commanding officer. "Uriah, I am tasking you with this private message to Commander Joab."

He held up a small scroll stamped with the king's seal. But he didn't pass it to Uriah. "I am also sending back with you the same trusted messenger who carried your summons, Reuel, son of my advisor Hushai, who is also a scribe. He will keep the message safe until its seal is broken solely by Commander Joab and bring back to me any return communication from Joab."

King David turned his hooded gaze to Reuel. "If you will come with me, I have an additional message for your ears only."

Reuel followed King David to the council chamber where he'd received his previous unusual instructions from the king. King David handed him the small scroll.

"This is to be delivered only into Joab's hands. But as before, I do not want any response from Joab to be written down, no matter how long that answer may be. Your father has spoken much of your gift of total recall since early childhood. He and I have long waited until you were of an age when this gift would be useful to the kingdom. Today is that day. It is urgent you receive Joab's response, then bring it word for word to my ears alone. Not even your father can be told. Can I trust you to obey your king's command?"

"Always, my king." Though increasingly confused by King David's cryptic words, Reuel tried to put all but his king's command from his mind. He'd grown up with a father who as the king's closest advisor was privy to many things of which all around were ignorant. If Reuel were to continue using his gift on behalf of the king, he should remind himself that he was but a lowly messenger and those to whom he carried the messages knew far more than Reuel was aware, including what the king's puzzling words actually meant.

Two evenings later, Uriah's party rode into the Israelite encampment. As his men scattered to their own campfires, Reuel followed Uriah to the command tent. While Uriah gave a brief summary of the trip to Joab, Reuel opened his travel case. It had rained much of the trip, and Reuel was dismayed to discover that water had leaked into the case, wetting the scroll along with his other writing materials.

A mistake he'd know to ensure against on his next adventure. But at least the seal remained unbroken, and the thin animal skin should still be readable on the inside. He dug out the scroll and handed it to the commander.

"I still have no idea why David summoned me to Jerusalem!" Uriah grumbled as Joab broke the seal. "I spent no more than half of an hour reporting on what was new with the siege. The greenest messenger like this one here—" Uriah threw Reuel a derisive glance. "—could have done the same without dragging me and my men away on the eve of the spring offensive. Especially since we were kept lingering in Jerusalem three days only to do nothing but feast and drink with the king. If we were to be given an unnecessary respite, I would have preferred one that did not involve four days hard ride."

"Well, we are thankful for your return as our spies tell us King Hanun is making preparations to break out and attack us in the open." Joab crumpled the small scroll and tossed it into the bowl of the nearest lamp, where the edge immediately caught fire in a puff of flame and smoke. "Your mighty sword will be appreciated. Should the attack come in the morning, I am assigning you to lead the charge."

Joab turned to Reuel. "And you, young man. It seems you have earned the king's trust. Walk with me."

Joab led Reuel away from the command tent until they were safe from listening ears. Then he ordered, "So tell me what it is David has sent for my ears alone."

"Only that I am to bring him no written communication from you, just your spoken words alone."

"Ah, yes. Hushai told me of your gift and why he has you training as a scribe rather than fighting at my side. A wise thought by the king." Joab looked Reuel up and down, his eyes resting on the sword at Reuel's waist. "At least your father has ensured you know how to use a sword as well. You will follow Uriah as my eyes and ears in battle so that you may report all you see and hear to the king. Meanwhile, get some rest and report back to me before daybreak."

The following morning, Reuel presented himself to Joab in the full battle gear he wore for training: helmet, breastplate, greaves, shield in his left hand, and sword slung from his belt. Joab cautioned, "Let me make abundantly clear you are not to fight in the battle. I would not want to explain to the king or your father why the king's messenger has not returned as ordered. You have but one task—to observe Uriah's assault from a safe distance and report to me immediately once the battle is over. That said, you must not reveal my instructions to Uriah so you must also obey Uriah's battle commands while remaining at a safe distance.

"Yes, sir!" Reuel responded, though he had no idea how he was to obey what appeared contradictory instructions. He would just have to trust the way would become clear once in the chaos of battle. Not that he had any clear idea what a battle was like.

"Now, go join Uriah and his men. You will find them gathering at the edge of the encampment. My own company will guide you under the command of my armorbearer Nahari as I am sending them to aid Uriah in the attack."

Thousands of Israelite soldiers were amassed at the edge of the no-man's zone that separated the encampment from the city walls. Following Igal, one of the younger of King David's famed Mighty Men and Joab's personal assistant, Reuel quickly found Uriah and his company at the front of the army. The dawn was just brightening the sky when he approached. The stocky Hittite looked annoyed to see Reuel. "What are you doing here, boy? This is a battle for experienced warriors, not a child."

Reuel wanted to point out that the same had been said of King David as a lad before he'd fought the giant Goliath. But he had a feeling Uriah would find the comparison as inaccurate as it was boastful. Instead, he said humbly, "Joab has commanded me to stay with you to be able to report on your exploits to King David."

"Hmm." Uriah looked pleased. "In that case, just stay out of the way and don't get killed!"

Chapter 28

Uriah was interrupted just then by a blare of trumpets from the city walls as the massive gates of Rabbah suddenly swung open. A large party of mounted horsemen raced out followed by hundreds of armed soldiers yelling battle cries. With a bloodcurdling cry, Uriah raced toward the mob, his own company's and Joab's at his heels. He slashed the underbelly of the closest horse, sending its rider catapulting into the path of the charging cavalry, then slashed another horse. Soon the cavalry charge had ground to a halt, horses and horsemen quickly slaughtered alike.

All around, Reuel heard the clash of swords, whizz of spears and javelins, groans and screams as bodies were pierced with sharp blades. As an attacker rushed at him, Reuel raised his own sword, finding his combat training effective as he parried the blow with his sword, then ran the attacker through with his sword.

By now so many Israelite soldiers were pushing past to engage the Ammonites that he soon had no adversary. As Joab had instructed, he hung back, recording mental images in his mind. An Israelite soldier beheaded by a sword. A warrior coming to a comrade's aid. The screams of a dying horse.

And always out front, Uriah fighting like a man possessed, all foes falling before him. Reuel watched in awe. No wonder the Hittite was counted one of King David's greatest Mighty Men! Joab's armorbearer Nahari and the other chosen warriors of the two Mighty Men companies also fought with a skill that made Reuel ashamed he'd ever prided himself on his combat training. Already, the surviving Ammonites were fleeing back to the city gates.

But just then Reuel spotted the grave danger facing the heroic warrior. While Uriah and his close companions had chased the remaining Ammonites almost to the city wall, Nahari and his men were falling back. Seeing their retreat, the rest of the Israelite force followed suit, streaming past Reuel so that he was suddenly once again at the front of the battle.

The city gates ponderously slammed behind the retreating Ammonites, leaving Uriah and just a handful of his company alone outside the wall. Just as Uriah realized his danger and raised his shield, a party of archers above the gate loosed a fierce volley. Uriah and every remaining man with him fell, each pierced with a multitude of arrows.

Reuel observed the disaster, stunned. Who could possibly have given the order to fall back, especially once it was clear Uriah had been left exposed? More so when the Israelite force had a clear advantage once the Ammonites were in the open.

The battle was over. Behind a protective wall of raised shields, the Israelite forces were dragging wounded and dead back to the encampment. Up on the walls, the Ammonite archers weren't even bothering to lift their bows. The mighty Uriah was carried from the battlefield on a bed of lifted shields. There were cries of grief and anger as the Israelite soldiers recognized their fallen hero.

Reuel trudged beside the makeshift byre back to the command tent, exhausted and bewildered. Just yesterday he'd been excited about participating in his first battle. Now he perceived the cost in bloodied, maimed, and dead countrymen. Above all, the courageous, daring warrior who had fought so bravely and successfully with David, Joab, and the other Mighty Men for long decades only to be cut down now so needlessly in a skirmish already won.

Sick at heart, Reuel waited in the command tent to make his report to Joab, who was outside conversing with a gathering of company commanders. He suddenly noticed a wad of parchment thrusting up from a nearby lamp. Tugging it free, he realized from the remnants of broken wax that it was the message he'd delivered to Joab. The commander must have assumed it had burned completely in the lamp's flame, but its sodden state had left it only blackened on the outside with the interior a knot of animal skin.

Reuel spread the tiny wad flat, shedding ash as he did so. Part of the interior was black and other parts partially burnt, but a number of symbols remained. Reuel pieced together the remaining words. *Put Ur…front…whe…fighting…fierc… withdr…be struck…wn…die*

Studying the gaps and partially burnt symbols, Reuel started over, filling in the missing letters from long experience to form full words. *Put Uriah in front where fighting is fiercest then withdraw so he will be struck down and die*

Reuel suddenly realized he'd broken a cardinal law as a king's messenger. He had no business reading the king's private message to the commander of his armies. If Seraiah knew, not even his father's position would save Reuel from severe punishment. King David would have every right to decree his execution, the penalty for a scribe breaching the king's seal.

But that thought troubled Reuel not at all compared to the horror and fear he felt as he took in the message's shocking contents. Then he hadn't been mistaken that the other soldiers had intentionally pulled back from Uriah. And by the order of King David himself! Joab must have instructed Nahari to pull his men away after having helped lead the charge within reach of the Ammonite archers. But why?

Reuel started as he heard a sound at the tent flap. Hurriedly, he shoved the betraying parchment into his case. Joab was alone when he entered. He gave Reuel a sharp glance. "You look distraught."

"I apologize. I have never actually seen battle before," Reuel said stiffly. "Above all, Uriah and his men. To see them killed."

He choked, afraid he was about to shame himself by spilling tears. But Joab looked sympathetic as though Reuel's brief show of weakness had wiped away any possible suspicion.

"The first battle is always the worst," the commander commented bluntly. "I was no older than you when I began fighting the Philistines at David's side. And we are of course all distressed that such a mighty hero has returned to dust this day. King David will want to know without delay that his friend has fallen, so I am sending you to Jerusalem immediately to give the king a full report of the battle as requested."

"And — if the king asks how it is that such a mighty warrior fell?"

Joab gave him a long, thoughtful look, and Reuel feared he'd given away his illicit knowledge. But Joab simply responded calmly, "If the king asks why our forces got so close to the city wall knowing how many of our men have been killed by Ammonite archers or stones like the one that killed Abimelech son of Gideon when a woman dropped it on him from the wall, explain exactly what happened in the battle. Then say to him, 'Moreover, your servant Uriah the Hittite is dead.' Now leave immediately and deliver this message to King David. I will send Nahari and a squad of my own men with you to ensure you arrive safely back to Jerusalem and your father."

Reuel thought he detected a note of derision in Joab's tone as though the commander saw Reuel not as a soldier who had survived his first battle but a boy good for nothing but to ferry secret messages between two plotters. Was the commander sending his own armorbearer to make sure Reuel didn't speak to the wrong person? The pride at being chosen as the king's own message bearer had evaporated. Instead, he felt dirty as though he'd been used as a pawn in some wicked scheme.

Two days later, Reuel entered King David's throne room, hoping against hope he was wrong. That perhaps the scroll he'd delivered to Joab hadn't been written by the king. That maybe even it had been switched by someone before it was turned over to Reuel's safekeeping. Dully, he gave the battle report to a hall packed with the king's top advisors, tribal leaders, and city officials, all eager for news from the battlefront.

"My king, the Ammonite army came out against your men from the city into the open. Their forces overpowered ours, but the Israelite army fought bravely, led valiantly by Uriah the Hittite, and drove the Ammonites back to the entrance of the city gate. Many of the enemy were killed. But then the archers shot arrows at your servants from the wall, and some of the king's men died. Your commander Joab is deeply distressed to send the news that among the dead is your servant Uriah the Hittite."

Reuel needed only the brief satisfaction in King David's eyes to know his worst fears were true. The king had been expecting this news, hoping for it. The king of Israel had indeed ordered the murder of one of his dearest friends and staunchest allies. But why?

Already, King David was intoning somberly, "Send word back to Joab. Don't let this misfortune upset you. The sword devours one as well as another. Losing good men in battle is the unfortunate cost of waging war against those who would destroy our people. But the Ammonites and their king will not get away with the murder of Uriah, our brother, nor any of our men. So do not delay further. Press your attack against the city of Rabbah and destroy it utterly."

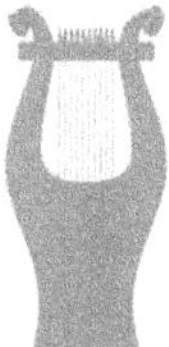

Chapter 29

Naamah followed Chinua and Hushai from the harem to the throne room, where her presence had been requested to play for a visiting delegation from King Hiram's court in Tyre. The very thought made Naamah smile with joy. She'd grown worried in the weeks since her one visit to King David's quarters when he'd dismissed Naamah's services to entertain the beautiful woman named Bathsheba, whom she now knew to be the wife of Uriah, one of the king's top battle commanders. Not once since then had the king requested that Naamah entertain him personally, all calls for her music coming through his assistants.

Naamah was at first simply grateful King David showed no interest in her physical attributes. Each day she felt less fear that her secret would be uncovered. But when she was no longer called to the king's presence in his pensive moods, another fear arose. Naamah was a concubine, not a wife, and in her case a concubine who had never been in the king's bed nor borne him a child.

In other words, a possession to be used or disposed of at will. What if the king was so displeased with her that he chose to gift her to some other man who did choose to exercise his rights to intimate relations? If the king didn't find Naamah attractive enough for his bedchamber, why oh *why* could he not have allowed her to simply be a musician in his court as Hushai and Asaph had originally planned? Or at least sent her home to her family, even if such a rejection would be a disgrace for her family as well as Naamah.

Still, while King David wasn't calling for Naamah personally, she was being summoned increasingly to the throne room and banquet hall to play for larger and more prestigious gatherings, whether court nobles, assemblies of tribal leaders gathered from across the nation, or delegations from neighboring nations. She had even sung her latest composition to the accompaniment of the tabernacle choirs the previous Sabbath at the weekly worship celebration in the courtyard of the tabernacle. Her music was now so renowned she'd been informed that King Hiram's own envoy had specifically requested to hear the woman said to be outmatched only by King David himself as the sweet songster of Israel.

"And in truth," Chinua had whispered to Naamah as they followed Hushai through the palace halls, "they only said outmatched so as not to offend the king. He may have been a fine singer in the days he played for King Saul, but that gift is long-gone. No voice in Israel can surpass yours today — or in Tyre, it would appear."

Neither Semere nor Chinua were Naamah's appointed guides when she left the harem these days since her almost daily excursions cut too deeply into their own duties. Instead, a newly-arrived eunuch barely in his teens had been assigned as her permanent escort and body servant. He'd been among the spoils from the sacking of Aramean cities for their support of the Ammonites against Israel.

But Chinua still claimed the privilege of escorting Naamah if an event was prestigious enough. It would seem a glimpse of the Tyre envoy fell into that category. The small, plump man suddenly twisted around as a group of half-a-dozen women emerged from a side corridor they'd just passed. "Hey, did you see that?"

Looking back, Naamah saw that the harem overseer Semere was leading the group in the direction of the women's section of the palace. One woman far more finely dressed than the others looked vaguely familiar to Naamah even from behind, tall and graceful with tumbling black curls spilling from under her head shawl, her very stride the definition of self-assurance.

Naamah was just about to turn away when the woman turned her own head to look back. Their eyes met. Naamah recognized that smoldering gaze, the flawless perfection of pale-gold skin, the derisive half-smile on wine-red lips. This was the woman named Bathsheba who had come to King David while Naamah played for him. The woman who turned out to have a husband! Was Semere taking her once again to the king's bedchamber?

"I heard the king has taken a new wife!" Chinua whispered as the group turned another corner and disappeared from sight. "I wonder if that is her. She is certainly beautiful enough. I can hardly wait to get my hands on her beauty regimen."

Naamah didn't have opportunity to answer as they approached the throne room. The next hours were exhausting as she played composition after composition, her own, King David's, some of Asaph's, and popular psalms of worship, all to the awed murmurs and applause of the Phoenician delegation. Chinua had long since slipped out to return to his own duties.

Naamah was just setting down her lyre as the throne room emptied when Hushai stopped by, her new body servant hovering timidly at his heels.

"Beautiful as always," the older man said smilingly. "I have a request for you from my wife. I will be helping David keep our guests entertained until well into the night. Not the sort of entertainment for your kind of music. In fact, I'm told the Phoenicians have a Moabite temple dance troupe they are bringing out this evening in exchange for our hospitality."

He grimaced. "All to say, you shouldn't be here any further, and Nasya was wondering if you would like to share the evening meal with her since I will not be here. If you are free, Elihu can escort you and I'll send a pair of palace guards as well."

"Of course," Naamah responded. "It has been far too long since I have visited your lovely wife. It will be my absolute pleasure."

Her new body servant at her heels and a guard on either side, Naamah made her way from the throne room onto the palace terrace and down the short, steep street separating the palace grounds from the compound of the king's advisor. Elihu wasn't the young Ammonite slave's actual name, which gave homage to one of the demonic entities the Ammonites worshipped. As was custom, he'd been given an Israelite name reflecting his new identity and allegiance. Elihu meant "my God is He."

Thin and short with almost feminine, very pretty features and the longest eyelashes Naamah had ever seen, Elihu had been made a eunuch and sold as a male concubine while still a young child. Naamah had at first felt guilty to think of another human being as her own personal accessory. But though Elihu's Hebrew was still rudimentary, it was clear the boy far preferred his life with Naamah than whatever he'd endured as an Ammonite sex slave.

Chinua had at first displayed jealousy toward the newcomer. But the youth was so timid and grateful for the smallest kindness that it wasn't long before Chinua took Elihu under his wing, treating him as a combination adoptive child, pet, and apprentice. Elihu in turn was happy to run errands, do the more tedious tasks of creating beauty treatments, and obey Chinua's peremptory orders any time Naamah wasn't in need of his services. From Chinua's satisfied smiles, it was clear he considered *he'd* been the one to acquire a full-time servant.

Hushai's wife warmly welcomed Naamah into her comfortable living area, where a delicious meal was already laid out. Nasya quickly settled Naamah on a cushion and thrust a cup of wine into her hand. "Hushai told me you'd be playing and singing for the envoys from Tyre, so I can only imagine how tired you are. Don't even think of talking for a bit, much less singing. In fact, I have a treat for you instead."

Nasya's plump face practically beamed with delight at Naamah's expression of astonishment when Reuel walked into the room, a scroll half-unrolled in his hands.

"You are always making music for others while they eat," Nasya went on. "Since we have a scribe in the family, I asked if he would be willing to read one of his scrolls so you in turn could be entertained while we enjoy our meal."

Chapter 30

Seating himself away from the low table to give the two women a feel of privacy, Reuel began reading from what Naamah immediately recognized as the first book of the Pentateuch. "In the beginning Yahweh created the heavens and the earth. Now the earth was formless and empty, darkness was over the surface of the deep, and the Spirit of Yahweh was hovering over the waters. And Yahweh said, 'Let there be light,' and there was light. Yahweh saw that the light was good, and He separated the light from the darkness. Yahweh called the light 'day,' and the darkness He called 'night.' And there was evening, and there was morning—the first day."

Naamah listened bemused as Reuel read through the record of creation, stopping only when the account reached where Naamah knew the story would turn dark as the serpent entered Paradise. By then, her hunger was slacked and her throat no longer parched. She looked over wistfully to where Reuel was rolling up the scroll.

"That was so very beautiful. I will never be able to remember every word. I wish I could learn the trade of a scribe. Not just to be able to write down my own songs but to read all the scrolls

I have seen in the palace scriptorium as you have."

As Reuel's expression suddenly stiffened, Naamah added hastily, "I didn't mean that as a request. I understand now that it would not be proper to learn from a man or to continue visiting the scriptorium except when I have been ordered. It is just—"

She stared down at her hands. "—well, I did as you suggested and inquired whether there might be one of the eunuchs with the knowledge to teach me. But I was told that there are but few who can read and write and they are fully occupied with the sons of the king."

She lapsed into silence, keeping her gaze on her clasped hands. Reuel was equally silent, his eyes intent on the scroll. But Nasya suddenly spoke up. "I have a wonderful idea! Of course it would not be appropriate for you to visit Reuel's workplace or for him to teach you alone or in the company of other men. But you are welcome here in our home. I have thought of you as a daughter since we believed you would be living with us. And here is Reuel with a scroll at hand. There is certainly no impropriety for my son to teach his mother the symbols on that parchment while my daughter of spirit sits beside me!"

"Why, that would be wonderful!" Naamah exclaimed. "That is, if your son has time and is willing."

"Of course! What son doesn't have time for his mother? Come, let's clear this off." Nasya called the servants, and within moments the table was cleared of dishes and wiped clean. In the meantime, Nasya left the room and came back with a well-worn length of papyrus, only partially covered with writing.

"This was a message Hushai received from King Hiram's chief architect many years ago when he was making arrangements for cedar logs and other materials to be sent for the building of David's palace. It has been gathering dust ever since. It seems just right for putting to use to learn the symbols Reuel is always writing. After all, he was but a boy of six when he began." Nasya smiled widely at Naamah. "I think we two grown women are capable of doing the same."

The rest of the evening was not one Naamah had ever expected. She covertly glanced at Reuel, bent over the parchment, a quill in his hand, a pot of ink nearby, as the scribe sketched out one symbol after another, patiently identifying them. "Alef, Bet, Gimel, Dalet, Heh, Vav" and so on all the way to "Tav." If Nasya's son was annoyed with Naamah for dragging him into such a chore, his expression didn't show it. In fact, the further into his instruction, the more relaxed he seemed, patiently correcting the two women's mistakes and even smiling briefly at his mother's patent excitement.

Finally, Nasya called a halt. "Enough! My mind will not hold another symbol. But we will do this again soon. That is, if you wish, Naamah."

"Wish? This has been a beautiful dream to me!" Naamah exclaimed, her smile so wide she could feel it stretching her cheek muscles. "I cannot thank you enough, Nasya." She glanced quickly at their tutor. "And Reuel, of course."

Reuel got hastily to his feet. "It is nothing. As I have said, anyone should be able to learn. If my mother wishes to learn and for you to learn as well, good." He broke off, hesitating for a full breath before continuing, "Though not all believe a woman is capable of becoming a scribe. Perhaps we should keep this between family and not speak of it outside this room."

Nasya's smile was shrewd. "Like your father, you are wise in the ways of men, son. This will be a game between Naamah and me when she comes to visit, nothing more. Is that not so, dear one?"

Naamah nodded, too overcome with joy and gratitude to speak. She was walking out of the chamber with Nasya when she remembered she had news and questions Nasya might be able to answer. Stopping in her tracks, she said, "I saw a woman at the palace today. Her name is Bathsheba. They are saying she is King David's newest wife. I saw her once before at the palace when I was playing for the king. It was just after I arrived. But when I saw her, she was married to a man named Uriah. I think her house is the one just down from yours right below the palace wall. Do you know her? Is she truly the king's new wife?"

Naamah was surprised to hear an audible gasp from Nasya. But she was even more surprised at the sound that came from Reuel. If Naamah had to guess from past interactions with male family members, it was one-third shock, one-third comprehension, and one-third fury.

"You saw Bathsheba at the palace?" Nasya demanded. "Yes, I know Bathsheba. She lives in the house you spoke of. Her husband Uriah was one of David's finest Mighty Men and a close friend for many years with the king and Hushai, so I have known Bathsheba since she was given in marriage to Uriah. He was killed not two weeks ago during the battle at Rabbah. Bathsheba has been in seclusion completing her time of mourning. If you saw her at the palace, her mourning period must be complete. Did she seem distraught? In tears?"

"Not at all. She looked quite happy and pleased with herself." Naamah's confusion had compounded. "If she is a widow now, I suppose it is possible for the king to take her as his wife as he did after Abigail's husband died. She is certainly beautiful enough to catch a king's eye."

"But why would Bathsheba have been at the palace when you saw her before?" Nasya asked with slow emphasis. "Uriah was at the battlefront when you first arrived. Was it in the women's quarters you saw her? Or his throne room?"

"No, it was his bedchamber. I was playing there for the king alone when a guard brought Bathsheba to the room. The king seemed to be expecting her and immediately told me to leave."

Naamah broke off, suddenly aware how much she'd given away. She didn't dare glance back to see if Reuel was listening. "I don't think I should say anything further. After all, who am I to question? Is it not so that a king may do whatever they wish? I just wondered if the gossip I heard today was true."

"Well, you can be sure I'll find out just as soon as my husband walks through the door! And if it is true, I am sure you will hear as soon as you are back in the palace."

& & &

Reuel walked with furious strides back to the palace, taking an alternative route to ensure he didn't cross paths with King David's concubine. So that was it! The entire ugly truth had become as clear as a stream of pure water. The king's antics in trying to get Uriah drunk and coax him to spending the night with his wife. The plotting with Joab to murder the Hittite when that attempt failed. The king, known as a man after Yahweh's own heart, who had turned the hearts of Israel back to the true faith, had committed adultery with another man's wife!

And not just any other man. One of David's most loyal

comrades who had fought staunchly at the king's side during all the years of exile. Who was fighting the very king who had disrespected King David and mutilated his envoys while the king of Israel lounged around his palace lusting for his close friend's wife.

Reuel's heart was anguished. He'd deeply revered the king since his earliest childhood. He'd grown up running around the palace, treated by the king like a nephew if not another son. His father counted David his closest friend, and the king counted Hushai his most valued advisor.

How had it come to this? And why the extreme of murder? After all, if the king had brought Bathsheba to his chambers, that alone was no evidence of adultery. A king had only to speak for his word to be truth. There had to be something more here that Reuel wasn't seeing.

Chapter 31

Amaris was sound asleep when Naamah returned to her room. Shiphrah was propped up in her bed, feeding baby Gia.

"Where have you been all day?" Shiphrah asked drowsily. "Even for the delegation of Tyre, I didn't expect you would be wearing down your fingers this long. In fact, I began wondering if the king had called you to his quarters. Though with a new wife, that seemed unlikely."

"I was invited to dinner with Nasya after playing for the Tyre envoys." Even with Shiphrah, Naamah decided it would be best if she didn't mention her reading lesson. Instead, she latched onto Shiphrah's last statement. "Then it's true the king has taken a new wife? Is it the woman named Bathsheba? If so, then Chinua and I saw her this morning on our way to the throne room."

"Yes, that is her name. Bathsheba is the widow of David's Mighty Man who was killed in the battle of Rabbah not two weeks ago. All are saying the king has taken her so quickly as wife to honor her husband, who lost his life fighting the king's battles, just as he took Abigail." Shiphrah giggled sleepily. "Not that David married Abigail to honor her beast of a husband, quite the contrary. But he did so as soon as Abigail's week of mourning was over."

Naamah didn't respond, and thankfully, by the time she'd readied herself for bed, Shiphrah and Gia were both sound asleep. After her indiscreet words to Nasya, she'd made up her mind to say nothing else of her previous encounters with Bathsheba. Especially if Uriah's widow was now the king's wife, to whom a lowly and still unbedded concubine was no more than a grain of dust under the woman's sandals.

That didn't keep Naamah from wondering just how great a coincidence it was that the woman she'd first glimpsed on a rooftop sharing an enraptured gaze with King David had moved so quickly from the king's bedchamber to widow to wife. Or had Bathsheba's speedy rise involved a helping hand?

& & &

When Naamah and Shiphrah entered the harem bath chamber, several other concubines were already wading about. Even after several months, Naamah still felt awkward to disrobe completely around so many other women. She slid hastily into the water, thankful for even that minimal cover.

Three concubines were lounging on the steps, showing no self-consciousness over their nudity as they took turns rubbing each other's shoulders and feet. Naamah had come to know well two of them—the harem midwife, Jytte, and Brielle, who had helped with Gia's delivery. They waved to Naamah and Shiphrah. "Come join us! Chaya has brought us some news about the king's newest wife. She got it straight from visiting

Abigail in the wives' quarters."

Shiphrah immediately plopped herself down beside Jytte while Naamah came close enough to listen while remaining chest-deep in the water. Jytte moaned with pleasure as Brielle dug her fingers into the midwife's right instep before summarizing, "Chaya tells us David has called for Bathsheba every night since her arrival two months ago. Or so Abigail's maidservant told her. The other wives are furious."

Chaya leaned forward, speaking unnecessarily just above a whisper. "And that's not all! They say Bathsheba hasn't menstruated once since she got there. Unless she's washing her own rags and drying them somewhere outside the harem."

"Like that woman would perform a servant's chores!" Brielle scoffed. "They say she won't even scrub herself when she bathes but has her maid do it. No, she is definitely pregnant!"

"As we all know, the king's seed is strong," Jytte said peaceably. "Perhaps she conceived as soon as she entered David's bed."

"Well, as the youngest in the harem—" Chaya broke off to throw Naamah a glance. "I mean, the youngest *mother*, I would certainly like to have some of that seed as well! A son for the king!"

Though several years older than Naamah, Chaya was much shorter with a boyishly slim frame and high-pitched flutelike voice that made her seem little more than a child though in fact she'd borne two daughters to the king. Her personality made up for her size as she was full of life and laughter rose easily to her lips.

"None of the rest of us will have a chance for another son if King David only calls for Bathsheba," Brielle said gloomily.

"Perhaps the king will tire of her once she is large with

child," Jytte commented wryly. "He always does eventually."

As one of the oldest concubines, the midwife no longer had any expectation of being summoned to the king and had never had a child of her own. Like Abigail, she'd found contentment caring for her harem sisters and their children.

"I pray that may come soon," Chaya interjected. "My maidservant just gave me a new perfume to put on my bed linens that I am hoping will add to my allure."

The concubines continued chatting of ways to attract the king's attention from new beauty treatments, perfumes, and dress styles. To Naamah, it seemed these women were desperate to have the one thing with King David she wished to avoid above all else — an intimate physical relationship.

The conversation moved on to methods by which a woman could make a man believe she was still a virgin while having relations. Naamah felt her face burn with embarrassment, but she listened avidly. At least one suggestion seemed feasible enough she took mental notes even while she wondered if she'd ever have the courage — or deceit — to carry it out. She could just see herself bursting into tears and blurting out the truth.

The conversation left Naamah feeling extremely uncomfortable. Once back in their room, she asked Shiphrah, "Why would any woman in a king's harem need such knowledge about pretending to be a virgin? After all, none of the women here are virgins and none have opportunity for relations with other men. If they did, they would be killed!"

Shiphrah's expression was almost pitying as she shook her head. "Do you truly believe every woman who finds herself here was a virgin when the king summoned her? Many of the concubines were spoils of war, others sold against their will. By Israel's laws, female captives are spared if still virgin while those who have known men are put to the sword. Do you think there is a harem where such knowledge is not freely shared? And who are we to judge the circumstances by which another woman finds need of it?"

Who indeed? Maybe Naamah's situation wasn't as unique as she'd already assumed. At least she'd had a loving family to turn to for consolation. And a current situation in no degree as terrible as she'd expected. What if she'd been Elihu, mutilated and sold into sexual slavery at just six years of age? Or Akilah, with her entire family slaughtered? Or worse, one of those even in this harem who had survived the slaughter of her people only to be given as a sexual toy to their killer?

Yahweh, I have seen only the hurt I've known. But now I know many have been hurt far more than I even here in this place. Thank You for Your salvation from my attacker. Thank You for restoring my music to my soul. Whatever happens, even should my secret be revealed, I give You thanks for Your blessings, and I pray that I may be a blessing in turn to others who may be hurting in this place.

Chapter 32

"We have a new arrival in the harem," Shiphrah announced loud enough for all to hear, entering the courtyard where Naamah sat on a bench in the shade of a fig tree softly picking out a new melody on her lyre. "Bathsheba, the newest wife, just had a baby."

Naamah looked up with surprise. "Are you sure it wasn't one of the other wives? I heard Bathsheba was pregnant, but she has only been in the palace six months. Or did the baby come early?"

Silence suddenly fell over the courtyard as a dozen pairs of eyes suddenly focused on Shiphrah. Balancing her own youngest daughter on her hip, Shiphrah hunched her shoulders. "Not that I have heard. Adah was there helping Jytte with the delivery. It was from her I heard the news after the king arrived and all the women were shooed out so he could be alone with his beloved and their firstborn. She said it is a son, healthy and full-sized."

The caustic note in Shiphrah's response echoed a general sentiment in the women's quarters, as much among the king's wives as his concubines. Since Bathsheba's arrival, King David might indeed be married to a single cherished bride since not one of the other women had been summoned to his presence over the past six months.

Then the murmurs began.

"It can't be David's son. She must have been three months pregnant when she arrived here. Is she trying to pass off her husband's son as the king's?"

"No, Uriah was off at war for half a year when he died," one of the older concubines, Eglah, commented. Shiphrah had told Naamah the woman's story. A dark-skinned, tall woman with almost kinky hair, she had been with King David from his earliest exile, a gift to him from the king of Gath when David and his men along with his first two wives, Ahinoam and Abigail, had lived in exile there. Her skill had been as an exotic dancer with an acrobatic dexterity trained to arouse a man's passions, and she'd attracted David's attentions long enough to bear him a daughter.

Eglah was now overweight and far from agile. But thanks to her long sojourn in exile among David's Mighty Men and their women, she always seemed to have the latest gossip about what was going on in the inner circles of David's court. She went on, "No, whoever the father is, it most definitely wasn't Uriah. In fact, he has never fathered a child on Bathsheba though they were married almost ten years."

She leaned forward conspiratorially. "Or from what I've heard, on any other women. It was whispered among the women when we were still in Hebron that Uriah's seed must be dead because he had several concubines before Bathsheba, and believe me, he was not always away at war!"

A titter swept the courtyard. Then Chinua spoke up slyly from where he was working with Chaya's hair, using carven bone combs to create a new style he'd been working on.

"But Uriah was not at war the entire time before his death. I remember well when he and his fiercest fighters rode valiantly in from the siege of Rabbah to be honored by King David. The king feasted to their great deeds right here in the palace. Naamah can attest as I escorted her there to play for them."

The small, plump eunuch sighed as though in envious admiration of the brawny, stalwart warriors he'd never be able to emulate. "It was at least eight months ago, long enough to account for a healthy birth. Perhaps Uriah fathered Bathsheba's child then."

Eglah shook her head. "Not so. I heard from several sources who were present that Uriah refused to go home to his wife. He said that while his men were at war and unable to be with their own wives, who was he to take comfort at home before the battle was won?"

Eglah looked shrewdly at Naamah. "If you were there, you must know. Is it true what I was told?"

Naamah nodded reluctantly. A knot tightened her stomach, then rose into her throat. She alone knew the truth that it must indeed be David's son he and Bathsheba were celebrating. Not fathered since Uriah's death, but on that night almost exactly nine months past when she'd witnessed the searing passion as David and Bathsheba stared at each other before she'd been ordered out of the king's bedchamber.

She could also now guess why David had been urging Uriah to go to his wife's bed while she'd played for that drunken party a month or so later. Had Bathsheba felt safe going to the king, never having conceived before? Did she believe like Sarah and Rebekah of antiquity that she was sterile? If so, she must have been shocked and terrified to discover she was pregnant.

And when the king's clumsy effort to cover up their adultery hadn't worked, was it unthinkable to believe King David had gone a step further to ensure Bathsheba's husband died in battle so he could cover their sin through marriage? Naamah didn't want to believe it. How could the man who wrote songs of such passions and praise to Yahweh stoop to such evil? But how could she deny the evidence before her?

Chaya piped up. "I have heard more. It is being whispered that the child is the king's, conceived before Bathsheba's husband died."

She lowered her childlike voice to barely audible. "My maidservant told me just this morning that a guard she has been dallying with told her that he escorted Bathsheba once to the king's bedchamber. It was while Uriah was still at the siege of Rabbah and some weeks before Uriah was killed in battle. She didn't think more of the guard's tale until Bathsheba birthed a full-term child claimed as son by King David."

A silence again fell over the courtyard, but this time it was a heavy one. The knot in Naamah's throat grew to the size of a pomegranate. It seemed a king could do what he chose, even to breaking the laws he himself was tasked with enforcing. But King David was renowned for ruling in righteousness. If he broke Yahweh's laws with impunity, what did that mean for the kingdom? And whether or not Naamah herself held her tongue, it seemed the truth was seeping out.

Shiphrah finally spoke up somberly, "If this is correct—and there seems little doubt it is if all told here is correct—word will spread throughout the palace like fire."

"And throughout the kingdom," Eglah added soberly. "The name of our king and our God will be reviled for this sin. May Yahweh have mercy on our nation!"

Chapter 33

King David listened impatiently to a report Reuel was reading from Joab, who had wiped the Ammonite countryside clean of adversaries but had yet to break through to the royal citadel of Rabbah, a fortress as heavily fortified as Jerusalem had been. The entire council, tribal leaders, and regional military commanders filled the throne room to hear the latest from the battle front. The king showed minimal interest in Joab's progress, and Reuel wondered if he was in a hurry to return to his newest wife, who according to the latest gossip he'd overheard between his mother and Naamah had recently borne a son.

Reuel's visits home while Naamah was there were no longer strictly necessary. Over the past months, she'd mastered both reading and writing the Hebrew script with the same proficiency with which she'd learned to play instruments and compose music. While his mother still struggled with both, Reuel could have easily turned her instruction over to Naamah. But he'd come to anticipate these teaching sessions with a feeling as though he were coming home.

Perhaps it was because Naamah had become to him the sister

he'd never had. Either way, her presence with his mother and sometimes his father in their living quarters had begun to feel like family. So he still arranged to pop in at least briefly each time his mother told him she'd scheduled another visit with Naamah. Which wasn't so frequently these days as Reuel was more and more in demand to handle communications with the battlefront, covertly surveil certain men, caravan movements, locations, and bring back trustworthy oral and visual reports.

Now eighteen, he had reached his father's height, and his combat training gave him a lithe strength. But his features were still boyish and his frame slim enough to allow him to project an illusion of being younger, especially since he kept his face smooth-shaven like an Egyptian. On such journeys, he traveled overland and dressed like a humble shepherd.

All of which had come in handy more than once when foes had grabbed him, searching for evidence of written communication or that he was a spy. Reuel had learned a dozen variants of Moabite, Edomite, Syrian, Aramean, and Ammonite dialects, and could act the terrified peasant boy in all of them. On the rare occasion he'd traveled beyond such borders, he could also resort to a mute idiot able to turn his hand to any hard labor but capable of nothing more than grunts.

In consequence, King David's commander Joab had been calling on Reuel's services with growing frequency. All to the disapproval of Seraiah, who objected to his best scribe spending more time out of the scriptorium than in it. Though he kept that disapproval unvoiced, knowing full well that the commander of Israel's armies would always have priority over its chief scribe.

Reuel had neared the end of the report he'd written out as soon as he returned from the battlefront when quick footsteps interjected. He broke off as a worried-looking duty guard approached the throne to murmur something to the king. Reuel exchanged a surprised glance with his father, standing to King David's right side. It would generally take something as catastrophic as an Assyrian invasion for a guard to interrupt a royal council briefing.

But King David simply looked annoyed as he raised a hand in an imperious gesture. "Let him in!"

It was too late to give permission. The throne room doors flew open, striking the wall with a thud. All heads turned to face the entrance as sharp footsteps and the loud thump of a staff striking mosaic tile filled the silence. Lowering the scroll he'd been reading from, Reuel swiveled to see who had interrupted his account.

The elderly bearded man with a long, unkempt white beard who strode forward wore a plain beige tunic covered by a cloak, also plain but with sleeves striped in several colors. He wore a belt of rough hemp rope and well-worn leather sandals on his dusty feet. Only when he drew near did Reuel recognize the man as Nathan, the kingdom's most renowned prophet of Yahweh. Reuel had read some of the prophet's fiery writings and prophecies from Yahweh, but he hadn't seen the prophet in person since he was a small child at Hushai's side when Nathan joined the Levite priests in the consecration ceremony after King David triumphantly brought the Ark of the Covenant to Jerusalem.

This time there was none of the joy of that occasion as Nathan strode up to the throne and launched without preamble into a story that seemed completely immaterial to the occasion. It was about a rich man who owned vast flocks of sheep and a poor man who had but one little ewe lamb that was a beloved pet to the man and his children. When the rich man had an unexpected visitor, he didn't bother butchering one of his own many sheep to offer the visitor a meal. Instead, he seized the poor man's lamb, killed it, and had his servants roast it as a feast for his guest.

If true and not some instructional parable, the whole incident certainly displayed unjust behavior. But in the context of a nation still at war with their powerful neighbors the Ammonites, the event hardly rose to the level of bursting into the king's throne room and interrupting vital matters of state.

But then, Reuel had never been a shepherd with a flock of cherished sheep, something perhaps the prophet had well in mind. He'd barely finished his heartrending story when King David roared out furiously, "As surely as the Lord lives. Any man who would do such a thing deserves to die. He must repay four lambs to the poor man for the one he stole and for having no pity."

For a long moment, Nathan was silent. Standing just one pace away, Reuel felt his heart chill to high mountain snow at the suddenly implacable, accusatory expression on the prophet's face. As if in slow-motion, Nathan raised his right hand and pointed it directly at the location of David's heart. His tone held angry contempt as he spat out, "You, David, are that man!"

A collective gasp and horrified murmurs filled the court. Nathan raised his voice to ring out above the noise. "The Lord says to you, oh, David, why have you despised me by doing what is evil in My sight? I anointed you king over all Israel and Judah. I delivered you from the hand of your predecessor Saul when he tried to kill you. I gave you all Saul's possessions and the women of his household. How many wives and concubines do you now possess? If you wanted more, I would have given them to you."

Nathan lowered his arm, his voice now saddened. "So why have you despised My word and My laws? You have broken my commandments given to Moses on Mount Sinai for the instruction and obedience of my people. You have coveted your neighbor's wife. You with many wives and concubines stole his only wife and committed adultery with her. You murdered her husband, Uriah the Hittite, with the sword of the Ammonites and lied to cover your actions. In so doing, you blasphemed My name before the nations!"

King David's head was now down, his face whitened above his trimmed beard, his hands visibly shaken. The prophet thundered on. "This is what the Lord says. Because of what you have done, the sword will never depart from your house, and I will bring calamity out of your own household. Before your very eyes, I will give your wives and concubines to a man who is close to you. You committed your sins in secret, but he will go to bed with them in broad daylight in the sight of all Israel."

From the throne, David let out an agonized groan. "You are right! I confess to all these things! I have sinned gravely against Yahweh. I deserve to die for my sins."

The harshness ebbed slightly from Nathan's expression. His voice gentled. "Yahweh has heard your contrite heart, David. He forgives your sins. You will not die. But the son Bathsheba has borne to you in adultery will die."

Letting out a howl of deep pain, King David fell from his throne onto his knees before the prophet. Tears poured down his bearded cheeks as he cried out, "No, no, not my son! He is innocent! Let me die instead! I pray, Nathan will you not intercede with Yahweh to spare my son? Do not put my sins upon him!"

But Nathan didn't even look down at the sobbing king. Turning with a swish of his prophet's cloak, he strode from the throne room. Behind him was absolute silence. Then King David raised his hands high and turned his grief-stricken face toward heaven. With unmistakable sincerity, he cried out, "Have mercy on me, O God, according to Your unfailing love. According to Your great compassion, blot out my transgressions. Wash away all my iniquity and cleanse me from sin. The sacrifices of God are a broken spirit. A broken and a contrite heart, O God, you will not despise."

The tortured anguish in King David's voice contracted Reuel's own heart, bringing to his eyes the first tears he could remember in years. Never had he witnessed such heartfelt contrition as he saw in the king's penitent expression, and it felt as if his own soul would break at the sight of it.

Chapter 34

Naamah was sitting cross-legged on her bed, softly strumming her latest revisions to a new song when Shiphrah rushed in. "Have you heard? They are saying Bathsheba's new baby is very ill. Jytte was with them, and she has called for the royal physician. People are saying the baby is not likely to survive."

Naamah didn't even have time to process how she felt about the news when Semere's large, dark face thrust itself into the room. "Naamah, the king is calling for you. Take your lyre and come with me."

Clutching her lyre, Naamah stumbled from the bed to her feet and looked down at her wrinkled tunic. Her music hadn't been requested since Bathsheba's son was born, and Naamah had neither dressed for public appearance nor had Akilah or Chinua do her hair.

"I'm not fit to appear before the king!" she protested.

Semere glanced impatiently over Naamah's disheveled appearance. "Just throw a cloak on. In his condition, the king will not care or even notice what you look like."

Shiphrah was already tugging a deep-yellow robe of some delicate, fine fabric over Naamah's shoulders and smoothing a gauzy matching scarf down her hair. Grabbing her lyre in one burly arm, Semere tugged Naamah out the door with the other. Mouthing a "thank you" to her roommate, Naamah followed Semere at the fastest pace she'd ever seen the head eunuch employ, almost a trot.

She soon realized Semere was leading her to an area of the palace she'd been in before. A few more turns brought them to a familiar hallway just outside the antechamber to King David's bedchamber. Hushai was standing there, apparently waiting for them. The same guard Naamah remembered from her previous visit stood at attention outside the door.

"Here is the concubine with her lyre." Handing the lyre to Naamah, Semere bowed deeply and retreated.

Hushai looked down at Naamah, his gaze somber. "Naamah, King David is asking for you. I don't know if you have heard what happened a few days ago. The … the visit of the prophet Nathan."

Hushai broke off and looked away, but Naamah glimpsed tears shimmering in the chief advisor's eyes. The whole palace knew of Nathan's proclamation condemning the king's iniquities and pronouncing judgment against his house. In fact, the entire kingdom likely knew by now. David's words of contrition had also been repeated. Remembering the passion she'd glimpsed between the king and his friend's wife, Naamah could only hope that part of the story was true.

"Yes, I have heard. What is it you wish from me? To sing for him?" As with Bathsheba, Naamah wasn't sure how she felt about being summoned here. Her music was the one thing she still had, the thing most precious to her. It wasn't just entertainment to distract a man, however powerful, from his guilt.

But the sadness and shimmer of tears in Hushai's eyes softened her heart. Whatever else, King David was Hushai's dearest friend, and in turn Hushai, Nasya, and Reuel were the closest to family Naamah had in this place. Softly, she added, "Whatever you need of me, you have only to ask."

Hushai let out a deep sigh. "It is not just for your music the king has asked for you, Naamah. I will say no more of what has happened. But in his pain, David's gift of music has left him. Especially since word came that Bathsheba's son is gravely ill. He can lift prayers to Yahweh, but he cannot find a tune to accompany them. He believes you can provide that for him."

Naamah remembered well the deep anguish she'd felt when her gift had abandoned her after the attack. Perhaps no other understood David's pain in this regard than she did. "I will do my best, Hushai."

"I know you will." Hushai smiled affectionately. "And your best, dear child, is better than anyone else I know. It is why I have summoned you and not Asaph or another of the palace musicians. Now go, and I will be praying that through you Yahweh will bring peace to our king's soul."

Hushai stood aside, and the guard opened the door, allowing her to enter before quickly shutting the door behind her. Inside, Naamah spotted King David lying prone on the hard mosaic floor, face down. Rather than the splendid robes she'd seen him wear on his throne, he was garbed in sackcloth, a coarse material woven from goat's hair, worn only by the poor and those in mourning. From what she could hear, the king was begging over and over for Yahweh to spare his son.

Naamah hesitated just inside the room. Should she speak, or should she just walk over to the couch where she'd sat on her last visit and begin playing? Before she could make a decision, the king rolled to his back and blinked up at her. "I can find the words, but the melodies have forsaken me."

It was the first time King David had spoken directly to Naamah since ordering her out of this very chamber. She looked down at the greatest personage in Israel, now a broken man, his cheeks and beard wet from weeping, his eyes reddened and swollen. Rolling to a sitting position, King David raised his hands and face toward the heavens.

"Have mercy on me, O God, according to Your unfailing love," he cried out with a hoarse, halting voice. "According to Your great compassion, blot out my transgressions. Wash away all my iniquity and cleanse me from my sin. For I know my transgressions, and my sin is always before me. Against You, Yahweh, You only, have I sinned and done what is evil in Your sight. So You are right in Your verdict and justified when You judge."

The contrition in King David's voice was so unfeigned, so sincere and anguished, that Naamah found tears overflowing her own eyes. It was as though the king was truly crying out for forgiveness and mercy to a deeply loved friend he knew he'd inexcusably betrayed. What would it be like to have such an evident close relationship with the very Creator of heaven and earth? This was the man Naamah had believed her king to be!

As King David continued pouring out his soul, Naamah sank to the floor beside him, already hearing melody rising to her mind. She tentatively touched the strings of her lyre as David continued his prayer.

"Cleanse me with hyssop, and I will be clean. Wash me, and I will be whiter than snow. Let me hear joy and gladness. Let the bones You have crushed rejoice. Hide Your face from my sins and blot out all my iniquity. Create in me a pure heart, O God, and renew a steadfast spirit within me. Do not cast me from Your presence or take Your Holy Spirit from me. Restore to me the joy of Your salvation and grant me a willing spirit to sustain me."

By now, Naamah was playing softly, a hauntingly beautiful minor melody that somehow perfectly matched David's words rising effortlessly to her fingers.

"Then I will teach transgressors Your ways, so that sinners will turn back to You. Deliver me from the guilt of bloodshed, O God, You who are God my Savior, and my tongue will sing of Your righteousness. Open my lips, Lord, and my mouth will declare Your praise. You do not delight in sacrifice, or I would bring it. You do not take pleasure in burnt offerings. My sacrifice, O God, is a broken spirit. A broken and contrite heart You, God, will not despise."

By the time David's prayer trailed into silence, the song had become clear in Naamah's soul. She began again, this time singing David's own words. "Have mercy on me, O God, according to your unfailing love. According to your great compassion blot out my transgressions."

By the second line, David's voice had joined with Naamah's. It was the first time Naamah had heard the king sing, a sweet, deep tone like the lowest strings of a great harp, perfectly harmonizing with Naamah's higher tone. She could now understand it was far more than his Yahweh-blessed lyrics that had made David renowned as the sweet psalmist of Israel when he wasn't so many years older than Naamah. This was the voice that had once soothed King Saul's own demons.

They finished the song together, then started again. This time Naamah increased the complexity of her chording and added new harmonies, allowing David to carry the melody.

When the last notes died away, they smiled at each other, no longer king and concubine, but two musicians doing what they loved, exercising the gift Yahwah had given them. For one moment, it felt to Naamah that for the first time David saw her as a human being, not the concubine he'd so heedlessly seized for his own desires without a thought as to Naamah's own well-being or wishes.

Then a hard knock came at the door. It swung open, and the guard stepped aside to usher Hushai into the room. He glanced around before looking down to spot David and Naamah still seated on the floor.

"My king, Bathsheba is calling for you," Hushai said urgently. "The child is worse. The royal physician has requested you be informed."

Chapter 35

Before Hushai had finished speaking, King David rushed out the door and down the hallway. Hushai attempted a smile for Naamah before he left to follow King David. The guard beckoned a servant to take Naamah back to the harem.

The next few days were difficult as Naamah was often called to play for King David. She rarely saw Hushai, upon whose shoulders all administrative matters had fallen. Elihu now knew the way well and would escort Naamah to the king's chambers and back, waiting outside in the hall however long it took.

After that first day, King David paid little attention to Naamah except to angrily tell her to leave him in peace when he tired of her music. He rarely moved from his prone position on the floor and still wore the same coarse, now filthy sackcloth garment. Hushai tried to coax him to eat, but from what Naamah had witnessed, he hadn't eaten a morsel since he'd received word of his new son's illness. Only the occasional sips of wine Hushai coaxed into him kept the king from collapsing repeatedly.

Naamah no longer sang when she was brought into King

David's presence, not even the beautiful song of repentance they had created together. If anyone spoke, the king grew agitated, his own mumbled prayers never ceasing. Instead, she played familiar songs of worship, including King David's own psalms of praise, hoping the words he already knew would offer some comfort. She was softly playing the tune to King David's well-known psalm from his own youth as a shepherd when Hushai and the royal physician entered the room with two others of the king's close advisors.

As they whispered together, Naamah caught a few phrases. "Who is going to tell him? If he has been so distressed thus far, how can we tell him now? What if he does something desperate?"

They had not been quiet enough. King David suddenly rolled over, his words coming out in a harsh growl. "Why are you all whispering? Is the child dead?"

The others fell silent, but Hushai took a hesitant step forward. "Yes, my king, I am deeply sorry to inform you that the child is dead."

Naamah's fingers stopped playing. She half-expected King David to rip his clothes and begin screaming out his fury. Instead, he struggled to his feet and commanded, "Call my servants and have them draw me a bath. When I am cleaned and changed, we will go together to the tabernacle to worship. Tell the high priest to meet me there. I wish to offer sacrifices of praise to Yahweh. And have a meal prepared for my return. I must eat to regain my strength."

Naamah could feel the shock in the room. As one of the advisors opened the door and began shouting orders, Naamah heard Hushai's quiet voice asking with bewilderment, "I don't understand why you are acting this way. While the child was alive, you fasted and wept. In truth, we feared for your life and sanity now that the child is dead. Instead, you get up to bathe and eat!"

King David clapped Hushai on the shoulder. "It is not so hard to understand, dear friend. While the child was still alive, I fasted and wept, hoping perhaps the Lord might be gracious to me and let the child live. Now that he is dead, why should I go on fasting? Can I bring him back again? Someday, I will go to him, but he will not return to me. Now it is time to give thanks to Yahweh for His mercy and forgiveness and to give comfort to the child's mother, my wife."

As Elihu escorted Naamah back to the women's quarters, she could hear women wailing, Bathsheba's voice above all the others. Even the other wives and concubines who had no reason to feel affection for Bathsheba could sympathize for a mother's loss of a child. Too many of them had endured similar pain.

The next afternoon following the infant's burial, Akilah entered Naamah's bedroom. "Bathsheba is asking for you. She says she has heard so much about how your music has helped the king and others that she thought perhaps it might sooth her in her sorrow."

Naamah immediately reached for her lyre. "Of course, I will play for her. But I have never been to her quarters."

"Her maidservant will arrive shortly to guide you."

Naamah followed Bathsheba's servant to her quarters, a spacious set of rooms far more luxurious than anything the concubines enjoyed. Naamah found Bathsheba sitting on the floor next to an empty cradle, a tiny blanket clutched to her breast. She raised a beautiful face wet with tears. "Naamah, come and sit with me."

Though she felt awkward, Naamah sat on the floor next to Bathsheba and placed her lyre on her lap. Bathsheba looked at Naamah. "I know everyone is gossiping about me. And they have reason. But as my child lay dying, I sought Yahweh's forgiveness for giving birth to a son who was not my husband's. Many in the harem will not understand, but Yahweh has forgiven me."

"It does not matter what they think, Bathsheba," Naamah responded warmly. "All that matters is the mercy that Yahweh shows us."

"Despite Yahweh's grace, I just cannot conquer my sorrow." Fresh tears spilled down Bathsheba's cheeks. "I know I must overcome this. The death of a child is nothing new to we women. I thought your music might begin to sooth my soul."

"Then I will sing." As Naamah lifted her lyre and began singing, other wives and servants squeezed into the doorway to listen, "Have mercy on me, O God, according to Your unfailing love. According to Your great compassion, blot out my transgressions … The sacrifices of God are a broken spirit. A broken and contrite heart, O God, You will not despise."

As Naamah finished the song and continued with others of her own composition and King David's, Bathsheba's heartbroken sobs gave way to a calm silence. Gently placing the tiny blanket in the cradle, she turned to Naamah. "Thank you, Naamah. Yahweh has used you to give me peace. I would like to lie down now and rest."

Those at the doorway evaporated away without a sound. Naamah arose, took her lyre, and with a soft smile at Bathsheba left the room. She was glad she'd been able to bring some comfort to the bereaved mother. But perhaps the sheer intensity and stress of the day's grief and her pouring out of comfort to Bathsheba had exhausted Naamah more than she knew. For the first time in months, she found herself back in the familiar nightmare of her assault. Only this time in her dream, the rape had left her pregnant. After an arduous labor, she gave birth to a stillborn child.

Naamah gasped awake. She discovered that her cheeks were wet with tears as though like Bathsheba she mourned the loss of a dearly-wanted child. Only this child was the product of rape, so how could Naamah possibly want it even in a dream? Would she have loved even such a child if it had been born to her? Or was she too broken for love? Was that why Yahweh had placed her in a loveless situation where she would likely never have a child of her own?

Naamah searched her mind for something to distance herself from the darkness of this dream. The words of King David came to her. "The sacrifices of God are a broken spirit. A broken and a contrite heart, O God, you will not despise."

"I have had a broken spirit," Naamah whispered into the night. "My heart has been broken."

The words finally sank into Naamah's soul, and she realized what she hadn't in all these long months. She'd done nothing wrong when she was raped. The sin was on the part of the rapist, not her. And even if she had sinned, there was still forgiveness. Unexpectedly, Bathsheba had been the one to teach her that.

"Yahweh does not despise me!" Naamah softly declared. "Yahweh loves me!"

In the comfort of that assurance, Naamah fell into a restful sleep.

Chapter 36

Dipping her quill into an ink pot, Naamah carefully drew the final symbol onto a scrap of parchment. Only when she lifted the quill from the parchment did she let out her held breath. She pushed her stool back from the table where she'd been working, which Akilah had managed to squeeze to one side of the door at the end of Naamah's bed.

"You did it!" Shiphrah applauded, leaning over Naamah's shoulder to examine the text. "It looks so—real!"

"It *is* real," Naamah said with a laugh. "The first song I have written down completely on my own. It came to me in the night."

"Then read it to us!" Akilah urged. "Better yet, sing it."

Naamah set the parchment to one side to dry. While pleased with her efforts, she didn't need to read her own words to sing her new song. Nor was she completely happy with the wavering lines of some of her symbols. She was growing increasingly adept at reading, but writing took more dexterity, a different dexterity than playing a lyre, and curving her fingers around the quill grew tiring after even a short time.

Which was why she hadn't attempted to write her new song

in the scroll Reuel kept for her in the scriptorium. She would take the song there later to allow his nimble fingers to add her words in his elegant calligraphy to the dozen or more songs now documented as Songs of Naamah.

Assuming Reuel was back in Jerusalem. When in town, he always stopped by the lessons Naamah was now giving Nasya to take a look at their handwriting efforts and occasionally clarify a word they hadn't yet mastered. He'd also started bringing home scrolls, which Naamah and Nasya took turns reading to each other. The scrolls were always well-worn and even sometimes ripped, and Reuel had assured his parents they were historical accounts he'd personally had copied onto new rolls for the palace archives.

Seraiah had given the scribes permission to use the discards as their own revolving library. When Nasya and Naamah finished one, Reuel would exchange it for another. Most recently, they'd finished reading the account of Deborah, Israel's only female judge. When they'd get another, Naamah had no idea as on her last several visits to Nasya, Reuel had been traveling somewhere his mother couldn't say or didn't know.

Picking up her lyre, Naamah added melody to the words. "It is good to praise the Lord and make music to Your name, O Most High. To proclaim Your love in the morning and Your faithfulness at night to the music of the ten-stringed lyre and melody of the harp. For You make me glad by Your deeds, O Lord. I sing for joy at the works of Your hands. How great are Your works, O Lord."

Naamah broke off as Chinua thrust his head into the room. "Your visitors are here, Naamah."

Naamah knew what this meant since she'd had only one set of visitors in the eighteen months she'd been in the harem.

Joyously, Naamah set down her lyre and hurried to the small outer courtyard that opened onto the palace terrace. She rushed first into Alzbetah's embrace, then her sister's. But at the feel of Zahara's no-longer-slim frame, Naamah stepped back in surprised delight. "Zahara, you are with child!"

Her sister smiled widely. "Yes. After three miscarriages, we were in despair. But Yahweh has blessed me again! This pregnancy is a full two months beyond where we lost the others, and the child is strong and active. So we have much hope."

Grabbing Naamah's hand, Zahara held it to her rounded belly. To her delight, Naamah felt a tiny kick against her palm. "Indeed, active! Perhaps he will be a warrior."

"Unless he is a she," Zahara smiled.

"Then perhaps she will be a wise prophet like Deborah, who once led all Israel."

"I will be happy for a healthy child, whatever he or she grows up to be."

Zahara and her betrothed Amos had married four months after Naamah entered the harem. It had been Naamah's only trip outside Jerusalem since her arrival. Chinua and Akilah had both accompanied her in the same finely-carved cart in which Naamah had left home along with a detail of four palace guards on horseback. While her family had seemed as delighted to see Naamah as she to see them, she'd felt awkward at the gawking and envious stares her fine attire and entourage had prompted.

Naamah hadn't been back to her childhood home since. She'd seen her father and other family members when they'd come to Jerusalem for the three annual festivals that required all Israelite men to appear before Yahweh — the festival of Unleavened Bread, or Passover, celebrating Yahweh's deliverance of Israel from Egypt, the festival of Shavuot, or Weeks, exactly seven weeks after Passover, and the Sukkot festival, which had always been Naamah's favorite as they slept in their makeshift hut for a full week, worshipping and enjoying the tabernacle music and reading of Yahweh's word.

Alzbetah and Zahara had come on their own several times in the long months between festivals, enough that the two guards knew them by sight and made no objection to Naamah taking her visitors from the reception courtyard back into the harem compound. As they strolled through the halls, Alzbetah spoke up. "Your fame continues to spread, daughter. You would not believe that even in our village I hear your songs, though few know that they are yours."

"Yes," Zahara added excitedly. "I heard the one you sang for us on our last visit sung by several women at the well when we were drawing water. They said their sister had learned it from the tabernacle choirs when she traveled with her husband to Jerusalem to offer the required sacrifice for their firstborn. They didn't believe me when I said that my own dear sister had written it. Not until Aunt Antje assured them it was true."

Naamah flushed with embarrassment. Glad though she was that her songs were being used in the tabernacle worship, she continued to feel self-conscious at such praise. "If you wish, I finished another just as you arrived. I wrote it down, the first time I've done so all by myself. I would be happy to teach it to you so you can sing it for the family when you get home."

"That would be wonderful!" Her mother caught Naamah in another quick embrace. "I am so proud of you, my daughter, and how you are using Yahweh's gift to serve Him. And how you have learned to read and write. I only wish that was permitted for women in our village."

"I can teach you!" Naamah said eagerly. "Why shouldn't women learn?"

"No, no! It is much too late for me," Alzbetah laughed. Zahara too shook her head firmly, "I have no interest in the craft of a scribe. My only desire is to fill my home with children to raise, and if I have hours to spare, I would prefer to weave a beautiful design of blanket or rug than scribble symbols. It is different for you, Naamah. You create words that must be written down so others can sing them. And—"

Zaharah glanced around at the ornate murals and pillars they were passing. "—in truth, dear sister, you have far more leisure for such pastimes than we do these days!"

It was a subtle reminder of the vastly different lives Naamah and her sister now lived. Naamah might regret not having a real husband or children, but she could hardly deny the relative luxury of her surroundings and the servants who made it possible for Naamah to spend long hours making music and reading scrolls. In her room, she retrieved her lyre and sang her new composition repeatedly until Alzbetah and Zahara felt confident they could reproduce it at home. Then for the next several hours, she engaged in small-talk on every extended family member, childhood friend, and village happening.

Alzbetah and Zahara bantered together about Gavriil and Rivka and their struggle to control all the children with which Yahweh had blessed them. Much though Naamah loved her mother and sister, it soon became apparent the passage of time had affected her relationship with them. The connection between Alzbetah and Zahara was effortless. They finished each other's sentences and laughed at jokes between the two of them that Naamah did not understand.

Alzbetah and Zahara eventually rose to their feet. "We must

leave if we are to be home by dark."

"Let me request a cart to take you," Naamah said eagerly. "Then you could stay longer."

But her mother was already shaking her head. "No, that isn't necessary, daughter. Can you imagine what people would think if we rode into the village in a palace cart?"

Another reminder of how different their lives now were. Naamah felt her cheeks grow hot. "But Zahara is pregnant, and you are no longer so young, mother. I just wanted—"

"I know you want to help, dear sister," Zahara said firmly. "But Mother and I both have the same strong legs we've always had. If Mother walked to the festivals when she was pregnant and with young children, then I can too. And if need be, Mother will help me."

Alzbetah and Zahara smiled at one another and touched hands. "And now we really must go."

Walking her mother and sister back to the smaller courtyard, Naamah hugged them both fiercely as the guard opened the door onto the palace terrace. "I love you both so much!"

"And I love you too, dearest daughter," Alzbetah assured her lovingly.

"We will come again after the baby is born so that he can meet his aunt. Or she." Zahara put her mouth close to Naamah's ear. "I continue to pray that your secret is safe. Since you are prospering here, I am guessing it is."

Aloud, she added. "And I love you too, dearest sister."

Naamah wrestled with her emotions as she watched her mother and sister exit the courtyard and head across the terrace, their voices mingling in chatter and laughter. She whispered to the sky above, "How can a heart be filled with such joy and sorrow at the same time, Yahweh?"

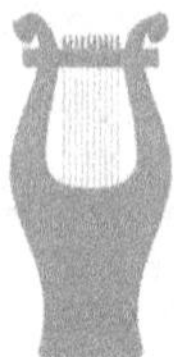

Chapter 37

When Naamah arrived back in her room, Shiphrah was on her bed, nursing a squirming Gia, now a rotund toddler. "How was your visit with your mother and sister?"

"It is always wonderful to see them." Sinking down on the edge of her own bed, Naamah added. "But it was also somehow sad."

"What do you mean?"

"I guess I realize that our lives have moved in very different directions. They do not understand my life here, and I have lost touch with what is going on with my family. And the bond between my mother and Zahara is—well, it makes me jealous."

Shiphrah maneuvered Gia so she could lean over and hug Naamah. "At least we have each other. And there are others in this place who love us, and we love them."

"You are right, Shiphrah." Naamah began to climb out of her despair. Just then, Amaris bounded into the room with Akilah in hot pursuit. The little girl ran straight for Naamah and gave her a big hug before hugging her mother, almost squashing baby Gia in the process. Naamah couldn't help laughing. "And we also have your children. Yahweh has indeed blessed us."

"Come on, Mama! Come on Naamah!" Amaris tugged at both women. "It's a beautiful day. Let's go outside and play."

Chuckling, Shiphrah released her hold on Gia, who instantly scampered for the door, and lumbered to her feet. "Sure, why not? Coming, Naamah?"

Naamah banished any lingering sadness by playing for Shiphrah and other women gathered in the courtyard the new composition that had been interrupted by her visitors. The rest of the day and evening passed in warm fellowship with her companions. But perhaps Zahara's mention of her secret had triggered something because that night she once again found herself in the bushes along the road fighting for her life, her body in pain from thorn scratches and vulgar hands touching her body. "Help me! Yahweh, help me!"

"Wake up, Naamah! Wake up!"

The nightmare instantly evaporated. Naamah opened her eyes to the dim light of an oil lamp. Blinking, Naamah realized Akilah was holding the lamp, and that the towering servant woman and Shiphrah were both looming over Naamah's bed, similar worried expressions illuminated by the lamp's soft yellow glow.

"Are you awake now?" Shiphrah demanded. "The entire harem heard you screaming. I thought you'd been hurt, but when Akilah came and lit a lamp, we saw you were screaming in your sleep. Whatever frightened you so?"

"It's a recurring nightmare." Naamah sat up and shook her head hard, trying to get her wits about her. "I am so sorry. Did I wake up the girls?"

"No, they are fine," answered Shiphrah. "They can sleep through a sirocco wind along with all of the infants in the harem wailing around us."

Shiphrah's response brought smiles to all of their faces. Naamah could feel the nightmare fading back to the shadows where it belonged. "I am feeling better. Thank you for waking me from my nightmare, but please return to your own slumber. I will be fine now."

"That is what friends are for." Shiphrah gently hugged Naamah before crawling back in her own bed.

"You are welcome, mistress." Akilah squeezed Naamah's hand, then left, restoring the room to night. As soft breathing told Naamah that Shiphrah was once again asleep, she prayed silently, *Yahweh, thank You for the friends You have provided for me here in the harem. They are a reminder, Abba God, that even in the dark times You provide us with beacons of hope. Please help me to look for and grasp those beacons instead of dwelling on the darkness.*

& & &

Naamah followed Elihu from the hall antechamber into the throne room. She stopped with surprise to see how full it was. Most of the men were in full armor. But far more than battle-tempered warriors were the chests and crates piled high in the center of the large hall, all overflowing with plunder. Gold and silver chalices, platters, neck collars, bracelets, and coinages. Jewels of sparkling red, blue, green, and amber. Fine fabrics shot through with copper and gold embroidery.

King David strode through the tall entrance doors from the palace terrace just as Naamah entered. He looked more bronzed and fit than Naamah had ever seen him. On his head, he wore a massive gold crown inset with numerous jewels. It looked too heavy for any man to wear, even one as tall and powerful as King David. At his side as he strode toward the throne was Reuel. He too looked powerfully muscled and filled out, a full-grown man rather than the teenaged youth Naamah had first met more than two years earlier.

It had been months since Naamah had seen either the king or Reuel. Joab and his forces had finally conquered the royal citadel of Rabbah. Naamah had been playing in the throne room when Reuel brought a message from Joab for the king, announcing that he'd captured the Ammonite water supply, and the city would soon fall. If King David wanted to receive credit for Rabbah's conquest, he needed to be there in person or the victory would be attributed to Joab himself.

This admonition had finally drawn King David from Bathsheba's side long enough to muster Israel's full fighting force from all twelve tribes and march on Rabbah. Reuel had gone with him as the king's personal scribe and messenger. The army had been mobilized for almost three months, first overseeing the final destruction and plundering of the Ammonite capital, then taking captive the remaining Ammonite towns. David was returning to his own capital city in great triumph, his reputation never higher among the tribes of Israel and surrounding nations.

Striding up to the throne, King David lifted the heavy crown from his head and handed it to Reuel. "A pretty thing I cut from King Hanun's head myself. But it gives me a headache. Add it to the collection in the treasury. Right next to the Amorite crown. Those are two conniving traitors who will never threaten Israel again."

Glancing around, King David spotted Naamah and called out exuberantly, "Songstress, play us some joyful music today.

This is a time for celebration."

He turned back to his gathered men. "And not just because our enemy has been wiped from the earth. I have just come from my wife Bathsheba. During the night, she granted me the gift of another son! The prophet Nathan has sent word that the child has received Yahweh's blessing and shall be called Jedidiah, beloved of the Lord, to signify Yahweh's special favor."

David turned back to Naamah. "Come child, play something lively. How about the song you composed before I left for the battlefront."

Dutifully, Naamah began singing, "It is good to praise the Lord and make music to Your name, O Most High. To proclaim Your love in the morning and Your faithfulness at night to the music of the ten-stringed lyre and melody of the harp. For You make me glad by Your deeds, O Lord. I sing for joy at the works of Your hands. How great are Your works, O Lord."

As she sang, she wondered about the prophet's declaration of special favor on the king's new son. It had already become clear Bathsheba was now David's favored wife over all those who had borne him children over the years. And now Bathsheba had a son favored by Yahweh Himself? What would this mean to King David's existing sons?

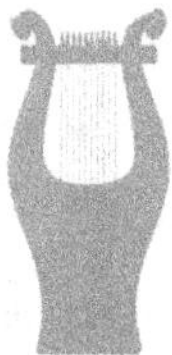

Chapter 38

Hushai looked around the table at his wife and son, who sat with him this evening. It was good to be all together again. "I have missed you these last months, son, though I am proud of the man you've become during your time serving Joab and at the king's side. Someday you will take my place, if not as David's advisor, then his son's. In the meantime, there is something your mother and I wish to discuss with you now that you have returned."

Reuel noticed that Nasya immediately sat forward as though anxious to see his reaction. Hushai began, "Reuel, you are now a full twenty years, past age to marry. I believe I have found the perfect wife for you. I have waited only for your return to approach her family and arrange a betrothal."

Reuel sat in silence. He shouldn't feel so surprised. After all, most of his peers were married and even fathers. With his constant travels, he'd given the matter little consideration. He knew his parents had been patient to wait this long. He could only hope this strange woman would have some semblance of the gifts, intelligence, and beauty of his adoptive sister Naamah.

"Go on, husband!" Nasya interjected eagerly. "Tell him

about Channah."

"Well, she is from a good family, but even more importantly, a devout one committed to following Yahweh and his laws fully. In fact, she is a niece to Asaph, the king's chief musician, by her mother. Her father is of the tribe of Ephraim, and the family lives in the north of their territory in the town of Shiloh."

Shiloh was the town where the tabernacle had been pitched during the time of Israel's judges before Samuel had appointed the last king. Asaph's clan had been among the Levites appointed to serve there until they'd accompanied the tabernacle and Ark of the Covenant to Jerusalem.

Hushai continued, "The girl has rarely visited Jerusalem but is willing to move here. Asaph tells me she is kind, hardworking, and gracious. In fact, her name even means gracious."

"As though your son doesn't know that!" Nasya teased. "He is an expert in words, after all! What matters more is that she is said to be pretty of face and healthy, both an asset to producing many children, believe me!"

Reuel flushed at the innuendo. Hushai cut in hastily, "Asaph tells me that even though she is but sixteen, she is already famed in Shiloh for the beauty of her weaving and fine designs. It was for this reason he thought of you, and I agree. Knowing your own creative gifts, I have always believed a wife with gifts of her own would provide common ground for your marriage. Especially if she is also devout of faith and kind in character."

Hushai let out the slightest sigh, and Reuel wondered if his father's thoughts had gone to Naamah. Nasya had never been one to hold in her thoughts, and in one of their reading sessions when Naamah wasn't present, she'd let slip that Hushai had once considered Naamah as Reuel's bride before the king had taken her for himself. The very thought of what might have been was one reason Reuel had focused so hard on seeing Naamah as a beloved younger sister. And perhaps too why he'd ended their study sessions and spent more time than absolutely necessary away from Jerusalem.

"I am sure your choice will be satisfactory, Abba! I trust your judgment," Reuel said aloud. Silently, he prayed, *Yahweh, help me be a loving, good husband to this woman whatever and whoever she turns out to be.*

& & &

"Zahara, it is so good to see you again! And Eilis! He has grown so big. I love that you and Amos have chosen a name meaning 'Yahweh is my God.'"

Naamah cuddled her nephew, enjoying the softness of his hair against her cheek, though the toddler squirmed to get away. Naamah hadn't seen Zahara's firstborn enough for Eilis to remember her from one visit to the next. "And where is Mama? Is she not well? And the rest of the family. Surely you and Amos didn't come to the Sukkot festival alone this year."

"No, the others are still setting up our shelters across the valley. They will all make sure to visit you during this week. But I couldn't wait to show you how much Eilis has grown. And to give you my news."

"Yes, I noticed you are pregnant again." Zahara must be close to six months along by her bulging belly. "I suppose that means I will not see you until after the child comes. Are you hoping for a daughter this time?"

"Just a healthy child. I waited again until I was sure the child was active." Zahara's pretty features showed pain. "I have had several more miscarriages since Eilis. I no longer share with anyone but Amos when I find myself pregnant. But as with Eilis, I am now beyond the previous miscarriages, and I can feel the baby's vigor, so I am hopeful."

"And as with Eilis, I will pray every day for a healthy child, girl or boy." Naamah stifled a pang of longing. Happy though she was for her sister and that her own secret remained undiscovered, she found herself wondering more with each passing year what it would be like to cuddle a child of her own womb.

Aloud, she went on gayly, "If the Sukkot festival is here once again, then it will soon be four full years since I arrived in the palace. I cannot believe my nineteenth birthday has already passed. And you are now twenty-one and soon to be a mother of two!"

Zahara knew her sister too well not to see beneath Naamah's cheerful words. "I wish you could know the joy of motherhood. Though I remain grateful that the king's distance means your secret remains safe. And I rejoice that every time we come to the festivals, we hear more of your compositions being sung. They have become as popular as King David's and those of Chief Musician Asaph."

Naamah appreciated Zahara's attempts to change the subject. She smiled wryly. "In truth, I am in good company. Do you know there has not been a single pregnancy in the harem other than Bathsheba since she arrived? There is her firstborn, Jedidiah, though his mother insisted on calling him Solomon, so that is how he is known. Then a second son, Nathan, named after the prophet. Just four months ago, she birthed a daughter, and I have heard she is pregnant again. It is not that the rest of us are infertile, but that the king has called none but Bathsheba to his bed since she arrived."

Naamah shook her head in commiseration. "At least I have my music. I feel sorry for others in the harem with no new babies and no other pastimes. Nor does Bathsheba allow the rest of us to help mother her children as the other wives and concubines are happy to do."

Chapter 39

Reuel headed down the hall to the palace scriptorium, his first day back in two months after a long and circuitous tour of more than twenty fortified cities from Sidon in the north to Ezion-Gever on the shore of the Red Sea. Joab had decided he needed a precise record of layout, population, defenses, and top officials, and for once Reuel worried his prodigious memory would fail by the time he got it all down on parchment.

Rounding a corner, Reuel heard jovial banter and immediately recognized the voices. King David's firstborn son Amnon and one of his cousins, Jonadab, son of King David's older brother Shimeah. Having grown up in the palace as the son of King David's chief advisor, Reuel knew well many of the king's sons. But Amnon had been born while the king was still in exile, son of Ahinoam of Jezreel, the king's first wife except for Saul's daughter Michal, who had been married off to another man when King David became a fugitive. Amnon was more than a decade older than Reuel and like all the king's older sons had been given his own household and landholdings once he reached adulthood.

Jonadab was in turn several years older than Amnon and

served as his cousin's advisor in much the same way Reuel's father served King David. All the king's adult sons had been given administrative tasks in the kingdom. Absalom, a handsome, charismatic man with a facile tongue, often served as the king's envoy to tribal leaders and even foreign courts. Amnon was theoretically in charge of overseeing the royal storehouses and herds. But even as a young child, Reuel had been aware of Amnon's reputation for drunkenness and carousing with women, the reason King David had appointed his clever nephew as Amnon's advisor.

Reuel had once overheard a conversation between his own father and the king, who hadn't realized the young boy was playing under the council chamber table. King David was bemoaning his firstborn's weak character. "Jonadab handles every responsibility I've given Amnon. But he also procures anything Amnon wants. I fear for Israel once Amnon is seated on my throne."

Hushai had hesitated before asking, "Must Amnon be your choice? After all, you were the youngest of your brothers when God anointed you king."

"He is my eldest," David had replied vaguely. "He expects it. It is the way of other kingdoms."

"Israel is not like other kingdoms," Hushai had replied before turning the conversation back to topics less interesting to a listening six-year-old. By the time Reuel himself was working in the palace, he'd come to realize that Jonadab did indeed do all the work for which Amnon claimed credit but also went out of his way to make sure Amnon got anything he wanted. Not as a wise advisor, the way Hushai served the king, but because Jonadab had clearly set himself to become indispensable to the future king of Israel, regardless of what that took.

"What is it, cousin?" Reuel now heard Jonadab say down the corridor. "You've been moping like a sick dog for days now. I came in here this morning looking for you. As I walk in, you look all dejected again like a sad puppy. Every morning, the same! Well, what is it, Amnon?"

Amnon let out a loud sigh. "It's my half-sister Tamar, my brother Absalom's sister. She is now full grown and exquisite. I am mad with love for her!"

"Ohhh, so that is it?" Jonadab laughed. "I wondered why you have been visiting the palace so often. I believed perhaps you desired to begin taking more seriously your duties so as to be prepared when your father goes the way of all flesh and you ascend the throne."

"Why should I take my duties seriously when I have you to look after me?" Amnon scoffed. "No, it is Tamar. I am sick with love for her! If I cannot have her, I will wither away! And now I have learned that her marriage to the prince of Moab is just a month from now. Once she is gone, I will have no further opportunity to slack my thirst for her."

"I have a brilliant idea, cousin! This is it!" Jonadab spoke up enthusiastically. "Go to bed and pretend to be ill. I will make sure the king learns of your condition. When your father comes to see you, tell him you have no appetite, but perhaps if Tamar visited you and prepared a meal in your presence, the sight of your dear sister might restore your appetite. Just make sure you are convincingly ill. Once alone with her, you may do what you will."

Reuel was stunned at what he'd just heard. He remembered Tamar well, though he hadn't seen her for several years. Seven years younger than himself, she'd been a beautiful little girl who loved to chase after her older brothers and the son of her father's advisor when the wives and children of the royal court enjoyed excursions to the countryside or to float in the Dead Sea. Even for a man as lacking in character as Amnon, that the king's firstborn could lust after his own sister when he had an entire harem of concubines at his disposal was vile. Reuel could only hope the two were joking.

Should I warn Absalom of what I just heard? Reuel wondered. Or would the king's third-born consider it impertinence for someone like Reuel to be repeating overheard gossip about one of the king's sons? He would think about it after he wrote down all he'd uncovered of Israel's adversaries over these last two months. And once he'd stopped by his own home to greet his wife after his long absence.

No, he was probably making much out of nothing. After all, a king's daughter had her own protections. And from Amnon's words, the girl would be out of his reach within another month. It was hubris for Reuel to think his own intervention was necessary. Or that any of the king's sons would hurt a sister, however much they might jest like soldiers in a battle encampment when none but their comrades-in-arms were around to hear profane boastings.

& & &

"Do you hear something?" asked Shiphrah. Naamah stopped her playing and Shiphrah her weaving to listen to the sounds of the harem.

"I think I hear someone sobbing," replied Naamah.

"Or wailing," continued Shiphrah. "Has someone died?"

Other women around the courtyard were turning their heads in search of the heartrending cries. These grew louder and a moment later burst into the courtyard along with their maker, Maacha, Tamar's mother. She no longer had the look of a royal princess or wife, something she fiercely preserved. Her grand robes and hair were completely disheveled, her face bleeding from fingernail scratches such as self-inflicted by those in mourning.

Maacha rushed straight over to the bench where Naamah and Shiphrah were sitting. "Naamah, I need you to come and comfort Tamar. I must go immediately to speak with King David, and I do not want to leave her alone. She speaks often of you as her friend since you began teaching her to play the lyre. Perhaps you can remove the pain in her as I cannot."

"Of course!" Naamah rose to her feet, but her confusion was on her face. "But what has happened? Has Tamar been injured? Is she ill? Should we call the physician?"

"It is none of that, and there is nothing a physician can do!" Tears spilled down Maacha's cheeks, and she once again scratched at her face with long nails before screaming out in anguish, "My Tamar was raped!"

The shock took Naamah's breath away. No one knew better than she the pain of what Tamar had just experienced, and tears overflowed her own eyes as she stood there frozen, lyre clutched to her breast.

"Naamah! Are you all right?" Shiphrah touched Naamah's arm. "Maacha is waiting to take you to Tamar."

Her roommate's gentle touch unfroze Naamah's limbs. Breathing in deeply to dispel the stench of evil that seemed to hover over her, she followed Maacha to the wives' quarters. Like all their bedchambers, Maacha's room was large and elaborately furnished. But Naamah's eyes focused only on Tamar.

The younger girl was lying curled up in a fetal position on her mother's bed, her ornate robe ripped and ashes strewn throughout her tangled tresses. Tears streamed from Tamar's eyes, but unlike Maacha's loud wailing, Tamar was emitting only quiet whimpers like a dying puppy. At the sound, Naamah felt her heart might break.

Chapter 40

Placing her lyre on the bed, Naamah sat down beside Tamar. Tamar immediately grabbed Naamah's hand. "Oh, Naamah. It was so terrible! I just want to die!"

Through her own tears, Naamah saw Abigail standing in the doorway, "Come, Maacha, I will accompany you to speak with King David. He must know what his son has done."

His son! Naamah was confused and even more shocked at the words. One of the king's own sons had done this? As Abigail escorted Maacha from the room, Tamar sat up on the bed, clutching knees to her chest. Wrapping a blanket around her, Naamah embraced her young friend close as Zahara had once done for her. After a few moments of silence, Tamar began to speak of the horror she'd endured.

"My father asked me to visit my brother Amnon because he was said to be very ill and refusing to eat. He thought he could eat if his little sister prepared the meal for him. Amnon was one of my favorite brothers when I was small. He was always so affectionate and purchased me fine gifts. But since I became nubile last year, I … I just didn't like the way Amnon's eyes followed me around a room. Not like the brother I loved but

… but like my father with Bathsheba!"

Tamar shuddered with distaste before continuing. "All this last year, I have tried to stay away from Amnon. I have looked forward to my marriage next month, when I will finally be safe from his lustful stares. But how could I say no to my father, the king? So I went to Amnon's house. I prepared bread for him as he asked in his presence. But instead of watching my kneading, he watched my body! And when I brought the bread to where he lay on his sickbed, he wouldn't even taste it. Instead, he ordered his physician and attendant from his bedchamber."

Naamah held her young friend even tighter as the story now came through sobs. "Then Amnon grabbed me and demanded I come to bed with him. I don't think he was ill at all because he was so strong! I begged him to stop. I told him if he desired me so greatly, he could ask our father to give me to him in marriage instead of to the prince of Moab as our forefather Abraham married his own half-sister Sarah. But he didn't listen! He overpowered me and … and raped me."

Tamar gasped for breath, her entire body trembling uncontrollably. She broke into a wail. "The worst is that after Amnon raped me, he threw me off the bed and ordered me to leave! I begged him again not to be so cruel. Now that he had taken my maidenhood and perhaps made me pregnant, surely he would ask the king to give me to him in marriage. But he called his attendant and had him drag me from the room and throw me outside in the street. Now I am an outcast. The son of the king of Moab will never marry me now."

Tamar's wail dropped to a whisper. "My own brother has destroyed my life. I am no longer a virgin daughter of the king to remain in the palace. I will go now to my brother Absalom's household to live as a desolate woman."

Naamah stroked Tamar's hair gently, trying to think how she might comfort her young friend. Perhaps a song as had so often soothed the horror of her own memories. She began to sing softly, "Hear my prayer, O Lord. Let my cry for help come to You. Do not hide Your face from me when I am in distress. My days are like the evening shadow. I wither away like grass. The Lord will respond to the prayer of the destitute. He will not despise their plea."

As the words flowed from Naamah, Tamar began to relax into Naamah's arms. After a time, Naamah could hear the even breathing of someone who was at rest. Gently guiding Tamar's body to lie on the bed, she covered the younger girl with the blanket.

Rest is what she needs right now, Yahweh, Naamah prayed silently, picking up her lyre and tiptoeing from the room. *And she will need You for comfort, Abba, God. Help her to heal, Yahweh. Help her to heal.*

& & &

Reuel was in the council chamber at his father's side, taking notes on the discussions between King David, Hushai, and others of the king's council, when the king's highest-ranking wife Maacha, daughter of King Talmai of Geshur, stormed in. Documenting the king's words for the Annals of the Kings had become Reuel's regular role since the months on the battlefront as the king's personal scribe. Reuel had never seen the mother of Absalom and Tamar less than exquisitely and expensively styled as befit a king's daughter, much less unkempt and blood-streaked like a battlefield survivor. Just behind her was the king's second wife, Abigail, who no longer held much influence outside the harem now that her only son, David's second-born, was dead.

As a shocked silence fell over the council chamber, King David jumped to his feet. "What is it? Has Absalom suffered harm? If someone has hurt him, I swear they will taste my vengeance!"

That only injury to her son and the king's second-born could justify such an intrusion was a rational conclusion. All there knew how much David loved and depended on Absalom, far more than his wayward firstborn. But Maacha grabbed at her hair, pulling out a fistful by the roots, as she shouted out scornfully, "Not Absalom. Is he my only child? No, it is our daughter Tamar. And the person who has hurt her is your son Amnon at your own connivance. She tells me *you* were the one who ordered her to visit him in his home, where instead of being ill as he claimed, he raped her, then threw her like garbage into the street!"

His face whitening, King David dropped back into his chair. He opened his mouth and closed it without a sound coming out. Hushai rose to his feet. "This council meeting is over. We will convene again tomorrow."

He turned to Abigail. "Take the princess back to her quarters. I will speak to the king on her behalf."

Abigail led the distraught mother from the room. The rest of the council were already obeying the advisor's instruction. Reuel began rolling up his scroll to follow suit. He felt sickened at what he'd just heard. If only he'd gone to Absalom when he'd first overheard Amnon and Jonadab. But it had been late by the time he'd completed his transcripts for Joab. And when he'd arrived home to his wife's loving arms, Channah had shared the wonderful news that she was expecting their first child. How could he rush from her side then?

That was a week ago. Reuel hadn't seen Amnon at court since while Jonadab had been his usual industrious self, so he'd dismissed his inadvertent eavesdropping as idle talk. No one to Reuel's knowledge had mentioned Amnon being ill. But then, Reuel had been so busy catching up at both the palace and at home after his long absence he'd paid little attention to the doings of the king's sons.

King David looked with anguish at his closest friend. "She is right. I sent Tamar to visit Amnon at his request. He did indeed claim to be ill. He has always been fond of his sister. I thought it would help him."

Hushai's expression was uncharacteristically stern. "You know Yahweh's law, David. If Amnon did indeed rape his sister, then he must receive the penalty of the law."

King David's head fell into his hands. He muttered, "Yahweh's law calls for death. How can I punish my firstborn so harshly when I have been no better? If Yahweh forgave me for Bathsheba, will He not equally forgive Amnon?"

"You repented before Yahweh and all Israel," Hushai said bluntly. "Has Amnon done the same?"

Reuel slipped out of the council chamber. *Yahweh, forgive me for my own failing in not doing what I should have to prevent this!*

But even as he sought surcease for his own feelings of guilt, Reuel's perfect recall flashed back to the words of the prophet Nathan after the king's own great sin. "Because of what you have done, the sword will never depart from your house, and I will bring calamity out of your own household."

Was the prophet's forewarning now coming to pass?

Chapter 41

Walking in from the palace terrace to the throne room on the heels of the king's nephew Jonadab, Reuel could hear his father's voice raised jovially. "So you decided not to attend Absalom's big celebration. He seemed quite set on you being there."

"I considered it," King David replied. "But if I attended, Joab would insist I take a full company of soldiers. He keeps reminding me I am not as young as when I slayed Goliath. Absalom has done well building his own wealth with his flocks. But he has already invited all of my sons, which between my wives and concubines number more than thirty not counting those too young to travel. I told him I didn't want to place such a burden on him, but I gave my blessing for all of my grown sons to attend. Including Amnon. I was pleased Absalom urged him to come. I am hopeful this means a repair in their relationship."

Reuel knew what his father and the king were referencing. In the two years since Amnon had raped Absalom's sister, life at court had continued as though it never happened. Amnon rarely appeared at the palace, but the king had levied no punishment against him. More surprisingly, Reuel had heard of no reaction from Absalom. But then perhaps the past closeness between the king's two eldest sons had transcended the justifiable anger Reuel would feel if Tamar were his own sister.

Absalom had boasted of a bumper crop of wool from his growing flocks and had been openly speaking of the great feast he planned at his country estate in Baal-Hazor near the border of Ephraim a half-day horse ride from Jerusalem once the shearing was finished. In truth, Reuel had expected Jonadab to accompany Amnon, but the commander of Israel's armies had demanded that Jonadab complete a long over-due tally of weapons and armaments the king had assigned to Amnon. Reuel had spent the last week at Jonadab's heels since Joab also considered the army's resources to be restricted information he trusted none but Reuel to document.

Reuel and Jonadab were just a few paces into the throne room when a palace guard burst into the room. "I must speak to the king at once. Urgent news has just arrived."

Behind the guard entered a sweaty, dust-covered man in armor. Reuel recognized one of the company of guards which had provided a protective detail to the party of king's sons who had ridden out to Absalom's celebration.

The travel-worn soldier barely took time to bow down before blurting out, "Absalom has killed all the king's sons! Not one is left alive!"

Horror and pain erased the smile from King David's face. He immediately leapt down from his throne, and threw himself on the ground with a cry of anguish. Others around the throne room ripped at their own robes in a gesture of solidarity.

But Jonadab hurried forward, calling out loudly enough

to be heard above the commotion. "Do not believe it, my king! Absalom would never hurt his brothers. Only Amnon. Absalom has hated Amnon since he raped his sister Tamar. I have feared he might plot to hurt my cousin. But I am sure we will discover your other sons are not all dead, only Amnon."

Through the open throne room doors, another guard shouted out from the terrace. "I see a party of men on mules riding hard from the direction of Baal-Hazor."

"See?" Jonadab said. "It is undoubtedly the king's son's arriving just as his servant said."

Reuel grimaced inwardly at Jonadab's obsequious tone. If Amnon was indeed dead, it seemed clear Jonadab was ready to curry favor with another benefactor, even if that meant ingratiating himself to a grieving father.

But he was also correct, as the king's shrewd nephew usually was. By the time Jonadab had solicitously helped his uncle to his feet, the first of King David's sons were bursting into the throne room, led by Adonijah, next-born after Absalom. Wailing loudly and tearing at their robes in customary mourning fashion, they chorused, "Absalom's men have attacked and killed Amnon."

Adonijah raised his voice above his brothers' wails. "We barely escaped with our lives. But I saw signs that Absalom and his men already had their mounts saddled to flee. My guess is that Absalom will seek sanctuary in Geshur at the court of his grandfather King Talmai."

Reuel saw Jonadab's nostrils flare with disdain at Adonijah's words. With Amnon dead and Absalom a fugitive, Adonijah was unmistakably angling to be next in line for his father's throne. Reuel also caught the moment a new thought occurred to Jonadab.

Striding over to Adonijah, Jonadab said pleasantly, "I am sure you are right, cousin. And let me just say how glad I am to see that you managed to lead your brothers unscathed in your escape. If I can serve you in any way or offer sound counsel as I did your brother, you have only to ask."

The two scheming cousins deserved each other, Reuel told himself as he left the throne room without trying to deliver the report he and Jonadab had spent so much time compiling. No one would be interested in it today. Instead, he'd spend some time with his young daughter and wife, due any day with their second child.

One thing today's events had made clear. Not only had calamity continued to come upon King David's household as the prophet Nathan had declared, but now the sword had descended as well.

& & &

Reuel was seated at a small table to one side of the throne, an open scroll and ink pot in front of him, as King David conducted his monthly public audience. In the three years since the death of King David's firstborn and exile of his second-born, Reuel had begun routinely accompanying his father to such events when he wasn't on the road at Joab's orders or carrying out some commission from King David himself. All of which had made it clear to the entire court that Reuel was being groomed as a future royal advisor like his father.

The monthly audiences were the only time when even the most lowly of Israelites could approach the king with a claim for justice or a plea for assistance. This time Joab himself was in the throne room, standing on the opposite side of the throne from Hushai, who stood between Reuel and the king. Both men occasionally leaned in to offer King David advice or information on the case at hand. It was already mid-afternoon, but the line of those waiting to address the king still snaked out the throne room entrance and clear across the terrace. Reuel stretched one leg and then the other. It was going to be a long, tiring evening.

He swallowed a yawn as a merchant from Jericho stomped out angry that the king had rejected his request for an adjustment of his levied taxes. The next person stepping forward was a gray-haired woman with the rent robes and ash-strewn disheveled hair of someone in mourning. Falling on her face before the throne, she cried out, "Help me, Your Majesty!"

King David's expression showed compassion as he leaned forward on the throne. "What is troubling you, good woman?"

The woman raised her head to look directly at the king. "I am a widow from Tekoa, Your Majesty, and I had just two sons to support me. They got into a fight while working in our fields, and one struck the other so hard he died. Now my clan wishes to put my remaining son to death for killing his brother. But it isn't for reasons of justice. They wish to rid themselves of my husband's only living heir so they can seize his land for themselves, thereby leaving me destitute and my husband without any remaining descendants on this earth."

"That will not happen," King David said calmly. "Return home, and I will issue an order on your behalf."

He nodded toward Reuel, who noted the decision on the scroll. It would be his responsibility to follow up and ensure the order was written up and sent to the council of elders in Tekoa, a small town not far from King David's birthplace of Bethlehem. But instead of rising to her feet to leave, the woman cried out even louder, "Let the king invoke the Lord his God to prevent the avenger of blood from destroying my only remaining son!"

"As surely as Yahweh lives," King David assured her patiently, "not one hair from your son's head will fall to the ground. If anyone says otherwise to you, bring them to me, and they will not bother you again!"

This time the woman rose to her feet, but instead of exiting, she straightened herself, no longer looking distraught but oddly authoritative. She spoke boldly. "Then, Your Majesty, let your servant speak a word to my lord the king. When the king says this, does he not convict himself, for have you still not brought back your own banished son? God devises ways so that a banished person does not remain banished from Him. So today I thought, 'I will speak to the king, and perhaps he will agree to deliver his servant from the hand of those who seek to cut off both me and my remaining son from God's inheritance.' For my lord the king is like an angel of God in discerning good and evil. May Yahweh your God be with you."

King David looked thoughtfully from the woman to the commander of his armies, standing at his left hand. Reuel settled his quill back in the ink pot, unsure whether he should be recording the woman's plea after all. Then King David spoke. "Just give me one answer, good woman. Did Joab put you up to this?"

The woman gave a reflexive glance toward Joab before speaking. "As surely as you live, my lord the king, you have wisdom like an angel of God, knowing everything that happens in Israel to the right or the left. It was indeed your servant Joab who instructed me to do this."

King David gave Joab a hard look, but nodded curtly. "Very well, go and bring back the young man Absalom. But not to the palace. I will not look upon his face after what he has done. He may return to his own dwelling."

Reuel was astonished to see the tough, unyielding commander of Israel's armies fall prostrate before the throne. Joab's voice was choked with emotion as he cried out, "Bless you, my king, because you have granted your servant's request. Today your servant knows that he has found favor in your eyes."

Chapter 42

"**D**id you hear that Absalom is back in Jerusalem?" Chinua chattered as he thrust a bronze comb into Naamah's hairdo. "They say the commander of Israel's armies, Joab, traveled all the way to Geshur to escort him in person from King Talmai's court."

"That isn't all I've heard," added Eglah, who sat on a nearby bench in the courtyard, waiting for her turn at Chinua's administrations. Though far from the only harem attendant available for such services, the small, plump eunuch had developed a reputation for being able to make the plainest, aging woman look attractive. "You know the woman who appeared before the throne on Joab's behalf to prompt the king to return Absalom from exile? Well, I have learned she is the wise woman from Tekoa! That must be how Joab knew to seek her out. Tekoa is within eyesight of Bethlehem, where Joab and King David grew up."

While few women had positions of authority in Israel, some did become renowned and even tribal leaders for their gifts of foresight and wisdom. Some were devout followers of Yahweh like Deborah, the prophetess and judge. Others were rumored to practice divination and even witchcraft. Naamah wondered which was true of this woman who'd been willing to practice deceit before the king on Joab's behalf.

Chinua sighed longingly. "I have seen him since his return riding through the city in his chariot. He is so handsome from the top of his head to the soles of his feet. His hair alone—it is so thick and curly no woman's can compare. If only I could get my combs into those locks!"

"Well, I for one am so tired of hearing about Absalom's hair and how handsome he is that I could scream," exclaimed Eglah. "Maacha is constantly bragging to the other wives about how brilliant and handsome her son is and that the king's summons back to Jerusalem means Absalom will now be his heir. Poor Ahinoam. She dares say nothing after what Amnon did, but I see her pain every time Maacha brings up her own son's killer. And she had no other child. Every day, she grows more ill and frail from her grief."

It was but a month later after a visit with her mother, sister, and Zahara's now three healthy children that Naamah heard of Ahinoam's death. The last time Naamah had seen the older wife, she'd been gaunt and wasted as though she'd stopped eating or caring for herself at all.

Yahweh, I pray that she will have found peace with you, Naamah prayed as she entered her room.

Shiphrah, who was sorting through her chest of robes, immediately detected Naamah's melancholy. "Did your visit not go well? Is your mother ill?"

"No, she isn't ill, but it is getting difficult for her to walk long distances. It may not be many more years before she can no longer travel to the festivals or to visit me. Especially since she still will not allow me to request a cart to convey her."

Tears misted Naamah's eyes. "I am happy that Yahweh has blessed Zahara and Amos as well as Gavriil and Rivka with many children. My mother is thrilled to be the grandmother of such a clan. But it also reminds me I will likely never provide my mother with a grandchild."

"Yes, we live a very different life from our families," Shiphrah agreed. "But even if you were to have a child here, your mother would rarely see the young one. My family lives so far from here only the adult males travel to the festivals as is required by Yahweh's law."

"My life here reminds me at times of a song of King David's I learned as a child. They say he wrote it while hiding from King Saul." Wiping at her tears, Naamah picked up her lyre and began the familiar song. "I cry aloud to the Lord. I lift up my voice to the Lord for mercy. I cry to You, O Lord. I say, 'You are my refuge, my portion in the land of the living.' Listen to my cry, for I am in desperate need. Set me free from my prison, that I may praise Your name."

"That is truly beautiful!" Shiphrah complimented when Naamah had finished. "But we are not in prison."

"No, you are right, dear friend," Naamah replied. "Yahweh has been good to us here."

That evening, Naamah was called to sing for King David in the king's personal living quarters. After a second daughter, Bathsheba had just borne a third son, Shobab, and so for once was not spending the evening with the king. Leaning back in a padded couch, King David closed his eyes as Naamah adjusted her lyre. His thinning hair and beard now liberally streaked with gray, his features lined and weary, he looked far older than the stalwart, muscular warrior he'd been when Naamah arrived at the palace ten years earlier.

Naamah chose her newest composition, one she'd sung several times already in the throne room. "Shout for joy to the Lord, all the earth. Worship the Lord with gladness. Come before Him with joyful songs. Know that the Lord is God. It is He who made us, and we are His. We are His people, the sheep of His pasture. Enter His gates with thanksgiving and His courts with praise. Give thanks to Him and praise His name. For the Lord is good and His love endures forever. His faithfulness continues through all generations."

As Naamah finished, King David opened his eyes. "That song is a gift to all who hear it. I have come to have a deep appreciation for you, Naamah. Your music is a great blessing to me and all of Israel."

"Thank you, Your Majesty." Naamah smiled as she chose her next song. Perhaps she was not a true wife or even a concubine and would never be a mother. But she did have a place in King David's life and in his kingdom. *Yes, Yahweh is good, and His love truly endures forever.*

& & &

Reuel looked up as Joab entered the council chamber. The commander of Israel's armies was uncharacteristically late for a scheduled meeting with the king. Joab dropped into a seat. As King David's nephew and close companion since the king's earliest years in exile, Joab didn't bother with formalities except in public. "Forgive the delay, but I've ridden hard this morning from Baal-Hazor."

"What were you doing there?" Hushai asked. "You know

the envoys from Damascus are due here this afternoon."

"I rode there because I discovered my barley fields had been set ablaze just as they were ready for harvest!" Joab said testily. "And I found out who did it. The fields lie beside those of Absalom's, and it was his servants at his orders who set them afire."

"Why would he do that?" King David demanded. "Were you not the one who brought him back to Israel? And whatever his past sins, he has stayed out of trouble these last two years since his return."

Joab sighed. "I went to his home to ask him that question myself. He told me it was because I'd stopped responding to his requests to ask you to see him. He said he might as well have stayed in Geshur if he was to continue in exile right here in Jerusalem."

Joab looked directly at his uncle. "He also gave me an ultimatum. He says he'd rather be dead than remain separated from his own father. He insists on meeting with you face-to-face, and if you judge him guilty of a crime, then so be it. You can put him to death. But he doesn't want to keep living if you will not reconcile with him."

Reuel caught the wearied expression on King David's face. Once again, his nephew had put him in a hard spot. Then the king sighed tiredly. "It has been five years since I've seen Absalom's face. I have missed him too. Fine. Make a time for him to appear before me."

Joab jumped to his feet. "He is right outside. I will bring him in now."

"Of course he is," Reuel heard Hushai mutter.

Then Joab ushered Absalom into the council chamber. Approaching his father, Absalom prostrated himself face to the ground in a stance of utter submission. With a cry of pain, King David rose to his own feet. Leaning down, he pulled Absalom upright and into a tight embrace, kissing him on both cheeks.

"My son, my son, it is with joy that I see your face again. Let us forget the past and start anew together."

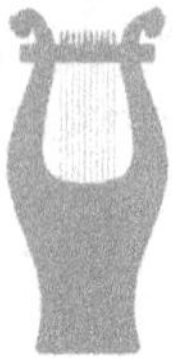

Chapter 43

"**S**on, you have returned! How did the children enjoy the trip? And how is your lovely wife?"

Reuel and Channah had been gone for over a month visiting Channah's family in Shiloh a full two days north of Jerusalem by ox cart. While some of Channah's family members had traveled to Jerusalem since their wedding for the festivals, this had been Reuel's and Channah's first trip to Channah's family home since their wedding ten years ago. For their eight-year-old son Kywan, five-year-old daughter Abi, and two-year-old son Noah, it was the first time they'd met many of their uncles, aunts, and cousins.

"They are all well. The children enjoyed the wide-open countryside and all the flocks, herds, and donkeys Channah's family owns. I was worried we wouldn't get them to come back to the city," Reuel said with a laugh. "I will bring them over to visit as soon as Channah has our household settled again."

The trip had been the longest time Reuel and Channah had spent together without Reuel having to travel, and it had made him fall even more in love with his wife. Loving, kind, caring, and as talented with weaving and embroidery as her uncle

Asaph had once boasted, Channah had proven herself a delight in every way and worked diligently to make a comfortable home for Reuel and their children. His father had indeed chosen well when he'd selected Channah as Reuel's bride.

After a few minutes of catching up on family news, Reuel looked sharply at his father. "You look as though you have a burden weighing on your mind. Is anything wrong?"

Hushai gave a quick glance around as though making sure no one could overhear, though Nasya had already rushed over to see her daughter-in-law and grandchildren and no servants were in sight. Lowering his voice, he said tensely, "I didn't want to alarm you so soon upon your return, but it is Absalom!"

"Again?" Reuel demanded with exasperation. "What has he done this time?"

"Well, you know how he has behaved since returning to Jerusalem," Hushai responded. "You remember when he hired dozens of men to run ahead of his chariot, clearing the streets for him and shouting his praises. Then for more than a year now, he started holding his own public audiences outside the gate on days when the king is not in session, listening to all who come from the tribes with complaints."

Not being blind, Reuel had known much of this. With his handsome physique and charisma, Absalom had always been popular, and his years of representing the king's interests to tribal leaders had made him highly respected before his years of exile. Reuel had overheard enough talk to know that many of the Israelites believed the king had treated his eldest remaining son unjustly after Absalom had done what the king refused to do in executing his sister's rapist as the law required. By Levitical law, family members had the right to execute judgment as their forefathers Simeon and Levi had done to the prince of Shechem who raped their sister Dinah.

"Yes, I have seen that Absalom has stolen the hearts of all Israel." Reuel agreed. "But it does not seem to distress the king. Perhaps he believes Absalom is getting experience for judging once he is king. It is not as though he executes actual judgments without the king's authority or contravenes the king's own verdicts."

"Perhaps. But whatever the actual merits, I have learned that Absalom tells all of them their claims are just and that if only he were appointed the king's representative, he would ensure they receive justice."

Hushai sighed. "Still, that is not what concerns me now. I was in Gibeon this past week, listening to a complaint against the descendants of King Saul, who had tried to annihilate them though Joshua swore on Yahweh's name to leave them in peace. I only returned last night myself to find that Absalom has left Jerusalem. He told his father he'd made a vow while in Geshur that he would offer sacrifices to Yahweh in Hebron if Yahweh restored him back to Jerusalem and that he wanted to travel there now to keep his vow."

Hebron was the city where David himself had been crowned king and ruled for more than seven years before conquering Jerusalem. It was also the burial place of Israel's founding patriarch Abraham and Absalom's own birthplace during the years King David ruled there. Abraham had built an altar there to the Lord after God had promised the land of Israel to his descendants in perpetuity, and many Israelites still traveled there to offer special sacrifices to Yahweh.

"After four years?" Reuel commented skeptically. "Still, I am not understanding why this is a concern. After all, the king lifted all restrictions from Absalom. Perhaps it is a good thing if he is absent from court for a while."

"I am less concerned at Absalom's absence than that Ahithophel and more than two hundred others traveled with him as did both his wives and their children and his mother, the king's wife Maacha."

Ahithophel was Hushai's counterpart as one of King David's top advisors and had been with the king far longer clear back to when the king was reigning in Hebron.

"I can understand wanting his family to witness the fulfillment of his vow. But it does seem unusual to take such a large company to honor a vow," Reuel responded thoughtfully. "Hebron is two days on foot or one long day on horseback. The supplies alone for such a party would be extensive!"

If there was one thing on which Reuel had become expert in his years of inventorying military stockpiles for Joab, it was the necessary provisions to feed a company of two hundred. He added caustically, "Well, I certainly hope the cost is to come from Absalom's pockets and not the king's treasury!"

The two men were interrupted by Hushai's doorkeeper, who burst into the living-room out of breath and looking frightened. "There is an urgent message from the palace, my lord!"

Hard on the doorkeeper's heels was one of Joab's top captains with whom Reuel had traveled on several occasions. He bowed to Hushai. "The king requests your presence immediately. He has just received word that Absalom has declared himself king in Hebron and that the king's counselor Ahithophel is advising him. Commander Joab is mustering those companies still loyal to King David, but it appears much of Israel is with Absalom, and his forces will enter Jerusalem within the day. The king is preparing to flee the city with those loyal to him."

Reuel whitened at the thought of Channah and his children caught in a crossfire between the king and his son. He had no real fears for the general population of Jerusalem. Absalom wanted to rule Jerusalem, not annihilate it. But seizing the families of those officials remaining loyal to King David to hold as hostages was just the kind of thing Absalom might do. Or the advice King David's traitorous counselor Ahithophel might offer.

"Go to Channah and my grandchildren!" Hushai ordered urgently. "Nasya is with them. Get them to safety to your mother's clan in Bethel, then join King David's forces wherever they may be by then. I will see you there."

Bethel was twelve miles, or a half-day's hard travel, to the north of Jerusalem, the opposite direction from Hebron. Reuel nodded assent. If they could leave the city in the next few hours, they should be long gone before Absalom and his forces arrived. As he left at a run, his thoughts flickered to his sister of spirit Naamah, who would be in far more danger in the palace than Reuel's family faced. *Yahweh, help her and keep her safe. Help us all!*

Chapter 44

"The last four years seem to have gone in a blink," Naamah told Shiphrah as they strolled through the courtyard. It doesn't seem possible Amaris is married and little Gia is almost fourteen. I suppose she will be the next of the harem children to be betrothed."

They were heading to their room when Naamah heard panicked shouting and the pounding footsteps of running men. Harem women and their children rushed out of rooms into the courtyard. Brielle called out frantically, "What is wrong? Naamah, you always know what is happening in the court. Are we under attack?"

At that moment, Semere burst in, as flustered and out of breath as Naamah had ever seen the stately harem overseer. He called out, "All of you pack belongings but no more than you can carry. Absalom has rebelled against the king and is on his way here. The king has ordered his household to evacuate immediately or Absalom will put us all to the sword!"

The large eunuch suddenly looked melancholy. "Not all of you are to accompany the king. Since his officials are leaving along with his wives and children, I have been instructed to leave ten of his concubines to oversee the servants and upkeep of the palace until his return."

As sobs and wailing broke out, Semere added quickly, "Not you, Naamah. The king wishes his personal musician at his side. But Shiphrah will remain as she is the best-qualified to keep the others organized."

Semere proceeded to name off nine other concubines. Several had already burst into tears even as the other concubines and wives scattered to pack bundles.

"Why must it be Shiphrah who stays? She has a young daughter still." Naamah stepped up to Semere, her blood chilling at the thought that what had happened to Tamar might happen to Gia at the hands of Absalom's invading force.

Semere's expression gentled. "Gia is King David's daughter. She like all the king's children will go with the rest of the household. As to Shiphrah and the others who stay, I am remaining behind as are the other eunuchs and servants except for those few tasked to help the king's wives who have small children."

Meaning Bathsheba, Naamah thought sourly. In the fourteen years since her arrival in the palace, Uriah's widow had borne four sons and three daughters to King David. A handful of concubines had also borne children since King David had not denied himself bedchamber pleasures during the seasons Bathsheba was too advanced in pregnancy or recovering from another birth to share his bed. To her disappointment, Brielle had not been among them.

Naamah turned to Shiphrah. "I will look after Gia as though she were my own. I just wish you were coming as well."

Shiphrah managed a sad smile. "I know you will watch over her, Naamah. And in some ways she is as much your daughter as mine the way you have loved her and cared for her all these years. In any case, I am sure the king will crush this rebellion quickly and you will all soon be home."

Semere left the courtyard. Behind him, Abigail called out calmly, "Come, sisters, let us all work together to prepare. We will meet back here within the hour to leave as one. And do not despair. Yahweh is with us, those who are leaving and those who are staying, and we will all help each other to get through this calamity."

Shiphrah and Naamah embraced each other, tears spilling down both faces. Naamah pushed through her fear and sadness. "I love you, dear friend. I will pray to Yahweh that we will soon be together again."

"And I love you," Shiphrah responded, finally releasing Naamah. "May the love of Yahweh always be between us. Now I must go and find Gia. I will bring her to you. Then I must go with Semere to see what needs done."

Naamah managed a smile. "You will do well running this palace. I am sure we will return soon to find it running far more smoothly than it does now."

Hurrying to her room, Naamah gathered the basic items she would need to take with her, wrapping them in a spare cloak to form a bundle. She carefully set her lyre in its special case and placed her mother's blanket on top before shutting the case. Arms full, she stepped back into the confusion that filled the courtyard. Women were attempting to balance bundles and manage wailing children. Bathsheba's youngest daughter and a concubine's son, conceived during Bathsheba's latest recovery from pregnancy, were still small enough to be carried. Naamah found Shiphrah, Gia at her side.

"Be safe, daughter," Shiphrah told Gia as she gave her a

final embrace. "Be obedient to Naamah and do not leave her side until you return home. I will be praying day and night for you both."

Counting off to ensure all were present, Abigail led the women out through the smaller courtyard and onto the palace terrace. A company of guards escorted the group to the king's gate. Carrying her pack over her right shoulder and her lyre under her left arm, Naamah wished for the strength she'd once had when she'd carried water daily from the well. Thankfully, the other women and children were moving slowly with their own burdens, but she alone carried a heavy lyre along with her personal belongings.

Once through the king's gate, Naamah spotted King David surrounded by his officials and a company of fierce-looking warriors. The soldiers wore full battle gear, but the king and his officials wore the rent clothing and disheveled, ash-strewn locks of mourning, and Naamah immediately noticed King David was barefoot. She looked for Hushai but didn't spot him. A much larger company of soldiers were on foot, and a long string of ox carts, donkeys, and mules were heading out, loaded with provisions.

A dozen ox carts had been provided for the women of the harem. Abigail steered the oldest women and those with small children to those. Bathsheba and her children occupied the largest cart. The rest of the harem would have to walk, but at least they were able to place their bundles in the carts, including Naamah's lyre.

A guard shouted above the chaos of milling women and children, "Move back for the king!"

King David's men-at-arms led the way through the city gates. Along with a sizeable contingent from his own tribe of

Judah, this included six hundred tall, powerfully built warriors from Gath led by their commander Ittai as well as companies of Kerethites and Pelethites, foreign mercenaries that formed part of King David's royal guard along with serving as elite troops directly under Joab. All of these had pledged allegiance to King David during his sojourn in the land of the Philistines while a fugitive from King Saul and had returned with him when he was crowned king in Hebron.

Once the king's men were outside the city and spread out to provide protection, King David and his top officials followed. The supply caravan came next, followed by the rest of the king's household. Residents of Jerusalem lined the streets as King David and his party passed by. Even more gathered in the countryside, held back by the protective formation of King's David's forces, all wailing loudly. Naamah couldn't help but notice there were far fewer than might be expected. How many had already thrown their lot in with Absalom?

As they reached the long, narrow Kidron Valley that ran along the east rampart, separating the City of David from the Mount of Olives and other surrounding hills, Naamah felt a pang of nostalgia. How many times had she followed this very path with her family during festivals, climbing up these very hillsides to where they'd built their Sukkot shelter? How much simpler life had seemed back then!

Suddenly, a fanfare of trumpets drowned out cries of sorrow. At Naamah's side, Gia pointed. "Look! It is the Ark of the Covenant of God."

Sure enough, King David, his officials, and his men had spread out from the path to form a wide circle around a small clearing. There Naamah recognized Zadok and Abiathar, the two high priests who oversaw tabernacle sacrifices, standing beside a makeshift altar of stone where a fire had already been lit. To one side, a party of Levites hoisted the beautiful golden ark on long, ornate poles. Then harmonizing voices replaced the trumpet fanfare, and Naamah spotted Asaph directing a Levite choir.

The harem company was steered close to King David, the royal guard surrounding them, weapons unsheathed. Naamah was thankful for the rest as Zadok and Abiathar slaughtered several lambs and placed them on the fire. To both sides, the Levite choir lifted psalms of praise. Naamah sang along softly. She saw King David's reddened gaze shift her direction when he recognized her voice.

When the last lamb was placed on the altar, King David raised his voice to announce, "Take the Ark of God back into the city. If I find favor in the Lord's eyes, He will bring me back and let me see it and His dwelling place again. But if He says, 'I am not pleased with you,' then I am ready. Let Yahweh do to me whatever seems good to Him."

Naamah was close enough to hear when King David lowered his voice and addressed Zadok directly. "Return the ark to its place with my blessing. Take your son Ahimaaz and Abiathar's son Jonathan with you. Whatever you learn, send them to inform me. I will wait at the fords in the wilderness until word comes from you."

As Zadok directed the Levites to begin carrying the ark back toward the city gates, King David began trudging once again towards the Mount of Olives. He wept broken-heartedly as he climbed, and Naamah felt the tears spilling down her own cheeks. All around her, other women and officials were sobbing, and Naamah even saw the king's strong warriors weeping openly.

When they reached the top of the Mount of Olives, Naamah saw why Hushai hadn't been present at the sacrifices below. Robe torn and head, white with ash, he met the company on the flat summit where the tabernacle was pitched during festivals.

247

Chapter 45

Embracing his advisor, King David wept against Hushai's shoulder. Then, straightening up, the king said wearily, "Walk with me. I must speak with you so that no one else may hear."

The two men strode off to the center of the summit, where King David led the way into a huddle of pack mules and lowered his voice. "My dearest friend, I have made a change of plans. There is no real value in you coming with me. I have Joab and all my officials to advise me. But if you will return to the palace to meet Absalom and Ahithophel when they arrive, you can help me by frustrating Ahithophel's advice. You know how astute he is. From the beginning of my reign, the people have accepted his advice as though he were one of God's prophets like Nathan or Samuel. That includes myself and Absalom. Beyond you, there is no one better able to help my son succeed at his rebellion."

King David sighed unhappily. "There is no one else I trust as I do you to foil Ahithophel's evil counsel. You have known Absalom since he was a child, and you know how prideful he is, how convinced that all Israel loves him. He will believe you if you tell him that he is the better king and that you will be his loyal servant as you were mine in the past. I have sent back the priests Zadok and Abiathar as well with the Ark of Yahweh. Their sons Ahimaaz and Jonathan are with them. Whatever you spy out in the palace, you can send me news through them. May Yahweh turn Ahithophel's counsel into foolishness!"

"May Yahweh turn Ahithophel's counsel into foolishness!" Hushai echoed fervently.

& & &

Naamah waited until she saw Hushai leave King David's side and stride off back down the mountainside. Threading through the throng, she hurried to catch up with him. Tremulously, she asked, "Are you not going with us? And Nasya, Reuel, his family? Are they not joining us? Please tell me they are not staying in Jerusalem when Absalom arrives. He is … evil! I fear for all who have stayed behind!"

Hushai smiled kindly, but his eyes were sad. "No one is more powerful than Yahweh, my child. As for Nasya and the rest of the family, they are all safe. They are no longer in the city."

He hesitated, looking down at her as though making up his mind. Then he said quietly, "Since you may see Reuel again before I do, and we both trust you completely, please tell him that if he hears I am serving Absalom, it is not true. I serve the king as I serve Yahweh. It is at the king's own command that it appear otherwise. Please swear you will tell my son this should I not have opportunity myself."

Meaning should his mission go badly, Naamah realized.

She swallowed back fresh tears. "I will do so. And I will pray for your safety."

As Hushai trudged down the mountainside toward the city gate, Naamah whispered, "Help us, Yahweh. Help Hushai, Abba God. And Nasya and Reuel and Channah and the children and Shiphrah. Help all of us and bring an end to Absalom's evil!"

Catching up with the other women, Naamah spotted a new caravan arriving onto the summit, a long string of heavily loaded donkeys. Word soon spread among the women that a loyal follower of King David had brought extensive stores of raisins, dried figs, wine, and journey bread. At least the company would not starve.

"Thank you, Yahweh, thank you!" Naamah praised aloud, seeing how Abba God had already answered her prayer for help.

For the rest of the day, the procession inched forward. Naamah felt sorry for the mothers with small children and babies, whose frightened cries turned into exhausted whimpers as the day progressed. In contrast, Gia remained cheerful and unflagging.

The caravan finally arrived at the shallow wilderness ravine King David and his advisors had chosen for the night's rest. Naamah and Gia retrieved their belongings from the cart. By the time Naamah had taken care of her first priority — ensuring no damage had been done to her lyre — Gia had spread her cloak out to mark their sleeping spot and had headed over to where Abigail was supervising the distribution of dry rations to the harem company. Naamah had never been prouder of her surrogate niece. The baby she'd welcomed into her life that first year in the harem had become a responsible young woman and would make a wonderful wife and mother one day.

No fires were permitted for fear of spying eyes in the hills. And for such a mass of people, there was very little talking. Everyone was simply too tired to speak. Gia returned with her hands full. "Here is some of the bread, raisins, and figs that man brought for the king."

Naamah was so hungry she ate despite her fatigue and anxiety. Darkness had descended. The only light was the stars and a three-quarters moon that shone above. Naamah and Gia lay down on Gia's cloak, and Naamah spread her own cloak and her mother's blanket over them both. She soon heard soft snores from Gia and the other women sleeping around her.

But despite her exhaustion, Naamah couldn't find rest. With each star that blinked, she was reminded of someone she cared for, and her concern for them grew. Shiphrah. Nasya. Reuel. Channah. Little Kywan, Abi, and Noah. Hushai, who had become as much a surrogate father to Naamah as Nasya had become a mother. How could he possibly be safe living the lie of a spy in Absalom's court?

Just as Naamah's dark thoughts attempted to overtake her, her eyes fluttered open. No, she hadn't been mistaken. The deep, sweet tone she heard floating across the encampment was King David's own, accompanied by the expert plucking of harp strings. The song was not one Naamah had heard before, but its haunting chords and the pain of its lyrics told her it was a new composition fashioned with Absalom's betrayal in mind.

"Lord, how many are my foes! How many rise up against me! Many are saying of me, 'God will not deliver him.' But You, Lord, are a shield around me, my glory, the One who lifts my head high. I call out to the Lord, and He answers me from His holy mountain. I lie down and sleep. I wake again, because the Lord sustains me. I will not fear though tens of thousands assail me on every side."

The rest of the company was utterly silent as though all were listening with bated breath to King David's powerful voice rising in yearning entreaty. "Arise, Lord! Deliver me, my God! Strike all my enemies on the jaw. Break the teeth of the wicked."

Then the king's voice dropped to sweet surrender. "From the Lord comes deliverance. May Your blessing be on Your people."

The music stopped, and quiet fell over the camp, followed within moments by renewed snores. Pushing back her coverings, Naamah rolled to a sitting position, hoping to hear again the words that held both defiance and hope. But it seemed the king had put away his lap harp. Reaching for her case, she eased out the lyre. Softly pulling a new melody from its strings, she began singing the words Yahweh was bringing to her own mind.

"He who dwells in the shelter of the Most High will rest in the shadow of the Almighty. I will say of the Lord, 'He is my refuge and my fortress, my God, in whom I trust.' Surely, He will save you from the fowler's snare and from the deadly pestilence. He will cover you with His feathers, and under His wings you will find refuge. You will not fear the terror of night, nor the arrow that flies by day. A thousand may fall at your side, ten thousand at your right hand, but it will not come near you. 'Because he loves Me,' says the Lord, 'I will rescue him. I will protect him, for he acknowledges My name. I will be with him in trouble and show him My salvation."

Like children soothed by a mother's lullaby, the camp slumbered in peace all around her.

Chapter 46

As he descended the mountainside, Hushai could see Absalom's ornate chariot accompanied by a large force of armed cavalry and foot soldiers approaching the southern gate of Jerusalem. His steps were heavy as he entered the northern gate and trudged to the palace. A psalm of David he'd heard sung many times by the king, the Levite choirs, and most recently Naamah played comfortingly in his mind. "When I am afraid, I will trust in You. In God, whose word I praise, in God I trust. I will not be afraid. What can mortal man do to me?"

Absalom, his close advisors, and military commanders were already in the throne room by the time Hushai reached its tall heavy doors. Ahithophel stood beside Absalom, seated on his father's throne, as for so many years he'd stood beside David. Not a man there didn't know Hushai as they knew Ahithophel, and no one tried to stop him as Hushai strode forward to the throne.

There he bowed low to Absalom. "Long live the king! Long live the king!"

Absalom gazed at Hushai appraisingly. "Is this the love you show my father? Are you not his dearest friend? Why are you not with him?"

Hushai's heart pounded, but his voice was calm. "I will remain with the man who is chosen by the Lord and by the people of Israel to sit on Israel's throne. And that man is you. Just as I served your father, so I will serve you."

As David had predicted, Absalom complacently accepted Hushai's declaration as his due. In contrast, Ahithophel gave Hushai a suspicious stare. After so many years the two had advised King David together, Ahithophel was clearly mistrustful of Hushai's changed loyalties. On the other hand, none would have anticipated Ahithophel would betray the king, so it would be hard to convince Absalom that Hushai wouldn't make the same choice.

Absalom turned from Hushai to address Ahithophel. "Give us your advice. What should we do first to demonstrate I am now king in Israel?"

"Sleep with your father's concubines whom he left to take care of the palace," Ahithophel answered promptly. "And do so publicly for all to see. We can pitch an awning on the roof terrace and bring up the king's bed so that you will be visible across Jerusalem. Once your father and all Israel hears that you have affronted the king so greatly, those who are with you will be more resolute because they will know there is no turning back."

Hushai struggled to hide his distaste. It was not uncommon for a victorious king to take possession of his predecessor's harem, as the prophet Nathan had made reference in condemning David's adultery with Bathsheba. David had inherited King Saul's harem, though he'd left them cared for in Gibeah, King Saul's capital city, rather than adding them to his own harem in Hebron or Jerusalem. But to humiliate the king's women by public rape as though they were common spoils of battle? That would indeed be an unforgiveable act, far more so from King David's own son.

But protesting would have no effect and simply defeat his own mission. So he found an excuse to visit the palace archives, claiming to be searching for important military data of use to Absalom, while servants erected a large open-sided pavilion on the flat, terraced palace roof and laboriously dragged up King David's royal bed. A younger and very pretty concubine named Brielle was the first to be dragged up and raped before the eyes of every Israelite who could see into the palace grounds from surrounding hillsides and summits.

As though some festival, thousands crowded the hills and palace rooftop itself to watch, and cheers of support rose when the evil deed was complete. It might have been pagan debauchery before the Canaanite fertility goddess Astarte or the golden calf that had brought down God's wrath during Israel's sojourn in the wilderness. Hushai shuddered in horror to see so many of his countrymen gleefully taking part.

He was suddenly reminded of another part of the prophet Nathan's pronouncement after David's great sin. "Before your very eyes, I will give your wives and concubines to a man who is close to you. You committed your sins in secret, but he will go to bed with them in broad daylight in the sight of all Israel."

Though David had repented, his actions of adultery and murder still had consequences, and here was the fulfillment of that judgment. The man most beloved of the king, his eldest remaining son, was going to bed with his father's women in broad daylight before all of Israel. Had Ahithophel also remembered that prophecy when he'd suggested that Absalom carry out such a vile act?

Hushai had the scrolls in question spread out on the council chamber table when Absalom swaggered in with Ahithophel and his other advisors. "That accomplished its purpose, I believe, from the applauding audience! I will take the remaining concubines as well, one each night. But now to deal with my father."

Absalom looked from Ahithophel to Hushai. "You two know his mind best, having advised him for many years. What would you suggest?"

Ahithophel spoke up immediately. "I would set out this very night in pursuit of David so as to attack him while he is weary and weak. You have twelve thousand men available, far more than he has, which will strike terror in the king and all the people with him. His supporters will flee. I would then suggest slaying only the king, as once he is dead, the rest of Israel will turn their loyalty to you. But if you harm people who seek only to follow their king, many Israelites may turn their hearts against you."

"That is good advice," Absalom responded.

Every tribal commander present nodded agreement. Every tribe was represented except David's own tribe of Judah and the Levites. But now was time for Hushai to carry out the mission David had assigned him. He cleared his throat suggestively. Ahithophel glared at him, but Absalom gave him a thoughtful look.

"What do you say, Hushai? Should we do as Ahithophel advises? If not, give us your own opinion."

Hushai looked around the council chamber at the tribal commanders, most of whom he had met and even advised over the years. He then turned to Absalom, shaking his head in patent concern. "My colleague here is both wise and crafty, as we all know. But this time, his advice is not good. You all know your father and his men. They are fighters as fierce as a wild bear robbed of her cubs."

It was a shrewd reminder that King David was the warrior who had slain Goliath and defeated the Philistines and countless other enemies. Unlike Absalom, who had commanded only his own men in peacetime. The tribal leaders were now nodding agreement with Hushai.

Ignoring Ahithophel's angry expression, Hushai went on, "Besides, your father is an experienced fighter. Did he not successfully avoid King Saul for many years? He will not spend the night in the encampment with his household. Even now, he is hidden in a cave or some other place. If he ambushes your own troops, word will go out that there has been a slaughter among those who follow Absalom. Then even your bravest soldiers whose hearts are like the heart of a lion will melt with fear, for all Israel knows that your father is a great fighter and that those with him are brave."

Absalom was silent. But Hushai could see he was seriously contemplating Hushai's advice. He raised his words in silent prayer. *Ahithophel's advice was correct as always, O Lord on High! But let that good advice be frustrated to bring disaster on Absalom for the evil he has done this day!*

At last Absalom spoke. "So what do you suggest?"

Hushai kept jubilation from his face as he said solemnly, "Do not rush into battle and risk your own forces. Instead, let word go out to all Israel from Dan to Beersheba, calling for every loyal Israelite to be gathered to your cause. When their numbers like sand on the seashore pour into Jerusalem, you yourself can lead them triumphantly into battle. Wherever your father retreats, we will attack him as dew settles on the ground. Neither he nor any of his men will be left alive. And if he withdraws into a city, then all Israel will bring ropes to that city, and we will drag it down to the valley until not so much as a pebble is left."

Hushai could hear the murmurs of approval before he even finished. It was clear from Absalom's expression that the image of riding out at leisure before a vast army was far more attractive than a hard night march after an already strenuous day.

Looking around the council chamber, Absalom announced with kingly authority, "The advice of Hushai the Arkite is better than that of Ahithophel."

His dignified act was immediately spoiled when he added with a suggestive leer, "That might even give me time to finish with those ten concubines. Starting this evening."

Numerous arrangements remained to be made for sending out summons and messenger riders to all twelve tribes of Israel. But once the council meeting was dismissed and Absalom and his sycophants had headed to the rooftop for more entertainment, Hushai went directly to the tabernacle where Zadok and Abiathar were overseeing the evening sacrifices, crowded as always though many of the worshippers had been among those cheering Absalom's depraved behavior.

Lingering behind as worshippers streamed from the tabernacle courtyard, Hushai drifted close to the two priests, telling them quietly what he'd advised. Then he commanded urgently, "You must send a message immediately to King David, telling him he must not spend one more night this side of the Jordan River ford but cross over without fail. If he does not, the king and all the people with him will be destroyed because you can be sure Ahithophel will ensure a force is sent to strike the encampment regardless of what was decided. And tell him all that has been determined in summoning the tribes to Absalom's side."

"We will do so," Zadok responded. "But you must know that the message cannot go before tomorrow. Our sons cannot risk entering the city, so they are staying with a loyal servant of the king in En Rogel."

En Rogel was a tiny village clustered around a spring in the Kidron Valley some five hundred paces south of the city wall.

"We in turn do not dare leave the city," Abiathar added, "lest someone see us and report we are going to David. So we have made arrangements to send any message from you with a trusted female servant. The city gates are already closed for the night, but we can send her as soon as they are open in the morning."

That would have to do. In any case, with the drunken festivities going on among Absalom and his men all over the city, it would likely be well into the next day before Ahithophel could convince anyone to send a precautionary advance force.

I have done what I can! Hushai told himself. *We must now trust that the great wings of Yahweh will shelter His chosen one in the wilderness.*

Chapter 47

Reuel was exhausted as he pushed his horse on as fast as the animal could trot. He'd delivered his mother, wife, and children to the home of his maternal grandparents in Bethel. Once he was assured of their safety, he'd spent only long enough to call together the clan leaders and give them full details of the crisis before borrowing a fresh horse and heading back to Jerusalem.

By then, darkness had fallen. Though the road from Bethel to Jerusalem was well-used, traversing it at night even under a three-quarters moon was hazardous. The horse stumbled frequently so that Reuel had to keep the animal to a walk. Only with dawn staining the eastern sky was the road visible enough to push the animal to a trot.

Reuel had avoided the lush, well-travelled Kidron Valley along the west side of Jerusalem, which he feared might by now be choked with Absalom's men. Instead, he'd taken a far more precarious trail through the Valley of Hinnom, a long, shallow ravine that ran along the west side of the original Jebusite fortress before curving east to converge with the Kidron Valley a few hundred paces south of the walled city.

Hinnom was infamous during Canaanite rule as a place where children were sacrificed to the false gods of Molech and Baal, and it was well-known that even many Israelites had followed suit over the centuries though the laws of Moses forbade it. Under the prophet Samuel, the death penalty began to be enforced against such offenses. Once King David captured Jerusalem from the Jebusites, the gorge where such sacrifices were carried out had been turned into the city dump. It was now perpetually filled with rotting flesh, maggots, and ever-burning fires in an ongoing attempt to eliminate the refuse piles and stench.

Which made it a perfect route to slip unseen into the city as Absalom's men would not willingly go near such a hellish place.

The sun was just thrusting its first rays above the Mount of Olives as Reuel reached the spring of En-rogel, just north of where the two valleys converged. There a deep shaft had been sunk in ancient times, creating a well whose water was deemed the sweetest in all Israel. Pausing to water his horse and himself, Reuel pondered his options.

The city gates were still shut and would be till full light. More so, his father had given strict orders to seek out King David, not to return to the city. But how to find out which direction the king and his company were heading without speaking to his father? He couldn't simply ask bystanders without raising suspicions.

Reuel stepped back under a nearby fig tree as a slim young woman in the plain clothing and head covering of a servant hurried past him down an alley. She disappeared inside a small dwelling. Reuel lingered in the camouflage of dawn's long, deep shadows to make sure she didn't return before stepping out to gather his horse.

The precaution turned out to be wise as Reuel suddenly spotted a familiar face peering cagily out the door the young woman had entered. This became a tall, lanky familiar frame as a man his own age slipped outside into the alley. He was followed by another familiar frame, this one short and stocky.

Reuel stared with disbelief. Jonathan, son of Abiathar, and Ahimaaz, son of Zadok, had grown up in the palace since the two priests had overseen the transfer of the Ark of the Covenant and its appointed dwelling place, the tabernacle, to Jerusalem. Since their fathers too were part of King David's closest circle, Reuel had run around the palace with the other two boys until their paths took them into training for the priesthood and Reuel's to the scriptorium.

It was there that Reuel had read more of the two priests' stories in the archives of the kings. Abiathar had been the only surviving tabernacle priest when King Saul ordered their slaughter after they'd unwittingly helped David escape. Abiathar had fled to David's side, serving as priest for David and all his men during the years of exile. Zadok had been appointed chief over the priests when the tabernacle was still pitched at King Saul's capital, Gibeon. Since David was crowned king in Hebron, Zadok and Abiathar had served equally as chief priests.

So why were their sons still here rather than at King David's side? Had their fathers turned against the king to support Absalom? That seemed like neither priest nor his childhood friends.

On impulse, Reuel left his horse at the well and slid from shadow to shadow as the other two young men headed at a hurried pace further down the alley and into a stand of olive trees. Slipping closer, Reuel caught fragments of their low, urgent conversation. "We must get to King David at once … The messenger insisted the warning came to our fathers directly from the king's advisor Hushai … Then perhaps he has not after all defected to Absalom as has been rumored … Others might say the same of our fathers. I have never believed Hushai would betray the king … It won't matter if we don't reach him before Absalom's men do."

Zadok and Abiathar still in Jerusalem? His own father defected to Absalom? His two old friends clearly spying on behalf of King David? What had happened since Reuel left Jerusalem less than twenty-four hours previously?

Either way, it confirmed that Jonathan and Ahimaaz were loyal to King David and had the answers he sought. Slipping close behind them through the trees, Reuel called out in a low voice, "Jonathan, Ahimaaz, old friends! It's Reuel! What news of the king? And my father?"

The other two spun around, daggers sliding into their hands. They relaxed when they recognized Reuel. After the three men had exchanged a quick summary of the last twenty-four hours, Ahimaaz explained, "We must get to King David at once with your father's warning to cross over the Jordan River before nightfall. My father's servant girl who brought the message gave additional news that Ahithophel has convinced the usurper to send an advance force to catch the king's company before they can cross the Jordan even as they send out couriers to summon the tribes of Israel to Absalom's banner."

"We left our horses hobbled in the ravine ahead in case we needed to make a quick escape," Jonathan added. "We know they fled over the Mount of Olives into the Jordan wilderness toward Jericho, beyond which lies the closest fords, so we thought to follow the same route if we can do so unseen by Absalom's forces. Would you like to join us? We could use an extra sword."

"Even better," Reuel responded. "I can take you on a route Absalom's men will avoid like Hades itself!"

Even with headscarves wrapped around their lower faces, the three horsemen were soon wrinkling their noses as they picked their way through the smoldering refuse pits of Hinnom. It was even worse now that Reuel could see. Rotting, bloated corpses were undoubtedly animal but could have easily been the mounded human sacrifices to Baal and Molech. Thankfully, the light also allowed them to move more quickly, and as Reuel had predicted, no human beings moved through this perdition except the unclean, lowest of all social classes, tasked with disposal of waste.

Their cover diminished drastically once they left the Hinnom Valley north of Jerusalem and turned east. A main west-east caravan route, the road from Jerusalem to Jericho was steep and winding through a narrow conduit formed by a natural rift in the hills. Which meant that the road was crowded with carts, caravans, horsemen, and foot traffic. Including Absalom's men. A sizeable party of soldiers was galloping toward Jerusalem when they came abreast of Reuel and his companions, who had tucked themselves among a slow-moving camel caravan until they were through the pass and could leave the main road.

"Hey!" One soldier suddenly shouted out just as he passed Reuel. "That is the son of Hushai! Where is he going?"

Reuel had recognized the soldier as well, a captain in Israel's armies and son of a tribal leader from Benjamin to whom Reuel had carried messages from Joab in the past. He and his men must have chosen to throw their lot in with Absalom over the aging king. Of all the poor timing, he groaned inwardly, kicking his mount into a run.

Thankfully, Absalom's men had been swept past the snarl of loaded camels by the time they were able to turn their mounts around. By then, Reuel and his companions were beyond the caravan. Ahimaaz pressed his horse alongside Reuel and called out, "I know a place we can hide! Follow me!"

Just beyond the pass, the terrain flattened, and the road ran through a sizeable town. Reuel knew its name—Bahurim—from his extensive travels this direction, though he'd never actually visited the place. Yanking his horse from the main road, Ahimaaz wove at a fast trot through a crowded roadside market, then made several turns through alleys beyond, Jonathan and Reuel close behind. When they were well out of sight of the main road, Ahimaaz drew up.

"There is a merchant here who is very devout, always bringing double the required sacrifices to the tabernacle. He and my father have become good friends. I know he will give us sanctuary if those soldiers come looking for us."

"Then we'd better make sure no one can inform them we've been seen entering his house," Reuel pointed out.

Stripping their horses of any identifying harness, the three men turned the animals into a large corral of horse, mules, and donkeys being offered for sale at the market. Reuel could only hope they would still be there to retrieve later, but that was a risk they'd have to take. Ahimaaz led the way to the rear of a two-story house not far from the market, its size indicating its owner's wealth.

"Wait here." Climbing a sycamore tree that overhung the wall, Ahimaaz stepped across onto a second-story balcony and disappeared from view. Reuel kept a tense lookout as he and Jonathan waited. He had picked up angry shouts from the direction of the market when a small door in the wall opened. Ahimaaz waved at his friends urgently. "Hurry! I think Absalom's soldiers have entered the town!"

The courtyard inside was large—and empty of any residents except an elderly, sun-darkened man and woman. The man beckoned the three newcomers toward the ultimate household luxury in that dry land—a well in the center of the courtyard. The cover was already removed.

"Climb inside," he urged. "It will be dry until rainy season so you have nothing to fear. Once you are hidden, Rachel will spread grain so no one will guess you are here."

He gestured toward his wife, who hefted a half-filled grain sack in one arm. She grinned toothlessly at her guests. "Like Rahab and the spies at Jericho. She was an ancestor of our king, you know!"

Despite the danger, Reuel smothered his own grin. Rather than fear, it was clear this elderly woman was relishing an unexpected adventure. The three men climbed down hurriedly. Then the well cover slid noisily closed above them, and Reuel interpreted sounds of the grain being spread out across the cover as if to dry.

And just in time. Already, fists were pounding against a door. "Open in the name of King Absalom!"

The three men barely breathed as the courtyard above filled with pounding feet and harsh shouts. But in fact, it was only a few minutes before Reuel heard the Benjamite captain he'd recognized call out, "Nothing here! Let's move on."

The captain must have been standing very close to the well because Reuel heard him add more quietly as though to a subordinate, "The caravan drivers concur Hushai's son was riding with two others, but their description could be half the men of Israel. We will search every house in this town, but I fear they have slipped our trap while we linger here and are long gone by now. At least we can take a report to the palace. They will know whether Hushai's son is on a mission for Absalom or has betrayed the new king."

Though the courtyard quickly fell silent, it was a good two hours later before the merchant removed the well cover.

"They are all gone, headed to Jerusalem," their elderly ally reported. "Do not go back to the main road. I have had a servant lead fresh horses for each of you to a pasture east of the city, and I myself will lead you there by back paths."

It took another hour of meandering hike along hillsides and through ravines before Reuel saw three horses at pasture ahead, all three already saddled and bearing small packs. The merchant explained, "There is food and drink for your journey. And a full skin of my finest wine for the king himself. There would be more, but you need to ride light and swift. May Yahweh be with you."

"And with you." Ahimaaz embraced his father's friend fiercely, and the other two followed suit. Reuel found himself dumbfounded at Yahweh's unexpected provision. Truly the Almighty was fighting on behalf of His anointed king.

As he hugged the old man, Reuel added his own pledge. "You are a true son of Israel, as we will inform King David. And we will make sure the king knows it was you who brought us safely to his side!"

Chapter 48

The second day's travel seemed easier to Naamah, or perhaps she was simply growing accustomed to more strenuous exercise than she'd known in years. There was a certain camaraderie between wives and concubines that didn't exist in the palace as they fled together the same evil. Naamah was fascinated with the resilience of the children. Yesterday, they'd been overcome with fear. Today, they raced around the convoy, dodging hooves and cart wheels with squeals of excitement. Naamah wished she had their energy and fortitude.

Even so, the day was exhausting, the sun blazing overhead. Naamah was relieved when Abigail brought word they would camp as soon as they reached the Jordan River. Darkness was falling when they reached the ford. A guard trotted over to let the harem's protective detail know which spot had been assigned to the king's women and children near his own camp. Naamah and Gia were spreading out their bedding when a trio of horsemen galloped past. Naamah's heart thrilled with delight to recognize the strong voice that called out.

"We must speak with King David! We've been sent with an urgent message from his advisor Hushai!"

Across the meadow, the horses drew up outside the battlefield tent that served as portable command center and personal quarters for King David. Even favored Bathsheba did not share the tent as it was where the king met for confidential discussions with his military commanders and advisors. Thankfully, the Jordan Valley was bone-dry this time of year so sleeping under the stars was no real discomfort. In fact, it reminded Naamah of the crowded fellowship of the Sukkot festivals.

Naamah resisted the impulse to rush in to pass on the message Hushai had entrusted for Reuel and demand news of Nasya and their family. Maybe she could catch Reuel after he'd finished communicating Hushai's missive for the king.

Yahweh, let it be good news! she pleaded silently. Perhaps Absalom had already been deposed and they could all go home.

But instead, shouts and running feet spread swiftly through the camp. The harem's guard detail strode through their camp, calling out, "Everyone up and moving. We are crossing the Jordan tonight!"

Trusting Gia to take the initiative to repack their belongs, Naamah hurried to look for Abigail. Finding the harem's de facto leader in conversation with the captain of their guard force, she waited only for the captain to stop speaking before asking urgently, "Abigail, what is wrong? I saw Reuel arrive. I know what Hushai has been doing in Jerusalem. Is Absalom on his way here? What can I do to help?"

Abigail raised her voice so the other women crowding around could hear as well. "There is no immediate danger. But word has come that Absalom has sent a large force after us. Thankfully, the plan was discovered and we have received warning in plenty of time. But we must cross the fords tonight if we are to be alive by morning."

Instantly, Naamah knew it was Hushai in his role as a spy who had learned of Absalom's plans and sent warning. *Thank you, Yahweh! You have snatched us from Absalom's snare and covered us with the shelter of Your wings!*

"But what of our children?" a concubine with a young daughter called out. "It is too dark to even see where the fords are!"

"You do not need to worry," Abigail responded. "There will be torches to mark the fords and many strong soldiers to help us across. But gather your things quickly as we must cross immediately. But first, let us pray to Yahweh."

She raised her voice even louder so that all the worried, chattering women could hear. "Yahweh, we have a big undertaking this night. Keep us safe as we cross this river. Keep our fear at bay. Give us the calm, strength, and poise we need to accomplish this endeavor."

Naamah's respect for Abigail increased further. Would she ever be as wise and godly a leader as the king's eldest remaining wife continued to prove herself?

She hurried back to Gia. As expected, the girl had already repacked their belongings and was returning them to their assigned cart. Naamah snatched her lyre from the pile. "This isn't crossing anywhere but in my hands!"

"It is too heavy in its box!" Gia protested. "What if the weight causes you to fall into the river! I fear you will be swept away!"

"You are right," Naamah replied. "Which is why I will leave the case and carry only the lyre. At least if it falls into the river, it will be my own fault and not a clumsy oxen."

Knowing how important her instrument was to Naamah,

Gia didn't try to argue her out of it but took her place close to Naamah's side as though determined to single-handedly protect her surrogate aunt and lyre both. The harem company fell into the same order of march they'd maintained the last two days as their guard detail led them toward the river. Soon, Naamah could see torch lights ahead. As her segment of the procession reached the water, she saw that soldiers spaced at intervals of an arms-length apart lined both sides of the ford, their torches held high.

The ford itself was the width of a main road to permit for constant passage of carts, caravans, mounted companies, and foot traffic. This was made possible by building up the river bed with large boulders covered by smaller and smaller stones to provide a solid surface just far enough beneath the surface for the river to flow unimpeded and shallow barges to traverse the ford. But the water on either side was chest high on horses being ridden across to speed up the evacuation. When one horse stumbled on the downriver side, the current was strong enough to sweep it a hundred cubits before its rider managed to urge the animal to the far bank.

The stones underfoot were also slippery, the water coming up almost to Naamah's knees as she took her turn stepping out onto the ford. Women with children clutched them tightly by the hand as they splashed across while soldiers carried the smallest ones. The carts were already on the other side, and Naamah wondered if she'd been foolishly reckless in insisting on carrying the lyre herself.

The answer came when she stepped into a gap amidst the rocks and stumbled forward, falling to her knees in the water. But just as the lyre slid from her grip, Gia snatched it up, holding it high above her head until a soaking-wet Naamah scrambled back to her feet. They both reached the other side without further adventure. Searching out their belongings, Naamah and Gia found a place among the other women to spread out their bedding as the last of the company crossed the river, followed by the men with torches. Naamah dug out a dry tunic and discreetly changed under cover of cloak and blanket.

"Look, Naamah! See what they are doing!" Still on her feet, Gia pointed excitedly toward the ford.

Dropping her wet clothing, Naamah pushed herself back to her feet. The torches now lined the near bank. Out in the river starting on the far side of the ford, hundreds of soldiers were digging at the crossing with sword, spears, and various tools. Smaller stones were allowed to flow downriver. Medium-sized rocks were tossed into the water on either side. Bigger boulders were rolled up or carried onto the near shore. To Naamah's amazement, it took less than an hour for the crossing to be replaced by swift rapids glittering gold under the light from the torches.

Once the soldiers had all splashed ashore, they spread out in their ranks along the bank. Supply carts created a barricade. Archers were unloading sheaves of arrows and stringing their bows.

Stepping up beside Naamah, Abigail said quietly, "I remember times like this in the years we lived in the wilderness fleeing from Saul's sword. The nearest ford now is many leagues from here. With the crossing gone, it will take days for Absalom to rebuild enough to bring his forces and supplies across. And if they attempt to swim the river, the king's archers will pick them off before they can get across."

Abigail let out a contented sigh. "We will sleep without fear tonight, and come tomorrow, the king's men will have no difficulty holding the ford long enough for all of us to reach safety. Yahweh truly is our fortress!"

It was a reminder of the new song Naamah had composed the previous night. Settling her lyre, thankfully still dry, in her lap, she pulled words and melody from her memory, not softly this time but letting Yahweh's promises ring out triumphantly as the camp settled around her.

"He who dwells in the shelter of the Most High will rest in the shadow of the Almighty. I will say of the Lord, 'He is my refuge and my fortress, my God, in whom I trust.' … You will not fear the terror of night, nor the arrow that flies by day. A thousand may fall at your side, ten thousand at your right hand, but it will not come near you. 'Because he loves Me,' says the Lord, 'I will rescue him.'"

As the last notes of the song died away, Naamah heard with astonished delight a new song wing its way through the camp. "Many are saying of me, 'God will not deliver him.' But You, Lord, are a shield around me, my glory, the One who lifts my head high. I call out to the Lord, and He answers me from His holy mountain. I lie down and sleep. I wake again, because the Lord sustains me."

Halfway through the song, Naamah picked up the harmony on her own lyre and joined in the song. "I will not fear though tens of thousands assail me on every side. From the Lord comes deliverance. May Your blessing be on Your people."

For the next hour under brilliant constellations and golden moon, Naamah and King David sang the encampment to sleep.

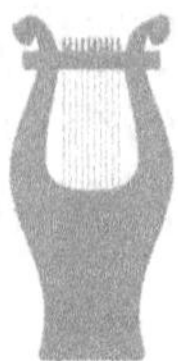

Chapter 49

After one more day of travel, Naamah was thankful to finally arrive at their destination. Mahanaim was a small walled city set in a valley among rugged foothills. Naamah knew from listening to Abigail regale the court women with its history that Mahanaim was among the sanctuary cities set aside for the Levites in the territory of every tribe since as God's priests the Levites had no territory of their own.

Mahanaim was in the territory of Gad, one of the three tribes that had been given land on the east side of the Jordan River. As a sanctuary city, it was under the authority of the Levites, not the tribal leaders, and any fugitive who reached sanctuary safely could not be turned over to their enemies so long as they remained inside the city boundaries. Whether Absalom would respect the law of Moses was another matter. He'd already broken God's laws in rising up against Yahweh's anointed king and his own father.

But sanctuary was irrelevant. They were only here as long as it would take King David's loyal forces to muster so they could give battle against the usurper and his men. Couriers had already ridden out calling loyal Israelites to defend their king. The race would be whether enough reinforcements would reach them before Absalom arrived with his own army. If King David's men won the day, they would all return to Jerusalem. If Absalom carried the battle, Naamah had no illusions he would respect the ancient laws of sanctuary.

The unwieldy camp of thousands narrowed into a neat procession to enter the city gate. King David rode first with his personal guard, followed by the women and children of his household. Naamah had spotted Reuel riding to the left of the king, the army commander Joab to the king's right. Other officers brought up the rear. The rank-and-file soldiers were already pitching camp outside the city walls by the time Naamah, Gia, and other concubines entered the gate at the heels of the king's wives and their children.

As typical in a fortified city, the entrance opened onto a sizeable public square where market days and other town business would be transacted. On the far side of the square, another wall and gate led into the residential parts of the city, allowing a defense to be mounted between the two gates should enemies attack. The outer wall was wide enough for sentinels to walk along it, and above the outer gate, watchmen kept a sharp eye on the valley beyond the city walls and the steep, rocky slopes rising on either side.

The area between inner and outer gates was currently empty, the townspeople clearly commanded to stay clear. All but three prosperous-looking men, presumably town elders. They bowed in deep respect as the king's company filtered in. Behind and to the other side of the three were at least a dozen carts piled high with supplies. Joab dismounted and approached them, the king's personal guard spreading out in front of King David's horse in a protective shield.

After a short murmured conversation, Joab approached the king, the three locals at his heels. Joab announced loudly enough for the entire company to hear, "My king, may I introduce Shobi son of Nahash, Makir son of Ammiel, and Barzillai the Gileadite. Knowing of your coming and that your people would be weary, hungry, and thirsty, they have brought from their own lands an assortment of supplies to honor the king. Various grains, beans, lentils, honey, curds, cheese, and sheep to slaughter. Bedding and vessels of all sorts as well. They ask where their offerings should be delivered."

Off to one side, Naamah saw King David's face light up with the first real smile she'd seen there since Absalom's rebellion. The king called out warmly, "My thanks, good men, for this kindly welcome. Your service to your king will not be forgotten. As to where—"

He glanced around as though wondering just who had been making his command tent and meals appear as if by magic every evening. Abigail hurried forward. "My lord, I will find out where you and your council will be lodged and make arrangements to have fresh food and bedding laid out shortly."

She turned to the closest of the three men, Barzillai the Gileadite. "If your servants can direct us to the accommodation that has been arranged for the king and all his household, we will put your generous gifts to good use. But perhaps you could first direct the king and his men to the stables so they might dismount and refresh themselves."

Naamah hid a grin. Whether the palace, a refugee camp, a strange city, or for that matter an abusive husband and vengeful warlord, Abigail would always have the poise to take charge and do what needed done. Catching her eye, Abigail waved Naamah over.

"Naamah, someone will need to let the king know where we are setting up accommodations for him. Could you request Reuel to accompany us to where the king will be housed, then return to the king and guide him there? It will take us some time to get organized, but we will make sure accommodations for the king and his council are made ready by the time he arrives."

Looking around, Naamah saw that King David and his party had all dismounted. Reuel was holding his own reins as well as those of King David and Joab's horses as Joab spoke earnestly with the king. Reuel smiled as Naamah approached. "I was hoping I would have opportunity to bring greetings before I am sent elsewhere. My mother and wife both send their love and said to let you know they will be praying for you every day you are away."

"Thank you, and please return my own greetings and love when you see them again. Does this mean they are safely out of Jerusalem? Your father told me why you were not with the king and company when we left."

"They are safe with my mother's family, who are all doting on the little ones." Reuel spoke heartily, but a flicker of worry crossed his face as he added in a lower tone, "As safe as they can be anywhere until Absalom's rebellion is crushed—may that come swiftly!"

"And your father? Is he well? Did he send any messag—"

Reuel's abrupt hand gesture cut her off. "I haven't seen my father since I took my family to Bethel. I assumed then I would find him here with the king. I only learned he was in Jerusalem with Absalom when I met up with Jonathan and Ahimaaz and joined them to deliver their message to the king."

"Reuel, you can't possibly think—" Naamah faltered briefly,

then raised her eyes to look earnestly into his. "Reuel, you do know your father would never betray his king. Hushai is in Jerusalem at the king's own command serving the king's purpose. I only hope Absalom has not guessed that purpose."

"Oh, it's okay!" A grin lit up Reuel's face. "Who more than I know my father's loyalty to King David. I know what he's doing there—and the source of the warning Jonathan and Ahimaaz received which ensured your company crossed the Jordan in time. But I wasn't aware *you* knew why he'd remained with Absalom. A spy does not remain safe if too many know his true role. Does the rest of the harem know? If so, one can't count on any secret remaining so with as much gossip as goes on there."

"Abigail may know. Not from me, but she does seem to know everything about everyone. Hushai told me before he left only because—" Naamah broke off, swallowing before she said in a whisper, "He was worried if anything happened to him that you might believe—well, you know! He wanted me to tell you and your mother that he was with Absalom only to fight for the king in that role. I told him his family would have no doubt of his loyalty. But if anything went wrong for him or the king, he wanted all of you to know he stood by Yahweh's anointed to the end."

"It isn't going to go wrong!" Reuel put a brotherly arm around Naamah's shoulders as she wiped surreptitiously at wet eyes, then dropped it as though suddenly remembering she wasn't in fact his sister. "Yahweh is going to deliver King David, and we will all be home in Jerusalem in no time. Now, we'd better hurry up if we're going to find out where we're supposed to be going and get that message to the king."

He was right. The household company was already almost

out of sight plodding after the supply carts through the inner gate. Meantime, King David and Joab had remounted and were leisurely pacing between the outer and inner walls with the rest of the king's guard, presumably toward the stables. Remounting swiftly, Reuel leaned down to offer Naamah a hand. "Come on up here, and I'll catch you up with those wagons."

His strong grip hoisted her in one swift motion to sit sideways in front of him. It was the first time she'd sat on a horse with any man besides her father, and Naamah felt self-conscious as she grabbed at the horse's mane to balance herself. But Reuel seemed to find it nothing out of the ordinary. And maybe it wasn't for him. Maybe Channah rode like this with her husband on a regular basis.

For just a moment, Naamah let her thoughts linger on what it might be like to have a real husband to share daily life with—and a growing family. But that was self-pity. She deliberately banished her envious daydreaming with prayer. *Dear God in heaven, please protect dear Nasya, Hushai, Channah, and the children. Keep them safe until we are all reunited in peace!*

It took little more time than her prayer for the horse's canter to bring them to the rear of the household group. Reuel lifted Naamah down, then dismounted, leading the horse as they made their way through the gate at the steady but slow pace the carts permitted. Gia rushed out of the crowd to throw her arms around Naamah. "Where were you? I was afraid you'd gotten lost!"

It wasn't much further before the carts turned into tall wooden doors standing open onto a sizeable courtyard. Like Naamah's childhood home, the house was built around three sides of the courtyard with the streetside wall and gate forming the fourth side of a square. But this courtyard was at least four times the size of her home, and it rose two stories high with a wide balcony on the second floor roofing a tiled verandah.

At each corner of the verandah a curving staircase rose to the second floor balcony, then on to the roof with its red-brick parapet. The rooftop to Naamah's left would give a clear view of the outer gate and valley beyond. Naamah suddenly realized from the residence's size and position that the left wing of the house must abut the inner city wall. Or perhaps the inner wall formed part of this building. This must be what passed for a palace in this sanctuary city, if Levites possessed such luxuries. Or perhaps the highest-ranking priest lived here.

Either way, its usual inhabitants would appear to have been expelled to provide the best accommodations the town could offer to their king. Spotting Abigail looking weary and exasperated amidst the turmoil around the loaded carts, Naamah made her way through noisy children and equally noisy mothers to offer assistance.

Abigail's face lit up with relief when she saw Naamah. "There you are! We've been given this entire residence while we are here. The left wing will be for David and his council and officers. The center wing for his wives, their children, and servants. The right for the concubines and their children. I know you weren't allowed to bring servants along. So do you mind if I put you in charge of organizing the concubines into sleeping quarters? In truth, you are the only one I trust to do so impartially and without losing patience. If there isn't enough bedding inside, you and you alone have the authority to requisition what you need from the stores our kindly hosts provided."

Abigail's eye fell on Gia peeking out from behind Naamah.

"Gia, would you find Jytte for me?"

As the girl took off running, Abigail turned back to Naamah. "I am going to put Jytte in charge of the food supplies. She was an excellent cook before she was a midwife. I don't know what kind of help we'll have in the kitchens or if they have provided us with kitchen and serving staff along with the food goods. But all this will allow us to ensure the king has a proper feast in front of him tonight to celebrate escaping that vile son of his, even if we must all pitch in to play the part of servants."

You mean, we concubines! Naamah thought derisively. She couldn't even imagine Bathsheba or most of the other wives lifting a finger, fugitives or not. That Abigail could and did only increased Naamah's respect and admiration for the older woman. *May I one day be that wise, kind, and accomplished when I grow up — if I ever do!*

Chapter 50

Hushai waited impatiently for the morning sacrifice and worship to be completed. This was the fourth day he'd awaited word from Zadok and Abiathar of the situation in which their sons had found King David and his forces. He hadn't expected a reply the first two days since it would take that long for the two young men to have reached the king's camp and return. Especially with Absalom's own growing forces occupying every road.

But if they'd reached the king successfully with their warning and were still alive, surely they would have made their way back by now. As the final prayer was intoned, Hushai didn't approach the two priests overseeing the sacrifice. They'd agreed not to make contact unless absolutely necessary should spying eyes have been set on any of the three.

Then Hushai saw the signal he'd been waiting for. Turning from the altar, Zadok wiped the back of his right hand across his forehead as though removing perspiration dripping into his eyes. Hushai drifted to the far left of the worshipping crowd, lingering as the rest threaded their way out the open gateway.

A man in ordinary dress and prayer shawl wrapped across

mouth and nose as though shielding against smoke and dust walked slowly by. Zadok with priestly garments removed. He muttered just loud enough for Hushai to hear, "They reached the king in time. All are safe across the river and have reached the citadel of Mahanaim. Your son was in their company and remains with the king."

Raising joyful thanks to Yahweh, Hushai made his way back to the palace. By the time he reached the throne room, he saw captains and officers of the force that had raced to cut King David off milling around the verandah and inside the throne room. So the priests' sons weren't the only ones who come back to make their report. And from the fury on Absalom's face as he strode to seat himself on the throne, the king's son already knew the news wasn't good.

Absalom spotted Hushai and waved him forward. He spoke angrily. "It's about time you showed your face, Hushai! Have you heard the news?"

Hushai responded cautiously, unsure of how much he could admit to already knowing. "I see your captains have returned but have not yet heard their report. If they engaged with your father's warriors, I trust their losses were few."

Absalom waved a hand impatiently. "No, there was no fighting. My father was already long gone by the time my men reached the Jordan. Undoubtedly, your advice was right and it was for the best they didn't engage before I have time to build my own force. No, it is Ahithophel, the fool! From what his armor bearer had to report, he traveled out to meet our advance force with some idea of proving his advice was better than yours."

Absalom grimaced. "When he learned that my father like the sly fox he is had escaped, it wasn't enough to admit yours was the better advice this time. He went home and hanged himself in front of his entire family with his armor bearer as witness."

Absalom's shrug held indifference. "He was a brilliant strategist. I could have used his continued advice. But I guess that leaves you as my chief counselor."

Hushai bowed low with outward deference, but inside his soul was singing, *Oh, Yahweh, You have indeed frustrated the traitor's advice and delivered Your chosen servant David!*

& & &

King David listened and nodded from the ornate chair that was doing service as his throne. It had been a week since they'd reached the sanctuary city. Each day, reports came in of new companies of soldiers arriving to join his forces from various tribes and regions, first in the hundreds, then in the thousands.

Standing beside King David's chair as his father had so often done beside the throne in Jerusalem, Reuel ceaselessly panned the room for any possible threat to the king. The long, ornate hall where King David and his officers were holding council and its equally ornate furnishings demonstrated that the Levites did well for themselves on Gadite tithes and offerings. At least, the descendant of Aaron who was chief priest in this city. Reuel had visited kingdoms in his travels with palaces less grand.

Joab was speaking. "I don't think we are going to see our force grow much further. It has been almost a day since the last company arrived. And my scouts tell me Absalom has crossed the Jordan with a sizeable force under command of Amasa."

A ripple of disbelief swept the crowded hall. Amasa was King David's own nephew and Joab's cousin, both their mothers being sisters of King David. He had fought courageously at David's side during the years of exile and all the years since when the king was defeating the Philistines and bringing peace to the nation.

I guess he's Absalom's cousin too, Reuel reminded himself. *Still, I would never have believed he could turn on his uncle like this. Of course, I'd have said the same of Absalom not so long ago!*

"You're right," King David said heavily. "We can't wait any longer. Better to meet them on an open battlefield of our choosing than have them reach this city and put all its inhabitants in jeopardy. Joab, Abishai, Ittai, you will each take one third of our forces. Joab, you will take center, and you can choose who takes left and right flank. I will leave you to appoint the commanders and captains and lay out the strategy of your section."

The king directed his gaze at Joab. "But one thing I won't do this time is give you all the command and risk, then have you calling me to take the acclaim and glory after you've won the battle. This is my fight against Absalom and my actions that have brought us to this. So I will surely march out to lead you into battle as in the days of old."

This time it wasn't disbelief but dismay that swept the hall. The three commanders murmured swiftly to each other as cries of "No! It must not be!" rose to the high ceiling. Swinging around to face the king, Joab opened his mouth, but it was Abishai who stepped in front of him. Abishai was another of King David's nephews, older brother to Joab. Like Joab and Amasa, he'd fought beside David since the day he'd fled from

Saul.

"My lord, we all know of your courage. Who has witnessed it more than all of us here? You are the greatest warrior Israel has known. But you must not go out to fight this day! If we are forced to flee from Absalom, they will not pursue us. If half of us die, they will not care. And for us, it will be worth losing our lives if it is to save our king. But if you go and are captured or fall in battle, all is lost. You are worth ten thousand of us. So please, the best way you can help us is to remain here and give us support from the city."

A murmur of agreement accompanied Abishai's speech. Unspoken was the reality that the soldiers could not fight to their best capacity if they were distracted by trying to keep the king from danger. But King David was himself too savvy a warrior not to catch that undertone. He slumped back in his pseudo-throne. "I will do whatever seems best to you. Go with my blessing. Joab, you are in command."

The next morning, King David stood at the city gate with the three commanders, Joab, Abishai, and Ittai, as the soldiers marched out by their hundreds and thousands, each under a chain of command that placed them in one of the three companies with Joab as commander-in-chief. As Joab's aide-de-camp, Reuel remained at Joab's side.

As the last sections marched past, the three commanders swung onto their horses. Following suit, Reuel mounted his horse to remain at Joab's heel. King David took a step away from the gate. "Just one more thing. Be gentle with the young man Absalom for my sake."

Reuel couldn't believe what he'd just heard. Nor was he the only one. It was clear the final units filing past had heard the king's words, and those words were now being repeated from one soldier to the next with accompanying stunned and angry expressions. All these men had chosen to fight for their God-appointed king rather than join Absalom's rebellion like so many of their countrymen. They were risking their lives against Absalom's large and well-armed force. And they had just heard their king express more concern for the traitor than the loyal subjects who had already expressed their willingness to lay down their lives on his behalf!

Young man? He's got to be forty at least!

Beside Reuel, Joab's face had turned bright-red with fury. He didn't answer but kicked his horse into a trot toward the front of his company drawn up in neat lines in the center of the formation. Abishai and Ittai trotted left and right to their own companies. A small party of mounted soldiers awaited each commander, their personal guard as well as messengers for swift communication between the three battle fronts. Reuel glanced back once as he kept pace with Joab in time to see the aging king shuffle as though broken in spirit and flesh back through the gate into the city.

Chapter 51

After three solid days on horseback, Reuel felt deep fatigue settling over him. It had taken a day's march to reach Absalom's forces, encamped in Gilead on the east side of the Jordan and west edge of the forest of Ephraim, a rugged, hilly terrain where ravines were choked with brush and hillsides thick with trees. Not that Reuel had any right to complain considering he'd been on horseback, not marching up and down hills and slashing through brush. But he'd probably covered five times the distance running messages back and forth from Joab to Abishai and Ittai as well as to Joab's own commanders of thousands and hundreds.

A surprise attack had been too much to hope for since Amasa if not Absalom was an experienced commander who knew every trick his brother Joab could throw at him after decades of fighting side by side in King David's service. His advance scouts had alerted Absalom to Joab's army long before the king's men reached the forest. Joab had set up his own camp on the east edge of the forest, permitting his army a night's rest before going into battle.

Joab and his personal guard had remained with the command

tent, its banner raised high on a pole to let his men know their center remained unbroken. Abishai and Ittai had a similar setup on the north and south flanks of the battle, creating a pincher movement that trapped Absalom's force on three sides. For the first hours, the battle had raged evenly. But by noon, the lines had broken on both sides, scattering the combatants into the woods and ravines in small knots of furious hand-to-hand combat. By mid-afternoon, King David's men had unmistakably put Absalom's forces to rout, many of them fleeing into the hills or back toward the Jordan River.

"With these reports from Abishai and Ittai, it looks as though the total casualties is close to twenty thousand. At least two-thirds of those are Absalom's men."

Reuel broke off as he saw a man on foot running toward the open side of the command tent. It wasn't one of the regular field messengers unless he'd lost his horse in battle, and he was no one Reuel recognized. The man staggered to a halt just outside the tent entrance, panting and sweaty. "Commander! Commander! I bring word of Absalom."

The man broke off, gulping in air, until Joab said impatiently, "Well? What word do you bring?"

"I saw Absalom hanging from a tree!"

"You what?" Joab stared as though not sure if the messenger was speaking truth or a madman. "You mean, he's dead? He's been hung?"

"No, he's alive alright! He was fleeing our men on muleback. We'd killed most of his guard. He raced under a big oak and—" The man shook his head hard, expressing disbelief at his own words. "You know that head of hair he's so proud of. He had it tied up in braids for battle. A branch skewered it like a spear. Next thing you know, the mule is still going, and Absalom is hanging from that tree by his hair!"

"And you didn't kill him?" Joab exclaimed angrily. "Why didn't you strike him to the ground right there? I would have rewarded the soldier who killed him with ten pieces of silver and a hero's belt!"

The messenger began backing away, his mouth agape. He shook his head again, slowly. "I beg your pardon, commander. But I would not have killed the king's son for a thousand pieces of silver. We all received the order from King David to spare Absalom, his son, for his sake. If I had betrayed the king by killing his son Absalom—and the king would certainly find out who did it—you yourself, commander, would surely be the first to abandon me for defying the king's orders."

"Enough of this nonsense! Where exactly was this?"

"M-m-maybe tw-two lea-leagues straight toward the s-s-un," the messenger stuttered nervously.

"You will show me the way." Joab had already snatched up three javelins from a stack of weapons piled against the tent wall. "Reuel, you are with me! The rest of you as well!"

A dozen young men who constituted Joab's personal guard fell in as Joab strode furiously toward a makeshift stockade of brush where the guards' mounts were enclosed. Joab leapt with easy strength onto his horse, a fine black stallion. Reuel climbed wearily onto his own horse, which having galloped much of the day was as unenthusiastic as Reuel.

The messenger hung back as the group of horsemen exited the enclosure. "I … I can't ride!"

Reuel leaned down and offered him a hand. "You can ride with me."

They were riding for almost an hour through ravines, brush, and game trails before Reuel's companion called out and a knot of soldiers gathered around the base of a towering oak responded. That the messenger had covered this distance on foot gave Reuel greater respect for his feat.

Vaulting from his mount, Joab strode over to the base of the tree. As the soldiers scattered back from him, Reuel saw that there was indeed a man dangling from a tight interweave of branches, his feet dangling a cubit above the ground, his abundance of braided hair snarled in the branches. Riding closer, Reuel saw that the man was indeed Absalom and that Absalom was very much alive. Though not for long.

Approaching the dangling form, Joab raised a javelin and threw it with deadly force, piercing Absalom in the heart. He followed suit with the two remaining javelins. With whoops of glee, Joab's guard followed suit, stabbing at Absalom until the king's son was a mass of gaping red wounds, his life blood pouring out onto the ground beneath the tree.

Stepping back, Joab grabbed a ram's horn trumpet from one of his guards and blew a deafening blast. It was a signal to every one of King David's men still alive that the battle was over and they were to return to base camp. Several of the guards who'd participated in mutilating Absalom's body lifted it down from the tree and slung it over the nearest horse. Foot soldiers and mounted headed back toward the camp, but Joab called a halt when they reached a steep ravine.

"A traitor receives no honorable burial!" he called out.

Joab pitched Absalom's body over the edge. When it smashed into the ground ten cubits below, he grabbed a nearby small boulder and pitched it down on top of the body. Reuel watched aghast as Joab's personal guard joined in grabbing the largest stones they could find, aiming them at the bloody corpse with cheers and laughter until Absalom disappeared under a stone burial mound. Where did the commander find such men? Or was it because they were such men that Joab had chosen them for his personal guard?

He felt more fatigued and disheartened than should be the case on the eve of great victory as they rode back into the base camp. King David's men were already streaming in from all directions. Reuel's spirits rose when he spotted a familiar face among a growing crowd outside the command tent. Swinging down from his horse, he called out, "Ahimaaz! It is good to see you survived the battle! Have you seen Jonathan?"

The son of Zadok the high priest swung around, a smile lighting his face as he recognized Reuel. His limbs and clothing were liberally spattered with blood, but it didn't appear to be his own. His smile faded somewhat as he admitted, "Jonathan took an arrow in the thigh just as we heard the horn of victory. He is with a group of other wounded who will come as they are able, but he insisted I go ahead. We brought a troubling message to the king not so long ago, and it was my hope I might serve as runner to carry the good news of victory should Commander Joab permit. Though I hate to leave before I know Jonathan is safely in the camp."

"If my memory serves, your previous message saved the king and his household," Reuel reminded gently. "As to your comrade, I will track him down myself and bring him into camp on horseback. I will see what can be done to aid other wounded as well."

"I thank you from my heart! I will run more swiftly knowing that Jonathan is in your hands." Reuel at his side, Ahimaaz strode over to Joab and bowed deeply. "My lord commander, if it please you, let me run ahead to the king with the good news that the Lord has rescued him from his enemies."

Joab looked from one young man to the other thoughtfully. He had known the son of King David's high priest Zadok since boyhood just as he'd known the son of the king's chief advisor Hushai. With a frown, he shook his head. "Not this time, Ahimaaz. The king will not find the news of his son's death to be good. I would rather you not be the one to carry such ill news."

Joab turned to one of the foreign mercenaries who fought under Ittai. His complexion the hue of rich, dark loam, the mercenary was a Cushite, his origins from south of Egypt as many mercenaries were. "Go tell the king what you have seen this day."

The Cushite immediately took off at a run. Crestfallen, Ahimaaz pleaded, "Please, my lord Joab, let me go too!"

"Why do you want to go?" Joab responded with exasperation. "There will be no reward for such news as this. Did you not already earn honor bringing the news that permitted the king to escape the traitor Absalom? Is that not enough?"

"I don't care about a reward," Ahimaaz insisted. "I only wish to serve my king."

Joab threw his hands into the air. "I thought only to spare your father's son a hard race and unhappy welcome. But if you insist, so be it."

With a grin that stretched from ear to ear, Ahimaaz sprinted after the Cushite.

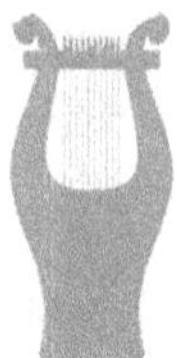

Chapter 52

Naamah and Abigail stood together at the parapet on the left side of the rooftop as they had done several times a day since King David's army marched away. As they'd worked together to keep the king's household in exile running smoothly, the two women had become increasingly close despite the difference in their age and status. Directly ahead rose the massive stone and wood of the city gates. Out of sight below to their left were the smaller inner gates.

"Surely, there must be word from the battle by now!" Naamah exclaimed anxiously. "Do you think the king has received reports we don't know about?"

"If there were news, I'm sure we would have heard," Abigail responded calmly.

They weren't the only ones anxious for word. Down below in the city square between inner and outer gates, King David strode restlessly back and forth, his personal guard detail spread out around the square only because he'd shouted at them when they'd tried to keep pace at his heels. In the last few days, the king had spent as much time striding around the square as in his temporary palace as though being a few paces closer to the gates would afford him news a few moments earlier than waiting for a message to be brought to him.

Others of the king's personal guard manned the city wall. They would be the last-ditch defense if the battle was lost and Absalom's forces attacked the city. Just then, shouts broke out from sentinels stationed directly above the outer gates. Naamah leaned forward, pointing. "Look! See that man running towards the city?"

"It must be a messenger and with portentous news to be running so hard." Abigail's tone was no longer so calm. "And look! There is a second man running behind him. They must be bringing news."

A sentinel turned and shouted down into the square, "My king, a man comes running!"

King David stopped midstride to shout up, "Just one man? Then he must have news."

The sentinel raised a hand to shield his eyes, studying the valley. He called out, "There comes another man running as well!"

"He too will have news," the king called back.

The sentinel suddenly grew excited. "My king, I recognize the first runner. It is Ahimaaz, son of Zadok."

"He is a good man so the news he brings must be good!" King David shouted out. "Open the gates for him!"

"Ahimaaz!" Abigail exclaimed softly to Naamah. "That is the high priest's son. He brought the warning from his father that allowed us to safely cross the Jordan."

Naamah remembered the name as one of Reuel's two companions on that night. She was sure the actual warning had come from Hushai, but she didn't argue. She leaned further over the parapet as the outer gates swung open. A man sprinted through. The moment he spotted the king, he prostrated himself face to the ground. Naamah had to strain to hear his words. "Everything is all right, my lord the king! Praise to the Lord your God, who has handed over the rebels who dared to stand against my lord the king."

All around, there was a patter of sandaled feet as others who had heard the sentinel's shouts hurried to the rooftop. Soon half the harem was crowding around Naamah and Abigail, their excited chatter making it hard to hear. King David's clear, deep tone rose above the noise. "What about young Absalom? Is he all right?"

Ahimaaz rose to his feet. He shook his head, looking confused. Naamah couldn't hear his response, but now the second runner was entering the gate, this one with the dark skin and tight curls of someone from lower Egypt or Cush. The second man bowed low and called out in the carrying tones of a practiced message runner, "I have good news for my lord the king. Today the Lord has rescued you from all those who rebelled against you."

"But what about young Absalom?" the king cried out. "Is he all right?"

This time such a silence fell over the scene that Naamah heard every word of the second runner's reply. "May all of your enemies, my lord the king, both now and in the future, share the fate of that young man!"

If he had expected praise for his news, he was disappointed. Naamah could see King David's body begin to tremble, and he suddenly wailed in anguish. His personal guard stepped forward to surround him and lead him away. Naamah could hear from the king's wails that they were leading him back into his temporary residence.

The king's bedchamber, which had been requisitioned from the city's top Levite, overlooked the inner gate and was just below where Naamah and Abigail stood. Naamah could hear the king climbing the stairway to the second floor balcony, then entering his bedchamber, all the while sobbing, "O my son Absalom! My son, my son Absalom! If only I had died instead of you! O Absalom, my son, my son!"

Naamah and Abigail looked at each other in shocked dismay. The other household members on the rooftop had fallen silent. To rejoice that the battle was won and they could all go home didn't seem appropriate in light of the king's anguish. But how could any of them join in weeping over the death of a traitor son who had attempted to kill their king?

In the end, they all filed quietly back down to their own quarters. Naamah picked up her lyre, but for once she had no desire to pluck out a song. She set it back down, her heart overflowing with confusion and sorrow for King David—and for the many who had fought and undoubtedly lost their lives for him.

& & &

Reuel trotted alongside Joab toward the city gates of Mahanaim. King David's foot soldiers were streaming back into the city as well. But though they'd just won a great battle, the troops were slinking through the gates heads drooping as though escaping a defeat. Once inside the gates, Joab pulled his horse alongside an officer leading one contingent.

"Why are your men not rejoicing in great victory?" Joab

asked. "One would think they'd fled in cowardice from battle rather than defeating the king's enemies."

"Haven't you heard?" The officer sounded surprised. "King David is weeping and mourning for Absalom. How can we rejoice when the king is grieving our victory?"

Joab kicked his horse into a gallop. Reuel had barely time to follow suit before the commander was disappearing through the inner gate. By the time Reuel caught up, Joab was dismounting in the courtyard of the large residence that served as King David's palace in exile. Sliding from his horse, Reuel tossed his reins to the same guard taking charge of the commander's sweating, wearied mount.

Joab was already racing up the stairs to the second floor wing where King David had his personal quarters. Hurrying to catch up, Reuel could hear the king's wailing cry. "O my son Absalom! O Absalom, my son, my son!"

Striding past the guard posted outside on the balcony, Joab didn't even knock before slamming the door open and storming into the room. King David was curled up in a fetal position on the huge bed that belonged to the city's top Levite. Joab's fists were clenched, his body stiff with rage as he stomped a sandaled foot against the tiles to be heard above the king's sobs.

King David raised his head, blinking reddened, tear-drenched eyes. "What is it, Joab?"

Joab glared around at the handful of personal bodyguards stationed around the large chamber. "I wish to speak with you alone, my king."

The guards immediately headed for the door. Reuel had started to follow when Joab called out, "Not you, Reuel. Stay with us."

Joab waited only for the door to close loudly on the last guard before bursting out furiously, "Today you have humiliated all your men in your grief over Absalom! You have disgraced the troops who have just saved your life and the lives of your sons, daughters, wives, and concubines. You have made it clear today that the commanders and their men mean nothing to you. I see that you would be pleased if Absalom were alive today and all of us were dead. You love those who hate you and hate those who love you."

Reuel had come to know the commander well and the close relationship between nephew and uncle that long predated King David's rise to the throne. Even so, he was startled at the harshness of Joab's words. The king was struggling to a sitting position, a hand wiping across his wet eyes. Joab leaned in so closely he was looming above the king.

Tersely, he ordered, "Now go out there and congratulate your troops. For I swear by the Lord that if you do not go out, not even one of them will remain here tonight. Not one will be loyal to you any longer. This will be worse for you than all the calamities that have come upon you from your youth till now."

It was so quiet in the room Reuel could hear a wind whistling across rooftops and through thrown-back window shutters. Finally, King David stumbled to his feet and sighed heavily. "You are right, Joab. Please accompany me to the city gate."

Joab's hard expression softened slightly. "It will be okay, uncle. We just have to get through this."

Reuel followed behind as Joab supported King David along the balcony and down the stairs, one strong arm around him as though the king were an old man rather than Israel's stalwart warrior. His personal guards and other household members fell in to form an entourage down the street and through the inner gate. Someone had been given orders or had the forethought to bring the ornate chair King David had been using as a makeshift throne.

The chair was set up just inside the outer gates. Joab eased him to his seat and stood back. Straightening himself with clear effort, King David called out in a voice that was loud and encouraging if still somewhat wavering, "My loyal warriors, you have done well this day. You have saved your king and your people. Victory is yours. Let us praise Yahweh and rejoice for this day!"

All around the city square, Reuel saw despondent soldiers straighten up, their faces brightening. Soon, officers were leading their troops to bow before the king and receive his personal thanks. Reuel and Joab stood behind King David for hours as he continued to receive and thank each new contingent arriving in the city. Among the last were Abishai and Ittai, who had overseen the rout of Absalom's remaining rebel force back across the Jordan.

When night fell and King David with his entourage made their way back to the makeshift palace, Reuel's thoughts turned to Channah and his parents. Perhaps soon he would be reunited with his loved ones once again. Fighting in actual battle alongside Joab and serving his king in exile had been a challenge Reuel didn't regret. But he looked forward to returning to a more peaceful life with wife, children, and the ancient scrolls whose contents were all the excitement he needed.

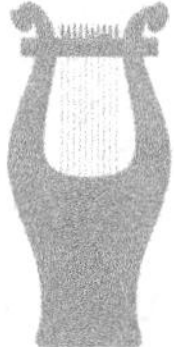

Chapter 53

The return journey to Jerusalem was far more comfortable than their original escape. Naamah and Gia sat at the rear of an ox cart, legs dangling off the end. Clutching her lyre in her lap, Naamah prayed aloud, "Thank you, Yahweh, that we are on our way home. Keep us safe from any remaining enemies of the king until we reach Jerusalem."

Naamah's excitement rose once they crossed the Jordan River and were approaching Jerusalem. All she could think of was seeing Shiphrah again. Around her in other carts and on foot, the women of the harem were talking louder and with more excitement the closer they got to the city. The city gates were visible ahead when King David's beautiful voice suddenly rose above the noise. All fell silent to listen to the king's song.

"Ascribe to the Lord, O mighty ones, ascribe to the Lord glory and strength. Ascribe to the Lord the glory due His name; worship the Lord in the splendor of His holiness. The Lord sits enthroned over the flood. The Lord is enthroned as King forever. The Lord gives strength to His people. The Lord blesses His people with peace."

Gladness welled up in Naamah to hear such joy and praise

once again pouring out from their king. The cloud of darkness had lifted. As their cart passed through the gate and jostled over the cobblestones up the steep road to the palace, she was elated at the thought of being reunited with Shiphrah. The oxen finally stopped on the palace verandah outside the door in the wall leading directly into the harem quarters.

Gia was so excited to see her mother she jumped down and rushed inside. Naamah lingered to grab her own bag of belongings and Gia's. Balancing both along with the lyre was a challenge, but that proved unnecessary. To her delight, Chinua bustled out onto the verandah and grabbed both bags.

Noise escalated as women and children poured back into the harem and resettled themselves in their living quarters. Naamah was surprised that Shiphrah had not come out to welcome them back. Stepping into her room, Naamah called out, "Shiphrah, are you here?"

Inside the room, Naamah immediately saw Shiphrah in a tight embrace with her daughter. She straightened up and reached to embrace Naamah. "Thank you, dear sister, for watching so well over my daughter. Gia has been telling me how you have been a mother to her while we were apart."

"Well, now we are back," Naamah said happily. "And all will be well with the king back on his throne."

The three chatted cheerfully, Gia pouring out the adventures she and Naamah had experienced. Moments later, Akilah and Chinua came into the room under guise of helping unpack. Naamah and Gia recounted their story again. But though Shiphrah nodded and smiled over their tale, Naamah sensed a sadness hovering over her friend. She'd expected Shiphrah to be more overjoyed at their return.

Naamah waited until Gia had scampered off to look up

her friends and Akilah and Chinua had run out of excuses to linger before confronting her friend. "Dearest sister, I sense something is wrong even now that the king is victorious and we have returned. If something has happened, I want to know what it is."

Shiphrah sank down on her bed. Naamah sat down on her own bed across from Shiphrah. With a heavy sigh, Shiphrah said in a low voice, "You know the ways of war, Naamah. As you know, Absalom took over the palace while you were all away with King David."

Naamah felt a pang of guilt she'd been so excited about their return she'd hardly given a thought to the story those left behind might have to tell. In truth, she like the other harem members who'd gone through the adventure of exile had assumed life for those left in the palace had continued in its usual monotony regardless of who occupied the throne room.

"Yes, I know the ways of war, dear sister," she said gently. "I thought of you and prayed for you every day we were away. But I apologize I didn't consider how Absalom's control of the palace might affect you. I guess we all assumed you were safe while we never knew when we might come under attack by Absalom's traitor army."

Shiphrah didn't respond. She was staring off in the distance as though lost in dark thoughts. Naamah felt panic rise within her, banishing the joy of being home. She leaned forward to grasp Shiphrah's hand. "My sister, tell me what happened here!"

Shiphrah shrank back, pulling her hands away. Her voice was a whisper, tears spilling from her eyes. "We were raped! All of us! By Absalom!"

"What?" Naamah mind was thrown immediately back to

her own attack. The hands touching her. The scraping of thorns across on her back. Her body violated.

Shaking her head to free herself from that nightmare, Naamah crossed over to the other bed to put her arms around Shiphrah. "I am so sorry! I am so sorry!"

"I will not let them win by controlling my mind with fear and sadness," Shiphrah whispered into Naamah's embrace. "I must move on!"

"I will help you," Naamah promised, tears spilling down her own cheeks. "I will help you."

She wondered if it was time to tell Shiphrah about her own attack. But sitting together in tight embrace after their long separation was a healing balm, and Naamah didn't want to break into the moment with her own sad story. Perhaps tomorrow, she would share with her dear friend that they had endured the same evil.

But the following day brought its own evil, and Naamah never did find opportunity to tell Shiphrah of her secret. They had just emerged into the courtyard on their way to breakfast when Semere entered the courtyard, a scroll in hand. He waited as the harem women were herded into the courtyard. Naamah immediately noticed that only the concubines had been summoned, not the king's wives.

When all were gathered, Semere broke the seal. He cleared his throat loudly before announcing, "I have an edict from King David. The ten concubines who cared for the palace while the king was away shall be moved into a house of their own. The king will provide for them, but they will no longer be deemed concubines of the king's household. They will live in seclusion until the day of their death as though widows of the king."

The entire group of women gasped in unison. To Naamah,

it felt like a nightmare. She like every other woman there knew well this was retribution for Absalom's rape. Why should it be the women who suffered that retribution when Absalom had been the sinner?

And yet Naamah had only to remember her own fear to recognize this was the way it was for women. She could be given in marriage to her rapist with no hope of divorce. If her rape were discovered by another husband, she could be stoned. These women had been defiled before the eyes of all Israel. However unfair, it was perhaps too much to expect King David to allow them to remain part of his household. Others would see such as weakness, and now above all, the king must appear strong. At least King David was treating them with the honor of royal widows rather than throwing them into the streets as some men might consider justified.

Rolling up the scroll, Semere announced "The ten concubines will immediately return to their rooms and pack their personal belongings. I will return with carts in one hour to transport you."

Turning to Shiphrah, Naamah began to weep. She choked out, "I would like to rage about that decree! It seems to me that you, Shiphrah, are an unfortunate victim of Absalom's sin."

"God's ways are not our ways," Shiphrah replied. "We must trust that Yahweh is doing what is best for us. My mother used to tell me that one of God's names is 'Jehovah Shammah,' which means the Lord is there for me. Yahweh is always there for us. You sing about such things, Naamah, and when we are parted, I will remember those songs and be comforted by their truth."

Too soon, a loud voice echoed down the hallway. "The concubines who are leaving must gather now in the courtyard."

Naamah helped Shiphrah carry her belongings out to the

courtyard. All the concubines had gathered to say farewell to the sisters of heart if not blood who had been their only real family through the years. Naamah attempted to smile as she gave Shiphrah a parting embrace. "I will miss you so much, dear sister. I will always cherish the memories we have made."

"As I you," Shiphrah choked out. "We will see each other again in our Yahweh's paradise."

Naamah lay on her bed weeping long into the night. A song that had begun to form during her time in Mahanaim rose to her mind. As words and tune came together, Naamah sang into the silent darkness. "Hear my prayer, O Lord. Let my cry for help come to You. Do not hide Your face from me when I am in distress. My days are like the evening shadow. I wither away like grass. The Lord will respond to the prayer of the destitute. He will not despise their plea."

With the song still echoing in her mind, Naamah called out softly, "Please, Yahweh, go with my dear friend, Shiphrah."

To the empty room, she asked, "What am I going to do now?"

Chapter 54

Naamah remained without a roommate. With ten fewer concubines and no new harem members or children being born to the king, there was no need to move in someone new. Several months after their return to the palace, Naamah heard that Bathsheba had born another son to the king, the fourth along with several daughters. As far as she'd witnessed, it didn't seem that the aging king called any other woman to his bedchamber.

Another six months passed before Naamah received a summons to play for King David, the first time since they'd sung together to the resting camp while fugitives in the wilderness. She'd begun to think the king had forgotten who she was. Or at least her music since he'd never seemed to notice Naamah as a person.

When Naamah entered the throne room, she saw King David standing in front of the mural with the scene depicting him killing the giant Goliath. Hushai and the king's army commander Joab were with him, but otherwise the throne room was unusually empty. Even the king's personal guards were stationed outside the doors.

The king was studying the mural with an expression of melancholy as though remembering that victorious moment. Joab and Hushai were to one side speaking to each other in low voices. But as Naamah walked past, their somber expressions made her wonder what unpleasant topic they were discussing. As she began to play, King David glanced up from his melancholic slump and walked to his throne, his steps like someone very old. Hushai and Joab followed, standing in silent attention as he climbed slowly onto the throne.

Naamah's soothing music continued through a dozen heartbeats before King David spoke up with a heavy sigh. "My heart tells me you are both right, my dear friends. I have done a very foolish thing and sinned greatly against Yahweh in demanding a census of Israel's fighting men."

Naamah knew what he was talking about. The harem might be isolated from public life these days, but Chinua's gossip as always had filled them in on the uproar within Jerusalem as census-takers numbered every healthy male between the fighting ages of twenty to sixty. He'd heard that the same census was being taken throughout the nation.

In truth, Naamah had no idea why this was such a controversial step. It seemed reasonable the king would want to know how many fighting men were available, especially after the great losses on both sides during Absalom's rebellion. But according to Chinua, the people were angry because it was believed numbering every male of fighting age was a next step to conscription.

To this point in the nation's history, Israel's warriors were under command of their own clan and tribal leaders, who chose whether to fight a common enemy in alliance with other tribes or not to fight at all. The prophet Samuel had warned the Israelites that insisting on a king would lead to a day when that king would conscript their sons to fight and daughters as servants. Not even Saul had dared to do such, and when the Israelites had faced a common enemy of Philistines and other surrounding nations, they had gladly followed Saul, then David. The internecine war between king and rebel son had ignited all those fears of Samuel's warning.

Abigail had another interpretation. She'd told Naamah quietly, "It isn't just about conscription. God has promised to be Israel's protector. Counting the fighting men as though he needs to know he has more soldiers than his enemies is like declaring publicly that Yahweh is not capable of protecting His chosen people."

Joab's expression showed he agreed with the king's self-assessment, but Hushai spoke up more gently. "That Judah has five hundred thousand men of fighting age and the rest of Israel eight hundred thousand is not what protects our people. It is the strong hand of our God. Yet your intentions were not intended for ill. Your concern was for the well-being of our people, both those who were loyal and those who rose up against you."

"I was thinking as a warrior in terms of men and supplies," King David admitted sadly. "I was not trusting the Lord, our Shepherd, Redeemer, and Fortress. But that is what I am—a simple shepherd who became a warrior. What am I if I am not a warrior?"

"You are our king! The leader of our people!" Hushai responded emphatically. "Yahweh anointed you Israel's king, not its warrior. And you must now step down from being a warrior and focus on your role as a leader. Consider it another way. When you were a fugitive from Absalom, Yahweh protected you through the help of others, not your own mighty strength. Let me speak bluntly. Your season as a warrior has passed. But there are still many things our nation will face. We need a leader anointed by Yahweh to get us through them safely."

A sudden upraised voice and loud tapping of sandals interrupted Hushai's words. A moment later, a man in a simple brown tunic and cloak strode into the throne room. Naamah didn't recognize him, but that the guards outside had allowed him to enter and neither the king nor his advisors raised any alarm at his presence meant he was more important than his appearance would suggest.

The man approached the throne with as much presence as though he himself were a prince. King David addressed him. "Gad, my seer. What word bring you from the Lord?"

Naamah's interest was immediately piqued. She'd once heard the prophet Gad addressing the crowd during a Sukkot festival. He was said to be Nathan's successor since that elderly prophet had retired to his hometown just a few years after confronting King David over Bathsheba. The king had named Bathsheba's third son after Nathan in commemoration of the prophet's faithful service.

"My king, the Lord has indeed sent me with a word for you." From the prophet's expression, whatever message from Yahweh Gad brought didn't look to be a joyous one. Dread clutched at Naamah's heart, and she stilled her fingers on the lyre.

Gad raised his hands in the air and declared somberly, "This is the word of the Lord to you! I, Yahweh, give you three choices. Choose one of these punishments for taking the census, and I will carry it out against you. Shall there come three years of famine on the land? Three months of destruction by the swords of your enemies? Or three days of severe plague throughout the land of Israel? Think this over and decide what answer I should give to Yahweh who sent me."

A groan left King David's mouth. As cries and murmurs rose, Naamah realized the guards King David had banished from the throne room during his discussion with Joab and Hushai had crowded in at the prophet's loud declaration. She couldn't stop her own panicked thoughts. Another war? Famine? A plague?

King David's head had fallen to his chest. The room seemed fixed in time. Gad continued to stand before King David waiting for a response. Joab looked even more furious than before, and all color had drained from Hushai's face.

Finally raising his head, King David said mournfully, "I am in deep distress. I am the one who sinned, I, the shepherd, the one who has done wrong. This punishment should be upon me and my family, not upon the people, the sheep Yahweh placed in my charge."

The prophet neither moved nor blinked. After a silent moment, King David threw up his own hands. "If I must choose, then let me fall into the hands of the Lord, for His mercy is very great. Do not let the human hands of our enemies be unleashed upon our people. Let Yahweh Himself choose who lives or dies."

"So be it! Yahweh will send a severe plague upon Israel that will last three days." With that statement, Gad turned on his heel and strode back out of the throne room.

Naamah sat motionless in her chair. She should be offering songs of comfort, but her throat was as dry as the desert. That Gad's proclamation was indeed from Yahweh and would come to pass, she had no doubt. How many people would die? What about her mother, Zahara, and all of her family and clan?

Chapter 55

"Suffering! Suffering!" Reuel shouted through clinched teeth as the horse beneath him galloped as fast as it could. "Yahweh, why are You doing this to us?"

When Hushai had told Reuel of the prophet's pronouncement that Yahweh was sending a plague upon Israel, the timing could not have been worse. Just a week earlier, Channah and their three children had left to visit her parents in Shiloh, twenty miles and two days by ox cart north of Jerusalem. Within the hour, cries of mourning were ringing out across the city as one person after another died of this mysterious plague.

Listening to his father's account, Reuel had to agree with King David that the king and his family should receive Yahweh's wrath, not those who had done nothing to deserve this. How was it that once again King David's sins and moral lapses were being visited upon the innocent rather than the sinner?

If the king hadn't committed blatant adultery, perhaps Amnon wouldn't have felt he could get away with rape. If the king hadn't neglected to punish Amnon for that rape, perhaps Absalom wouldn't have felt justified in murdering his brother and rebelling against his father. How many had died in that rebellion? So much suffering had resulted from King David's failures. And now once again, the king was sitting safely on his throne while others died on his behalf!

Night had fallen by the time Reuel pulled his exhausted mount to a halt outside his wife's family home. Channah's mother hurried out to meet him, an olive oil lamp uplifted. Reuel's world turned into a nightmare the moment he saw her face. Weeping, she led the way inside to the bedchamber where Reuel and Channah had slept on their previous visit. Reuel was overcome with grief as his gaze fell on the still, pale form of the woman he loved. He had arrived too late!

By the following day, there were sick and dying in every household across Shiloh. Over the next three days, many recovered, but a second distressing census revealed that a total of seventy-thousand lives had been lost throughout Israel by the time the plague burnt itself out. The only thing that kept Reuel from sinking into total despair was that his three children lived and needed their father.

In the palace, Naamah received the sad news that her father had been taken in the plague. The following day, a messenger arrived from Nasya. "Channah has died in the plague and was buried in her family tomb. The children survived, and Reuel has just brought them home. We are heartbroken."

Naamah's heart ached as she thought about those poor children without a mother. And how would Reuel carry on without the wife he loved so much? *Oh, Yahweh, help them! Please help them and all who are mourning loved ones this day!*

Naamah visited Nasya the following day. Hugging the older woman, she said fervently, "I am so sorry about Channah. How are you coping? How are little Noah and Abi and Kywan? And

Reuel? He must be devastated."

"The children are doing well," Nasya responded. "Children are resilient, in many ways more so than adults. Caring for them keeps my own mind off Channah. As for Reuel …"

Nasya shook her head. "He headed to the palace as soon as he left the children with us. He says he has much work to catch up with, but I think he is keeping himself busy so he does not have to think about Channah."

On her way back to the palace, Naamah prayed for Hushai, Nasya, Reuel, and the children, but she wished there was more she could do. Something that would bring comfort to Reuel in his time of great loss. If only she could play for him the songs of consolation and solace she played for King David when the king suffered melancholy. But it was no more appropriate now than it had ever been for a king's concubine to play for another man, no matter her motives.

Suddenly, a thought came to her as though Yahweh Himself were speaking. Reaching her room, she dug into a chest, pulling out equipment she hadn't used since returning from Mahanaim, when she'd written down the songs Yahweh had given her during their exile. She unearthed a segment of parchment Reuel himself had given her years ago to practice her writing. Mixing fresh ink, she painstakingly formed the first symbol of the song Yahweh had given her upon her loss of Shiphrah. When she was finished, she called for Chinua.

& & &

The next morning, Reuel came wearily into the scribes

quarters. He'd been up much of the night with three-year-old Noah, who wanted his mother and refused to be consoled by his grandparents or anyone but his father. Sinking into his chair, he reached for the pile of reports that had built up on his table during his week of absence.

He was opening the first scroll when he noticed a small scroll set off to one side. He immediately recognized the hand of the inscription neatly bordering the wax seal. Breaking open the seal, he began reading Naamah's neat writing.

"Hear my prayer, O Lord. Let my cry for help come to You. Do not hide Your face from me when I am in distress. My days are like the evening shadow. I wither away like grass. The Lord will respond to the prayer of the destitute. He will not despise their plea."

There was no personal message, but none was needed. For the first time since receiving warning from his father of the plague, a smile twitched Reuel's firm mouth.

Chapter 56

In the months that followed the plague, life at the palace slowly got back to normal. But Naamah became increasingly aware that the king had never truly recovered his strength and fire since Absalom's rebellion. His hair was now completely white, he shuffled when he walked, and there was a bend to his back that took away the imposing height Naamah remembered from their first meeting.

But as his body weakened, Naamah also witnessed that King David's zeal for Yahweh seemed to grow. He once again called for Naamah's musical giftings several times a week. As she sang or played her lyre, she often heard him call out to Yahweh. Other times, she saw his mouth moving and knew instinctively he was praying.

One day, Naamah realized it had been over a week since she was last called to play for the king. When a messenger came for her, it wasn't Chinua or Semere but Hushai. He didn't lead Naamah toward the throne room but down a corridor to a large ornate door she'd only passed through once before.

Pausing outside, Hushai said quietly, "King David is not well. The end is not imminent, but I fear it will not be long before Yahweh calls the king to His paradise. He has come to depend on your music to alleviate his discomfort, so you will remain with him in coming days except for your own sleep and other needs. I will ensure you are given ample time to rest."

Following Hushai inside, Naamah recognized the king's personal quarters where she'd played for the king until Bathsheba's arrival. How thankful that fourteen-year-old had been for the interruption. It had been years since she'd worried the king might require services of her that would betray her secret.

The king's quarters were crowded with people. Through the archway leading into the bedchamber with its huge bed, Naamah glimpsed Bathsheba hovering over King David, who was propped up against cushions under a mound of blankets. The king's personal physician was at the bedside as well. A number of advisors and personal attendants milled around the antechamber.

When Hushai led Naamah into the bedchamber, she suddenly realized there was movement under the bedcovers beyond the king's. A beautiful young face popped up to stare at Naamah. A girl who could be no older than Naamah had been when brought to the palace.

Naamah was stunned. At his age, how could even a king bring such a young girl into his bed in so public a fashion? And how was it that Bathsheba, the jealous wife who hadn't allowed another woman near the king in years, was looking on with such complacence?

Hushai must have heard Naamah's slight gasp of dismay. In a low tone, he explained quietly, "The girl is Abishag, a Shunammite. She is not here to lie with the king but to keep him warm as in his poor health he does not have the body warmth necessary so complains greatly of being cold."

That explained Bathsheba's complacency. This beautiful young girl was no threat to her own ascendancy. As she approached, Naamah could see that the king was indeed shivering under his mound of blankets despite the girl curled up close to his side.

Bathsheba nodded at Naamah with a more welcoming smile than Naamah had ever received from the older woman before. Though also showing her age with fine wrinkles around eyes and mouth and streaked gray in her dark hair, Bathsheba moved with a slim grace and composure that would keep her beautiful as long as she drew breath.

She gestured toward a small bench on the far side of the huge bed from where she stood with the physician. Hurrying over to the bench, Naamah began to play softly. She usually waited to see what mood the king was in before she selected songs she felt would be helpful to him. But the king's eyes were closed, his strong features looking aged and thin under an overgrown beard. So she began singing a new song that had been coming together in her mind during these last months of the king's growing fragility.

"In You, O Lord, I have taken refuge. Let me never be put to shame. For You have been my hope, O Sovereign Lord, my confidence since my youth. Since my youth, O God, You have taught me, and to this day I declare Your marvelous deeds. Even when I am old and gray, do not forsake me, O God, till I declare Your power to the next generation, Your might to all who are to come. I will praise You with the harp for Your faithfulness, O my God. I will sing praise to You with the lyre, O Holy One of Israel."

Naamah finished the song, then began singing it from the

beginning with more confidence, increasing the complexity of the lyre chords that accompanied the melody. King David's eyes were still shut, and Naamah believed him to be sleeping, but suddenly in a surprisingly strong and still beautiful baritone, King David's voice rose to match Naamah's. "Even when I am old and gray, do not forsake me, O God, till I declare your power to the next generation."

His words mumbled off, and this time Naamah was sure he'd fallen asleep. She shifted to soft instrumental. Across the large bed, Bathsheba sank into an ornate chair. From her expression, she was enjoying the music as well. Naamah could see the dark top of Abishag's head where she was burrowed close to the king's side, providing her body warmth.

Naamah had been playing for about an hour when a messenger entered the bedchamber and whispered to Bathsheba. Only then did Naamah realize Hushai had slipped out of the room. Fury banished Bathsheba's relaxed expression. Jumping to her feet, the king's wife almost raced from the bedchamber.

The physician left on some errand, leaving Naamah and the young girl Abishag alone with King David. The king snored softly, and Naamah quieted her music even further. She could see the girl running her hands across the king's chest under the blanket, then reaching for his hands lying on the bedcovers. Abishag massaged each finger, drawing warmth down to his extremities.

Suddenly, the tranquility was broken as Bathsheba stormed back into the bedchamber. And she was not alone. Hushai was at her heels. Several other court officials crowded in behind. The king's physician hurried back to King David's side, holding a draught of liquid in a silver cup.

"My lord, my king!" Bathsheba called sharply.

Her voice roused the drowsing king. Opening his eyes, King David struggled to sit up, but he was too weak to lift himself. Abishag immediately emerged from the blankets and helped prop him against the cushions with her own well-muscled young arms. "What is it you want, my wife?"

Bathsheba dropped to a prostrate position on the ornate rug beside the bed. Naamah heard genuine anguish in her voice as she cried out, "My lord, did you not make a vow before Yahweh that my son Solomon would surely be the next king and sit upon your throne? But now Haggith's son Adonijah has made himself king! He has sacrificed many fattened cattle and sheep, and he has invited your sons and all of Israel to join in a great feast proclaiming him king. But my son Solomon was not invited. My lord the king, all of Israel is waiting to learn from you who will sit on your throne after you. But if you do not make public your vow to place Solomon on your throne, then be assured that the moment my lord the king is laid to rest with his ancestors, I and my son Solomon will be treated as criminals!"

Chapter 57

Naamah drew in a sharp breath. Had nothing changed since the defeat of Absalom? She knew Adonijah, at least by sight, more than most women of the harem since he was frequently at banquets and court events where Naamah had been summoned to play. He was as handsome as Absalom and as charming but even more undisciplined and narcissistic. Absalom at least had been given court responsibilities while Adonijah had been overindulged by King David and his mother Haggith since infancy.

"Are you sure of this?" King David demanded querulously. He clutched at the bedcovers as though striving to hold his thoughts together. "How is this possible? Where is the army? Where is Joab?"

Hushai stepped forward. Sadly, he responded, "Your commander Joab is at Adonijah's side as is the priest Abiathar. During your illness, it seems Adonijah copied a scroll from Absalom's actions, riding through the streets of Jerusalem with fifty men running before his chariot proclaiming him king. It has been so long since the people have seen you, my lord king, and he is the next-born after Absalom. Since you have not publicly named an heir, it is only natural the nation believes Adonijah will be the next king. They fear chaos if your successor is not in place when—"

He broke off with a cough. King David finished grimly. "When I join my ancestors. I understand the people, but I will not forgive Joab and Abiathar for their betrayal. I did not choose Solomon as my heir. Yahweh Himself revealed the choice. Though young, Solomon is wise and capable. Adonijah is a fool who has never grown beyond childhood!"

Naamah's heart skipped a beat as she listened. Joab had fought for the king during Absalom's rebellion. Abiathar with Zadok had been Hushai's co-spies working in the king's interests inside Jerusalem. How could they now betray their king?

"My king! I can add my word to the testimony of Bathsheba!"

Naamah was even more stunned to recognize the man who pushed past Hushai to bow face to the ground before rising to his feet to address the king. It had been at least a decade since Naamah had seen the tall, thin man with a long, unkempt white beard dressed in the beige tunic of a peasant belted with rough hemp rope. The prophet Nathan had seemed ancient then, and Naamah had somehow assumed he was no longer among the living since Gad had been palace seer for numerous years.

"Right now Adonijah is eating and drinking with all the king's sons, the commanders of the army, and Abiathar the priest in his own residence not far from here," Nathan went on. "Abiathar has anointed Adonijah king, and Joab has proclaimed the support of the army. They are crying, 'Long live King Adonijah!' That he did not invite me, your servant, or Zadok the priest, or Benaiah, commander of your Mighty Men, or your son Solomon can only be because we are faithful to you alone, my king, and this action is not by your orders. Or is this indeed something my lord the king has done without letting his servants know who should sit on the throne of my lord the king after him?"

By now, King David was sitting up strong and erect against the cushions. His face was ruddy with anger, and the hands that had lain limp against the bedcovers were curled into fists. Reaching out to take Bathsheba's closest hand, he roared out with the power of his younger self, "As surely as the Lord lives, who has rescued me from every danger, your son Solomon will be the next king. He will sit on my throne this very day!"

The king addressed himself to Hushai, "Find Zadok the priest and Benaiah son of Jehoiada. From this moment, Benaiah is commander of Israel's armies in Joab's place. Then take Solomon to the Spring of Gihon. There Zadok the priest and Nathan the prophet are to anoint Solomon king over Israel. Blow the ram's horn and shout, 'Long live King Solomon!'"

Naamah needed no explanation to understand the king's instructions. The Spring of Gihon was just outside the original city walls, bubbling up from a cave in the Kidron Valley. The water was the reason for building the original fortress and then the city of Jerusalem as it was one of the few reliable sources of water in that dry, dusty region. The underground tunnels that brought its water into the city was the route by which King David had conquered Jerusalem.

The spring also fed into the Pool of Siloam, where the high priest gathered water in a golden pitcher for tabernacle worship ceremonies. Except during Sukkot and other festivals, when the tabernacle was moved to the Mount of Olives, the tabernacle was kept pitched at the spring year-round, and that was where the Ark of the Covenant was housed. It was also where the sacred perfumed oil for the altar of incense, seven-branched menorah, and ceremonial anointing was kept, so it was the logical and most public location to anoint Solomon king.

King David sank briefly back against the bed cushions, the strength leaving him. It took several long, struggling breaths before he could continue. He panted out, "When my son Solomon has been anointed king, escort him back here. He will sit on my throne and succeed me as king. I have appointed him to be ruler over Israel and Judah!"

Within moments, the bedchamber was empty again except for Naamah, Abishag, the physician, and King David. The king slumped back, eyes closed, as though the tense excitement of the last minutes had been more than his frail body could handle. The physician hurried forward to place the silver cup to the king's lips. Naamah's fingers glided across the strings of her lyre quietly.

For a long time, her music was the only sound in the room. She was close to nodding off herself when suddenly a commotion broke out beyond the bedchamber's open shutters. Though at a distance, Naamah could make out joyful shouts. "Long live King Solomon!"

Trumpet blasts punctuated the shouts. King David's eyes flew open, and he sat up suddenly. He looked over at Naamah. "My child, will you not look out the window and tell me what you see?"

Setting down her lyre, Naamah hurried to a window that looked out two stories above the palace verandah, giving a view of the rooftops and narrow, steep streets zigzagging down from the palace to the eastern gate where the Spring of Gihon and Pool of Siloam were located. A large procession was moving uphill toward the palace, Solomon at its head riding the king's own snow-white ceremonial mule. A great crowd of people were dancing behind him to the blasts of trumpets, clanging of cymbals, and playing of hand-pipes.

"What a wonderful sight!" Naamah whispered.

"What sight do you see?" King David demanded.

"Your son Solomon approaching. A great crowd is with him! It looks as though all the city is rejoicing that Solomon is king."

Over the next minutes, the noise grew louder as the procession approached until the very ground shook with the sound. The blast of trumpets shifted to the melody of one of King David's own well-known psalms.

"I love you, Lord, my strength. The Lord is my rock, my fortress and my deliverer. My God is my rock, in whom I take refuge, my shield and the horn of my salvation. The Lord lives! Praise be to my Rock! Exalted be God my Savior! He is the God who avenges me, who subdues nations under me, who saves me from my enemies. Therefore, I will praise you among the nations, O Lord. I will sing praises to Your name. He gives his king great victories. He shows unfailing kindness to His anointed, to David and his descendants forever."

It was the perfect song to celebrate the anointing of King David's successor and defeat of yet one more enemy. Hurrying to snatch up her lyre, Naamah played along as the procession spilled onto the palace verandah and disappeared toward the throne room where she could no longer see its progress.

There was a final trumpet blast, then silence fell again. Above her own soft strumming, Naamah could hear King David praying to Yahweh. "Praise the Lord, the God of Israel, who today has chosen a successor to sit on my throne while I am still alive to see it."

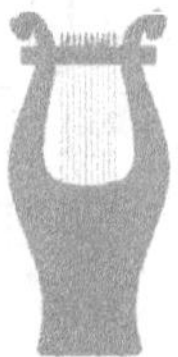

Chapter 58

"Reuel, you must come with me!" Jonathan, son of Abiathar, burst into the scribes quarters as though a Nubian lion were at his heels.

Reuel looked up in surprise. He'd remained good friends with the sons of Zadok and Abiathar since their spy mission to save the king's camp from Absalom's forces. But since Channah's death, he'd seen little of them as he spent every spare moment from his duties with his children. In contrast, Jonathan and Ahimaaz were single young men who spent their free time in revelry with their peers.

Reuel had heard commotion beyond the thick walls of the palace, some sort of festival though this wasn't one of the usual feast days. He'd assumed some foreign dignitary must be visiting Israel's capital, but he'd just returned from a month-long trip spying out which of the tribes were now solidly behind King David and where rebellion might still be brewing, and he was determined to finish his report before heading home.

His young friend Jonathan looked ashen with dismay. Dropping his quill, Reuel asked sharply, "What is it?"

"I fear my father is in great trouble. Please, you must come with me now to the house of Adonijah. There are few others I trust. I need you as witness that I am no traitor to my king on this errand. I will explain on the way. I have a horse waiting outside the palace gates. It will be quicker."

People were milling in the streets as the two men emerged from the palace gates, some in excited celebration, others looking somber. Reuel rode behind Jonathan, who headed his horse downhill at a breakneck speed that had Reuel hoping they wouldn't both break their necks. All the time, Jonathan was shouting an explanation over his shoulder that made little sense to Reuel.

"I know my father would never betray the king. He must have been told this was at the king's request. I believe it must have been the commander of the king's armies, Joab, because my father would never doubt the orders of the king's nephew."

Jonathan finally skidded to a stop outside the large compound Reuel recognized as the private residence of King David's eldest remaining son. Above the walls rose the laughter, boisterous talk, and background music of what sounded like a feast. Guards were posted outside, but the double gates stood open on a large courtyard garden filled with dozens of long tables littered with the remains of a lavish feast. Reuel immediately spotted Adonijah flanked by Joab at the head table. Jonathan's father, Abiathar, was nowhere in sight.

As Reuel entered at Jonathan's heels, Joab raised a wine goblet and called out, "What's the meaning of all the noise in the city? Have the people already heard we have a new king?"

Adonijah lifted his own goblet with a broad smile. A golden band circled his brow, not the crown King David wore for ceremonial occasions but equally ornate. "Come in, come in, Jonathan! A worthy man like you must be bringing good news!"

As with Reuel, son of King David's chief advisor, the sons of the king's two chief priests had grown up around the king's sons, though like Absalom and Amnon, Adonijah was a good decade older than the new arrivals.

Jonathan shook his head, his expression grave. Reuel suddenly realized that Jonathan had brought him along as more than a witness to his own loyalty. He was deeply worried at the reaction his news would provoke. Hushai had been a close ally to Joab and Abiathar both. Did Jonathan believe the presence of Hushai's son would be some kind of protection? Was Abiathar missing from this feast because he'd realized this wasn't sanctioned by the king after all?

"The rejoicing is not for Adonijah," Jonathan blurted out somberly. "Our lord King David has made Solomon king. The king sent Zadok the priest, Nathan the prophet, Benaiah son of Jehoiada, and all of Commander Ittai's Kerethites and Pelethites to anoint Solomon king with the sacred oil of the tabernacle at Gihon. The noise you hear is the city cheering. Moreover, Solomon has taken his seat on the royal throne, and even now the royal officials have gathered to congratulate our lord King David, saying, 'May your God make Solomon's name more famous than yours and his throne greater than yours!'"

There was a stunned silence, then a scramble of activity as every guest rushed to exit the compound. Adonijah raced through the gates. Grabbing a horse from among those tethered there by his guests, he took off at a gallop. Jonathan and Reuel hurried to follow. By the time Reuel realized Adonijah was aiming for the eastern city gate, he had a good idea of the prince's intentions.

Sure enough, Adonijah slid to a dismount at the tabernacle entrance. Sprinting toward the altar of sacrifice, he grabbed onto one of the horns. Beyond the altar, Reuel spotted Jonathan's father Abiathar, who not long before had anointed Adonijah king. His mouth agape, Abiathar retreated inside the tabernacle tent. By this point, soldiers were pouring into the courtyard. Adonijah clutched even more tightly to the altar. Reuel slid from his seat behind Jonathan and strode over to the prince.

"I have sanctuary, I have sanctuary!" Adonijah shouted. "You dare not touch me here or Yahweh Himself will strike you down."

The soldiers encircled the altar but made no attempt to touch Adonijah. Reuel said reasonably, "You cannot stay here forever, my lord. Surrender and throw yourself on the mercy of your brother, the new king."

"Only if King Solomon swears to me today that he will not put his servant to death with the sword," Adonijah shouted back.

Looking around, Reuel spotted the unit's commanding officer, a man he'd fought beside in the battle against Absalom. He said quietly, "Take a message to the king. I will remain here with your men to ensure Adonijah does not escape."

The officer galloped through the eastern gate up the steep streets toward the palace. Adonijah remained standing in the hot sun, clutching the altar and sobbing. It was a full hour before an additional troop of soldiers returned with the officer, who announced, "The king says if you show yourself trustworthy, not a hair of your head will fall."

Reluctantly, Adonijah released his grip on the altar and allowed himself to be led away. Reuel looked around for Jonathan, but his friend was gone. Reuel could only hope he'd reunited with his father and both would be in no further trouble. He could testify to Jonathan's loyalty if need be. Snagging Jonathan's mount, he followed Adonijah and his entourage back to the palace and into the throne room.

The great hall was packed with officials offering their allegiance to the new king. On the throne, the teenaged firstborn of Bathsheba looked far too young to be a king, but his steady gaze held wisdom and intelligence. Adonijah prostrated himself on his face before the throne, visibly shaking in fear. He mumbled, "My king, may Yahweh bless your reign with greatness and make your throne even more famous than your fathers!"

King Solomon gazed steadily at Adonijah for a long moment, then said with stern authority, "My brother, you have nothing to fear from me so long as you remain true to your oath. But if evil should be found in you, be sure you will die! Now arise and go to your home."

Chapter 59

Over the next few days, Naamah never left the king's side except to sleep and deal with personal needs. She played and sang. Abishag hugged the king and gave him massages. The physician hovered with potions. Hushai occasionally visited, but the advisors who had crowded around before were now all in attendance on King Solomon.

Somewhat to Naamah's surprise, Bathsheba rarely left the king's side either. Perhaps the older woman's love for King David was as genuine as the king's, however iniquitous their relationship had initially been. What might have happened, Naamah wondered, if King David and Bathsheba both had refused to give in to their illicit passion outside of marriage. Would Yahweh have eventually blessed their love and brought them together in a godly union that would have avoided such dark repercussions on so many lives?

Naamah paused her singing as two of David's bodyguards ushered King Solomon into the king's sitting chamber, Hushai and Reuel at the new king's heels. Reuel's eyes met Naamah's shy glance, and he smiled warmly. Naamah hadn't seen Reuel except at a distance since their return to Jerusalem. He'd moved with his children back into his own home and hadn't been present the few times Naamah had visited Nasya.

But one day not long after she'd sent Reuel the scroll with its prayer of distress to Yahweh, she'd received a cloth-wrapped package delivered to her room. When she'd opened the package, it contained a scroll in Reuel's deft writing that was a copy of Joshua's conquest of the Promised Land she'd once expressed a desire to read. She knew this was his way of thanking her.

King David had been bathed, dressed in royal robes, and settled onto a wide lounging couch in preparation for Solomon's visit. Abishag sat on the floor at one end, rubbing the king's feet. Bathsheba sat in a nearby chair. A table and stool had been set up nearby. Settling himself behind it, Reuel laid out a clean parchment and writing supplies. Everyone there knew why the king had summoned his son.

Reuel picked up his sharpened quill and dipped it in ink as King David began. "My son, Solomon, I will very soon pass from this life. This is my final charge to you. Show yourself to be a man by being strong and courageous. Keep Yahweh's decrees, commands, regulations, and laws written in the Law of Moses. You must have obedient fellowship with Father God. If you do these things, you will be successful in all you do and wherever you go. If you observe Yahweh's requirements and follow Father God with your heart and your soul, Yahweh will keep His promise to me to always have a descendant of mine—and yours—upon the throne of Israel."

Reuel diligently wrote down the words exactly as King David said them. As Naamah listened, it occurred to her that these instructions were not just for kings but all men and women. As Reuel inscribed the final symbol, King David said weakly, "Now, please, all leave me except my dear friend and advisor Hushai."

& & &

Solomon stepped forward to embrace his father before leading his mother from the room. Naamah took Abishag by the hand, and the two young women retreated out of the king's bedchamber, closing the door to give the king and his advisor complete privacy.

Once they were alone, King David raised a weak hand. "Hushai, my friend, come close to me."

Hushai fell to his knees beside David's couch. They were two old men who'd gone through decades of adventure, pain, and victory together since long before King David had made this city his capital. Hushai knew what this moment meant, and tears trickled down his cheeks into his beard.

"Do not weep, my friend," King David said softly. "I go to my ancestors and my God. I am content. But when one is nearing death, many things become clear."

The king took a labored breath. "Above all others, you have been my faithful friend and wise advisor, Hushai. If I had listened to you, my troubles would be fewer. I want to apologize to you, Hushai, for not listening to your counsel about Bathsheba, Amnon, the census. Yahweh has forgiven me my follies, but I know my actions also caused you much pain. Above all, the death of your son's wife and your grandchildren's mother. Her loss should have been my punishment and not yours. For that too, Hushai, my friend, I beg your forgiveness."

Hushai bowed his head. "There is no need to ask. All is forgiven, my king and my friend."

"You are a man of mercy and grace," King David responded. "Now I have another request of you, and I wish you to be completely truthful. Do not try to spare my feelings."

"But of course! What is it, my king?"

"It is Naamah, she whose music has so greatly blessed my heart and all of Israel." The king broke off, staring into the distance for several heartbeats before continuing. "I have so often been so selfish in my life, Hushai. I realize now how greatly I wronged the girl in snatching her for my harem as though she were an ornament rather than a human being. It is not as though I had any interest in her as a woman. I was already rashly enthralled with Bathsheba, who has been the love of my life. I simply reached out and took Naamah to have her music at my every summons without thinking what that meant to her. Never to have a husband or children."

King David looked intensely at Hushai. "It is only in recent days as the curtain of Paradise is being pulled back that it occurs to me I wronged you as well. You brought the girl to me to be a blessing in my melancholy. But I am not blind that you see her as a daughter, and perhaps it was not my household's but yours for which you first brought her to Jerusalem. If so, I am truly sorry."

The king sighed and smiled slightly. "It is perhaps too late to make amends. But I think you are aware I have never taken Naamah into my bed in all these years. And I know that your son is once again in need of a wife. Upon my death, I have given orders that she is to be freed from the harem so that she can be married. If not to your son, I will leave her in your hands to ensure she has the future she deserves."

Hushai was too stunned to respond. He finally stammered out, "How … how can I possibly thank you enough for this?"

King David reached over and touched his dear friend's bowed head. "Yahwah has given me so much. How can I not give so little?"

The king began singing softly a melody Hushai had heard him sing many times over the years, a reminder of God's own mercy and forgiveness.

"The Lord is gracious and compassionate, slow to anger and rich in love. The Lord is good to all. He has compassion on all He has made. The Lord is righteous in all His ways and loving toward all He has made. The Lord is near to all who call on Him, to all who call on Him in truth. He fulfills the desires of those who fear Him. He hears their cry and saves them. The Lord watches over all those who love Him."

Gradually, the king trailed off. Seeing his stilled face and closed eyes, Hushai knew the sweet psalmist of Israel would never raise his voice in song again. Reuel was just leaving the scribe quarters when Hushai spotted him. Hurrying down the palace corridor toward his son, Hushai burst out as soon as he was close enough that passers-by couldn't listen in, "Reuel, I am on my way home to give your mother some good news. I wanted to tell you as well."

"What is this good news that has you so excited, Father?" Reuel asked teasingly.

"It is Naamah. King David is freeing Naamah from the harem upon his death. She will be free to marry."

The expressions of shock, joy, then determination that chased each other across Reuel's face filled his father with warm satisfaction.

& & &

The following morning, Naamah was called to play for King David before the sun was even up. Entering the antechamber, she saw that it was packed with physicians, priests, advisors, and the king's sons moving in and out a few at a time. This time it was King Solomon who sat enthroned in an ornate chair at his father's bedside.

So many people gathered in one place would normally be very noisy. But the silence this morning was deafening except for the patter of rain on rooftiles outside the open windows and an occasional rumble of distant thunder. Hushai walked over to Naamah. "The king has been unconscious since last night, and the physicians say it will not be much longer. Play something that will ease him to his final resting place."

What did you play to give comfort to someone nearing death? Naamah had no idea. Settling herself on her usual bench, Naamah breathed a simple prayer, the same she'd prayed so many times over the years. *Help me, Yahweh, help me!*

A psalm of King David she'd learned when she herself was still a small child rose to her mind. One the king had written while still a shepherd boy with no inkling he would one day be Yahweh's anointed king. Softly, she touched the lyre strings and began to sing. "The Lord is my shepherd. I shall not be in want. He makes me lie down in green pastures. He leads me beside quiet waters. He restores my soul."

As Naamah sang, the physicians stepped away from King David's bed. There was clearly nothing more they could do.

The rise and fall of the king's chest was barely perceptible. King Solomon's eyes never left his father's face. Standing behind him, Bathsheba let out a soft sob.

Naamah continued. "He guides me in paths of righteousness for His name's sake. Even though I walk through the valley of the shadow of death, I will fear no evil, for You are with me. Your rod and your staff, they comfort me. You prepare a table before me in the presence of my enemies. You anoint my head with oil. My cup overflows."

King David's last, deep breath escaped his lungs as the final words of the psalm left Naamah's lips. "Surely goodness and love will follow me all the days of my life, and I will dwell in the house of the Lord forever."

As the song died away, lightning flashed through the room, followed by a deafening peal of thunder. There were gasps of awe. Hushai said quietly, "It is as if Yahweh in His own voice is calling King David, the man after Yahweh's own heart, to his eternal home!"

Chapter 60

Naamah was both exhilarated, exhausted, and battling fear as she returned to the harem. What would happen to her now that King David had joined his ancestors in Paradise? To all of the wives and concubines? Would they be consigned to living the remainder of their days in confinement and under guard like the ten concubines Absalom had raped? Would the new king be as generous in providing for them as King David had been?

Or would it be as she'd been warned? The wives might be given consideration as widows, but the concubines would become Solomon's property to use as he willed or even to give away as gifts. Could she hope the gift of her music would spare her such indignity? And what about a young girl like Abishag, as young as Naamah had been when she'd arrived in the palace and unlike Naamah still a virgin? Would she be allowed to return to her family? Marry and have children?

Naamah sighed internally and lifted her thoughts upward. *Forgive me, Yahweh! You have taught me through so much these past years to trust You. No matter what happens next, I must trust that You will care for me and for my sisters in the harem. And no matter what happens, I will not lose my music again because You have shown me I can sing through the greatest of sorrows as in the greatest of joy.*

Chinua met Naamah in the corridor outside the harem. "I have a message for you from the household of Hushai. They wish you to visit as soon as you are free. Hushai sent the message through Semere so that you would be appointed someone to escort you."

Naamah sighed again with a tinge of frustration. Even with the king gone, it would seem the women of his harem were still not free to come and go on their own. "Let me bathe quickly and change into fresh clothing, and I will be ready."

Within the hour, Naamah was following Chinua through the familiar streets she'd traced so many times over the years to visit Nasya. When she arrived, she was startled to find Reuel and his three children waiting in the courtyard with Hushai and Nasya to welcome her. Reuel's seven-year-old daughter Abi ran forward to throw her arms around Naamah's waist. Naamah knew the boys less well since Abi had often joined the women when Naamah visited Nasya and Channah while boys typically visited separately with the menfolk once they were weaned.

Naamah didn't glance at Reuel, not wanting to see pity in his eyes, as she greeted each of the children. Not that her own situation compared to his loss of a dearly beloved wife. She was really no more alone than she'd always been, especially once Shiphrah had been taken away.

Hushai whispered to Nasya. To Naamah's surprise, the two of them gathered their grandchildren and herded them across the courtyard toward the verandah, leaving Naamah and Reuel standing alone together. Memories flashed through her mind.

Reuel reading back to her word-perfect the compositions she'd sung. His patience teaching her to read. His tall, erect frame on horseback galloping into camp to bring warning of Absalom's treachery. His brotherly arm around her shoulders and strong hand lifting her to his horse in Mahanaim. The love on his face when she'd glimpsed him with Channah and the children.

Reuel had now surpassed his third decade, but he was as tall, muscular, and, yes, as handsome as the seventeen-year-old she'd met during her first days in the palace. What did she at twenty-nine look to his own searching eyes? Did she seem old and worn to him, or was there anything of the fourteen-year-old girl passionate about singing to Yahweh and eager to learn to write down her own music?

"I'm sorry," she said awkwardly. "I'd better go see what I can do to help Nasya with the children."

Reuel put a hand out, touching her arm just briefly before dropping his hand. "No, stay. Mother and Father—" His firm lips twitched in a half-smile. "This is their doing. They know I have a question to ask you."

Naamah stood still, puzzled. Reuel took a deep breath. "Naamah, will you marry me? Would you be my wife? Mother to my children?"

Naamah was speechless. Finally, she got out the words. "But—I do not understand. How can I marry you? I am the king's concubine! Even now, I am not free!"

"Yes, you are," Reuel responded gently. "My father told me last night when he returned from King David's side. The king set you free before he died. He told my father you had never been a true concubine to him. That he regretted taking you for his selfish enjoyment of your music rather than permitting you marriage and family. He knew—"

Reuel broke off, then continued diffidently, "The king knew, he'd come to realize that my father's plan all those years ago was to choose you as my bride. With my gifts of writing and drawing and your gifts of music, my father believed you and I would be a strong partnership as husband and wife. He saw too your heart for Yahweh, which I share. It was what he wanted in the wife of his only son."

Reuel hunched his broad shoulders. "When Father brought you to sing for the king, he never dreamed the king would take you as his possession. He had thought to house you as a daughter in our home so you could develop your talents of music until you and I were old enough for marriage. Instead, well, you know what happened. All these years—"

Naamah finally found her voice. "Yes, all these years Yahweh gave you a wonderful wife in Channah and three beautiful children. As for me, I do not regret the years of playing and singing, not just for the king but all of Israel as my songs have spread from Dan to Beersheba. It is a miracle of its own I would never have thought possible when Hushai brought me to Jerusalem."

"You are right, Naamah. I have deeply loved my wife and been very happy with Channah. And I have rejoiced to see Yahweh using your gift of music to bless our people and the king." There was a gentle earnestness in Reuel's voice. "But Yahweh took Channah home to His presence. And He has set you free as I would not have dreamed possible. I do not have the right words to explain it, but it seems to me that in His infinite love Yahweh has given us opportunity for a new path together. A new love."

Reuel took a step closer to Naamah. "I do not expect you to love me immediately. I have loved you as a sister. As a friend.

And I know the love of a husband and wife will blossom between us if you will only give it a chance. Most importantly, you and I both have absolute trust in Yahweh. I know it may take some time for you to even see me as a possible husband, and I am willing to wait. But I believe wholeheartedly that Yahweh is leading us together."

For one last time, Naamah's dark secret tried to flash through her mind. But Reuel's words swept it away as she realized that with Yahweh at the center she and Reuel could work through anything together. As fear of her past faded into shadows, Naamah allowed her delight to grow. Reuel stood before her, patiently waiting for her answer.

Seeing the anxious yearning in his eyes, Naamah allowed joy to light her face with a smile. "You don't have to wait, Reuel. I would be delighted to marry you and be the mother to such wonderful children. Our Father God has shown me how much He loves me through the gift of you. I look forward to building our life together."

Reuel closed the gap between them, taking Naamah's small hands in his strong ones. His touch made Naamah's spine tingle, and the passion in his gaze filled her heart with an unfamiliar happiness. It wasn't possible for Naamah to feel emotion without music flooding into her mind, and without even thinking she burst into song. "The Lord is my strength and my shield. My heart trusts in Him, and He helps me. My heart leaps for joy, and with my song I praise him."

Naamah blushed and broke off as she realized Hushai and Nasya were still standing with Kywan, Abi, and Noah on the verandah, watching Reuel and Naamah's entire exchange. The newly-betrothed couple smiled at each other, then smiled and waved at their family. Reuel caught Naamah's hand in his.

As he led her over to join the others, Naamah heard Nasya murmur to Hushai, "Just think, my husband! We will be blessed for the rest of our lives with the songs of Naamah."

Hushai looked to the heavens. "Thank you, Yahweh! Thank you!"

About the Author

Gayle Walhof's occupational background is in executive administration as founder of a business that provided contract secretarial services to city agencies, law enforcement, medical clinics, banks, attorney firms, churches, and more. But her passion has been music, God's Word, and writing, including chorales, poetry, women's Bible studies, and Christian articles. Reading King David's poetic writings in Psalms and curiosity as to why a man whose sins were so obvious could be called "a man after God's own heart" led her to research and write this book.